# TRAITORS AND TYRANTS

**RUSSELL JONES**

Copyright © 2005 by Russell Jones.

All rights reserved. Printed in the United States of America.

No part of this book may be used or reproduced in any manner whatsoever without written permission except in the case of brief quotations embodied in critical articles or reviews.

Book design by Misti Tracy

ISBN: 0-9773354-0-2
LCCN: 2005909175
HNKS Publishing
P.O. Box 6677
Boise, Idaho 83702-6677

www.hnkspublishing.com


Printed in the United States by Morris Publishing
3212 East Highway 30
Kearney, NE 68847
1-800-650-7888

*To Barbara*

# — 1 —

THE WHIP DREW BLOOD WITH EACH LASH.
The five captives bore the blows mostly without protest. They had no choice. As condemned men they expected little mercy and none was offered. They flinched under the blows, but refused to give the guard the pleasure of a cry or yelp. They simply clenched their teeth and hid their anger so as not to provoke him further.

A biting wind pressed in from the north, the remnant of a storm that raged through western Missouri the night before. This too the captives ignored except to wrap themselves in light coats and blankets. The cold lingered until late morning when the clouds broke up and the sun burst upon them, but the flogging continued at the guard's pleasure.

Creech, the youngest of the guards, handled the whip expertly, coiling it up after each lash and then waiting until the prisoners relaxed before he assaulted them again. To him the whipping was a game and he laughed each time he struck. His windblown red hair framed a chubby, freckled face and a mouthful of crooked, twisted teeth. His eyes hid beneath heavy, droopy lids and a ragged scar snaked down his right cheek to his jaw. His uncle, Toad Ward, drove the wagon.

Opposite Creech to the right of the wagon rode a third guard, a squat, fleshy man on a swayback palomino. He screamed wildly and goosed the swayback into a hard gallop around the wagon when Creech lashed the prisoners. He and Creech assumed it was their duty to keep the prisoners occupied and thinking about anything but freedom.

Tucker, an olive-skinned man with long black hair and a mustache, warily led the procession usually keeping half a furlong between his horse and the wagon.

Fifty yards to the rear Tyrone Glaze casually watched his young guard and protégé whip the prisoners. The sight pleased him. He liked seeing the prisoners wince and ache. He hoped one would try to escape. Blood sport would break up the monotony of their journey.

Raw muscle covered Glaze's six-foot, two hundred pound frame. Stringy blonde hair and three days growth of beard covered his head and face. As chief guard, he felt in control at the rear, keeping prisoners, the wagon driver and the other guards in view so that if unexpected trouble sprang up he would see it immediately. He expected trouble. Under the right circumstances he'd welcome it. A little trouble would end this charade. It would give him the excuse he wanted to kill the prisoners.

A sixth man shadowed the procession. Glaze didn't count him as one of his men. He wasn't a guard. He didn't join with Glaze's men and he didn't associate with the prisoners. He appeared to Glaze to be nothing more than a big, dull-witted farm boy. The sixth man kept his distance and watched. He followed for reasons only the governor knew and Glaze only could guess. That made Glaze nervous. The sixth man's name was Harmon — Otis Harmon.

As Glaze watched, one of the prisoners, now warming in the mid-morning sun, slid to the edge of the wagon and leaned against a side rail. Creech pretended not to notice until the trail narrowed as it threaded through a stand of cottonwood trees naturally pushing the buckskin close to the wagon. Suddenly, Creech lashed at the prisoner, but before the leather struck, Ol' Joe, the lead prisoner, leapt forward, caught the whip in his right hand and jerked. Creech who was leaning forward awkwardly in his saddle was caught off balance. And rather than let go of the whip Creech held on and tumbled from his horse face first into a wagon rut filled with muddy water.

Ol' Joe stood up in the back of the wagon holding the whip in his manacled hands. The prisoners cheered as the wagon rolled to a stop. Creech struggled to his feet angrily spitting mud and dirty water and pulling a pistol from his belt. He pointed the gun at Ol' Joe.

Glaze and Harmon spurred their horses forward until they flanked Creech.

"Put the gun away Creech," Harmon said.

"Don't tell my men what to do," Glaze yelled at Harmon.

"He had it coming," Harmon said. "It's time for him to back off."

Glaze hated to admit it, but he knew Harmon was right. He couldn't let Creech start shooting. Not here. Not now.

"Creech," Glaze said. "Let it go."

"I'm going to kill him," Creech said, his gun hand shaking. "Before this trip is over, I'm going to kill him."

"Maybe," Glaze said. "But not right now. Not while everybody's watching."

Creech lowered the gun.

"You're going to die today," he said, pointing at Ol' Joe.

Ol' Joe slowly coiled the whip and tossed it into the mud hole.

"If you don't put away this whip, you're the one who's going to die," he said.

Ordinarily, a threat from a prisoner in chains would have had Glaze and his men rolling on the ground clutching their stomachs as they laughed their guts out. But this man was no ordinary prisoner. He was known and feared throughout Missouri and, it was said, the governor himself prayed for his early execution.

Creech, however, was not one to be cowed by mere words. The wagon had not proceeded another mile before he found an opportunity to use the whip again, this time raining down blows on all the prisoners as they ducked and dived to escape. Then, he rode alongside the wagon laughing.

"Ya gonna kill me now? Maybe you could break my neck. Come on now. Jump up here and break it. It's easy as eatin' pie. Just jump right up here and snap it off."

The taunting kept Creech occupied and the prisoners angry. Glaze liked that. In his judgment any pain Creech dished out represented only a fraction of what they deserved. The procession continued throughout the morning non-stop.

About mid-afternoon, Creech wheeled the buckskin and spurred it on a dead run toward Glaze. Whenever he could Creech rode at a dead run. He seldom let his mount trot or lope. He whipped it as much as he did the prisoners. As a result, the buckskin never settled into an easy walk. It pranced, danced, reared and kicked. When the buckskin came within ten yards of Glaze, Creech heaved back hard on the reins and the buckskin put on the brakes leaving long, straight skid marks in the mud and dirt with its hind legs and hooves. Lather streaked the buckskin's neck and front quarters. A bloody froth dripped from the corners of its mouth where the sharp bit cut sores. Creech wheeled the buckskin expertly and it fell into its dancing walk alongside Glaze's chestnut stud.

"One of the prisoners is sick. Just puked all over the wagon," Creech said. "He wants to stop."

Glaze wasn't surprised. One of the prison guards at Liberty confided the prisoners went days without food. Then, as a joke, the guards offered them the half-cooked flesh cut from the thigh of a dead Indian. All but one of the prisoners refused to eat. Though he did not feel sorry for them, Glaze thought it a miracle they lived, given their treatment at Liberty.

"Wight?"

"Yeah. It'd be too bad if he died, wouldn't it?" Creech said, his lips curling in an unsympathetic smile.

Glaze shrugged and watched the bloody froth drip from the buckskin's mouth. Hunger pangs tore at his stomach too.

"Tell Tucker to find a spot with some water," Glaze said. "We won't stop long. I want to be in Gallatin before dark."

"Yessir," the freckled young man said, then whipped the buckskin into another hard gallop past the wagon to where Tucker rode on the point.

The wagon stopped twenty minutes later near a small stream. The guards watched gravely, guns ready, while the prisoners stiffly crawled from the wagon, slowly stretched their legs and drank from the stream taking every second the guards gave them. Despite the steel manacles and chains on their feet and hands, the guards studied their every move carefully until they finished. The guards then pushed them roughly into a tight group near the wagon. The wagon driver produced a bag of corn dodgers and some dried meat. The guards ate first and the prisoners devoured the leftovers.

Glaze watched Ol' Joe closely as they ate. His brother, also one of the prisoners, sat nearby. The family resemblance was striking. There was something about both men that Glaze hated, but the reasons eluded him.

Ol' Joe wasn't old at all. The citizens at Independence gave him the nickname, but he wasn't old. Glaze guessed the man was his senior by only a few years and that would have put him in his early thirties. His eyes peered out over high cheekbones and a curved nose. He chewed his food while staring intently at the ground. The look on his face worried Glaze. As Glaze watched, Ol' Joe looked up, propped his right shoulder against the side of the wagon and stared back. He was a large man, six feet tall with broad shoulders and long muscular arms. He threw around the heavy manacles as if they were nothing. His eyes were clear and intelligent and Glaze wondered what schemes cooked inside his head. The man scared him as few men ever had and he didn't like that feeling one bit.

Missouri ministers and preachers called Ol' Joe the son of Satan. Others believed he was the devil himself. His enemies accused him of every possible outrage from stealing to murder and everything in between. He denied all charges, but Missouri collectively hated him. Glaze placed little stock in preachers, but Ol' Joe was one man with whom he would take no chances.

Ol' Joe's steady stare made Glaze uncomfortable and finally, after a supreme effort to hold eye contact, he broke his gaze and looked away. Though Glaze matched the condemned man physically, the steel chains on Ol' Joe's arms and legs made Glaze feel much more secure.

Glaze noticed Ward, the pot-bellied wagon driver, eying Ol' Joe closely. Toad spent most of his time complaining or whining, but now his usually doleful eyes danced with mischief. The guards' recreation on this trip consisted of insulting and taunting the prisoners and this break presented a perfect opportunity to goad them more.

"Tell us a prophecy Joe," the wagon driver said politely in his worn, raspy voice. The guards never said anything pleasant or respectful to the prisoners, so everyone knew his amiable words and demeanor were bogus.

Ol' Joe shifted his eyes from Glaze to the driver who was seated on the ground about ten feet to Glaze's right.

"No point in it," he said quietly. "You wouldn't believe me."

"Sure we would, wouldn't we boys?" the wagon driver intoned contemptuously. "We'd believe any prophecy you want to tell us."

Glaze laughed as all four of his men in mock solemnity vowed to believe Ol' Joe's words. Creech even held his hand over his heart. Then they looked back at him expectantly. All except Harmon who stood about ten yards away, apart from the group, watching and saying nothing.

"What do you want to know?" the chained man asked.

Silence. The question stumped them. They looked back and forth at one another puzzled. What in the future could they find profitable to know? Not that they'd believe Ol' Joe, but the thought intrigued them. Finally, Ward spoke up.

"Tell me how I'll die."

Ol' Joe shook his head.

"Oh come on," the wagon driver said. The other guards needled Ol' Joe too.

"Show us a sign Joe."

"Yer no prophet."

"Yer a fake Joe. You don't know nothin'."

Ol' Joe sighed and shifted his weight.

"It's been my experience that people who want signs are adulterers," Ol' Joe said, looking squarely at Ward. "Wicked and adulterous men seek signs."

Ward sat stone-faced and speechless.

"He is," Tucker bellowed. "I caught him with that James widow two weeks ago, you know the old, gray fat one."

"So what?" Ward snarled.

The guards laughed heartily at each other, nevertheless, the coaxing and taunting for a prophecy went on for several minutes without success. Creech snapped his whip angrily and Pepper spit tobacco onto Ol' Joe's pant leg. The chained man tore a handful of prairie grass from the ground and wiped the tobacco from his pants while chewing calmly on a corn dodger. He went on staring at the ground.

A stream of profanity exploded from Creech. It was almost funny. Glaze knew Creech's temper and figured the blowup would result in some sort of violence, but he decided to do nothing. He found Creech's wildness and meanness endearing. If things got too far out of hand he'd stop it, but all Creech could do was kill a prisoner and that wasn't a bad idea anyway. Drawing a knife from his belt Creech grabbed Ol' Joe's brother by the hair and pinned his head against the ground. Placing the knife against the chained man's throat Creech looked up at Ol' Joe.

"Are you going to tell us a prophecy or am I going to have to cut your brother's throat."

Ol' Joe's eyes glowed. Harmon stepped into the circle.

"Let him go," Harmon said.

"Not until he tells us a prophecy," Creech yelled at Harmon. Then to Smith. "Are you gonna tell us a prophecy?"

"Yeah. I'll tell you a prophecy," Ol' Joe said. "Now let him go."

Creech released the man, who slowly righted himself, unhurt and apparently unperturbed by his brush with death. All eyes fastened on Ol' Joe who slowly rolled onto his knees. His chains rattled eerily. Pointing to the wagon driver he became very businesslike.

"This was your idea so I'll start with you. You'll be dead in five years. Your guts are rotting because you drink too much."

Glaze and the other guards burst into laughter for they all knew that Ward drank heavily and most Missourians they knew regarded heavy drinking as a cherished right and virtue. Even Harmon smiled. Ward staggered clumsily to his feet, bowed and held out his arms to quiet his comrades.

"This calls for a drink," he said. "Does anyone have one?"

Tucker pulled a bottle of whiskey from his saddlebag and tossed it to the wagon driver who held it in his hands reverently. Then, to the other guards' delight, he twisted the cork off and gesturing a contemptuous toast to the chained man who prophesied his demise, took a long swig. Glaze and the other guards roared and clapped merrily. When he finished Ward recorked the bottle and handed it back to its owner while staring at Ol' Joe defiantly.

"Probably more like three years," Ol' Joe said.

For a few minutes everyone, but Ol' Joe, Harmon and the prisoners teased the wagon driver about his imminent death. But soon the chatter died and Pepper, the flank man opposite Creech, spoke up.

"What's gonna happen to me?" Pepper asked.

"You'll go west across the plains to the Rocky Mountains," Ol' Joe said quietly. "But you won't come back. Your scalp will decorate an Indian's tepee and your bones will be crushed by wild animals."

Creech laughed, but the other guards grimaced and fell silent. An uneasy spirit settled over them and they sulked.

"Anybody gonna die of old age?" Tucker asked. In his mid-twenties, Tucker had robbed a Tennessee bank several years earlier, then fled to Missouri to avoid prison. An amiable companion, he enjoyed both hearing and telling stories.

"Not unless you change your ways," Ol' Joe said, fixing his gaze on Tucker. "You'll live longer than these first two, but your life will be a waste and when you finally die there will be no tears shed for you and the grave diggers will gather your body parts in a gunny sack. You won't get a coffin."

Suddenly Ol' Joe looked very tired. He shifted from his knees and sat on the ground next to his brother. Leaning his head against the wagon, he closed his eyes. He obviously didn't want to talk anymore, but the guards weren't finished.

"Tell us what's going to happen to Creech and Glaze and Harmon," Tucker demanded. The others joined in and as Ol' Joe kept his silence their voices got louder, angrier and more insistent. The chained man ignored them and didn't even open his eyes.

Creech lost his temper again. He walked to where Ol' Joe sat and booted the man in the thigh. Ol' Joe barely winced. Creech grabbed the chained man by the throat and pulled him to his feet.

"I wanna know when I'll die," he demanded. "And I wanna know now."

A tense silence fell over the group. Guards and prisoners alike sat spellbound. The wild young guard appeared ready to snap, but Ol' Joe seemed unafraid.

Suddenly Harmon appeared at Glaze's side.

"You've got to stop this before somebody gets killed," Harmon said to him.

"Mind your own business," Glaze yelled at Harmon.

"You don't need to know and you really don't want to know," Ol' Joe said calmly to Creech, shaking his head.

Creech pulled the pistol from his belt, cocked it and shoved it into Ol' Joe's face so that the end of the barrel made a dent in the prisoner's left cheek.

"Don't tell me what I want or don't want," Creech said menacingly. "Say it. Now."

Glaze knew he should intercede before Creech completely lost control, but decided against it mainly because Harmon suggested it. He didn't care what Harmon reported to the governor. He wanted to see what Ol' Joe would do.

Ol' Joe didn't blink. He gazed calmly along the barrel of the gun into Creech's eyes.

"Okay," he said softly. "If that's what you want."

Creech lowered the gun, then smiled at his comrades to celebrate his victory. They cheered and waited for Ol' Joe's prophecy. Ol' Joe shook his head and sighed. Looking Creech straight in the eye, he said, "You won't live to see the sunset today."

Creech's face turned ashen. He stood in front of Ol' Joe like a child expecting to be whipped when his father got home. No one moved or spoke. Finally Creech laughed, tucked the gun back into his belt and walked to the buckskin.

"You better be right," he called back. "And here's a prophecy for you. Tonight after I watch the sun go down I'm going to cut your throat."

Creech put his left foot in the stirrup and swung onto the buckskin. Glaze ordered the prisoners back into the wagon. The guards took up their positions and the procession got under way again, everyone now paying close attention to the sun's position.

For most of the afternoon Creech rode sullenly alongside the open wagon. He forgot to lash the prisoners. They relaxed and talked quietly amongst themselves. From his position at the rear Glaze saw Ol' Joe speak from time to time, but couldn't hear what the man said. As the sun dipped toward the horizon Glaze sensed his guards growing nervous. The game to goad the prisoners had been turned on them. He and his men now worried about Creech wondering how it would happen. Interesting, Glaze thought, since none of them including himself, believed anything Ol' Joe said. A moment later he cursed out loud when he found himself glancing nervously at the horizon.

As time wore on Creech awoke from his somber thoughts and became loud and boisterous. He lashed at the prisoners again and occasionally raced his horse around the wagon screaming savagely. In the late afternoon, he removed a hunting knife from its sheath and flamboyantly honed its edge over a whet stone in full view of Ol' Joe and the prisoners. Glaze loosened the reins on the stud and drew close to the wagon.

"See this knife," Creech said, slicing it through the air as the wagon rumbled along. "It's sharper than a barber's razor. I broke it in last fall. I was with the Livingston boys when they shot up Haun's Mill. So were Glaze, Pepper and Tucker."

Creech pointed at Glaze with the knife and all the prisoners stared. Seventeen of Ol' Joe's men died at Haun's Mill.

"I cut some of your friends' throats with it," Creech went on proudly. "Just the wounded ones that were gonna die anyway. I'd have done more but Glaze shot 'em first with his pistol."

The prisoners shifted nervously. Ol' Joe's brother rapped his chains on the wagon floor angrily.

"Those were peaceful people, simple farmers," Ol' Joe hissed, but Creech ignored him.

"I tried to catch a girl, but all the females ran into the brush too fast," Creech said, grinning, his crooked teeth poking out. "But I caught one a week later at Far West. Hooey. She was pretty. And you'll be happy to know that I wasn't selfish. I shared her with my friends here."

Ol' Joe stared sickly at the wooden floor of the wagon, shaking his head. Glaze saw Harmon look at him disgustedly.

"Yeah. She fell in love with Creech there," Pepper teased from the other side of the wagon. "She hid a sharp rock in her fist and gave him that little love mark on his cheek."

The prisoners squinted up at the ugly red scar on Creech's cheek.

"Good for her," Ol' Joe's brother said loudly.

Creech grinned on.

"When I finished I put my own little love mark on her," he said, flashing the knife in the air again. "I cut her hair off and put a little notch in her ear, so that she'd remember me forever. She had long hair, but not anymore." Then, pointing the knife at Ol' Joe, he added, "Tonight I'm gonna do worse to you."

"Creech, you talk too much." said Tucker, who appeared near the wagon. Shaking his head, he spurred his horse to its original position.

The wagon rumbled on, and though the sun still shone brightly in the west, the day took on a dark and sullen mood.

Several miles remained in their journey to Gallatin, but Glaze determined to get there without stopping again. His orders to move the prisoners to the Gallatin jail came personally from Governor Boggs. He wanted to finish the job.

An hour before sundown, as the glum parade topped a small rolling hill, Tucker glimpsed movement in a stand of cottonwood trees right of the trail one hundred yards away. Tucker signaled Glaze who called an immediate halt and ordered his men and Harmon to form a line on the west side of the wagon so that the prisoners stood between them and the trees. The governor said Ol' Joe's friends might attempt to free him. Now, Glaze's heart pounded and Ol' Joe's prophecy of Creech's death thundered in his ears.

"Somebody check that grove," Glaze ordered, pointing to the trees. "And make sure your guns are loaded. If anything happens, kill the prisoners and scatter."

Without hesitation Creech reined his horse around the wagon and spurred it to a dead run straight at the grove.

"That kid has guts," Tucker said loudly. "He may be stupid and half crazy, but he has guts."

Creech and the buckskin covered the distance in seconds. At the edge of the trees he stopped, then spurred the horse forward again disappearing in the bushy clump of trees. All eyes watched and ears strained expecting any moment to hear gunfire. Instead they heard Creech's buckskin crash through the heavy brush. At the edge of the grove opposite the side Creech entered a whitetail doe appeared followed by two fawns.

"Ah hell, it was only deer," Glaze said with a relieved laugh. "Doesn't look like Creech's gonna die today."

A moment later Creech exited the grove. Seeing the deer he spurred his horse in playful pursuit while the prisoners and other guards watched. The doe and fawns disappeared in another brushy outcropping. Creech stopped and watched them for a moment, then wheeling the buckskin he whipped it to a dead run back to the wagon.

"Won't see the sunset, huh?" Glaze heard himself say.

An instant later, only twenty yards from the wagon, the buckskin's right foreleg disappeared in a prairie dog hole and the mare smashed nose first into the ground and tumbled forward doing a complete somersault. Creech's face hit the ground a split-second after the mare's and then the full weight of the mare's hind quarters landed squarely on his back and neck.

The mare rolled off of Creech and staggered with difficulty to its feet, and then stood awkwardly on three legs. Its right front leg hung limply, obviously broken. Creech shuddered, twitched and lay still. Glaze dismounted and ran to him but there was nothing that could be done. As Glaze rolled him onto his back Creech's eyes fluttered and went blank.

The procession arrived at the Gallatin jail well after dark and found no one there to meet them. The jail turned out to be just a school, but Glaze appreciated that. Remembering his youth in Georgia, Glaze considered jails and schools about the same thing.

After Creech's accident, Glaze had ridden near the wagon glaring at Ol' Joe. He truly wanted to kill him. Glaze thought briefly about stopping the wagon and slitting the prisoners' throats. Had it not been for Harmon's presence and his own orders from Boggs, he would have. But if there was a man he feared more than Ol' Joe, it was Boggs. The prisoners had become a political liability for the governor, who now didn't want them anywhere near Independence.

"Get them to Gallatin quickly and don't kill them," Boggs had said. Apparently, some people actually considered Ol' Joe innocent. Ol' Joe sat in the wagon after Creech's accident with his eyes closed. He said nothing. The other prisoners, sensing the guards' anger, remained quiet too.

Glaze told Tucker to find the sheriff and ordered the prisoners out of the wagon. Creech's body lay in the back of the wagon covered by his own bedroll. His head rested on his saddle and other tack, all his worldly possessions. The buckskin now lay dead back on the trail. The broken leg flopped around pathetically until Harmon unsaddled it and put a bullet through its brain.

When Tucker returned with the sheriff, they herded the prisoners toward the school door. Ol' Joe, as usual, brought up the rear, and before he entered Glaze seized his shoulders from behind and pushed. The prisoner, his legs tangled in chains, fell against the outside wall. Glaze pressed a knife to his throat.

"We're gonna hang you," he said quietly.

"You won't," Ol' Joe shot back.

"Then I'll slit your throat," Glaze said.

"You won't do that either."

Ol' Joe's expression showed no fear.

"That kid was just like you," Ol' Joe said. "His life was a waste just like yours is. And I'll tell you this. If you and your ilk don't leave me and my people alone, there'll come a day when you'll sit in puddles of blood and wish you'd never been born."

Glaze hit Ol' Joe in the face, then pulled the man to his feet and pushed him inside. The only light inside came from one small candle. It illuminated the door to a windowless room that served as the jail cell. The sheriff, Harmon and the other guards waited for Ol' Joe to enter. Glaze shoved Ol' Joe toward it. At the door he put his foot in the man's back and kicked. Ol' Joe tumbled forward into the darkness. Glaze heard the man crash into something and then fall to the floor.

Once the cell door closed Harmon exited the jail quietly, closing the outside door gently behind him.

Glaze's pent-up rage suddenly exploded. Seizing a wooden chair by its legs, he crushed it against the wall. He grabbed an open Bible from the table in the middle of the room, ripped it in half, then overturned the table as his men scrambled to get out of his way.

"I hate you Mormons," he screamed, shaking his fist at the darkness and the prisoners he now could not see, "Joe, I'll cut off your head one day and put it on a pig pole. Mark my words."

# — 2 —

THE HEAVY, POWERFUL ROAR OF A FIFTY-CALIBER RIFLE rolled out of the river bottoms about an hour after sunrise. Otis Harmon spit a stream of tobacco juice onto the ground, then looked up from his task of digging post holes. He knew who was shooting.

Ma.

Libbie Harmon left the house about daybreak determined to find something different from their usual fare of venison and catfish. She spotted a wild turkey a week earlier and mentioned it several times over the next few days saying it looked plump and probably would make a tasty meal. He offered to help.

"I'll do it Oat," she said with the brutal frankness that always made him wince. "You couldn't sneak up on a turkey if you had wings."

She was right. Although he enjoyed hunting, he often felt clumsy trying to slip silently through heavy brush. Anyway, today other tasks occupied his time and his mother hunted as well as any man he knew. The walls of their barn and house, covered with deer and bear hides, testified of her prowess as a hunter.

A half hour after the shot his mother walked into the front yard with a tom turkey draped over her back. She laid it on the ground and walked into the house to put the rifle away. Oat took a break to inspect the turkey as his mother exited the house.

He spit on the ground near the bird, realizing his mistake the moment the juice left his mouth.

"That's a filthy habit and you know I hate it," his mother said acidly. "Don't be spittin' near our food or I'll whup ya."

His mother hadn't whupped him since he was fifteen and she certainly would never do it again, but her rebuke always unsettled Oat.

"Where's its head?" he asked, although he already knew. His mother was good with a rifle. Maybe as good as his father had been.

"Shot it off," she replied. "Didn't want to waste any of the meat."

"How far away was it?" he asked.

"'Bout forty yards."

"Didn't give it much of a chance, did ya?" he teased.

"It shouldn't have let me see it," she said without humor.

The two surviving members of the Harmon family lived along a trail that, according to the trappers who often drifted past, eventually reached Oregon and California. To the southeast a few miles lay the little township of Independence. To the north across the Missouri River small towns and settlements dotted the countryside homesteaded by farmers moving to Missouri from all over the country. More settlements and farms occupied the lands on their south. To the west great plains and wilderness, deserts and mountains lay mostly unoccupied except for Indians, fur trappers, buffalo hunters and a few daring settlers.

Libbie Harmon dressed the turkey while Oat returned to his post hole digging, a long day's work ahead. He needed a new corral. Molly, one of his prized draft horses, had given birth to a colt several weeks earlier which now moved in lock step with Molly. Separating the mother and foal was nearly impossible but Oat often had to work the big mare and the colt got in the way. He was worried it would be injured so he was building a safe pen where he could keep the colt when Molly was in harness. Besides the colt, the Harmons owned five horses — the draft team and three saddle horses.

Oat spent most of his time working. Aside from an occasional trip to Independence for supplies or to see his neighbor Clovis for a few drinks, he spent almost every waking hour on some task. He loved the land the way his father had. He saw more than a log cabin and a few crops surrounded by virgin land, untouched sod and trees. He saw acres of corn, wheat, vegetables, fenced pastures, corrals and barns for cattle and horses. He planned to spend his life building it.

Oat's father, Andrew Harmon, had settled the area with his wife and three young sons in the spring of eighteen twenty-six. Oat, the oldest of the sons, turned six that year, old enough to remember the hardships.

Life dealt cruelly with his father. Over the years Oat pieced together stories about his father's early life and how he came to live in Missouri. Some things he learned from his mother. Some from family friends like the old buffalo hunter Bufflehead, as well as things his father said before his death.

Oat's father spent his early years in a Baltimore orphanage. Oat knew least about that time. His father did not remember his parents. At thirteen, he ran away from the orphanage. He supported himself doing odd jobs and manual labor. He ranged far from Baltimore relying on a strong back and sharp wits. He prospered because the nuns at the Catholic orphanage taught him to read and do elementary math.

Obviously young and alone, he learned many of life's lessons the hard way. Some employers cheated him. Older men conned and swindled him at times, but he learned as he went, working his way south and west, saving a little money with each job and living off the land.

He often found himself working side-by-side with slaves. But as a white man, plantation foremen trusted him with horses. He soon developed an appreciation for well-bred horses, as well as a talent for handling and training them. When he reached New Orleans in the fall of eighteen fourteen, he had become a brawny seventeen-year-old man, strong enough to break the right arm and three ribs of a drunken soldier who tried to rob him. The injured soldier's commanding officer offered him a Springfield flintlock rifle with a broken stock if he would fight against the British who were pressing the city. Having learned never to back down from a fight, Oat's father climbed into the trenches and alongside thousands of other men repulsed wave after wave of British soldiers. When the British retreated he scavenged two British-made muskets, an American-made McCormick flintlock pistol, and a heavy, wool coat.

Over the next four years he continued his journey, traveling north on the Mississippi and then west on the Missouri. He hunted, trapped and worked any job he found, all the while searching for a place to call home. He found his land where the Missouri River took a sharp curve to the north near a small town called Independence. On the surface the land didn't look any different from the thousands of miles over which he had traveled, but it beckoned to him. The soft, green topsoil felt spongy to his feet and when he dug into it with his hands, it turned up black, warm and alive. He decided to live there. With his savings and one of his muskets he purchased one hundred and sixty acres from an old settler and trapper who called himself Bufflehead.

Andrew Harmon then did an odd thing by Missouri standards. He returned to Baltimore to find a wife. He found the few eligible daughters of the old settlers unattractive, even homely. Further, few of them could read or write, and those were skills he now knew his children must have.

He returned to the Roman Catholic parish which operated the orphanage from which he ran away. No one recognized him and he didn't volunteer that he lived there once. Remembering the kindness and the discipline of the Catholic nuns who raised him, he determined to find a wife in a church because he knew by experience, and later taught Oat, that women of character are more commonly found in churches than anywhere else.

He drew no distinction between churches and finally settled on a small Methodist church in a quiet neighborhood. There he found his future wife, Oat's mother, on his first Sunday in Baltimore.

She was the fourth of eight children, having five brothers and two sisters. Seventeen and physically mature, she possessed a fine-boned face and slender strong body. Though not strikingly beautiful, she entertained many suitors mainly because of her sassy wit and happy personality. As it turned out Elizabeth, or Libbie, Hunt discriminated as vigorously as her prospective husband. Andrew's intentions were clear immediately. He did not understand the subtleties of courtship in a place like Baltimore. But his innocent forthrightness attracted her. That, and his rugged bearing. Still, she resisted several months before he won her heart and her hand.

Her family remained suspicious of him for some time. The idea of Libbie marrying a man they didn't know, who had no family and wanted to take their daughter into the western wilderness, alarmed them. Yet, in the end her family warmed to his innocent persistence. Libbie fell in love with him and accepted his marriage proposal. They married in the same Methodist Church where they met. After their marriage, they remained in Baltimore more than five years. Andrew worked in the Hunt family's hardware business, growing increasingly agitated and impatient to be off and working his own land. During this time Libbie gave birth to three sons — Otis, George and Sherman. After saving a sufficient amount of money, the little Harmon family moved west to Independence in the spring of eighteen twenty-six.

Hell greeted them. Though the soil was fertile the tough prairie sod resisted their efforts to raise crops the first year. They grew little food. They survived the winter on potatoes they purchased from neighbors and venison Andrew shot in the river bottoms. They purchased a milk cow from a neighbor on credit so they could have milk for the children but it bloated and died a month later. That first winter Oat's youngest brother, two-year-old George, died of pneumonia.

Despite their setbacks, Andrew and Libbie persisted. The land started to yield to them, but it took its toll. Oat's other brother, Sherman, died of cholera four years after their arrival at age nine. Though Oat contracted the cholera too, he survived.

The most tragic event, however, occurred a short distance from their cabin in December of eighteen thirty-three, the night Andrew failed to return home from hunting. Oat found his father's body the next morning lying in the middle of the trail about a quarter mile from the farm. Someone had shot him in the chest. Whoever did it left his rifle and hunting gear in a pile near his body. Now, six years later, the death haunted Oat and his mother.

Oat's mother often pined away her time in the little family cemetery only a hundred yards from the house. The whole community at Independence expected Libbie Harmon to take her remaining son and return to Baltimore. She sensed pity from some and from others pleasure at her predicament. Maybe that's why she stayed. She refused to let anyone enjoy the satisfaction of seeing her family beaten, especially whoever murdered her husband. Returning to Baltimore symbolized defeat. She remained too stubborn and proud to "go crawling back to her family" as she put it. Now, after six years of living alone on the frontier with her only remaining son, no one could doubt her tenacity. But Oat worried about her. He grew to adulthood seeing her change. His childhood memories included recollections of a soft, sensitive woman who sang and laughed. He seldom saw that in the years following his father's death. Now, her personality included coarse, blunt outbursts not entirely unlike those he heard from men who worked in the fields. Oat knew she suffered and he often wished he could make life better for her.

When Oat turned eighteen his mother hinted, none too subtly, that it was time to find a wife. Oat ignored her, but on reflection he wondered if she wanted him to marry so she could leave without guilt. Her family still lived in Baltimore and she often spoke of them. She never said she wanted to return, but she talked about Baltimore constantly.

The Harmon house was a square log hut, with a dirt floor and a mud-plastered chimney. The house included two windows with no glass. The window doors swung shut at night and in times of storm or bad weather. Their barn housed their large animals. Pigs and chickens occupied small pens. Adjacent to the house the Harmons had cleared almost twenty acres for corn, wheat and a few vegetables. They produced enough to feed themselves and their animals and sold or traded the excess to travelers who passed by, mainly trappers.

In the spring and summer, long pack trains of trappers and buffalo hunters arrived from or departed to the west. These curious looking men wore fur caps and leather clothing. Their hollow, lonesome faces seldom smiled. They talked little and when they did they weren't always understandable. They spoke a mixture of French, English and Indian languages. A few claimed to be criminals who came west to escape a noose or prison and spoke openly of their crimes. Oat heard them on occasion. Some, like Bufflehead, boasted of their crimes. Bufflehead bragged he killed a man in Mississippi for calling his mother a whore. Sadly, he never saw her after running to Missouri to escape punishment.

Sometimes the Harmons saw Indians, but not often. Once seen, the Indians disappeared quickly, like wild animals. On more than one occasion Oat saw Indians staring at him from a bushy vantage point. Many people said Indians killed his father. His mother scorned those who did. And though the thought and tales of savage Indians made Oat nervous sometimes, no Indian ever had threatened him.

Within an hour, the smells of cooking turkey drifted from the house. Out of the corner of his eye Oat saw his mother exit the house and walk slowly to where he worked. She watched quietly for a few moments. She usually did this when she wanted to talk. He ignored her until she spoke.

"I got a letter from Emily yesterday," she said suddenly. She had traveled into Independence the day before, but hadn't mentioned mail. That was her way. She revealed news on her own timetable. Oat figured all women did the same.

"Aunt Emily? You didn't say anything last night."

"I was thinking what I should do," she said. "John is sick, probably dying. She wants us to come live with them."

Uncle John and Aunt Emily lived in Baltimore. John was his mother's oldest brother and she often talked of him fondly. She seldom heard from the rest of the family, but Uncle John wrote several times each year. Oat knew his mother wanted to see him. Oat let his shovel stand in the post hole. He didn't remember his Uncle John. The last time he had seen him would have been thirteen years earlier when he was five years old. Uncle John would be more than fifty.

"I think you should go," he said after a moment's reflection. "We've got enough money saved. Uncle John needs you and you should go see him. I can take care of things here."

"I want you to come with me."

He shook his head.

"Who'd look after the farm? It won't keep by itself. Besides, there's nothing for me in Baltimore."

"We can sell the farm and there would be work for you in Baltimore," she said. "Uncle John owns that little tavern near the wharf and some of my cousins still have a hardware store in town. You could work there and you'd have a chance to meet some girls your age. You're old enough that you need to think about marrying."

"There are girls here and I'm not going to travel a thousand miles so I can wash dishes for somebody else."

His mother scowled.

"You're a man now Oat. If you don't find a woman to settle down with soon you're going to be chasing after whores and silly, empty-headed women like Sarah Riley."

His mother's bluntness always made Oat uneasy. He didn't like talking about women with her. She thought he liked Sarah. He really didn't, but for some reason he wanted her to worry about it.

"When the time comes I'll find a good woman Ma."

"And no Mormons. I can't stand Mormons."

"No Mormon girls," Oat agreed, nodding his head.

"Mormons are trouble," she continued. "Stay away from them."

"Boggs chased all the Mormons out of the state, Ma," Oat said patiently. "I couldn't marry a Mormon if I wanted to."

"I wish your father was alive," she went on. "He could tell you how to act around a woman. How to be a gentleman. I feel like it ain't proper for me to tell you."

"Ma, I know what to do. I'm not stupid."

"You haven't shown much aptitude up to now. With a woman it takes a little more than just snorting and then jumping on her like the stud does with Molly."

"Ma, when the time comes I'll figure it out." Oat felt himself growing impatient.

"I hope you figure it out soon. I want some grandchildren."

She stood silent for a moment looking into the hole he was digging.

"I'll worry about you here alone. The same men that killed your father might kill you. You should leave here."

"I've lived here most of my life and I'm still alive," Oat said. "Whoever killed Pa is long gone. They won't be back."

"You're wrong," she said. "Boggs is still here and one of these days he's going to come after you too. He didn't like your Pa. Last week when you went to Gallatin with that good-for-nothing Glaze I worried every minute. I had nightmares all week. I was afraid you wouldn't come back — like your father."

When Oat helped move the Mormon prisoners to Gallatin, his mother had gone into town and threatened the governor that she'd kill him if anything happened to her son. She acted like a crazy woman and it embarrassed Oat.

The common belief at Independence held that Indians killed Andrew Harmon. Even Oat wondered if that might be the truth. His mother firmly maintained Boggs was responsible, yet she had no proof.

"If Boggs was going to do anything to us he would have done it already," Oat said. "I can take care of myself. This is where I plan to spend my life. Pa, George and Sherm are buried here."

Invoking the memory of his father and brothers seemed almost unfair, but he felt cornered.

"Your Pa could take care of himself too," she said quietly. "And you are young and you don't have the experience your father did."

He knew she was right. Few men would have challenged Andrew Harmon face to face. Oat resembled his father physically, but he had never fought anyone.

"I feel like I should go to Baltimore," she said a few moments later. "Emily wouldn't ask unless she truly needed the help and I do want to see John again before he dies. But Oat, you shouldn't live here all alone. If anything happened to you there wouldn't be anyone nearby to help."

"Clovis lives just a few miles away," Oat said. "He's my best friend and he'll check on me."

"You know what I mean Oat," his mother said, a touch of impatience in her voice. "Quit avoiding the subject. You need someone, not only so you're not alone, but so I can have some grandchildren before I die. You're my only hope. Your father went to Baltimore to find a bride, you could too."

Oat leaned on his shovel.

"Ma, you're not going to die anytime soon," he said. "I promise you grandchildren. In fact, I am going to have so many kids you'll get tired remembering all their names. You'll have to have a house as big as a church if you invite us to Sunday dinner and you'll have to cook a buffalo to feed us all."

# — 3 —

THE SEVENTEEN MINISTERS ANSWERED YES WHEN called upon to vote. They reasoned that since God chose them, then they must be right especially if they agreed. Most assented vocally; others simply nodded. Some shouted eagerly while a few hesitated, but in the end not one dissented.

No names were used because as everyone had agreed, this meeting didn't take place. No minutes would be taken nor records kept. If anyone outside this group asked if such a meeting was held, the question would be answered by puzzled blank stares or ridicule. And God help the man who couldn't keep his mouth shut or who got in their way. The memory and fate of Andrew Harmon lingered in their minds and built a giant, invisible wall of secrecy.

The red-headed reverend, who hosted the meeting, put the proposal to words. Common feelings burned in all their hearts. All voiced the same sentiments many times before in a variety of places and circumstances. Any could have, and would have, said the same thing.

The seventeen assembled from Richmond, Liberty, Kingston, Breckenridge, Gallatin, Independence, even as far away as Columbia. They represented a variety of denominations. Some traveled all night and day to attend and all arrived at the barn within minutes of the others as a dark, menacing thunder cloud eclipsed the soft light of the early evening.

Lightning cracked the gathering darkness followed by the pounding of distant thunder. A slight wind pressed in from the southwest steadily growing in intensity. Thunder swelled and rolled over the western Missouri frontier. The rain started slowly in sparse spitlike droplets, but as the wind and thunder increased so did the rain until it fell in torrents as the men arrived.

These men, familiar with all the problems and dangers of frontier living, found the rainstorm trivial. Upon entering the barn they stomped, kicking mud from their boots and shaking rainwater from their coats like rangy, wet animals. They spoke little to one another mainly out of weariness and because the atmosphere and business did not lend itself to that of a social occasion.

They chose the barn as a meeting place because it was spacious and remote. The participants wanted secrecy because some individuals would misinterpret their good intentions. They posted a guard outside.

The seventeen main participants sat in a circle. As the premature darkness settled around them the red-headed reverend placed a lantern on the floor. As each man took a chair, huge black shadows danced on the walls behind them like incomprehensible demons.

Other guests sat outside the main circle. Glaze, a special invitee, took one of these chairs and watched as others arrived. They included important and significant men in Jackson County. Bill Brown and Tom Pitcher, the constables, stood together in the corner. County judge Sam Lucas and James Flourney, the postmaster, seated themselves near Glaze. Cleo Barker, the livery owner took a seat along with state and county officials, businessmen, farmers and even one newspaper man. Most importantly, Governor Lilburn Boggs sat quietly near a wall by himself, his head bowed.

Glaze's invitation came directly from Boggs, who a few years earlier made it plain he could destroy Glaze with one stroke of a pen. Survival to Glaze meant remaining in the governor's favor. Glaze intended to survive.

Though Boggs didn't say it, Glaze clearly understood that a core group that included Boggs orchestrated the proceedings. Boggs explained the meeting gave this group a chance to force key individuals, the entire community and state into line by putting an ecclesiastical blessing on their plans. They thought if the ministers of all the religious groups agreed, then God must be in agreement too. This allowed the conspirators to justify their acts even when they appeared contrary to everything they preached from the pulpit or decreed in the courtroom. They used this rationale often.

The red-headed reverend was a barrel of a man, about medium

height, heavy set, but certainly not fat. His round, pink face and red hair gave him a rather jolly, boyish look. His deep, practiced voice easily filled the room.

Glaze watched transfixed as the meeting unfolded, the main players speaking and slowly moving the group toward its predetermined conclusion just as Boggs predicted.

Glaze understood Boggs. They thought alike. No moral code bound them. Each lived to serve his own ends and would do anything at all to further his personal goals and enrich himself, even the sorts of acts and deeds that repulsed weaker men. Though Boggs made all the decisions and gave the orders, Glaze found the terms suitable. A willing accomplice, he carried out Boggs' will to the letter.

The meeting revolved around the group's plans for a man who was not even present, the same man Glaze had transported to Gallatin a week earlier — Joseph Smith. The mysterious Mormon prophet frightened Boggs and every man in the barn though not one would have admitted it. But Glaze knew fear and he sensed it now.

Smith and his followers had come to Missouri by the thousands. The old settlers nicknamed them Mormons because of a book Smith claimed to have translated from golden plates and published. Smith called it the *Book of Mormon*. The Mormons intended to make Missouri into Zion, a paradise that Ol' Joe said would be God's kingdom on earth. The old settlers laughed at them at first, but the Mormons kept coming, continually spouting their obnoxious beliefs and intentions. They grew in number so quickly that the old settlers soon realized they could lose political control of the state to these newcomers. That could never be tolerated, not in Missouri.

A year earlier this same group approved a plan laid out by Boggs to rid Missouri of Smith and all of his followers. The diabolical plan was carried out in meticulous detail. It began with carefully concocted rumors designed to ignite the old settlers' hatred toward the Mormons.

"The Mormons are thieves," the first rumor raged. "Mormons have horns and cloven feet," another popular rumor went. And then probably the most damning rumor of all: "Mormons want to free the slaves."

The defamation of the Mormons was easy. The old settlers, who came from mountainous southern regions of the country where slavery was accepted, were naturally suspicious of the Mormons. Since the Mormons hailed mainly from the New England states, their speech and mannerisms seemed peculiar in Missouri. As it turned out the Mormons did harbor abolitionist ideas and their anti-slavery sentiments bubbled into the public eye on occasion. The rumors and the abolitionist talk riled the old settlers. The final straw, however, turned out to be Joseph Smith himself, who claimed to have seen God Almighty. Evidently, all the new people believed Smith and, in most things, followed him unquestioningly. The Mormons' boldness and their proselyting activities engendered a seething hatred among the other churches in the region.

A few inflammatory words uttered by the right people at the right times ignited Missouri into a boiling cauldron of hatred. These same ministers, now seated before Glaze, provided the perfect medium to purvey the hate. These clergymen twisted and slanted Mormon views against slavery and their beliefs in a future Kingdom of God to scare the old settlers. The resulting rumors flashed and raged through the countryside quicker than an Indian scare. As Boggs intended, tempers flared. Fist fights broke out. More extreme violence followed. Old settlers tarred and feathered Mormons. Their houses were torn apart or burned. The conflict produced a human powder keg ready to explode just like Boggs planned. When tensions reached their apex, Boggs gave Glaze his first set of secret orders.

"Attack both sides brutally," he had said. "The Mormons will think the old settlers did it and the old settlers will think the Mormons did it. Before long Ol' Joe and his bunch will collapse simply because they're outnumbered."

Boggs' assessment turned out to be perfect. His willingness to sacrifice some of his own citizenry made the plan work. Glaze and his men attacked and burned several Mormon farms in two succeeding nights. A few nights later, masked and unrecognizable, they burned three non-Mormon farms, actually killing a man who months earlier had cheated Pepper in a horse swap. Soon the old settlers and the Mormons drew battle lines. The old settlers rode together in groups of up to one hundred men. The Mormons formed a group called Danites who fought back. After that, the newspapers blamed the Danites for every unexplained, evil act that occurred in Missouri. Boggs saw to that. And Glaze operated without fear of being held responsible. A few weeks of midnight raiding gave Boggs ample reason to call out the Missouri militia to restore peace. The call-up was brilliant. No one, except Boggs apparently, realized the militia would turn into a murdering, plundering mob. The Mormons suffered dearly.

By the end of October several thousand Mormons gathered at Far West, the main Mormon community in Missouri. They intended to defend themselves against the militia that now numbered more than six thousand. Boggs made the most of their resistance, issuing an executive order to exterminate or drive them from the state.

At Haun's Mill, near Far West, a score of Mormons holed up in a blacksmith shop to defend themselves from two hundred militiamen. Missouri called it a battle. Glaze witnessed and participated in the massacre. The Mormons called it murder.

After that, both sides prepared for war. But the Mormons avoided an all-out war when Ol' Joe, under a flag of truce, rode into the Missouri camp. In a strange twist, the military commander Smith appointed himself, handed Ol' Joe and several other Mormon leaders over to the Missouri militia as prisoners of war. Glaze wondered later if Smith devised that plan to avoid a battle. In any event Boggs' predictions turned out to be exactly right. With Smith gone, the mob looted Far West and drove the Mormons out of Missouri. As far as Glaze knew they were still running.

Glaze suppressed a laugh as the red-headed reverend read a list of Smith's crimes. Half of them Glaze committed himself. He did his job well, making the Mormons appear responsible for the attacks on the old settlers. Those deeds included three murders Glaze and his men committed. They cut one man's head off and shot the other two. The deaths angered all of Missouri and confused the Mormons. Glaze glanced at Boggs, who appeared to be dozing. Glaze knew he wasn't. He heard every word.

As he watched Boggs, Glaze felt a cold, hard fist of fear. He hoped he and Boggs never got crosswise. Boggs' political skills and ruthlessness scared him. He nurtured the power to have others kill for him. Few men possessed that power; even fewer used it.

When the red-headed reverend finished reading he asked the other ministers to add personal testimony to illustrate Smith's delinquent personality. The ministers obliged and for another hour they took turns using their abundant ministerial talents to ridicule Smith's teachings and his so-called revelations.

"No man amongst us has seen God or angels or been given holy stones or golden plates," one minister screeched. "No man can know the things Ol' Joe claims to know and do the things he claims to do." Others said the same thing in different ways.

No one argued in Smith's behalf. The consensus held that Smith was incorrigible. So the ministers talked and deliberated and then, finally, after what seemed to Glaze like hours of discussion they reached a conclusion.

"Brothers," the redhead said. "If I understand you correctly every man here believes Joe Smith is going to hell."

Affirmative grunts went around the room.

"If that's the case, then why don't we help him on his way?"

More agreeable noise pulsed through the group. Hearing this, the red headed minister beckoned to Boggs who rose.

"I have listened closely to your concerns tonight," he said. "It's obvious that you feel Joe Smith's soul is irretrievable. I agree with you. He is an infidel, his ideas so radical that even the most liberal of us recoil at the thought of such dogma. His soul is lost, far beyond the reach of even your most sincere and faithful efforts. Preaching to him is out of the question. Such a man can't be taught or rehabilitated, not even by you and if you were to try any effort to preach, it would meet with failure. He would respond to your faithful efforts arguing word for word, idea for idea, doctrine for doctrine. He would not appreciate your mercy or your prayers. And if we were to release him right now from the jail at Gallatin he would continue in his same damnable direction. The laws of this great republic have not yet been written to tell us how to deal with men as evil as Joe Smith. He is beyond our law. So we must be creative. I am your elected servant, here to do your bidding. Tell me what you want me to do and I will do it."

Boggs sat down and the red-headed reverend slowly rose to his feet and again took command. He started softly.

"Brothers, we have a duty. As ministers of righteousness and protectors of our flocks, we each have a solemn, sacred obligation to shield our people from this heretic and his dangerous ideas and influence. He is evil, a troublemaker who will never go away unless we put an end to him. Even though he is in jail and his people scattered we can't stop now. They will return when given the chance. They have said so openly. We have to stop this man now while we can."

He paused and looked down at the floor as a murmur of agreement rippled through the room. When the murmurs died, he said: "Reason demands that we act. We know what must be done and we can't shrink from our duty."

He paused again and closed his eyes as if in prayer. All eyes fastened on him. He filled his lungs, opened his eyes and slowly panned the room. Then his voice thundered:

"If we don't act now God will hold us responsible. Our course is simple and direct. Smith must die. Only then will the Mormon Church become extinct."

The room fell silent for long seconds as the preachers stared back and forth at each other, absorbing the words, knowing what they meant and wondering if they had the courage to see it through.

Then one very low, quiet voice said, "Amen." A louder "Amen" followed. Soon everyone in the room repeated the Amens until the rafters of the barn shook with Amens.

And so the seventeen beacons of Missouri charity and piety condemned 'Ol Joe to death, uniting their voices and resources in a solemn and secret oath, swearing by Almighty God to destroy him.

When the meeting broke up after midnight, Glaze made his way back to Independence slowly letting the chestnut pick its way through the darkness. As he rode, he heard another horse draw near from behind, probably someone else from the meeting on his way home, but because of the blackness of the night Glaze could not see who followed until the rider spoke.

"Can you come see me Monday morning? We have plans to make." The voice belonged to Boggs.

"Where?"

"My house. Early."

They rode on silently the only sound the thumping of the horses' hooves on the wet ground.

"I wonder if Ol' Joe has any idea what's about to happen?" Glaze said.

Boggs remained silent for a moment, then said: "Believe me. He does."

# — 4 —

HANNAH GENTLY BRUSHED HER MOTHER'S HAIR MAKING sure each wavy brown lock fell in place. Martha Wheatley lay on her back under a sycamore tree, eyes closed, her worn, calloused hands folded neatly on her stomach. She often fell asleep when Hannah brushed her hair. As Hannah brushed, she studied her mother's ruddy, tanned complexion, complemented so perfectly by a small, upturned nose. Her lips, usually full and pink, pursed downward this morning into an odd frown. Hannah adored her smile because her whole face lit up and beamed warmness and sincerity. It made people happy to see it. Hannah remembered those who said Hannah looked just like her. She felt happy when people said that because she knew her mother was beautiful.

Nearby movement caught her attention and Hannah looked up to see her father approaching, a pointed stick in his hand.

Jerome Wheatley seemed small this morning. His strong, wide shoulders sagged and his eyes drooped sadly. He always appeared so in control. Few things troubled him. When the family needed food, he supplied it. When the roof leaked, he fixed it. When they needed money, he earned it. No problem stopped him. He never whined or complained and taught Hannah to shoulder her responsibilities without whimpering. He knew how to fix everything. At dawn, only a few hours earlier, Hannah heard him cry. The sound shocked her and she never would forget it. But he had good reason. He awakened to find that his wife, Hannah's mother, had died quietly in the night.

"I'll go over by those trees," he said, pointing to a small grove of aspen. "We'll lay her there. You get her ready."

Hannah nodded. While tears flowed down her cheeks hate boiled inside her breast for the people who inflicted this terrible tragedy on her family. She couldn't speak without crying. Her father leaned down and stroked her head.

"We'll get through this," he said, his voice strong and confident. "Don't lose hope."

Hannah knew his hurt matched hers. She watched his back as he walked to the designated grave spot. He walked slowly, head bent, shoulders trembling and shaking as he muffled his sobs. The pathetic sounds eerily drifted to her ears. She wondered how much more he could take and what toll the full truth would have. He didn't know everything, and he never would know. Hannah, the only person who knew the full extent of her mother's trauma, never would tell him.

"I'll take care of him for you Mama," Hannah said, patting her mother's still shoulder. "We'll be okay, but it's going to take us some time, maybe a long time."

Over the past three weeks the Wheatley buried three other family members, Hannah's younger brothers. One by one, they succumbed to fever, hunger and exposure or a combination of the three. The baby, Daniel, departed first. Born in late December near Far West, he arrived at least a month early, only weeks after the mob sacked the city. His birth sapped Martha Wheatley's strength. Daniel fared poorly from the start, but would have lived if not for an attack by the Missouri mob during a cold, winter storm at the end of February.

Over the years mobs had attacked Hannah's family three times. The first occurred years before when they were driven from Jackson County. The mob struck a second time only a few months earlier during the plundering of Far West. The last attack, though the least violent, bore the most vicious consequences.

Hannah remembered the day well. The men, a group of bearded, tobacco-stained pukes, entered their home without invitation or warning while her father hunted for food. Hannah attacked them with a kitchen pot, but they simply took the pot away and carried her outside, shooing her brothers along behind.

Compared with earlier mobs this group acted politely, at least they didn't kill or rape anyone. A few groped and leered at Hannah, but they took it no further. One stinking brute grabbed Hannah's dress and tried to tear it off. But their leader, a tall well-dressed man, scolded the attacker.

"Ain't got time for that today."

Hannah's mother lay on a bed with the baby, too weak to move. The men lifted the entire bed with its occupants and carried it outside. They deposited the bed on the ground in the cold open air. Hannah, intent on making sure her mother and tiny brother weren't harmed failed to notice the fire until it was too late, not that she could have stopped it. The mob stayed long enough to make certain the house couldn't be saved and then left them in the cold morning drizzle, without shelter, watching everything they owned burn to ashes.

The mob stole the family's mules and cow and as they left, their leader said: "You Mormons been warned more than once. Now get out."

In retrospect, Hannah felt it would have been more merciful if they had put guns to their heads and shot their brains out.

Upon her father's return, the family left Far West following a worn trail to the east left by the main body of the community weeks earlier. The Wheatleys would have traveled with them if not for the new baby and Martha's weak condition. They planned to leave that spring after her health improved and the baby grew old enough to travel. Now no one offered help. For the most part, the only ones still living in Far West had sold their souls to the devil or the governor. To Hannah, they were the same.

They moved slowly, sometimes only a few miles a day. With no animals they carried the few possessions they salvaged from the burned rubble of their home. The baby died two days out of Far West. It developed a cough and fever first and then got too weak to cry. He drifted away quietly one afternoon while Pete held him. Nine-year-old Pete departed four days later after developing a high fever. John followed. At thirteen, wiry and strong, he lingered almost a week as the family sought shelter in a glen near a small stream. Finally, a lack of good food and shelter combined with the sickness took him too. Now Hannah's mother was gone too, a victim of the same awful fever and probably a broken heart.

Hannah, now eighteen, knew life held disappointment and difficulties, but still did not understand why God let this happen to her family. She prayed so often during those dark weeks that her dirty knees bled. If God saw, he didn't respond. She pictured her father standing before her in the early morning light.

"Your Mama died."

And no one could do anything or say anything to bring her back. Tears welled up in her eyes. From where would her strength come now?

"Oh, God. How could you let Mama die?" she whispered.

Hannah smoothed her mother's dirty dress, the only clothing she had. Everything else burned at Far West. Hannah dipped a corner of her own skirt in a cupful of water. Papa salvaged the cup from the wreckage of their home. She washed her mother's face and hands, kissed her cheek and went to Papa.

The spot her father chose lay far enough away from the aspens that he did not have to dig through their roots. He dug slowly. First, he gouged at the soft soil with the stick to loosen it then he scooped it away with his bare hands as he did when he dug her brothers' graves. He was composed. The work probably helped him and he hardly noticed Hannah as she stood nearby. Over the next three hours Hannah walked back and forth between Mama and Papa, trying to think if there was anything she could do for her mother and trying to help her father. A few times she fetched water from a nearby stream using the cup. He gulped it down quickly and returned to his work. By midmorning the grave was ready.

Her father carried his wife to the grave and laid her beside it tenderly. He knelt there for a long moment in silence, tears quietly rolling off his cheeks. Hannah knelt beside him. She thought she had cried all her tears, but others appeared.

Tears we have in abundance, she thought bitterly. Kissing his wife one last time, her father got into the grave while Hannah wrapped her mother in the small blanket she laid under during the night. They both knew they should keep the blanket, but neither wanted to place her in the ground with nothing to cover her beautiful face. Finally Papa lifted her down and laid her gently on the earth and climbed out.

He stood at the head of the grave and motioned for Hannah to come to him. They knelt again. He prayed, but Hannah couldn't focus on the words. She wondered bitterly if God listened anyway. When he finished, her father began to fill the grave.

Hannah couldn't watch. She walked toward the stream. Once there she found six round, smooth stones. She carried them back and when her father finished filling the grave she arranged the stones at its head in a circle.

They stood over the grave for some time weeping. They found it hard to leave the spot. It was so peaceful. For the first time in several weeks the sun shone warmly on them.

"I suppose we should be going," her father said finally.

"Where are we going Papa?" Hannah asked.

"We're going to join the saints," he said, looking at her oddly. "Where else would we go?"

"I don't know," Hannah said. "Do you think they're all together?"

"Yes," he said. "Somewhere at the end of this trail."

They walked eastward.

# — 5 —

HUNDREDS GATHERED ALONG INDEPENDENCE'S MAIN street to enjoy the warm spring sunshine and the horse races. Racing provided the main social outlet for many of Jackson County's old settlers. A jug of corn liquor, aged just right, fast horses and spirited spectators livened some afternoons into all-out parties. Many went straight from church to the races still dressed in their Sunday best. Sometimes fiddlers played and couples danced. Everyone laughed and talked.

For Tyrone Glaze, the Sunday races provided one of life's greatest pleasures — the satisfaction of soundly beating an opponent in all-out horse race with few rules. Glaze loved the smell of leather and horse sweat, the betting and the gut-rending tension just before a race began. He reveled in the rumble of powerful hooves pounding the earth. He especially relished the feeling of victory and superiority upon seeing the sadness or misery in the faces of those who lost.

At the end of this spring afternoon as the shadows deepened four riders brought their horses to the starting line for the day's final race. A long-backed palomino gelding pawed the ground next to a bay mare ridden by an Independence teenager. A sorrel gelding with four white feet snorted nervously as it eyed Glaze's chestnut stallion. These four undefeated horses each had won earlier in the afternoon and this race would determine the day's champ. At the finish line, men placed bets on their favorites, but for this race Glaze knew relatively little money would change hands. Only fools bet against his chestnut because it never had lost a race.

Though thirty to forty pounds heavier than the other riders, Glaze rode the stud. His extra weight handicapped the stud and gave the other horses a small chance to win. As they waited for the starting signal, the sorrel gelding, rearing and snorting, edged too close to the chestnut. The stud laid back its ears and attacked, viciously biting the sorrel on the left shoulder and drawing blood. The sorrel squealed and reared.

"Keep that devil back," the rider snarled.

"Keep that cur out of his and my way," Glaze yelled back.

The sorrel's rider feared the stud for good reason. The stud had no tolerance for geldings or other stallions. Only a week before, a livery hand had made the mistake of penning the chestnut with a gelding and a young stallion. The stud killed the gelding and maimed the stallion so badly it had to be destroyed. Glaze had watched and laughed as it happened. One at a time, the chestnut had charged the other animals, ramming into them and knocking them to the ground. While the other animals struggled to regain their footing the stud kicked and trampled them.

Glaze stole the stallion from a Kentuckian named Turvey who rode it into Texas during the late winter of thirty-six, just before Texas' war with Santa Anna. Glaze wanted it the moment he laid eyes on it. On the run from for killing a Georgia plantation heir in a brawl over a whore, Glaze understood the value of a fast horse. Turvey rebuffed his offer to buy it.

"Can't sell this one," Turvey said brusquely. "Besides," he added arrogantly. "You don't have anywhere near enough money."

Glaze never wanted anything so badly, especially after seeing the stud run. No horse in Sam Houston's army could match it over any distance. Besides being incredibly fleet, the stud's unmistakably beautiful conformation belied a storied bloodline. Turvey cleverly earned a decent living betting on it.

Glaze stole the stud a week later, killing a ten-year-old Mexican boy who tended it while Turvey slept off a hangover. The horse represented a fortune. Glaze deserted Houston's army and left Texas traveling north as quickly as the chestnut could carry him, easily outdistancing any pursuers.

Glaze stopped in Missouri, far beyond Turvey's range, he thought. He kept the stud hidden for months, shaved his beard and changed his name. Until then Glaze had been known as Henry Garrison. Missouri knew him as Tyrone Glaze. He lived as Turvey had. The old settlers in western Missouri loved to race horses too, so Glaze made money betting on and racing the chestnut. He also made money breeding the stud. The more Glaze raced the more determined others were to have colts from the stud.

Glaze underestimated Turvey and the spread of the stud's reputation. One summer evening Governor Lilburn Boggs and two armed guards on horses surprised him at his cabin on the Blue River bottoms. The guards' held their rifles ready as they rode up to his hut. He saw the hammers pulled back on both guns. They waited outside the cabin while Boggs entered without an invitation.

"Can you read?" Boggs asked abruptly. Glaze shook his head.

"It's a letter from the president of the new republic of Texas, a fellow named Sam Houston," Boggs said. "It says a man named Victor Turvey is coming to Independence to retrieve his horse, a thoroughbred chestnut stallion stolen from him about a year ago. It also says the man thought to have possession of that horse is wanted for the murder of a boy. It asks me to arrest you and assist Mr. Turvey."

Boggs laid the letter aside and stared accusingly for a long moment at Glaze, who wondered if he could murder a governor and get away with it. Boggs read his mind.

"Please understand sir," he said, "that if anything were to happen to me while I'm here in your house that those two men outside are under orders to kill you."

Glaze nodded and Boggs smiled smugly.

"Horse theft and murder are serious offenses," he said. "When you get back to Texas, they're going to hang you."

Boggs let his words sink in for several seconds, then smiled again.

"But I can help you if you're willing to cooperate with me."

And then to Glaze's delight the governor, by candlelight, unfolded a plan that guaranteed Glaze's safety and allowed him to keep the stud. In exchange Glaze would help the governor with certain sensitive services.

Victor Turvey arrived at Independence a month later, carrying a bundle of important papers given him by Sam Houston. He called on Boggs who arranged accommodations in an isolated cabin near

Independence. No one at Independence knew Turvey so no one missed him when he and his papers disappeared that night. A week later a ferryman fished a headless body from the Missouri River many miles downstream from Independence. The local sheriff attributed the deed to Indians. The local populace soon forgot about it probably because the dead man remained unidentified and no one among them was missing.

A gunshot signaled the start of the race and the horses surged forward. The race would end on the Independence Main Street. The palomino started quickly and ran even with the chestnut for the first quarter mile as Glaze held the stud back. If he beat them too far he'd never get another race so he didn't turn the stud loose until the finish line came into view lined on both sides by a yelling horde of bearded, drinking men. Glaze loosed the reins and the chestnut responded by opening a lead of nearly five lengths before crossing the finish line.

Governor Boggs used the back room of his house for an office when the legislature was not in session. Visitors waited outside on a log bench concealed by bushes and shrubs. When Glaze arrived he heard muffled voices inside so he waited. Ten minutes later the door opened and a listless old man in buckskin leggings stepped outside, shaking his head.

"I'll think on it," the man said to Boggs as he limped out the door.

"Suit yourself," the governor called after him, "but don't think too long. This won't wait."

"I'll come back later and give you my answer," the old man said as he hobbled on. A beard adorned the old man's leathery face. He chewed tobacco and barely glanced at Glaze as he went past. Glaze had seen him about town but couldn't remember his name.

"Who was that?" Glaze asked Boggs.

"An old trapper. I've know him for years. His name's Bufflehead."

Boggs led Glaze into his office and shut the door. Sitting on a hard chair in front of a big wooden desk, he surveyed the room. It hadn't changed since his last visit. A sword hung on the wall near the hide of a giant black bear and the antlers of a four-point whitetail buck. A few trinkets and books sat on the desk alongside a pile of papers. A brass spittoon rested on the floor to the right of Boggs' desk. Tobacco spittle dripped down its exterior and puddled on the floor.

"You need to practice your aim," Glaze said, pointing to the spittoon.

The governor laughed easily, but Glaze always tensed in his presence. At fifty he remained a striking man. He moved about gracefully and elegantly. He demeanor oozed confidence. Power glowed in his eyes — cold eyes. Deadly eyes. The eyes of a predator. The governor arranged some papers on his desk.

"I saw the horse race Sunday," he said. "That's a fine animal you have. I'd probably kill for it too. When you steal a horse you go after the best."

Glaze grunted. He knew he hadn't been summoned to pass the time of day. The governor leaned back in his chair.

"We're ready to proceed," Boggs said. "I've heard from the judge at Gallatin. He's with us."

Standing, Boggs walked to the bear hide on the wall. He ran his fingers through the fur, then looked at Glaze curiously.

"The judge has misgivings about you. He heard that during the attack on Haun's Mill, you found a young boy hiding among the bodies in the blacksmith shop. The judge says he was scared to death and begging for his life, but uninjured. You, however, grabbed him by the hair, put a gun to his head and shot his brains out. The judge says he's willing to do whatever it takes to get rid of the Mormons, but he draws the line at killing kids."

Boggs sat down at his desk and stared directly at Glaze.

"Did you really do that?"

Glaze hesitated uneasily, wondering whether to lie. He decided not to. Too many people knew what he'd done. The governor, or the judge, apparently had been asking questions.

"Nits make lice," Glaze said nervously. Boggs leaned back in his chair and grinned widely back at Glaze.

"You are a man after my own heart," he said. "If I had been there I would have been in that shop with you shooting the hell out of things. But governors can't do things like that personally. We have to maintain a certain distance. You understand, don't you?"

"Yes sir," Glaze said. "I understand."

The governor still smiled at him.

"I have some other questions," he said, shuffling more papers about on his desk. "Last year on my orders you burned homes and killed men. Some were against the Mormons; some weren't. Have you told anyone you did them on orders from me?"

"The only ones that know are me and the four men who helped me. One of them's dead and the others know not to talk. If they do, I will kill them. They know that."

Boggs nodded.

"Of course if anyone ever does talk I'll deny it, and then you will pay the natural penalty. You understand that don't you?"

Glaze nodded. The natural penalty. In addition to all his other strengths, Boggs had a way with words too.

"I understand," Glaze answered.

"Do you regret killing that Mormon kid?"

Glaze didn't regret it for a moment and never had lost a moment's sleep over it. He returned the governor's cold stare, eyeball to eyeball.

"The only regret I have sir is that I didn't shoot that little sucker again before he hit the floor."

Boggs and Glaze stared across the desk at each other for a long, silent moment. Suddenly Boggs broke into a huge roaring belly laugh.

"Glaze," he said finally, after calming himself. "You're my man? Are you ready to go to work?"

Glaze leaned back in his chair tipping it onto two legs. He knew what Boggs wanted done, but he wanted Boggs to say it.

"Sir?" Glaze said.

"As we both learned the other night, Missouri wants Joe Smith dead," Boggs said leaning forward. "Can you do it and keep your mouth shut about it?"

Glaze let the legs of the chair come back to the floor.

"Sure, but I want you to explain to me again why I couldn't have done it when I took him to Gallatin. I lost a man on that trip and it would have been easy."

"We weren't ready," Boggs said.

"Why don't you just have a trial and hang him?"

Boggs squirmed in his chair. It was good to see. Glaze had never seen Boggs squirm.

"Unfortunately, the political climate is changing rapidly right now and it appears we no longer can count on a conviction and execution. In fact, it appears more likely that such a trial simply would be a huge embarrassment for me and all of Missouri. On the other hand we can't let Smith go. If we did, we would be admitting we were wrong in making war on the Mormons."

"So it's best just to kill him?"

Boggs nodded: "That's about right, but it can't appear as if I or any other state official had anything to do with it."

"If he's killed in jail, or even trying to escape from jail, that's exactly what it will look like," Glaze said.

"Yes, I know."

Glaze leaned back in his chair again and waited.

"We're going to give him a change of venue," Boggs said. "Ol' Joe's been asking for that anyway so we'll give it to him. While en route from Gallatin to Columbia he and his guards will be ambushed by Indians and wiped out. The guards have to be killed too. I want no witnesses, just dead men. That will draw the blame from me."

"Who do you plan to use for guards?" Glaze asked.

"I have someone in mind. A man I've been grooming for the job."

"Who? I hope you don't plan on using my men."

"Oh no. But you know him. It's Otis Harmon," the governor said.

Glaze stared appreciatively at Boggs for a long moment.

"You've been planning this for weeks, haven't you? That's why you sent Harmon with us to Gallatin. So he wouldn't be suspicious when you asked him to do this job. What have you got against Harmon?"

"He caused me severe embarrassment several years ago when he was just a kid," Boggs said. "He's a man now, old enough to get his comeuppance."

# — 6 —

THE PLOW SLICED DEEPLY INTO THE PRAIRIE SOD, burying the grass and leaving a pile of fresh dirt in its wake. The acreage the Harmons cleared and plowed over the preceding years made the prospects of a big crop promising. Oat expected a good year.

The horses plodded on in the direction of the house where Libbie Harmon busied herself with laundry and other chores.

Thousands of settlers arrived in western Missouri each year. Initially, they needed food, not only for themselves, but their animals as well. Oat sold his surplus each year. During the past two years the Harmons watched their meager savings grow.

The two giant horses trudged effortlessly on. They provided the engine for the Harmons' prosperity. In their prime, they did more work in a day than four yoke of oxen could in two. And they did it so effortlessly. Either could have pulled the plow alone. Together they made it sing. Jack, the cantankerous, skittish stud could be startled by the smallest noise or movement. Blowing and snorting constantly, he worked the left side of the harness. Molly, more amiable and gentle, kept Jack in line, often laying back her ears and nipping at him when he got too lively. The other Harmon horses kept their distance from Jack because he had a bit of a mean streak. He always had his way in the barnyard unless Molly stepped in his path. He didn't push her around.

Seven years earlier Oat's father traded four mules to a passing Frenchman for the two horses that were colts at the time. The Frenchman, on his way to California, shipped the two animals all the way from France across the ocean and up the Mississippi and Missouri rivers to Independence. When he finally gazed across the wide, lonesome expanse of prairie and heard the terrifying tales of hostile Indians he realized they were unsuited for a cross-continental trek that could demand speed. Had they been older and trained he might have risked it, but the filly was only two years old and the young stud was little more than a yearling.

"La percheron," the Frenchman said in broken English as if Oat's father should have known what that meant. "Ze King's horses," he went on. "Magnifique. Vorth ver' much. Purebred percheron. Ze warhorses of ze kings."

Oat's father rolled his eyes and refused to give up any more than the four mules. Still, the colts impressed Oat's father.

"I've seen horses like this before," he whispered to Oat. "In New Orleans, just before the battle. They pulled loaded wagons through axle-deep mud and didn't even break a sweat. They were the most powerful animals I ever saw."

At the time, the filly towered above the yearling that already was as large as a saddle horse. Only colts, they would require training and feed for at least a year before they would be good for anything. In the end the Frenchman agreed to trade for the mules. He needed pack animals, but he extracted a promise from Oat's father.

"You must not geld the young horse," he said most emphatically, a condition to which Andrew Harmon finally agreed reluctantly.

"I don't need a stud horse," he said, exasperated. "They're knotheaded, hard to train and always fighting."

Both horses were gray, although Molly was whiter than Jack whose coat had a bluish hue. The elegant filly displayed a broad powerful chest, large muscular hind quarters and an animated and lovely head. The yearling stud, though at the time fairly small side-by-side with the filly, carried his head high on a massive beautifully curved neck. The Frenchman predicted the young stud would grow larger than the filly, a guess that proved right.

"Look at those lines," Oat's father said. "Somewhere in their ancestry these horses have Arabian blood."

The Frenchman told the Harmons the two animals descended from separate bloodlines for he planned to breed them.

The Frenchman's name was Jacque Jacquard and his wife's name was Molinda. So in their honor the Harmons named the colts Jacque and Molinda which they soon shortened to Jack and Molly — the Jacquards.

Oat grew up with the colts. After his father's death he trained them to lead, broke them to ride, and eventually worked them in harness. He showered them with attention. They matured into big, gentle animals under his care. After spending so much time with them, they seemed like family members, taking on separate and definite personalities -- Molly, the stable, dependable one who almost never acted up and responded obediently to Oat's every command. Jack, temperamental, standoffish and hard to catch when he saw a rope in Oat's hand, but a sucker for a handful of grain.

Already Molly had given birth to two colts, one of which Oat sold for a nice sum to a farmer from DeWitt. The second colt, however, he planned to keep.

The tough prairie sod proved no match for the Jacquards. The plow ripped through the sod as easily as a canoe slipped through water. Small trees that got in their way were doomed. Oat simply cut the tree off at about shoulder height, hooked the Jacquards to it and yelled, "Jack, Molly, ha." The two massive animals laid their full weight and muscle to the task and whether green or dead, the tree always broke or came out by the roots. His horses never balked when challenged.

Oat stopped about mid-morning when the Jacquards reached the end of the field farthest from the house. He unhitched the plow and led them to a stream at the edge of his property. The horses drank a lot of water. They sweated profusely and their coats glistened from the moisture that dripped down their massive front and hindquarters.

The stream lay hidden by willows and brush that grew along its banks except for a worn path Oat and the horses used when he watered them. Oat used the same spot as a crossing when visiting Clovis Blackburn, his closest neighbor and friend. Clovis and Oat needed each other. Clovis, a blacksmith, helped Oat build his plow and at times put shoes on the big horses. In return Oat performed heavy work for Clovis with his horses. Oat had never seen anyone else use the crossing so he was startled when Jack threw up his head and snorted nervously, his ears pointed directly at a man mounted on a black saddle horse in the middle of the stream.

The rider waved. At first Oat didn't recognize him because his hat shaded his face, but as Oat drew closer the man's features became more distinct.

Governor Boggs.

The governor sat easily in the saddle, exuding a friendly, warm smile as Oat and the Jacquards reached the edge of the stream and the horses drank.

"Morning Oat," Boggs said. "How are you?"

"I'm well governor," Oat said, remembering the awful things his mother said about Boggs. According to her, this man was responsible for his father's death.

"What brings you this way?"

Though on horseback the governor wore a business suit, shirt and tie. It would have been unusual to see him dressed any other way.

"Official business."

"With me?"

The governor nodded, shifted in his saddle, and squinted up at the sun now high in the morning sky.

"We've got to move the Mormons again. Was wondering if you could help?"

"No," Oat said. "I don't get along with Glaze well. He's unnecessarily mean and he doesn't control his men."

"Glaze won't be going this time," Boggs said. "He can't be trusted. That's why I sent you along last time so you could learn what needs to be done and so I could replace Glaze."

"And all of his men?" Oat queried.

"And all of his men."

"Where do the Mormons have to be taken this time?"

"The court has arranged for a change of venue so they can be tried. They have to be moved from Gallatin to Boone County."

"That would take several days," Oat said.

Boggs folded his arms and looked out over the Harmon farm.

"You'll need to take change of venue papers to Gallatin and then act as a guard on the trip to Boone County."

"Why doesn't the sheriff do that?" Oat asked.

"The Daviess County sheriff will be in charge of the guards and prisoners on the trip from Gallatin to Columbia, but I need my own man along to make sure things go as I want."

"What's the pay?"

Boggs' horse finished drinking. He coaxed it ahead a few steps nearer Oat holding out a small sack of coins.

"That's ten dollars, half your pay. You'll get the rest when you deliver the prisoners to the jail in Boone County."

The cash tempted Oat. This money combined with their savings would give his mother enough money to get to Baltimore. The thought of his mother and her feelings about Boggs complicated things, however. And why would the governor go so far out of his way to have him do the job. Oat pushed away the thought that there was something sly and sinister about the offer. He knew Boggs was a politician, not a murderer like his mother said.

"I have some chores that will take the rest of today and part of tomorrow, but I could be ready day after tomorrow."

"That will work. You can pick up the papers tomorrow in Independence at the courthouse. Meet me there at noon. After that you can leave at your convenience."

His business done, Boggs spurred his horse back across the stream. A moment later the governor reined his horse around.

"I'd prefer you not tell anyone about this," he said. "It'll be safer. Some of my people think the Mormons plan to free Smith if they can. I think that's mostly just rumor, but you never know. For your own safety you may want to keep this quiet."

Oat nodded. Sounded like good advice. He wouldn't even tell his mother.

# — 7 —

THE HARMONS OWNED THE BIGGEST WOOD PILE IN Jackson County. It occupied a conspicuous spot about fifty yards south of the barn. It sheltered skunks, squirrels, rabbits and countless mice and gophers. It grew larger each year despite Libbie Harmon's pleas for moderation.

"That wood pile is bigger than the house," his mother complained at least once a week. They used the wood for more than just firewood. Oat cut posts and poles and built fences and outbuildings for his animals with the gathered wood. But his mother called it a wood pile and after a while so did Oat.

The wood pile grew mainly because gathering wood developed into Oat's main recreational activity in spite of the fact that two years earlier he lost two fingers because he yelled "ha" to Jack Jacquard before getting his left hand clear of the snaking chain. Jack lunged, the chain snapped tight around an oak tree trunk and lopped off Oat's middle two fingers at the first knuckle as cleanly as if he did it with an ax. That experience taught Oat to stand well clear of Jack.

The day of Boggs' visit as his mother prepared supper Oat took Jack after a pull of firewood. He led Jack to a giant fallen pine tree about a half-mile away near the old Wheatley place. Oat had been watching the tree cure after lightning struck it a year earlier and now it lay lifeless and dry, perfect firewood.

Though the tree lay on the ground a canopy of dead branches reached high in the air in every direction. A portion of the trunk remained attached to the trunk. All the better, Oat thought, Jack needs a challenge. Breaking a path through the dead branches with a small ax, he succeeded in getting a solid hitch to the tip of the trunk. After attaching the chain to Jack's harness he searched for a skid path. To the left in front of Jack lay ground with nothing to stop them. No good. To the right big, well-rooted green trees blossomed out despite the cool spring weather. A small opening provided enough room for Jack and Oat to wind their way through, but there wasn't room for them to drag a huge tree with wide branches. Just what Oat wanted.

"That's where we're going Jack," Oat said, pointing at the trees and turning the big horse by the harness bridle. "Right through the middle of them."

Oat slapped Jack on the rear.

"Ha Jack."

The big horse moved forward and felt the hitch tighten. He lunged, his huge muscular hind quarters exploding with the power of a barrel of gunpowder. Branches popped and cracked, followed by a loud snap as the last portion of the tree separated from the trunk.

As the tree slipped ahead, Oat led Jack between two healthy green trees with just enough room for Jack to fit through. Oat jumped out of the way. The branches from the dead trees ran up against the trunk of the two green trees temporarily halting Jack. The harness sagged for a split second as Jack steadied himself and lunged into the collar again. Branches snapped and splintered and the tip of the dead tree shot forward again. Jack increased speed and broke into a hard trot. The dead tree twisted as it moved ahead and ran up against other green trees. The big dead branches broke like small twigs. Within seconds Jack cleared the far end of the grove pulling a long, slender log, ready to saw into blocks and split into firewood.

"Whoa Jack," Oat called out and the big gray beast stopped. Oat walked to him and patted his huge neck. Jack jerked away like he'd been bitten. Nevertheless, Oat rubbed and scratched the horse's ears until the sound of steel shod hooves clanking against rocks behind him drew his attention. He turned to see a rider with four pack mules wending through the clump of trees on the path Jack cleared through the grove. The mule train, packed with traps and supplies, appeared to have embarked on a journey west to the Rocky Mountains.

"I have never seen anything like that," the rider said jovially. "If that old Frenchman could see that horse now he'd die of envy."

Oat recognized the stooped figure of Bufflehead, a buffalo hunter, trapper and friend of the Harmons years earlier when Oat's father lived. Since Andrew Harmon's death, neither Oat nor his mother saw Bufflehead much. Though Bufflehead wasn't tall he was large. He spent much of his time on the plains hunting buffalo. Years before he traveled far into the western mountains to trap beaver. When Oat was young, Bufflehead told marvelous stories about Indians, grizzly bears, wild rivers, monstrous mountains and herds of buffalo swarming like ants to the far horizon. For a time after returning from the west Bufflehead frequented the Harmon place. He taught Oat woodsman skills like how to skin a deer and tan the hide. But Bufflehead didn't visit the Harmons anymore and now seemed almost like a stranger.

"He's half mean. Jacquard might not want him," Oat said.

"Yeah. He does have a wild look in his eye. You be careful with him. A horse like that could maim a man without even trying."

Oat held up his hand with the two missing fingers.

"I learned that lesson. Luckily I only lost two fingers."

Bufflehead dismounted slowly and extended his right hand to Oat, who shook it.

"How are you boy?" Bufflehead said.

"I'm well," Oat said. "You haven't come around for a long time."

Bufflehead nodded, and as Oat looked into his eyes he saw a sad, beaten man, worn down by life.

"There are reasons," he said, and then sweeping his arm around. "You look well and prosperous. You've grown into a big, fine man like your father. How is your mother?"

"She's all right," Oat said. "She's at the house waiting with supper. Come share a bite with us?"

Bufflehead looked sullenly in the direction of the Harmon place and shook his head sadly. Then he clasped Oat's arm and held it. Oat again saw the pain in the man's face.

"No Oat, I've got to be on my way, but I must speak to you. Please sit."

Oat focused his full attention on the buffalo hunter. He had no idea what Bufflehead wanted so urgently, but it obviously was important.

Bufflehead sat down on the log that Jack had delimbed only moments earlier. He sighed deeply as though he carried the weight of the world on his shoulders. Oat sat down on the log too.

"If certain people find out what I'm gonna tell you they'd kill me without a thought, but it don't matter because by morning I'll be well out of their reach. I'm going west as far as I can get and I'm going to stay there until I starve to death or an Indian cuts my throat."

Bufflehead pulled a skinning knife from a sheath at his side and picked a stick up off the ground. He began to whittle.

"I learned today that you probably are going to be dead within a week," he said, looking squarely at Oat.

"Me?" Oat said. "What are you talking about?"

"Are you the Oat Harmon who agreed to go to Gallatin for the governor in two days and then help move Joe Smith and the other Mormon prisoners to Boone County for trial?"

"Yes," Oat said. "How do you know? It's supposed to be a secret."

"It is a secret," Bufflehead said sharply. "But you only know part of the secret. I know the whole secret."

He sliced at the branch.

"On the way from Gallatin to Boone County you're going to be ambushed and killed supposedly by a band of wild Indians, all of you, prisoners and guards. They will be led by Tyrone Glaze and whoever he and the governor can get to help him. Boggs asked me to go with them and that's why I know all about this."

"You aren't serious."

"I'm dead serious," Bufflehead said. "And so are they. Why they picked you to be a guard I have no idea, unless Boggs still holds a grudge over the Wheatley thing, but that's their plan."

"Well, I won't go then," Oat said.

"That's what I'd recommend, but if you don't they'll know you're on to them and they'll kill you anyway right here at this farm and probably your mother too."

"They won't do that," Oat said.

"Yes they will," Bufflehead said firmly. "And not care a lick. They are ruthless and spiteful. They will kill you."

"I'll speak to the sheriff," Oat said.

Bufflehead sighed and stood up, gesturing angrily, the pitch of his voice rising.

"You're young Oat. You don't understand what you're up against so I'll spell it out for you as plainly as I can. Governor Boggs, for whatever reasons, wants Joe Smith dead. He's gotten Tyrone Glaze to do it for him. This is the same governor who signed an extermination order last year for all the Mormons. Unfortunately, you've been drug into it. Neither of them can afford to let anyone know what they are doing. The sheriff is a weak fool and he certainly won't go up against the governor to help you. You have two choices — leave or die."

Oat sat on the log stunned, still unable to believe what he was hearing. Bufflehead sat down beside him. Bufflehead whittled and let Oat think. Several minutes passed.

"How do you know this Bufflehead?" Oat asked finally. "Maybe they're playing a joke on you?"

"It's not a joke Oat," Bufflehead said. "I know this because the governor asked me to help them."

"Why would he do that?" Oat asked.

"Because I've done this kind of stuff for him before," Bufflehead said, shifting his weight uneasily.

Oat stared at Bufflehead.

"Are you saying you've killed people for Boggs?" Oat said incredulously.

Bufflehead closed his eyes and nodded sadly.

"Several," he said, looking woefully at Oat. "And that's not the worst of it. I have to tell you this for my own peace of mind, but it ain't easy and I shrink from it because I am so ashamed."

He buried his face in his big hands. Finally he looked up.

"I killed your father for Boggs. I hate myself for it. It was the worst thing I ever did."

The revelation hit Oat like a sledge. He shook his head, hardly believing it and not knowing what to say. He stared back at Bufflehead for several long moments, as he fought to control his emotions. His mother was right. Bufflehead sat quietly as Oat tried to keep his composure.

"He didn't suffer," Bufflehead said. "He was a friend. I made sure he didn't suffer."

"My mother suffered," Oat said, his anger boiled up inside him.

"I know," Bufflehead said sadly. "And so did you. I wish . . ." His voice trailed off and he hung his head for several long seconds.

"I have suffered every day since and rightfully so. I haven't slept peacefully in years. I never will."

"Why did you do it?"

"I had my reasons, but none that are good enough. Your father crossed Boggs right here on this ground. Boggs paid me and blackmailed me. He knew things about me that would have sent me to the gallows or to prison. I was running from the law a long time before I met Boggs. He helped me stay out of jail and I owed him. So I did it. But when he asked me yesterday to help kill you I knew I couldn't. When he finds out I told you, and eventually he will, he'll try to kill me. By then I'll be far out of his reach. I'm hoping that by warning you I can partly repay you for what I took."

Bufflehead stood and walked to his horse. He removed a heavy, leather bag and offered it to Oat.

"This is for you and your ma," Bufflehead said. "It will help you build a new life somewhere else away from here."

Oat slumped back on the log, ignoring Bufflehead's outstretched hand. Finally, Bufflehead dropped the bag, mounted his horse and picked up the rope on the lead mule.

"You'll have to use all your wits to get away from here alive, Oat. I'd advise you to start now."

Bufflehead, his horse and mules moved away. Oat watched as they walked through the charred wreckage of the Wheatley farm a hundred yards to the west and disappeared in the brush and trees the other side of it. The old farm's wreckage suddenly loomed up like a ghost and awful memories flooded into his mind. The house's fireplace cast a firm, deep shadow in the twilight, over the scattered logs of the house's walls.

Hannah Wheatley's pretty, dimpled face smiled at him from his memory. The image startled him and he stood up again.

"Ha Jack, Ha," Oat said, without emotion.

The big horse obediently dragged the log toward home. He wouldn't stop until he got there, but Oat stopped and stared at the remains of the Wheatley place as the horse plodded on by itself in the gathering darkness.

Hannah and her family were Mormons. Oat discovered her while exploring the banks of the Blue River one day seven years earlier. She had been twelve then and he fourteen. She was lean, tanned and lithe as a cat. Although just a girl she was as bold as any boy he knew. When she looked him straight in the eye he knew she considered herself second to no one. She and her family were new settlers from Ohio. They purchased eighty acres of land bordering the Harmon farm.

Oat and Hannah became friends instantly. Friends were often hard to find for an only child on a farm far from town. Oat's shyness toward girls evaporated when she knocked down a badger with an egg-sized stone at twenty yards. The badger lay on the ground twisting and contorting in its death throes and bleeding from its nose. Oat and Hannah stood nearby and watched quietly as the animal shuddered and lay still. Oat finally walked to where the animal lay and rolled it over onto its back with his foot.

"You killed it deader 'n hell Hannah," Oat said, admiringly. "I wish I could throw like that."

Tears suddenly flowed freely down Hannah's cheeks and her chin quivered.

"I didn't want to kill it," she said. "I only wanted to scare it away."

She knelt on the ground next to the dead animal and stroked its lifeless head.

"I'm so sorry," she said between sobs.

Oat didn't know what to make of her behavior. She had a right arm like a sling. She'd performed a feat few men could do and if they did would have been pleased to brag about it. He didn't understand why she cried. The badger wouldn't be missed. It was a pest and there were plenty left. Either of their fathers would have shot it on sight. To further confuse Oat, Hannah prayed on her knees for a good five minutes asking God to bring that stupid badger back to life. Oat endured it, hands in his pockets, not knowing quite how to act. He nearly interrupted to tell her that praying for a dead animal was stupid when he saw the badger's hind leg twitch once and then twice. Hannah stopped praying and the animal rolled onto its stomach and stood up. At first it was unsteady, but after a few minutes it gained control of its legs and staggered off. Within a minute, to Oat's wonder and Hannah's delight it bounced away across the prairie and out of sight.

That summer Oat spent so much time hanging around the Wheatley farm that he neglected his own chores on occasion and got a few good scoldings from his father. He found the scoldings worth the trouble. Hannah radiated happiness. Her face lit up and her pigtails shook when she laughed. A dimple appeared on her right cheek when she smiled. She explained to him that the dimple appeared after she had fallen out of a tree onto her face. She hugged him when he did something that pleased her and she called him Oatie because she said Otis sounded too uppity. No one else ever called him Oatie.

Hannah turned out to be very good at praying things back to life. She prayed another miracle when his father's only mare at the time gave birth to its first foal, a colt his father promised to Oat. Though the colt stood up within seconds it wouldn't eat and no amount of coaxing by its mother helped. After a few hours the colt lay down in the shade of a tree near their house and Oat's father said sadly that it probably never would get up again. Hannah and her younger brother stopped by that evening. Oat remembered sitting under the trees near the colt trying not to cry. He feared the young horse wouldn't live through the night. Hannah knelt down nearby and stroked the colt's nose.

"He's so pretty Oatie," she said. "I'll pray for him."

Oat didn't pray much, but he was ready to try anything to save the colt.

Hannah prayed quietly with her head bowed and eyes closed while her brother and Oat looked on. When finished she stood up looking quite satisfied.

"We better get home," she said. "Don't worry though. He'll be okay."

The next morning Oat arose at dawn to find the colt sucking contentedly and, though wobbly, it walked steadily by nightfall. That had been seven years before. The colt, a bay with black legs below each knee, grew into a sturdy saddle horse.

The Wheatleys belonged to a community of hundreds of

Mormons who moved into Jackson County from Ohio during the preceding years. One Sunday morning Oat told his father he was going fishing and followed the Wheatleys to church. They called him Brother Harmon that day and teased him about getting baptized in the river. He sat with them in the open air near a grove of trees and listened to men preach about Jesus and something they called the gospel. They also spoke often with awe and reverence about Joseph Smith. They called him Brother Joseph, never Ol' Joe like everybody else at Independence.

"Do you know Joseph Smith?" Oat asked the Wheatleys on the way home that day.

"Yes we do," Mr. Wheatley said. "We joined the church after we met him in Ohio."

"He sounds like a good man," Oat said.

"He's God's prophet," Mr. Wheatley said firmly. "For the first time since Peter there's a prophet on the earth."

"So you'll do whatever he says?"

Mr. Wheatley nodded.

"I'd follow him into Hell if he asked me to. That's how much I believe."

Of course Mr. Wheatley had no way of knowing that within a few months that actually would happen.

While the Mormons held Smith in high regard, Smith's visions were a matter of mirth among non-Mormon members of the Independence community who hated the Mormons for their anti-slavery sentiments and their belief in Smith. When Oat's mother dragged him to the Methodist meetings, Oat heard Reverend Riley speak of Smith as though he was the devil. The whole controversy confused Oat.

In November of that year the conflict enveloped the Wheatleys and the Harmons. For weeks Oat listened to his parents talk of the increasingly harsh feelings of many of the old settlers toward the Mormons. Oat heard rumors that Mormons grew horns under the hair on their heads and walked on cloven feet. He found that to be untrue when Hannah allowed him to examine her head and feet closely. No horns or hooves. The Harmon family remained more or less neutral during this time even though the two families lived close to each other. The Harmons tried not to seem too chummy with the Wheatleys because the sabre-rattling leadership at Independence seemed suspicious of anyone who became friends with Mormons. Talk of violence soon turned to acts of violence. Armed men on horses raided Mormon farms and settlements sending shock waves throughout the county.

"You stay away from the Wheatley place today," Oat's father said one morning, a troubled look in his face. "I just saw a group of men riding that way. I don't want you getting hurt."

He might as well have given Oat a special invitation. Worried about Hannah, Oat sprinted to the Wheatleys to find the place surrounded and under attack by about twenty men their faces painted black so no one would recognize them. The Wheatleys' fences and corrals lay flat on the ground. Their livestock ran loose. Some of the men entered the house and carried away armloads of clothing and furniture. Smoke billowed from the house. Hannah's father lay on his back in the middle of the yard, blood running from his forehead. At the edge of the yard five men on horses looked on quietly like plantation owners supervising field work. One of them, Oat soon learned, was Boggs, then the lieutenant governor of Missouri.

In the confusion, Mrs. Wheatley and Hannah loaded Hannah's two younger brothers into a two-horse wagon near the house. As Oat arrived they drug Mr. Wheatley to it and tried to lift him into the back. Oat ran to their aid and with his help they succeeded in loading Mr. Wheatley into the wagon. Mrs. Wheatley grabbed the reins and started the team when two men dragged her struggling and screaming from the wagon. Another man tore at Hannah's clothing. Oat scooped up the only weapon available — an old shovel handle. He bashed the knee of the mobber who held Hannah. The man yelped, grabbed his knee and fell to the ground, but another seized the shovel handle and knocked Oat sprawling face first onto the ground. Oat expected the shovel handle to come crashing down on his head, but instead a gunshot brought the melee to an abrupt halt. Oat saw his father standing near the coral with his musket pointed at the stomach of the man holding the shovel handle. Without taking his eyes from the man, he handed the pistol he had fired to Oat's mother, who immediately reloaded it.

The noise and confusion ceased. Black-faced men looked for cover. Those with weapons touched them nervously.

Oat watched his father intently. He knew his father fought the British and the Indians, but Andrew Harmon didn't talk much about those times saying he'd rather forget them. Bufflehead once described a fearsome brawl at Independence when his father nearly killed two men in a fist fight when they tried to steal his rifle.

"You hurt my boy and I'll kill you," Andrew Harmon said softly, but everyone heard and, apparently, none doubted he meant it. Together the mob could have overpowered him, but they knew he would kill several of them if they tried and not a single one had the backbone to risk it.

The men struggling with Hannah and her mother released them and the man standing over Oat dropped the shovel handle and backed away. As he did Oat's father moved the musket until it was pointed directly at Boggs.

"Anybody else gets hurt here and I'll cut you in half," he said in the same soft voice. "Get these swine out of here."

Boggs stared defiantly at Andrew Harmon for a long moment, rage growing in his face. But his good judgment prevailed. Even though he was Lieutenant Governor with a score of men with him he didn't dare say a word.

Boggs signaled to his men to leave. They slowly and silently collected their horses. While they withdrew Boggs stared hatefully at Oat's father. Finally, he wheeled his horse and kicked it into a gallop.

Once the mob was gone, the Harmons helped the Wheatleys load their belongings into the wagon. Other Mormons, alerted by the smoke from the Wheatley house, appeared and silently escorted the Wheatleys away. Oat never forgot the sight of Hannah crying forlornly on the wagon as it disappeared. It was the last time Oat saw her. During the following days all Mormons who wouldn't recant their faith left Jackson County.

The Harmons feared they would pay dearly for their interference and they did. One evening two weeks before Christmas Oat's father didn't return home from a trip into Independence. Somehow during the long, lonely night that followed Oat and his mother knew he would never come home again. Oat found his body the next morning, a bullet in his chest. Since that day Oat and his mother struggled. Oat watched his mother age daily. She cultivated a bitter hate for the men who killed her husband and for the Mormons, who she blamed for dragging her family into the mess.

Though she seldom put her feelings to words Oat felt his mother's anger. He grew through his teenage years feeling cheated, angry and rebellious. He worked as a stable hand and for the blacksmith at Independence when he wasn't busy helping his mother run their own farm and over his mother's objections, learned how to chew tobacco and swig corn liquor from men much older than he.

Oat picked up the bag Bufflehead dropped and walked home. Coins jingled in the heavy bag, but it was too dark to count the money now. In the distance the outline of the Harmon's simple cabin came into view, a candle glowing from a window. He knew his mother waited up for him. She always did.

When he reached the house he unhitched Jack from the log, unharnessed him, and turned him loose in the new corral with Molly and the colt. He left the bag in the back of a stall in the barn. If he showed it to his mother he'd have to explain about Bufflehead. That idea did not appeal to him. Before he entered the house he stopped at the little family graveyard a short distance from the house. Three white headstones marked the graves of his father and younger brothers. Moonlight reflected from their smooth surfaces. The place always made him sad because he often saw his mother cry here. Tonight it fit his mood.

When he finally entered the house he found his mother sitting at the table reading by candlelight.

"I was beginning to worry about you," she said. "You're late."

"It was a big tree," Oat said.

"I saw it," she said. "Jack's been here a while."

She busied herself at the stove and soon set a turkey drumstick and a large piece of cornbread before him. He ate hungrily as she watched.

"I'm almost ready to go," she said. "There'll be a riverboat at the wharf day after tomorrow. Are you sure you won't come with me?"

A chance to escape. For a brief moment he thought about doing just what Bufflehead suggested. Leave. But the thought, he realized, wasn't that tempting.

"I'm glad you're going," Oat said. "You need to get away from here."

"Why?" she said, looking at him oddly.

He hadn't told his mother about the job he agreed to do for Boggs and now decided he wouldn't. And if he told her of Bufflehead's confession now she never would leave without him. In one day his life had gotten extremely complicated. He wanted to get her safely away from Jackson County and that meant telling her nothing.

"I just think it will do you good to see your brother," he said, wondering if not telling her the whole truth was a lie.

# 8

WHENEVER HANNAH AND HER FATHER HEARD HORSES or saw people in the distance they darted off the trail into the closest cover and hid. They foraged for edible plants and though their diet was meager they didn't starve. They passed some houses, but having no desire to confront any more pukes, they didn't stop.

The day Hannah first heard Missourians called pukes her family was on its way to Gallatin in the family's wagon so that Papa could buy supplies and vote in the election for county sheriff.

"Ma, will we see some pukes today?" Pete asked.

"Where did you hear that word?" Mama demanded.

"All my friends call em that," Pete said, and it was true. Papa laughed when Pete said it and Mama glared at him. The term had become more prevalent among Mormons as the animosity between the two groups increased. Still, Mama didn't like her children calling other people names.

"Please don't use that word today," Mama said. "And behave yourselves. We'll take care of our business and leave as quickly as we can without any trouble."

Gallatin teemed with people in town for the election and Mama's good intentions were doomed. As soon as the family tied up the wagon in Gallatin Hannah's brothers spied two greasy gobs of hair and tobacco spit walking down the street toward them. One had a round jowly face, a large, solid build and long greasy red hair. His companion was thinner and mostly toothless, his bearded cheeks sunken in under his eyes and a dark tan burned into his bearded face.

Evidently, neither liked soap and water. The hair on their heads and faces stuck together in clumps. Body odors, plus the putrid smell of liquor breath, surrounded both of them for ten feet in every direction. They swaggered down the street spitting out tobacco juice, sucking on a jug of brew and ogling every woman they saw.

The bearded one was a poor spitter. While the red head could lob an even load about six feet every time, the bearded feller could barely get it out of his mouth and most of it ran down his chin into his whiskers where it hung and dripped. While the family watched, the bearded man spit his tobacco spittle into his beard, took a drag on the jug and handed it to the red head. The red head lifted the jug to his lips and drank deeply without wiping the opening. They walked past the family staring at Mama and Hannah, but not saying anything because Papa stood right there watching them.

"Ma?" Pete said. "Are those pukes?"

"Yes Pete," Mama said patiently. "Those are pukes."

Unfortunately the pukes headed the same direction as the Wheatleys — toward the hardware store. At the store a young woman stood outside, uneasily waiting for someone doing business inside.

As the Wheatleys approached, the bearded puke stepped up to the railing next to her and smiled. Hannah still smelled the pukes from her distance so she knew the other woman must have been overwhelmed. The woman courageously stood her ground. The bearded puke chewed, and after glancing sideways at the woman, let go a load of tobacco juice out into the street. As was his style, he sprayed in every direction.

The woman turned white. Mama opined later that maybe she was pregnant and experiencing morning sickness, but it seemed more likely that the puke's smell and the sight of him spitting made her gag. In any case, she soon vomited over the railing spraying her breakfast right into the middle of Gallatin's main street.

The bearded puke backed away from the woman, his eyes widening, a look of abject disgust on his face as though he'd never seen anything so horrendously sickening in his entire life.

Papa held his stomach and howled, laughing harder than Hannah had seen him laugh since before Jackson County. He couldn't stand to look at anybody for at least an hour without breaking out in shrieks.

After that, even Mama called them pukes.

As she trudged slowly eastward along the trail out of Missouri,

Hannah wondered if her father ever would laugh like that again. Not likely. Extremely unlikely. Only a year before their family had been so happy and secure in Far West. They had overcome the tragedy of losing their home in Jackson County. They lived among the saints. Joseph arrived from Ohio and everything for a time seemed so right. Then all hell broke loose beginning a chain of ugly events that doomed Far West.

The same day the Wheatley family encountered the pukes in Gallatin there was a violent brawl between some of the brethren and other Missourians who tried to stop them from voting. In the days and weeks that followed armed mobs attacked Mormon farms and settlements at night in the outlying areas around Far West. Papa fought in a battle at Crooked River and brought home the sad news of the deaths of three of the brethren. Days later they heard of the awful massacre at Haun's Mill.

The battle for Far West was lost a few days later. Governor Boggs' army of six thousand men, loosely called Missouri militia, surrounded Far West. Alarm gripped the city as the news of Boggs' sinister extermination order spread from home to home as only bad news can. Though outnumbered five to one, Hannah's father and the other men prepared to fight. The mob, however, plundered and pillaged the city without any resistance.

The general consensus among Mormons after the Far West debacle was that Colonel Hinkle, the leading Mormon military officer, betrayed the entire city. Hinkle arranged a peace conference between Joseph and the leaders of the Missouri militia. Hannah remembered feeling so hopeful that they could make peace without fighting. If only they could talk she was sure the Missourians would see they were not bad people. But her hopes and those of all the other families in Far West were shattered when Joseph and several of the other leading brethren rode into the Missouri war camp and Hinkle gave them to the Missourians as prisoners.

"Hinkle betrayed us to save his own stinking hide," Jerome Wheatley reported bitterly to his family. Hannah often thought that if her father knew everything that happened in the ensuing days that he probably would have hunted Hinkle down and killed him.

The morning after the surrender Hinkle marched his troops,

including Hannah's father and all of the other men, out of Far West and the Missouri militia entered the town under the pretense of searching for weapons. An endless nightmare began.

About mid-morning Hannah's mother peeled back some boards in the floor of their home. Hannah recalled her words vividly.

"When the mob comes you get in there and don't make a peep, no matter what happens."

"What about you and Charlie and Pete?" Hannah asked.

"They won't hurt the boys, but you are young and pretty," her mother said. "And I'm pregnant. They won't harm me. Even if they do don't you come out or they'll do the same to you."

Hannah remembered the Jackson County attack several years earlier, how men in the mob grabbed at her and her mother. They had been saved only by the intervention of the Harmon family. She resolved to do as her mother ordered.

Part of the mob finally got around to their house about noon, five of them. Mama was right about Hannah's brothers. The mob didn't hurt them, but she was wrong about herself. While they rifled through the Wheatley's possessions outside the house, Hannah dropped through the hole in the floor and her mother replaced the boards. A few moments later Hannah heard the door burst open. After an awful silence, Hannah heard scuffling, a muffled scream and a piece of cloth ripping. The next hour became the longest of Hannah's life as she listened to her mother struggle with her attackers one by one. Hannah cried silently in her dark hiding place trying to cope with a variety of emotions from fear to anger to frustration to guilt.

Finally the men left. Hannah emerged from her hiding spot to find the house in a mess. What the mob hadn't taken they spilled, tipped over or broke. Her mother sat on the floor clutching a blanket. Her gingham dress lay on the floor ripped in pieces. Hannah hugged her and wept.

"I want to kill them," she wailed as her mother hung her head.

"So do I," her mother said.

Together, she and her mother cleaned up the house and as far as Hannah knew her father never learned what happened to her mother that day. Hannah thought the abuse her mother endured caused her last baby brother to be born early. It didn't matter now. Mama and the baby now lay dead, free from any more hurt from the Missouri mob.

Three days after burying her mother, Hannah and her father traversed a particularly narrow and brushy section of trail in their eastward journey. Rounding a corner in the road they came face to face with an armed man on horseback. They had no time to hide.

"What have we here?" the man bellowed lustily. "Mormons I'll bet."

Hannah knew immediately he would be deadly. Fat and red-faced with a swollen belly and a tangled matted beard, he dismounted and drew a pistol from his belt. Some men apparently lived for an excuse to kill and she knew instinctively that here was a Missouri puke in all his glory. Her heart filled with dread.

"Leave us alone," she pleaded. "We've got nothing for you to take."

"Boggs said to exterminate all Mormons," the man said loudly while studying Hannah lecherously. "But you're a fine looking woman. I think I'll get to know you first."

"You filthy dog," Hannah heard her father protest. The fat man aimed the pistol at Hannah's father and fired. The impact of the ball caused her father to spin and fall.

The sudden violence, so uncalled for and unjust, touched off an awful fury in Hannah. The abuse and battery of her family had no end it seemed and it maddened her to see it again. They had been robbed and all of their possessions stolen. They had been driven from their home twice and her mother raped. Her brothers and mother died one by one of hunger and cold and fever. For a brief moment rage overcame Hannah and she lost all sense of personal safety as her father fell and the puke bent to reload his pistol. Glancing around at her feet she found a round stone about the size of a potato. She picked it up and heaved it at the puke as hard as she could throw from a distance of only ten feet. She caught him completely by surprise. The man looked up just in time to catch the stone in his forehead right between the eyes. He dropped heavily to the ground and rolled back and forth on his fat belly until he lay still.

Hannah seized the pistol and rushed to her father, who sat upright holding his shoulder and looking at Hannah incredulously.

"Are you hurt badly?" she asked.

"I don't know," he said. "The bullet hit me just beneath my arm pit. It didn't hit a bone." He stared at the man lying in the trail. "Is he dead?"

"I hope so," Hannah said.

She helped her father to his feet and together they started down the trail again, but after only a few steps her father stopped.

"I'm tired of walking," he said tiredly.

He took the man's horse by the reins. Hannah helped him into the saddle and then climbed up behind him, still clutching the pistol. She hid it in the folds of her dress.

## 9

OAT TOLD NO ONE OF THE PLANS SWIRLING ABOUT IN HIS mind. Bufflehead's confession enraged him and the more he thought about it the more determined he grew to meet out some revenge for his father's murder. His pride and anger demanded action, but he knew he couldn't confront the governor face to face and win. The governor had too much protection.

The thought of shooting Boggs from ambush crossed his mind, a direct payback, an eye for an eye, but he had no time to wait for an opportunity like that. And, he doubted he could do it. He wasn't that good with a rifle.

The trip to Boone County with the Mormons, however, gave him an opportunity. He might at the very least cause Boggs some embarrassment — if he was smart and lucky.

Libbie Harmon's impending departure for Baltimore helped. Oat could carry out his plans without worrying about her safety. He needed only time for her to get downriver. He gave her no hint that anything was amiss. But her intuition blossomed uncannily at times and he kept expecting her to change her mind. If she suspected danger for him she would not leave, but if Oat's plan worked she'd be well on her way to Baltimore, far out of the reach of anyone in western Missouri, when the whole thing unfolded.

Bufflehead warned that he would have to use his wits. The idea of matching wits with a powerful, shrewd and murderous politician appealed to him. The challenge would test him. Did he have the wiles he would need to survive?

The day before his departure to Gallatin, Oat hitched Jack and Molly to the wagon and set off on the four-mile trip to Independence.

Molly's colt, now broke to lead, followed along tied to the back of the wagon. Oat didn't often take the Jacquards to town, but when he did it always caused a commotion. His huge horses fascinated businessmen, slaves, travelers, and especially farmers for they dwarfed saddle horses and mules. And though huge, they stood docilely while any number of people stroked, stared and touched.

Oat unhitched the Jacquards right on main street. Molly's left hind shoe had come loose a few days earlier. He led Molly and her colt to the blacksmith shop where he left them so the shoe could be refitted while he did his business. Meanwhile Jack, tied to a hitching rail, dropped his head, cocked his right hind leg and went to sleep.

As Oat left the Blacksmith shop on his way to the courthouse, his eyes fell on Sarah Riley, a conspicuous presence amongst the drab ambience of Independence's Main Street.

Sarah's flowing red hair, flirtatious eyes and slender figure set her apart as one of the most attractive women in Independence. Her beauty, however, did not compensate in Oat's mind for her poisonous tongue and mean wit. She victimized Oat on occasion with her venomous barbs. He avoided her now whenever possible. Oat's mother once observed dryly that Sarah's personality resembled that of a cornered bobcat. Despite all that Oat found himself gazing at her. In the past, he toyed with the idea of courting her, but that necessitated attending church. Her father, the Methodist minister, required her suitors to attend each Sunday and that didn't appeal to Oat. In addition, the thought of his mother and Sarah conversing on a Sunday afternoon conjured up images of bloodshed.

Sarah suddenly spied Oat too, and she and her younger friend strode regally, yet quickly, down the street on a course that intercepted Oat near the hitching rail where Jack slept. At one time Oat would have been flattered, but he knew Sarah probably wanted a verbal joust not a pleasant conversation.

"Where's your other plow horse Oat?" Sarah asked with a twinkle in her eye. She intuitively knew how to get under his skin.

"She's at the blacksmith," Oat said, knowing the best way to deal with Sarah was to ignore her jabs. He bragged to Sarah about his horses a year earlier in a moment of weakness while trying to impress her, a mistake he now regretted intensely.

"This is Oat's percheron draft stallion," Sarah said to her friend while pointing at Jack. "Oat raised him from a colt. He has a mare that looks just like this one."

"My goodness," said the friend who evidently took personality lessons from Sarah. "Is the other one as ugly as this?"

Sarah feigned surprise at her friend's question.

"Do you really think they're ugly?" Sarah said. "Oat thinks his horses are quite pretty."

"Oh I don't," the friend said meanly. "He's out of proportion from what a horse should look like. His neck is so big and his fetlocks so bushy. He's just too big. I'd bet he's terribly slow. I prefer saddle horses. They're sleek and pretty and fast."

"Oh, he wasn't bred for speed," Sarah said, parroting the words Oat used when he had told her about Jack and Molly. "He's bred for power."

"Why would you want a horse like this?" the friend went on shaking her head. "He's monstrous."

"Because he's more powerful than four full-grown mules," Sarah explained. "His ancestors were used in Europe as war horses. They were strong enough to carry knights and all their armor into battle."

Still unimpressed, Sarah's friend turned away.

"I would never own a horse like that," she said as she and Sarah entered a dry goods store having largely ignored Oat while insulting his horses.

Oat followed them inside, where he encountered Sarah's father, the Reverend Riley standing near a window looking out at Jack Jacquard.

"We missed you at church last Sunday Oat," the reverend said so everyone in the store could hear, including Sarah and her friend. "And the Sunday before that."

Oat didn't like attending church. He and his mother argued about it often and he sometimes attended just to humor her. His mother, a lifelong Methodist, attended services every week but Oat didn't see much point in it.

"You'll probably miss me this Sunday too," Oat answered. "And the Sunday after that."

The reverend scowled as Oat bought powder for his rifles and left the store headed toward the courthouse. As he neared the front door, Glaze rode into sight. This unnerved Oat for a moment. He hadn't expected to see his would-be assassin parading through town. Bile rose in his throat, yet he managed to check himself realizing he could not afford to give away the advantage of the secrets Bufflehead told him. Glaze rode to the courthouse where Oat planned to meet the governor.

Oat guessed Glaze's age at ten years older than himself. Muscular and tanned, he sat easily in the saddle. He obviously spent a lot of time there. Glaze stood an inch or two shorter than Oat, but he was heavier. His wrinkled brow and squinting eyes locked his face into a perpetual frown. A smile would never come easy for him. His entire demeanor radiated anger and said "stay out of my way."

The stallion pranced, snorted and blew as Glaze reined it up near the court house hitching rail and dismounted. Dropping the reins loosely to the ground, he let the animal stand untethered. He reached the courthouse door the same time as Oat.

They found the governor immediately inside the courthouse. Their appearance together didn't affect Boggs at all. Bufflehead's disclosures caused Oat to view the governor in a new light. He tried to read the man's eyes, but saw nothing unusual in them. The governor handled his business as smoothly as ever leaving Oat to wonder how a murderer could be so calm especially in the presence of a man he planned to have killed. Did he have no conscience? The governor handed Oat a bundle of papers.

"You care if I read these?" Oat asked.

"Yes, I do," Boggs said, "There's a sealed letter to Judge Birch. Don't open it. It's official business. You could be prosecuted if you do."

Oat wouldn't need to. He already knew its contents.

"Harmon is going to Gallatin to transport the Mormon prisoners to Boone County," Boggs said to Glaze.

"I'm glad it's him and not me," Glaze said. "Those people make my skin crawl. But I would like to see how Harmon here handles Smith. He didn't like the way I did it."

Oat didn't say anything.

Their business done, Boggs and Oat moved toward the front

door of the courthouse. At the door Oat realized suddenly that Glaze's stud horse had discovered Jack Jacquard.

"We're going to have a fight if you don't control your horse," Oat said. "My horse is a stud too."

Glaze made no move toward his horse.

"This should be interesting," Glaze said. His indifference caused Oat to wonder if he worried for no reason. As the three men moved outside they encountered Sarah and her friend. The governor and Glaze greeted the women but were diverted from a conversation when the chestnut snorted and neighed shrilly and angrily.

Jack, still tied to the rail, stood alert and erect watching the other stallion approach. Jack's ears pricked forward, his neck bowed and his nostrils flared. He nickered and pawed. The chestnut pawed the ground too and moved warily closer to Jack.

"That gray nag is yours Harmon?" Glaze asked incredulously. "I'm surprised you'd bring something like that to town."

"It's Oat's war horse," Sarah giggled, making Glaze and the governor laugh.

"Harmon, you best run along home if you're worried about your horse getting hurt," Glaze said.

"I think I will," Oat replied, hurrying toward the two horses, knowing he was too late, and wondering how Jack would react to the other stud. The chestnut stalked toward Jack, who grew increasingly agitated. He stretched the lead rope between his halter and the hitching rail until the rail bent into a bow.

Oat stopped.

"The hell with this," he said aloud and stopped. "Jack's gonna have to take care of himself."

The chestnut suddenly bared its teeth and attacked, screaming furiously. Jack responded, ears laid back, lips curled so that his great teeth gleamed like ivory. The rail snapped like a dry twig and Jack's huge bulk moved ahead freely the lead rope dragging a portion of the rail. The two horses collided shoulder to shoulder. For the chestnut, the collision must have felt like running into a rock wall. It immediately collapsed under Jack's superior weight and strength. As it tried to regain its footing, Jack, raging and screaming in a way Oat had never before seen, seized the chestnut's neck just above the withers with his teeth and shook. The chestnut squealed again, this time in pain. When it finally pulled free, a piece of hide about a foot long had been torn loose leaving a bloody gash.

"What the hell," Glaze yelled.

Within seconds the two horses collided again with the same result, but this time as the chestnut tried to regain its feet, Jack wheeled, lifted his huge rear haunches into the air and unleashed a vicious kick. Both steel shod hooves connected, one in the chestnut's left front shoulder and the other in his ribs. The chestnut collapsed again, a good thing for it because when Jack kicked once more he missed. Jack wheeled again and charged, but the chestnut, though injured, regained its feet and fled. It was quick enough to temporarily limp out of Jack's reach. Jack gave chase as Oat seized his lead rope. The big horse, blind with rage, jerked his head forward sending Oat flying through the air. Oat lit on his feet, however, and kept a tight hold on the rope until Jack calmed down.

"I'm gonna kill that devil," Glaze yelled angrily, after Oat stopped Jack. The big gray stud wanted to get at the chestnut and probably would have killed it if Oat hadn't held him back.

"You wanted the fight," Oat yelled at Glaze. "Get your horse under control or I'll let him go and we'll see who gets killed."

Besides the piece of hide that drooped loosely from the chestnut's neck, it favored it's left front shoulder. Oat guessed it probably had some broken ribs. A stirrup had been ripped from Glaze's saddle during the brief fracas and the cinch slipped allowing the saddle to fall sideways. Except for a small cut on his left shoulder, Jack was free of any injury and his harness was intact. He wanted to fight, however, and Oat decided to get the big animal away from the scene before he figured out that he could toss Oat around as easily as he could the piece of broken rail on the end of the lead rope.

Leading Jack to the blacksmith's shop, he retrieved Molly. The blacksmith hadn't fixed her shoe, but Oat didn't wait. Clovis would put the shoe on for him. He hitched the Jacquards to the wagon. When finished he looked around to see Sarah, the governor and about ten other people staring at the Jacquards. A crowd had gathered and now talked excitedly, some pointing at Jack. Glaze wiped blood from the chestnut as Oat drove the Jacquards past him out of town toward home.

# — 10 —

LIBBIE HARMON DEPARTED FOR BALTIMORE THE SAME day Oat left for Gallatin. She had no idea Oat planned to go anywhere which was how he wanted it. She didn't take much, her clothes, a few books and letters. There wasn't anything else she could take along that would do her much good in Baltimore. Oat packed the money Bufflehead gave him into her bag when she was occupied with other things. He had been surprised when he had counted it. There was nearly three hundred dollars worth of coins. She could use it in Baltimore. He promised himself to explain it to her in a letter.

During the preceding few days she spent several gloomy hours in the little family cemetery. She gathered wild flowers and placed them neatly near the headstones of Oat's father and brothers and then sat nearby crying. At dawn, Oat loaded her belongings into the wagon and drove her to the river boat landing near Independence. She planned to make most of the journey by boat, down the Missouri to St. Louis, then up the Mississippi and Ohio to Cincinnati. From there she would travel cross country by stage to Baltimore.

At the pier she nearly changed her mind.

"I don't want to leave you here Oat," she said. "I wish you would come too. I may never see you again."

"You worry about me too much," he said, but her words didn't do much for his peace of mind. "I'll write often and you can come check on me anytime you want. I might even come to Baltimore for a few days this winter if things go well here."

He hugged her and stood dutifully still while she held him tightly for several minutes before boarding the boat. When the boat departed he waited on the landing until it floated out of sight. A peculiar feeling settled over him. Somehow, his life never would be the same again.

Returning home he hastily made preparations to leave for Gallatin. Harnessing the Jacquards, he led them about two miles west to Clovis's farm. Molly's colt as always followed close by its mother. Since the Wheatleys fled Jackson County with the Mormons, Clovis was the Harmons' closest neighbor and Oat trusted him with the big horses. Clovis had plowing to do and would fix Molly's shoe and care for them while he was gone.

Clovis was an agreeable, good-natured man with a plump, happy wife and seven hungry youngsters ranging in age from two to fourteen. The Blackburns were a close-knit family and Oat liked to visit them because the smaller children climbed into his lap and onto his shoulders and treated him like their long, lost uncle. Clovis had round protruding ears and his nose wiggled when he spoke. When he wasn't farming Clovis liked to distill liquor in an apparatus he constructed behind his barn. He told Oat it was a skill passed down through many generations of Blackburns and he intended to keep passing it on. It also brought him a good source of income. His brew had gained a reputation as one of the best in the region and the local settlers' thirst for liquor helped Clovis build a nice little enterprise to complement his farm.

"It's been a wet spring Oat," Clovis said as they sat together on stools in front of the house sipping a cup of his latest batch. "Haven't had many good days. I'm hoping I can get the fields plowed soon."

"You're welcome to use the Jacquards if you want," Oat said. "I have some business over in Boone County so I won't be needing them for a few days."

"I will Oat. I can sure use them."

They sat quietly watching his children chase the chickens. Oat felt the liquor warming him and his head getting light after just one drink. Clovis made a strong drink.

"Do you have a jug of that real hard brew you cooked up last fall?" Oat asked. "The stuff that could take the rust off my plow."

"You're not a hard drinker Oat. I don't recommend it. The wife uses it to clean pots."

"It's not for me."

"Who then?"

"Some hard-drinking friends in Boone County. It's kind of a

joke I'm playing on em."

"I worry about that batch Oat. I'll give you some, but I'm going to put some honey in it to sweeten it up a little. I've been thinking of throwing it out. The drunks at Independence can't even stomach it without going to sleep for two days. I'm telling you, it's strong."

"Just what I want Clovis."

April truly had been a wet month. The preceding winter had been cold, but mostly stormless. In March and April, however, the weather pattern had changed bringing a storm almost every day. Daily deluges turned the countryside into a panoramic display of greenery. Prairie grasses were already belly high to most grazing animals and settlers who had been fortunate enough to plant their crops between storms watched with enthusiasm as their crops grew. Those who hadn't planted waited anxiously for the sun to stay long enough to dry out the soil.

At Gallatin, a brief, heavy storm turned the streets to a quagmire. The mud in places was ten inches deep making the act of just crossing the street a miserable and dirty task. The mud didn't stop the teams of oxen, mules and horses that pulled heavy farm wagons loaded with cargo up and down the streets. As the rain fell the animals' hooves and the wagons' wheels stirred, kneaded and churned the mud and manure into fine slimy grease. Pedestrians were at a distinct disadvantage if they wished to stay clean.

Oat arrived at Gallatin about midmorning, two days after leaving Independence. He rode his bay gelding and led his two other saddle horses. He brought them along for the prisoners to ride in case he couldn't find a wagon. Since he used the Jacquards so much he often neglected the saddle horses and this appeared to be a prime opportunity to work them some. He asked directions to Judge Birch's residence and soon found the judge's farm near a grove of sycamore. The large white log house was easy to spot and was unusual because it had glass windows and a whitewashed exterior. Fiel hands worked nearby in a newly planted field. The yard was neat and tidy.

Oat knocked loudly on the front door and soon the judge appeared. An average looking man, there appeared to be nothing remarkable about him except for a hollow, haunted face and liquor on his breath which wasn't unusual for any Missourian. Oat handed over the papers.

"These are from Governor Boggs," he said. "I'm to wait here until you read them and then follow your instructions."

The judge stepped outside and opened the bundle. He studied the papers for a good ten minutes, opening the sealed letter and glancing at Oat several times as he read. Finally he folded the papers.

"I'll go with you to the jail," he said. "But I have to write a letter first."

He called to one of the hands to saddle his horse and then disappeared inside the white house for another twenty minutes before emerging dressed in coat and tie. By then his horse was ready. He and Oat made a quiet journey to the Gallatin jail.

Oat remembered from his previous visit that the jail usually served as the community's school, but doubled as a jail because the town didn't have a permanent jail. The windows were boarded and the interior dark. Inside, Oat made out the forms of the prisoners, three sitting and two standing. He saw them stir and knew they watched as he and the judge entered. The prisoners heard every word. As his eyes slowly adjusted from the outside light, Oat made out the unmistakable upright silhouettes of the Smith brothers peering at him.

The sheriff sat in a wooden chair with his feet propped on a small desk, a badge fastened to his shirt. A shotgun leaned against the wall in a corner within arm's reach. A bearded deputy sat nearby holding a rifle in his lap. Both cast wary eyes on Oat as he came through the door behind the judge. The bearded man shifted ever so slightly so the barrel of his rifle pointed at Oat's stomach.

"Point that somewhere else," Oat said crossly. Tired and hungry, he recoiled at the idea of being gut shot. But the guard made no move until he got a stern look from the judge. He then shifted the gun in another direction.

The judge handed a folded sheet of paper to the sheriff.

"This is an order for a change of venue for the prisoners to Boone County," he said. "You and three deputies will accompany Mr. Harmon here to Columbia and you'll leave this afternoon."

The sheriff read the paper and scowled.

"There ain't no date, time or place on this," he said acidly.

"No, there isn't," the judge said, "But it's legal because my signature's on it."

"I don't want to ride all the way to Boone County with a bunch of lousy Mormons," the sheriff said, staring icily at Oat.

"Tough. That's your job and be sure you leave today," the judge responded. "If you don't it will be noon tomorrow before you get out of here. It's important this be done now."

The judge's cool, matter-of-fact tone amazed Oat. In a few terse sentences he had ordered the unsuspecting sheriff and his men to die. Oat clenched his teeth and looked over his shoulder at the prisoners. He wondered how many others knew of the conspiracy.

By mid-afternoon the sullen sheriff, still quite unaware that he and his men had been targeted for massacre, obediently secured a wagon large enough to haul the five prisoners and two horses to pull it. He drove the wagon through the mud to the front of the jail. Two surly men joined the bearded man from the jail, the sheriff and Oat as guards. The sheriff and the other men loaded their bedrolls and personals in the front of the wagon and then went after the prisoners. Oat mounted his own horse and watched the parade of prisoners as they got their first dose of sunlight and fresh air in several days.

As they marched out of the jail Oat studied them closely. Smith looked the same as he had the last time he'd seen him. But Oat had heard Smith described so unflatteringly by both strangers and friends that he always expected to see a monster. The two Smith brothers resembled each other, Hyrum being a little taller. Their coats, pants and boots remained dirty, tattered and worn.

Joe Smith's presence drew everyone's attention. Strikingly well-built, he stood as tall as Oat's father had been. His face featured a hooked nose and piercing eyes. He walked easily and gracefully despite a slight limp. The guards and sheriff paled next to him. He flung about the manacles that held his wrists and feet as if they were made of string yet he and his fellow prisoners appeared thin and gaunt.

Joe exited the jail last and got into the wagon, being pulled up by his brother, who extended an arm and a healthy tug. He sat down and leaned against the side of the wagon nearest the back, relaxed and amiable, as though he had not an enemy in the world.

The word of the prisoners' removal to Boone County had spread quickly about Gallatin and a curious crowd of locals gathered to watch their departure.

"Good bye and good riddance," yelled a stout, ordinary looking man sitting on the walkway near the school's entrance.

"Have a nice hanging," called out a shrill younger male voice.

Others stood on the front steps of the jail or draped themselves over the railings and stared disdainfully, saying nothing. The prisoners mostly ignored the onlookers until an old man with a brawny, grating voice began to harangue them. A tall, dignified farmer, he hadn't used a razor on his beard or scissors on his hair for at least a year. He came straight from digging a well or ditch, apparently, still covered with mud and dirt.

"Hey Joe, did you see any angels in our jail?" he called out contemptuously. Giggles and grunts rippled through the crowd.

Among Mormons, Smith's work of translating ancient records from golden plates, visitations by angels, tales of healings and speaking in tongues were legends. Oat vaguely remembered stories the Wheatleys told reverently of Smith seeing God. Among Missourians, however, these Mormon legends often caused great frivolity. They believed none of it. Here, he was a criminal, a prisoner known as Joe Smith, Holy Joe — or worse.

"Could be," Smith called back good-naturedly. "Get these chains off, give me a good meal and I'll tell you all about it."

The crowd laughed again casually and softened some when they realized that Smith looked and talked pretty much like any normal human being. That is, all except for the dirty farmer who drew closer, still loud and caustic. He walked to the back of the wagon until he stood next to Smith.

Speaking to the crowd the man said:

"This man claims to have seen God Almighty Himself. I think he's a liar."

"He is," another man shouted and many others in the crowd gave assenting nods and gestures indicating they agreed.

"Have you seen God, Holy Joe?" the man said contemptuously

looking squarely at Smith.

"Yes, I have," Smith said evenly and earnestly as the old man bristled.

"Well if you've seen him, what does he look like?"

The sheriff and guards listened without saying anything. Even though hostile, the question was a good one and everyone wanted to know the answer. Clearly, no one planned to move until he answered it. Oat strained to hear, but he needn't have bothered because Smith's retort came back loud and clear.

"I can tell you brother," he said happily, his eyes twinkling. "God looks almost exactly like you, only he's a whole lot cleaner."

The crowd on the jailhouse steps, including the sheriff and the guards, roared. The outmatched curmudgeon, unable to tell if he'd just been insulted or complimented, shook his head and threw up his hands as the crowd clapped and laughed. The sheriff climbed into the wagon driver's seat, clearly not enthused with his task. He slapped the reins over the backs of the horses and the wagon jerked forward down the muddy street leaving the crowd standing in front of the jail. The guards mounted their horses and followed.

From among the bystanders a small boy ran out into the street. Grabbing a handful of mud he formed a ball which he threw into the wagon hitting the prisoner sitting between the two Smith brothers. The prisoner patiently scraped off the mud and threw it over the side of the wagon. The act delighted the onlookers and soon a whole phalanx of men and boys pelted the wagon with mud. The prisoners held their manacled arms over their heads but had difficulty protecting themselves as the slow wagon drew away from the jail. Oat, seeing that none of the other guards was going to stop the barrage, spurred his horse into the midst of the mud throwers breaking their ranks and harmlessly hindering their fun until the wagon moved out of their range. He then galloped back to his place in the procession accompanied by the jeers of the crowd. He took two mudballs in the back for his trouble.

As he took up his place at the rear of the wagon he felt a pair of eyes settle on him. Joe Smith smiled and saluted.

Oat quickly looked away.

The slow-moving procession gave Oat plenty of thinking time. He believed the ambush probably would occur at the point in the trail where they would pass closest to the Missouri River. But that was the tricky part. He couldn't be sure. If he, the other guards and the prisoners were to survive the journey he had to put his own plan into motion before Glaze sprang the trap.

He decided not to tell the others that an ambush was imminent mostly because he didn't know how they would react. His plan would work best if no one but himself knew about it. The main ingredient to his scheme, Clovis's brew, hung in a bag tied securely to the saddle of one of his horses. Long ago, when his father was still alive, he had heard Bufflehead tell tales about how a good jug of whiskey could make even the orneriest men docile and cooperative when conducting business. The old trapper claimed it worked every time.

The first two days the group covered only about five miles a day and stayed overnight at farms located along the way. The weather was wet and windy and the trail was muddy. But on the third day as they moved onto the open prairie the sky cleared and the sun warmed them throughout the morning. The sheriff kicked the team into a trot and they covered about ten miles that morning. At noon they stopped near a stream to rest and water the horses and eat a lunch of bread and dry meat.

As they ate, Oat pulled the bearded guard from the jail aside so no one else could hear.

"You want a drink? I've got a jug of hooch stashed. Don't tell anybody and we'll sneak away from camp tonight."

The guard's eyes got big as corks.

"You've got a jug? Where? You bet I want a drink. Let's get it now."

"No, not now," Oat said. "Later."

Before the procession got under way ten minutes later, the other three guards and the sheriff knew about the jug and openly salivated for it, tobacco juice drooling down their chins. They were true Missourians who had been without whiskey for almost three days. The very thought of a jug of liquor made water or anything else ineffective in quenching their thirst. As the day wore on and Oat continued to hold out on them they grew thirstier and thirstier until as the sun set in the west they became cross and churlish, ready to fight, if necessary, for a crack at Oat's jug.

Finally the procession stopped between two small hills covered with trees and brush and flanked by a small stream, a perfect spot for an ambush. Somewhere out there Glaze waited. Oat sensed it and acted quickly. The sheriff and other guards looked on reverently as Oat pulled the jug from his pack and shook it so that the honey would mix with the liquor. The jug was full, and they were happy as pigs in slop.

Oat handed the jug to the bearded guard who popped the cork and sucked down a large gulp. Oat thought the man would die then and there. Immediately his face screwed into an awful contortion and his body convulsed as he bent over clutching at his stomach. His eyes watered and he blew out a long, hard gasp, while his legs buckled. Sitting on the ground he looked up at Oat solemnly.

"That is good stuff," he said.

The other guards and the sheriff jumped at the jug and soon all swilled it freely. They forgot entirely about the prisoners who sat in the wagon looking on wryly. Oat started a fire and cooked a wild turkey one of the guards had killed earlier and warmed some corn dodgers for the prisoners as the sheriff and others drank. Within an hour as darkness set in the sheriff and his men were pawing for their bedrolls. The sheriff walked uncertainly to where Oat sat eating.

"Judge Birch told me Ol' Joe was never going to make it to Boone County," he said, loud enough for the prisoners to hear. "I'm not sure what he meant by that, but I'm going to go over here and have another drink of your hooch and then I'm going to bed and you can look after these Mormons."

The prisoners whispered amongst themselves. Oat felt Smith's gaze following him. He could not remember feeling a pair of eyes search him more closely. Darkness gathered and the fire burned low. The sheriff and guards snored loudly and peacefully. They wouldn't wake until morning. Oat nervously looked out into the darkness. Somewhere out there Glaze lurked, waiting to strike.

He found a hammer and chisel in the wagon and handed it to the prisoners. They knew what to do with it. They immediately broke the manacles from their arms and legs, creating a racket that should have awakened the dead. It did not, however, disturb the sleeping sheriff and the other guards. As the chains came off Smith immediately took charge. He looked toward the horses tethered a short distance away.

"Do you own any of those horses?" he said to Oat.

"Three of them," Oat said.

"Can we buy them from you?"

"You can have two of them," Oat answered. "I'll need one to get home on."

"Good," Smith said. "We'll take them."

Oat saddled the two horses while Smith conferred with his brother and the other three men. When Oat handed them the reins Smith pushed a bundle of clothing at him.

"This should about pay for one of the horses," he said. "We will give you our note for the other one if you will accept it."

Oat nodded as he examined the bundle. It contained a wool coat and two pairs of cotton trousers in good condition. The bundle surprised him, considering the rags the men wore. He knew they carried a few bundles for their personal effects and realized the bundles contained the clothes. He expected to get nothing in return, a loss he would accept as long as he got some satisfaction at derailing Boggs. Someone produced a pen and piece of paper and a note was hurriedly written and handed to Oat. It promised payment for the remaining horse and was signed by Hyrum Smith.

Joe told the other four to start. They put Wight on the horse and the other three walked. Smith faced Oat.

"What is your name sir?"

"Otis Harmon."

"You got the sheriff and guards drunk on purpose so you could let us go," he said. "Why? Few people in Missouri would do that for us."

"Self preservation is one reason," Oat said. "There's an ambush waiting for us up the trail a ways. Boggs's plan is to kill us all and make it look like Indians did it. If you get away they have no reason to kill me and the others unless they find out I helped you."

"You have my deepest gratitude," Smith said. He turned to mount his horse then stopped suddenly.

"Boggs will find out what you've done and you'll be killed if you stay in Missouri. We won't tell anyone what happened here, but they'll know. You should come with us."

"No," Oat said. "My home is in Jackson County and I need to be there."

"Our home is Jackson County too," Smith said. "Get away from there. Boggs will kill you if you stay." A chill ran up Oat's spine because he knew Smith was right.

"God bless you Otis Harmon," Smith said. "You are always welcome in my home. You have a good heart. As long as it remains good you'll have power to defeat your enemies."

Smith's words sounded a little presumptuous, but Oat felt a warmth for the man.

"If things don't work out for me here I may be seeing you," Oat said.

"Well then I shall look forward to seeing you soon," Smith said seriously as he mounted the horse.

"I read in the Bible once that God sent an angel to free Peter," Oat said abruptly. "If you're a prophet, why didn't God send an angel for you?"

"He didn't need to. He knew you'd do it," Smith said. Then slapping the horse on the rear, he disappeared in the darkness.

# 11

Tying the bundle of clothing onto the back of his saddle, Oat left immediately after the prisoners disappeared into the darkness. He didn't want to be around when the guards and sheriff awoke, but judging from the amount of liquor they had consumed, it would be well after sunrise the next morning before they would rise.

For the next several hours he moved slowly through the darkness. At first light he found a good trail heading west and kicked the bay into a slow lope. He didn't stop all day. The full weight of his deeds settled on him as he rode. Glaze and Boggs easily would figure out what happened and they would come looking for him. If they found him they wouldn't be kind. He thought about his father's death, Bufflehead's confession and the things his mother always worried about. He wouldn't be safe at the farm any more. It wasn't an easy conclusion to come to and he fought with himself about it. Finally after miles of contemplation he realized that if he wanted to live, he had to leave Jackson County.

The realization nearly broke his heart. He hadn't thought of this when he planned to free Smith and spoil Boggs' plans. His desire for revenge had been too strong, too overpowering. Now, he'd have to leave the farm, the newly planted crops, the acres of ground he had worked countless hours to make productive. Worse, he'd have to leave his dreams. It was a big price to pay for a little bit of revenge.

By nightfall Oat arrived at the ferry and felt happy to stand still for the span of time it took to float quietly across the river. He let the bay walk the rest of the way home. After unsaddling the horse, he staggered into the house exhausted and slept soundly until sunrise when he awoke with a start. His muscles ached but he knew that he didn't have time to spare. The consequences of his actions in releasing the Mormons loomed larger in his mind. Smith had been right. As soon as Boggs found his plans foiled, Oat's future in Jackson County would be short lived. He must leave now or suffer the full weight of Boggs' wrath. He quickly made a decision. He would go north away from Independence, possibly into Iowa. It didn't matter where, it just had to be away from Jackson County. He really had no choice. Events now controlled his circumstances and he had to react to them. But he would have the slow-moving Jacquards and that meant he couldn't move as quickly as he wanted. Time was valuable. He didn't have any to waste.

He spent the next few hours loading farm tools and items from the house into the wagon. He couldn't take everything but he loaded the plow, all of his small tools and tack. His mother's possessions that she had left, he loaded into an old wooden trunk that had belonged to his father. He placed it in the front of the wagon. He was surprised how little time it took. By mid-morning, he was ready.

He left the loaded wagon at the house and rode the bay to Blackburn's to get the Jacquards. Clovis, planting corn in the middle of a freshly plowed two-acre field, didn't notice Oat's approach. When he finally saw Oat, a surprised, fearful look appeared in his eyes.

"They said you was dead."

"Who?" Oat asked.

"Barker and that Reverend Riley," he said. "They took the two big horses. Left the colt here. Said they'd be back for it."

Oat swore. Barker owned the livery in Independence and was Boggs' close friend.

"Why?"

"They said Indians killed you and they'd sell the horses and give the money to your mom."

So there were more people than just Boggs and Glaze involved, Oat thought. Not surprising and all the more reason to get away.

"Do you know where they took them?"

"To town."

Oat suddenly knew where his horses would be. At Barker's livery. Old man Barker would work them or try to sell them.

"When were they here?"

"Yesterday. Said they'd come back for the colt later."

That too made sense, although they acted too hastily. They generally knew when the ambush was supposed to take place, which probably was yesterday. They assumed it occurred as planned. Oat knew he must get to the livery before Barker sold his horses. He soon was pushing the bay hard again toward Independence.

"They'll kill you if you stay in Missouri."

Smith's words popped into his mind as he raced toward Independence. But he didn't care. His anger swept away his fear. Boggs could have taken almost anything else and he would have left without a whisper, but not the Jacquards. Too much of his life was invested in those two horses. Boggs wouldn't get them without a fight.

He found the Jacquards in the corral behind Barker's livery, standing calmly near one another with their big tails swishing at flies. Seven other mares and geldings milled about the corral but no one was at the stable. All appeared calm. Ten-inch posts sunk deep into the ground circled the corral with four rows of three-to four-inch poles nailed to them to form a generous circle, large enough probably for twenty horses. Some poles were nailed to the walls of the livery. A gate hung on enormous steel hinges and was fastened shut with a heavy steel chain and a lock. Barker had lost horses to thieves in the past and clearly he didn't want it to happen again. Oat looked about briefly for the key but couldn't find it. He guessed Barker had it in his pocket and Oat knew he would never get it.

The Jacquards' collars and harnesses hung on nails inside the stable. He carried them to the corral where he carefully strapped them onto the big horses. They stood patiently, well acquainted with the procedure. The process took about ten minutes. Inside the stable he found two singletrees with chains. He took them to the corral and fastened them to two separate posts, the one nearest the livery and the other one clear across the corral. He led Molly to the post nearest the livery where the single tree was fastened and attached her harness to it. He fastened Jack's harness to the other.

Oat sat down on a stool in a corner of the livery, bit off a chew of tobacco and waited. Barker soon appeared accompanied by two long-haired men dressed in leather — buffalo hunters. One drove an empty wagon pulled by a pair of broken-down mules. They apparently were getting ready for a hunting trip.

"Don't want nothing that's old and crippled," he heard one say. "We're going to have a big load coming back."

"I have just what ya need," Barker said, "but I hope you've got money cause these horses ain't cheap."

"We got money," one of them said.

The three men, unaware of Oat, walked slowly down the street right past Oat's bay, tethered to a hitching rail alongside the livery. They stopped near the corral.

The hunters eyes fell on the Jacquards.

"Them harses is bigger than range bulls," said the hunter who was doing most of the talking. "Where'd you get them things?"

"Once owned by a young man who met with some misfortune," Barker said lightly. He suddenly noticed the harnesses on the big horses. He glanced around and swore.

Oat emerged from the livery.

"Hello Barker," he said.

Barker stared.

"Don't worry," Oat said, slapping the grisly old man on the back. "It's me in the flesh. No ghosts here. I got back from my trip last night. Clovis Blackburn said you were kind enough to look after my horses while I was gone. I thank you, but I've got to get going now so if you'll open that gate I'll be on my way."

Barker stared stupidly at Oat and didn't move.

"The governor gave me these horses for some land," he said finally.

"Did he?" Oat said. "Well, he may be the governor, but those are my horses."

"He said it all was arranged."

"Sure it's arranged on condition that I'm dead, which I'm not and they weren't his horses to trade," Oat said. "They're mine and I'm ready to leave so open the gate."

Barker stubbornly refused.

"I'm going to go see the governor and we'll get this straightened out now," he said. "You just cool off and wait here a minute."

"I am not waiting Barker," Oat said. "Boggs wants me dead. You open that gate or I'll open it for you."

Barker grinned.

"I've got the key to that corral right here and I'm not opening that gate until I see the governor and I'll bet that within two hours you're in jail and those horses are still in this corral."

With that Barker turned and walked away from the livery leaving Oat standing next to the two buffalo hunters.

"Looks like yer gonna have to wait a while to get those horses turnt loose ain't ya kid?" the tallest hunter said, laughing. He spit a stream of juice onto the ground at Oat's feet. "I'll bet those big gray horses can haul a lot of buffalo hides."

Oat spit right back at the hunter. He walked to the bay, untied the horse's reins and mounted. He reined it around and walked it alongside the corral while the two hunters watched. Barker, still in sight, walked purposely toward Boggs' house more than a quarter mile away.

"Tighten it up Jack," Oat yelled, slapping the horse's big haunches with his reins.

The big horse moved slowly forward until the chain fastened to the corral post was taut. The hunters seated themselves on the top pole of the corral watching. Barker, on hearing Oat's voice, turned around to see what Oat was doing.

"Jack, tighten it up," one of the hunters said, mocking Oat.

The hunters sat just a little too close to Jack and for a moment Oat thought about warning them, but quickly decided against it. He didn't like them much. Jack leaned into his collar. The other horses in the corral, sensing the impending commotion, trotted around nervously. Molly tightened her chain.

"Ha Jack ha," Oat yelled and slapped Jack again with his reins.

The big gray percheron rocked backward allowing the single tree to drop about a foot toward the ground. Then he lunged forward. The chain snapped tight and the post broke off right at the ground like a dry twig, cracking loud enough to sound like a gunshot.

"Go Jack," Oat called. The big horse moved forward. Corral poles splintered and split and two more posts gave, one breaking and another coming right out of the ground. Within seconds the whole side of the corral lay flat on the ground. The buffalo hunters landed on the ground with a span of poles on top of them. The loose horses in the corral gingerly scrambled over the down fence leaving Molly and Jack standing alone in the ruined corral.

Oat spurred the bay over the fallen poles and jumped to the ground. He unfastened Jack's harness, grabbed the lead rope, mounted the bay again and led Jack out of the corral. Once clear he yelled to Molly.

"Ha Molly ha."

The commotion had spooked Molly. She dived forward and the chain snapped tight. The post broke off immediately allowing her to jerk forward about three yards, but the four poles fastened to the post also were fastened to the corner post of the livery. This stymied Molly for an instant. The big mare eased off for a second, rocking backward and then barreled forward again putting all of her strength into the collar. The chain snapped tight, the poles moved again, then the whole livery shuddered. The corner post snapped and the west wall of the livery broke free causing the roof and two other walls to cave in. The noise frightened Molly and she bolted over the top of the corral fence Jack had leveled still dragging about fifteen feet of livery wall. Oat knew it would be suicide to try to stop her so he got out of the way.

The big gray mare thundered down the Independence main street right past Barker still dragging the livery wall. Oat and Jack followed close behind.

"Next time I'll bet you open the gate," Oat yelled as he and his horses ran past Barker.

Molly missed her colt so she didn't slow down much until she got home. Oat found her in front of the house, sides heaving, the shredded wall of the livery still attached to her harness. Oat wasted no time. Barker and Boggs would have people after him soon, if not already. He loaded his guns and hid them in the wagon and then led both of the Jacquards to the watering trough where they drank briefly. Then he hitched them to the wagon and tied the bay's lead rope to the wagon. Pulling away from the house he didn't look back. No sense being sentimental now. He was in a race for his life with the two slowest horses in western Missouri pulling his wagon.

# — 12 —

GLAZE FOUND THE SHERIFF AND HIS MEN STILL SLEEPING about mid-morning the day after Harmon freed Smith. Glaze and his men waited about a mile beyond the campsite on the southside of a brushy swale until they couldn't stand it any more. They would have struck at dawn had the sheriff and his prisoners moved on schedule.

The campsite told the story of what happened. The sheriff and the other guards lay wrapped in their bedrolls. A jug of corn liquor lay on its side — empty. Flies buzzed around the partially eaten turkey carcass still fastened to a spit over some burned-out coals. A pile of broken manacles lay in the back of the wagon. The prisoners were gone and two sets of horse tracks led eastward and one led west.

"Well over ten hours old," Tucker said. "We'll never catch 'em."

Glaze dismounted near the ashes of the fire. Their talking and the sound of horse's hooves aroused the sleeping men.

"Who the hell are you and what do ya want?" One of them demanded.

"The governor sent us to give you boys a hand," Glaze lied, "but it looks like we're too late."

He held up one of the manacles and dropped it. It thumped noisily on the ground. The sheriff stumbled to the wagon and stared.

"Where's Harmon?" Glaze asked. "Wasn't he with you?"

"He guarded the prisoners last night."

"That figures." Glaze said. "How many of your horses are missing?"

The sheriff looked anxiously at the horses tethered in some trees near the wagon.

"Three. All Harmon's."

Glaze shook his head. Smith escaped with Harmon's help. Boggs would be furious. He spoke to his men who still were mounted.

"We're going to have to work fast to save our own hides. Follow those two sets of tracks for a while. You might get lucky. If you catch 'em, kill 'em. Don't waste more than a day on it though. Meet me at my place in two days. I'm going after Harmon."

A day later, about a mile from Independence Glaze's tired horse stumbled and nearly went down. The big-boned sorrel wasn't nearly as strong as the chestnut stud. The chestnut, however, was in no shape to be ridden. The wounds it received in the brief fight with Harmon's big gray work horse wouldn't heal for weeks.

Glaze, as tired as the horse, knew he had to report to the governor as soon as he arrived in Independence. He believed Harmon would return home, but couldn't be certain. He obviously wasn't as stupid as Boggs thought. Why had he let Smith go?

Glaze hoped Tucker, Pepper and Ward would be lucky enough to catch the Smiths again, but he doubted that would happen. They were too smart. After all the chances they had had to kill Smith and now to let him slip through their fingers like this was embarrassing. Boggs would throw a fit. The authorities in Gallatin would be furious when they learned Smith had escaped. And the people in Columbia, all primed for a big trial and hanging, would be angry too.

A crowd milled about the main street at Independence for some reason, laughing with one another as the old livery owner Barker ranted angrily up and down the street picking up ropes, buckles and leather straps. Something had been drug down the middle of the street leaving a mark like a ditch furrow.

"That man looks like I feel," Glaze said out loud to himself.

Boggs sat alone in his office when Glaze arrived. It was mid-afternoon. A purple vein on the governor's temple pulsed outwardly and his black eyes held a cold hard stare. Though he was badly in need of sleep Glaze sensed Boggs already knew their plan had failed.

Boggs let Glaze into his office and slammed the door. The governor literally shook as he made his way to his desk chair and sat down. He pressed his hands onto the top of his desk to keep them from shaking. The color drained from his face and Glaze heard the governor's teeth grinding together as he pieced together a report of how the Mormon prisoners escaped.

Boggs listened without interrupting.

"There's two things I hate worse than Mormons," Boggs said, after Glaze finished. "Uppity slaves and failures."

Glaze shifted uneasily. He wanted to be on Boggs' good side. People the governor didn't like often ended up dead. The operation would have gone as planned but somehow Harmon found out about it.

"The Harmon kid outwitted you," Boggs said accusingly.

Glaze didn't like the thought of being outsmarted by a farmer. He prided himself on his cunning.

"No. He outwitted you," Glaze said. "Because someone must have told him your plan."

"Obviously." Boggs said. "And if he knows that, then he knows a lot more. In fact he probably knows a lot of things that I don't want him to know about."

"One of your chums spilled his guts," Glaze said acidly. "This was not my fault. Harmon planned this. He probably knew the day he came to town to get those papers."

"The only person who would have talked was that old fool Bufflehead," Boggs screamed, slamming his fist on his desk. "This is very damaging to me. I could lose the election. You find Harmon, find out what he knows and how he knows and then shut him up forever."

Glaze threw up his arms and slumped in his chair. Boggs, unreasonable, vicious and angry, now asked the impossible. Tired and short-tempered himself, he was not willing to accept Boggs' demands.

"I have no idea where Harmon is. If I could get my hands on him I could make him talk," Glaze said. "But he could be anywhere. He might have come back here, but he's not that stupid. He's got to know that we'll kill him."

The corners of Boggs' mouth curled in more of a grimace than a smile.

"He's here," Boggs said. "About thirty minutes ago the whole town watched him and those two big work horses drag half of Barker's stable right down main street. Barker gathered up his horses yesterday and Harmon apparently wasn't too happy about that."

The tiredness drained from Glaze's body. He stood up.

"He's dumber than I thought then," Glaze said. "He should have stayed away from here. I'll run him down before dark."

Boggs followed Glaze to the door.

"Don't be overconfident and don't underestimate him again. He's not stupid. If he gets across the river you'll never find him and I promise you there'll be hell to pay if that happens."

"If he's got those two big horses he'll be moving slowly and leaving a real good trail," Glaze said. "I won't be back until I get him."

Glaze left Independence an hour later on a fresh mount with three other men. He recruited the old livery owner Barker, who was so mad he breathed out threats to put Harmon's head on a pole before they cleared town. The livery was destroyed. Halters, leather straps, rope, harnesses, buckles and broken boards littered the length of the street. Barker caught four of the horses that ran off when the corral fence went down, but it took an hour to find enough tack to outfit the horses. The other two were buffalo hunters Glaze didn't know. They came along with the understanding that once Harmon was dead they could have his horses.

They rode west about a mile before the trail veered north. From the sign it looked as though one of Harmon's horses still dragged a portion of the stable because it left a continuous scar in the road that was easy to follow, but they didn't need it. Glaze knew it would lead to the Harmon place.

Glaze expected to catch up to Harmon at his farm, but no one was there. Harmon had hitched his horses to a wagon and left on a trail heading west. They followed wagon wheel tracks to another farm where he found a woman and more kids than they had time to count.

"You know I honestly didn't see them leave," the woman told Glaze. "Clovis had a load of wheat he was taking to the mill. Oat may have gone along to help him."

The mill was five miles away. Loaded wagons had to use a ferry to cross the Big Blue River. Glaze knew of a crossing that would cut that distance in half, but he wished he could be certain that Harmon was at the mill.

"Are you certain Harmon went to the mill?" Glaze asked.

The Blackburn woman shook her head.

"I know that's where Clovis was going. And I'm pretty sure that's where Oat was going too. But I won't swear to it sir."

Glaze mounted and led the other men away from the farm at a gallop. About a quarter mile down the road they cut off the main trail and went west cross country right over Clovis's newly plowed and planted cornfield.

# — 13 —

WHEN CLOVIS REINED HIS MULES TO A STOP AT THE mill, four horsemen approached and he knew his decoy had worked. Glaze matched Oat's description — big, ugly and mean. One of the men with him was the livery owner Barker, but the other two he'd never seen before. Their vacant faces stared back at him like a couple of cows.

He had left Oat about three miles north of the mill. Oat had two miles to travel to the ferry and the big horses did not travel fast. He also had Molly's colt to slow him down. Clovis wanted to buy Oat all the time he could so he let the mules take their time getting to the mill. He liked Oat, always had. A big, honest, innocent farmer, Oat didn't have a mean bone in his body, but somehow he'd gotten himself into some real trouble that Clovis didn't understand and Oat didn't explain.

He asked for Clovis' help, but made Clovis swear to do as he asked.

"When you see Glaze you can't lie to him," Oat said. "If you lie and I get away, he'll find out and he'll come back and hurt you and your family and I couldn't bear that. He can't suspect you helped me."

Clovis agreed, but he wanted to do more. Oat just up and gave his entire farm to Clovis. He sat down at Clovis' kitchen table only an hour earlier and quickly wrote a bill of sale. The bill said Oat was selling Clovis his farm and everything on the farm including the bay and the rest of the livestock and all the buildings and tools.

"But I don't have any money to give you," Clovis said.

"I don't need money Clovis. I need feed for my horses," his friend said.

Clovis loaded four bags of oats into his wagon. So Oat wrote on the bill of sale that he was selling his farm and all his possessions on the farm for four bags of oats.

When his wagon rolled to a stop and took a place in line at the mill Clovis got nervous. He spotted Glaze and his men as soon as he broke out of the brush along the creek about a hundred yards from the mill. They were watching for him and Oat too apparently. He heard Glaze swear when he realized Oat wasn't with him and saw the man angrily throw his gloves onto the ground. Clovis smiled.

"What the hell are you smiling about?" Glaze called out angrily.

Clovis pulled a jug of corn liquor out from under the seat, popped the cork and took a sip. He patted the jug and set it down.

"I'm fifth in line so that means I have at least an hour to sit here and enjoy this jug," Clovis said. He could tell by the looks on their faces that they wanted his jug. He counted on that.

"Have you seen Oat Harmon?" Glaze asked.

"Oat and me are friends," Clovis said. "What do you want him for?"

"We just want to talk to him."

"He was at my place just a while ago."

"We know," Glaze said. "We talked to your wife. Where is he?"

"He's leaving the country and he's scared out of his wits. Says people are chasing him. You ain't gonna hurt him, are ya?"

"Did he tell you why we want to talk to him?"

"Nah. Said it was a long story and he didn't want to take the time."

Clovis popped the cork on his jug and took another sip. Before corking it again he held it out to the four men.

"You boys want a drink?"

Barker and the other two swarmed around the jug. Each took several large gulps. Glaze even took a big swig. The jug contained Clovis' heaviest brew, taken from the same batch Oat took a few days earlier, very strong and sweetened with honey. Within an hour, the four men would have difficulty sitting in their saddles.

"Where'd you last see him?" Glaze asked.

Clovis had milked all the time he could for Oat.

"North. He's gonna cross the river."

"At the ferry?"

"I s'pose. It's what I'd do," Clovis said. "You boys want another sip before you hit the road. Don't drink all of it though. Leave some for me."

The four men each took a turn at the bottle. When they gave it back there wasn't much left and that was just fine with Clovis. They mounted their horses.

"Thanks for the whiskey," Glaze said. "But you better be telling me the truth. We're going to the ferry now and we better find Harmon there or we'll be back for you."

The horsemen spurred their horses into a hard gallop and disappeared in the trees. They would be at the ferry within ten minutes. Clovis hoped Oat at least was on the ferry by now.

# 14

A DISAGREEABLE HOARY-HEADED MAN OPERATED THE ferry. Business was slow and Oat interrupted his late afternoon nap in the shade of a poplar tree. He slipped his suspenders onto his shoulders and scowled at the Jacquards. When he figured out that Oat was in a hurry he worked as slowly as possible.

The old man bummed Oat's last piece of tobacco. Oat hoped the tobacco would buy him some favor, but his only payment was a grin that revealed a mouthful of brown teeth. Oat was careful not to stand too close because he soon realized the man's breath could have killed a raccoon. A jug of Clovis's corn liquor hung from one of the raft's rails. The old man stopped every few moments to suck on it.

The Jacquards' sides heaved and they sweated profusely. The sweat lathered the parts of their huge frames covered by the harnesses, more especially around their collars. Plainly, they had been running.

"If you didn't have such slow horses you wouldn't have to be in such a hurry all the time," the curmudgeon said, and then laughed at his own joke.

Oat led the Jacquards still harnessed to the wagon onto the ferry. The colt, nervous and scared, followed Molly on and stood shaking near her. The ferry was nothing more than a large raft made of three tiers of logs and overlaid boards on the top tier to form a flat surface. The top boards lay buried under six inches of dirt and manure. A three-foot high pole rail encircled the raft and gave it the appearance of a floating corral. There was room for the Jacquards and the wagon, but there wasn't room for much more.

Once loaded, the old man started asking questions.

"Where you headed in such a hurry young man?" he said, then

spit. The spit sprayed out in a fan covering most of Jack Jacquard's left rear flank.

"I'm going north, maybe to Iowa."

"I see you got a plow on that wagon. A big plow. You must be a farmer."

"Yes, I am," Oat said.

"You're in an awful big hurry for a farmer," the old man said. "I suspect you're running from somebody. Maybe the sheriff."

Oat decided there wasn't much point in trying to hide his need to hurry.

"To tell you the truth, sir, there are a few men that I'd rather not see right at this moment and I'd appreciate it if we could get started across this river."

"You got any money to pay the toll to use this ferry?"

"Yessir," Oat said. He reached into his pocket and produced his bag of coins, realizing his mistake too late.

"That's good," Berry said. "Because the toll for taking you and these two big fat, ugly horses and that colt across the river today is ten dollars."

"It cost two bits yesterday," Oat said angrily.

"Times change," the old man said. "Either give me the ten dollars or get your horses off my ferry."

Oat thought for a fleeting moment about pulling one of his guns from its hiding place in the wagon and forcing Berry to take him across, but instead he swallowed his anger and gave Berry the ten dollars, all the money he had.

"This whole rotten raft wouldn't cost ten dollars to build," Oat said.

"That's about right." The old man grinned and shoved the money into his pocket. Then he untied the rope that allowed the raft to drift away from the bank. "That's just about right."

The river's current slowly pushed the heavy ferry across the river. The trip across took an eternity. Oat used the time and his nervous energy to check the wagon and the Jacquards' harnesses all the while keeping a close eye on the receding shoreline. He felt more comfortable once the raft was out of rifle range of the shore, but he knew he remained in danger, although he hoped his pursuers gave up. Maybe they decided killing him wasn't worth the effort, but when the ferry was nearly across the river, Oat spied four horsemen, one of them the unmistakable silhouette of Tyrone Glaze, rein up on the far shore.

The sour old man saw them too.

"So those are the fellers who're after you," he said. "Looks like they have fast horses, not slow ones like you. Probably will take about an hour for me to load them up and get them across the river and after you. They'll catch you before dark. Best say your prayers."

"You going to charge them ten bucks too?" Oat asked.

"Probably not," he sneered. "They don't look as desperate as you and they have guns. Besides anybody that's dumb enough to have such slow, ugly horses in Missouri deserves to pay ten dollars to use this ferry. I don't usually let such unattractive horses anywhere near it."

Oat moved to the edge of the raft as it neared the shore thinking what to do. The old man was right. The Jacquards couldn't match his pursuers' speed. They would catch him immediately. He could abandon the big horses and hide, but he entertained that thought less than a second. It wasn't an option. He glanced down as the shore drew closer and noticed a pair of steel rings fastened to a large bottom log. To its right was a second bottom log and another pair of rings. They obviously had been used in the past to pull the raft out of the water and to somehow drag it.

The ferry finally ran up against the north bank of the river and stopped. The old man jumped off, tied the raft and disappeared behind a clump of bushes. Oat led the Jacquards off the ferry and parked the wagon on a level spot away from the river's edge. He unhitched the Jacquards from the wagon and led them back to the river's edge to the raft. The old man was still in the brush.

Oat hooked the Jacquards to the hitches, Jack on the left, Molly on the right, then waited for the old man, who soon emerged from the bushes tucking his shirttail into his britches and pulling on his coat.

"You still here?" he yapped happily as he walked toward Oat. Seeing Oat's horses hitched to the ferry, he stopped in his tracks. "What you think you're doing boy?"

"I'm about to show you why these two fat, ugly gray horses are more valuable than a dozen saddle horses," Oat said.

"The last time I pulled that raft out of the water to fix it I had to get four teams of mules," the old man said. "I don't know how much that raft weighs but its wet and heavy and it's not worth getting yourself gut shot over."

"Molly, Jack," Oat called to the horses and slapped Jack on the rear. The big horses moved forward until the hitch was tight.

"We're going right between those trees," Oat said to the old man and pointed at two solid green maples at the top of the bank. A trail led from the river's edge up a tapered bank, between the two trees and out onto the prairie.

The old ferry owner grinned.

"No you're not," he said, pulling a pistol from his coat. "I think I've had about all of this I can stand. I think I'm going to shoot your guts out now."

He pointed the barrel at Oat's stomach.

"How you going to do that when you don't even have a cap on your gun?"

The old man took his eyes off Oat for a split-second to see if a cap was in place. As he did Oat snatched the gun out of his hands, shoved the old man backward and heaved the gun into the river.

"Jack, Molly, ha."

The big horses slammed forward their big hooves kicking up mud and then dirt. The edge of the raft ran up against the lip of the bank and stopped. For the first time in his life Oat thought the Jacquards would balk.

"Ha ha ha," Berry laughed. "Yer a big talker."

Suddenly Jack launched into his collar with a fury Oat had seen only once before — when he fought Glaze's stud. Molly echoed and together they ripped the ferry out of the water tearing away a foot of riverbank sod and mud that momentarily had stopped them. After that the raft slipped easily out of the water and through the loose sand and mud up the bank. Jack and Molly gradually picked up speed as the raft glided through the dirt and by the time they topped the bank and passed between the two maples they were kicking up a big cloud of dust and the ferry was slipping along easily behind them.

The raft was too wide to go between the maples so when it hit the trunks of the two big trees their branches shuddered, but the trees didn't give. Neither did the Jacquards. The rotten log timbers of the raft crumbled and snapped. The two logs to which the rings were fastened and which formed the raft's keel were torn away from the bottom tier of logs and without them the raft disintegrated into a pile of firewood. The Jacquards were headed towards Iowa with the parts that were still attached to the bottom logs when Oat stopped them. He unhitched and led them back to the wagon. The old man sat on the ground staring at the wreckage.

"I should have killed you," he said.

"No, you should have charged me two bits and acted like a decent human being," Oat said.

"I was going to give your money back," he said.

"Sure you were, right after you killed me," Oat said sarcastically. "You can keep it. It's not often I get to have ten dollars worth of fun."

# — 15 —

OAT KEPT THE JACQUARDS MOVING THE REST OF THE DAY and throughout the night relying on a clear sky and a full moon. He knew his pursuers would travel downriver several miles and find another ferry. By the time they crossed the river and picked up his trail he'd be far away. Still, they could track him easily. He needed some luck.

Toward morning, clouds gathered and at first light as he traversed a wooded swale a stiff wind whipped the trees violently. Twigs and leaves shook loose and branches broke. Flashes of lightning were accompanied by deafening claps of thunder. The noise spooked the Jacquards who, despite being spent, would have bolted had Oat not kept a tight rein on them. The lightning and thunder continued for several minutes and the wind grew colder. Oat searched for shelter in a tight stand of low hanging sycamores as the rain washed down on him. By the time he unhitched and tethered the Jacquards he was soaked, cold and miserable, but the storm was just what he needed. The rain washed away his tracks and Oat realized that if he was smart he would be safe from Boggs, Glaze and the Missouri mob.

He remained in the grove all day sleeping under the wagon and allowing the Jacquards to rest and feed on prairie grass and some of the oats for which he had traded his farm. At dusk he hitched the Jacquards up and let them slowly pick their way through the darkness along worn trails not caring which direction as long as it took him away from Jackson County. He traveled in a northeasterly direction along well-worn trails. The going was slow, but safe.

As he thought over his situation and the events that caused it he felt an odd kinship with Joe Smith. He and Smith did, after all, have a few things in common, the most glaring of which were their enemies. Though for different reasons, Boggs obviously wanted both of them dead. And they both escaped, losing their homes in the process. Oat reflected many times on Smith's invitation to live amongst the Mormons. Having heard so many unflattering things about them, he rejected the thought. Yet, he remembered the Wheatleys fondly and on reflection decided that if Joe Smith could find a haven safe from Boggs' then maybe Oat Harmon could find peace there too. That would give him the time and opportunity to decide where he would go. Besides, Smith still owed him for a horse.

For the next five days he traveled at night only. He passed by farms and towns in the night and saw lamps and candles burning in windows far off, but he didn't stop. At times he got so tired that he dozed and let the Jacquards pick their way along the trail. Once when he dozed he imagined seeing his father leading the big horses along the trail and pointing east, but then a wheel hit a rock and jarred him awake and he realized he was dreaming. Yet the dream warmed him so he kept following the same trail at night. He didn't want anyone to see him or the Jacquards because they were so easily recognized. Anyone would remember their size and color. Occasionally, at night, the gut-wrenching shriek of a screech owl sent shivers up his spine and cast an eerie pall over his thoughts. Sometimes he heard dogs bark, but mostly he heard only the howling of coyotes and wolves at night and the chirping of birds during the day. He was, after all, still in Missouri and he knew he wouldn't be completely safe until he was far away from Jackson County.

Once in the early morning light, exhausted and looking for a place to stop for the day, the Jacquards shied from something at the side of the trail. Jack pointed his ears at it and blew nervously. Oat stopped them and got off the wagon to see what it was. As he neared the object the stench of rotting flesh overcame him and he recognized the body of man. Not knowing what else to do, he got a shovel from his wagon and buried the body. He marked the grave and put the man's hat on a stick he drove into the ground, but there was nothing on the body to identify the man and Oat could not readily ascertain a cause of death.

By the end of the fifth day his food was exhausted and he was hungry. The dried meat and bread he brought along were gone. So were the oats, but the Jacquards could always eat prairie grass. Oat didn't want to shoot at game, but he might not have a choice soon.

At dawn on the sixth day the Jacquards topped a small rise and nearly walked over the top of a farmer and his mule laboring mightily to break through the tough prairie sod with a one-horse plow. The farmer wasn't having much luck. The mule could have pulled the plow through already broken ground but it was too weak to break the sod. The farmer and mule had circled a two-acre patch of new ground with a light scar, probably about as close as he would get to a plowed furrow. His mule was exhausted and the sun hadn't even come up. The farmer, upon hearing the Jacquards and Oat's wagon, stopped in the dim light to see who or what was coming.

Oat pulled his horses to a stop. He and the farmer's eyes met for a long second. They studied each other warily. Oat silently scolded himself. He didn't want to be seen. He wondered if the farmer would be friendly or would turn out to be an enemy. The man had a round face, a beard and a sly look in his eyes.

"Looks like pretty gamey sod right here," Oat said.

"Yah. Das a mule killer," the farmer said nodding.

"You been here long?" Oat asked.

The farmer nodded again.

"Bout a year ago. Ve from Germany, den Ohio. You?"

"I'm looking for a place to light," Oat said. "Might go up into Iowa and see what there is."

The farmer nodded eagerly.

"Good land dere, but many Indians."

Oat saw a small sod house about a hundred yards off with smoke curling up from a fire near the front door. A woman worked nearby, probably preparing food. Oat's mouth watered and he hoped for an invitation.

"Very large harses," the farmer said. "Vere you get harses like dis?"

"My dad bought 'em from a Frenchman years ago when they were colts. Had no idea they'd get this big."

"Can dey pull?"

Oat saw his chance for a decent meal.

"If I can talk you out of some breakfast and two buckets of oats I'll show you."

The house was fashioned of tree trunks stacked about six feet high and a sod roof. A few small outbuildings for animals and storage stood nearby. A cow and a calf fed on a small hill to the west of the house and a sow lay on her side in a pole pen fashioned to keep her from wandering away. Several other smaller pigs wandered about the place loose.

The farmer's name was John Muller. His wife's name was Sarah. They had seen no one else in days and were happy to have a visitor.

Sarah, a pleasant-looking woman with kind, soft eyes, peppered Oat with questions and chattered happily about everything from birds to the lack of neighbors and wondered about Oat's family. She seemed so excited to have someone new to talk with that she couldn't talk fast enough. Oat tried to answer her questions but never really got a chance to say anything. She served him a large plate of bacon, eggs and hot bread. While she talked Oat nodded and did what talking he could do politely with his mouth full while the woman kept dishing food onto his plate. Oat ate and listened to the woman talk while her husband fed the Jacquards a few gallons of grain and tended to a few small chores.

John didn't speak English well, but Sarah spoke the language easily and told Oat their story. They occupied this spot since the previous year coming from Ohio where her family lived. The previous winter, their only child died of pneumonia and Sarah herself had been sick. Oat saw the grave marker on the hill near the grazing cattle. Bouquets of wild flowers lay near it. While John appeared robust and healthy, Sarah was thin. Despite that, she possessed an energetic nature and Oat judged that she would be just fine.

About an hour before sunset, to the astonishment of the Mullers, Oat made a final pass down the field turning over the last piece of prairie sod in the circle that John and his mule started early that morning. A beautiful dark patch of freshly overturned earth lay ready to be planted.

Oat rested himself and the big horses that night enjoying the Mullers' hospitality and another fine meal. He slept in the open air near the Muller house. The next morning he hitched the horses to the wagon, loaded his plow and got ready to leave. John Muller looked on openly covetous of the percherons and the plow. Oat and the Jacquards had done in only a few hours what would have taken Muller and his mule more than a week. Sarah gave Oat a large sack of fresh bacon, two loaves of bread and a wet kiss on the cheek. She waved sadly as Oat slapped the Jacquards on the rump to continue his journey. John jumped onto the wagon seat and asked to ride along for a ways.

"How far do I have to go to reach the Mississippi River?" Oat asked as they moved away from the farm.

"Bout three days," John said. The man fidgeted restlessly on the seat occasionally glancing nervously at Oat, his worn hands clasped together tightly.

"I vould like to buy dese harses," John said abruptly after they had gone about a mile.

"I couldn't sell them," Oat said. "They're like family to me. I have raised them since they were colts."

"Dese harses are vorth ver much so I vill give ev'yt'ing I own," Muller said. "I vill give me farm, me house, me tools, me mule and me vife, Sarah. She vorks hard and vill give you children."

Oat laughed and pulled the Jacquards to a stop.

"Whoa. Slow down," Oat said. "You want to trade Sarah for my horses?"

Looking into John's face he realized that Muller did not mean his offer as a joke. John appeared completely and positively serious. Oat knew the Jacquards were valuable but he never imagined he'd ever get an offer like this. Oat shook his head slowly.

"Dat's all I have," Muller said.

"What would Sarah say about this?" Oat asked.

"She vould do it. She vould do it if I tell her to."

"Don't you love Sarah? How could you trade someone you love like a piece of property?"

"Dat's all I have," he repeated.

"It wouldn't be right," Oat said, shaking his head. "No. Good-by John."

Muller got down from the wagon and the Jacquards started up again. For the next several hours Oat looked back over his shoulder often. An uneasy feeling grew inside. He did not see anyone following him, but he made a point to be especially wary. A man who coveted his horses enough to trade his wife for them could be capable of almost anything. At dark Oat stopped, but didn't sleep well. He wondered if Muller wanted the Jacquards so badly he would murder for them. The thought kept Oat awake and tuned to every noise of the night. Before first light he was moving again.

Oat remained uneasy throughout the day as the feeling that someone followed him grew. He gazed for long periods at the trail behind but saw nothing. That night he again slept fitfully and before dawn had the Jacquards on the trail. As the Jacquards drew out of a brushy swale, Oat grabbed one of his rifles and ducked into the brush, allowing the big horses to plod on up the trail. He knew once they realized he wasn't at the reins they would find a grassy spot and graze. Oat found a secure hiding spot and waited. Nestled in the brush, he couldn't see well because of the undergrowth and it wasn't yet light, but he could tell if someone followed.

For nearly an hour he squatted in the brush seeing nothing and chiding himself for being so jumpy and anxious. Just as he prepared to emerge from the brush and catch up to the Jacquards he saw a figure moving along the trail. His heart thumped loudly in his chest and his hands sweat where he gripped the rifle stalk. When the figure drew near he stepped into the trail and pointed the rifle.

"Stop," he yelled.

It was Sarah. She screamed and dropped a small bag.

Oat lowered the rifle in astonishment and stepped toward her.

"What are you doing?" he asked. "I nearly shot you."

"I'm following you," she said defiantly.

"Why?"

"John beat me so I left him."

As Oat drew near he saw that the left side of her face was bruised and puffy and her lip was cut.

"Why did he beat you?"

"He wanted your horses and you wouldn't trade them for me."

She looked down at the ground.

"He said I was worthless and ugly, not even worth two horses. He got drunk and then he beat me."

She sat down on the trail and wept. Oat sat too, and tried to comfort her.

"He leaves me for days sometimes and travels to town," she said. "I hate being alone and he doesn't want me. He treats me like a slave and uses me badly. That's why I followed you. Let me come with you?"

"I don't really know where I'm going," Oat said.

"I don't care. I won't go back to John."

# 16

HANNAH HID THE PISTOL IN A HANDBAG SHE CARRIED everywhere. Though heavy to tote around, she soon grew accustomed to it. The feeling of security, power and self-sufficiency it gave her made it worth the trouble. She liked the feel of the cold steel barrel and the smooth sanded oak handle. With it in her hand she did not fear the hate and violence of the Missouri pukes. Though she no longer lived in Missouri, she knew someday she would face them again. She swore to avenge the death of her loved ones when that day came.

She actually enjoyed the thought of killing a puke. Hate swelled inside her breast whenever she thought about Missouri. She nurtured it. She often fantasized that someday she would see the men who attacked her family, or some like them. She never tried to tame her unruly thoughts so they often ran out of control and she imagined aiming the gun at some puke's chest and squeezing the trigger without remorse or regret.

Whenever she saw her father struggle with some task her heart swelled with love for him. At the same time the thought of Missouri, and the pukes who had treated her family so hatefully, set her teeth on edge. She realized she hated the pukes with the same intensity that she loved her father. All things have their opposites. She remembered hearing Joseph speak of that in Far West once and wondered if that's what he meant.

With the horse, she and her father reached the Mississippi only three days after the incident on the trail with the puke. Crossing the river at Quincy, they soon found themselves surrounded by old friends, who also had fled from Far West. Most had been taken in by the charitable citizens of Quincy, who were as outraged by the behavior of the Missouri mobs as the Mormons themselves. They dwelt in a state of poverty, having little to eat and hardly any shelter. Thousands found cover in tents, lean-tos, old sheds and out buildings, eating the meager provisions they foraged. They had lived like this most of the winter. Many died of exposure and disease. All suffered, some more than others. The Goddard family, whom Hannah had known in Far West, fared as badly as the Harmons. The mother and four children, including Sarah, a friend who was a year younger than Hannah, died of cholera brought on by lack of food and shelter during the cold winter months. Hannah wept for them and in their tragedy found more reasons to hate Missouri.

Hannah and her father arrived in Quincy in early May after the weather had tempered. They built a small lean-to on the outskirts of the town on the farm of a kind man named Taylor who offered them food and helped find materials for their shelter. He offered to let them stay inside his own home but they saw it already was packed with other refugees so they opted to build their own shelter.

Some of the refugees purchased land on credit and began to put in crops and build homes, but many did not know what to do, whether to continue their journey back to Ohio where most of them had lived earlier or to stay and try to build a new life again. The latest communications from Missouri said that Joseph languished in jail and likely would be executed. He encouraged them in letters that were read in church gatherings to remain together, but the uncertainties and difficulties of staying made them restless. It was time to be planting crops. Should they find land and plant? Should they go back to Ohio? What should they do? The uncertainty and the mourning for their losses of family and homes in Missouri weighed many down into a deep depression. Many died. Most wanted to do the right thing, but didn't know for sure what the right thing was. They needed Joseph, but after the events in Missouri they despaired of seeing him again. Nevertheless, Hannah prayed every night for his release. She suspected all the other saints did the same.

And then one day, miraculously, he appeared. The news pulsed up and down the river one morning from camp to camp and village to village. Joseph and Hyrum had escaped Missouri and crossed the Mississippi River on the Quincy Ferry. Hannah did not see him for days but others did. Those who saw him reported that he was thin and gaunt, his clothes in rags, his boots with holes in them. But he was alive and healthy and most important of all — free. Hannah immediately noticed a change in her own spirits as well as those of her father. Jerome Wheatley still mourned for his wife and sons and the gunshot wound would bother him for weeks. Though the wound didn't appear serious and had healed mostly, his arm remained mostly useless. Sadness and pain lingered in his eyes, but his spirits rose.

"We need to find another farm Hannah," he said one morning. "It's time to be putting in crops and we'll need to build a house."

He didn't have much energy but an occasional smile crossed his face. It usually didn't last long, yet it was good to see.

The story of Joseph's escape from Missouri soon was told in devotional meetings and around campfires wherever the Mormons gathered. Somehow Joseph and Hyrum and the men who were with them slipped away from their captors while being moved from Gallatin to Boone County for trial. Having experienced the murderous wrath of the Missourians Hannah thought it a miracle to see him alive. The Missouri mob had sworn to kill him, but for now he remained safely out of their control.

One evening two weeks later, her father returned to their small hovel after a meeting of the brethren with good news. Joseph had purchased land, enough land for everyone near a place named Nauvoo on the banks of the Mississippi a few days north of Quincy. The land lay on both sides of the river in Iowa and Illinois.

"The church has bought the land," her father said. "And Joseph's dividing it among all those who will gather."

"But how will we pay for it?" Hannah asked. "We don't have any money and I doubt if Joseph has any either."

"Joseph arranged it. We can trade the deed to our land in Jackson County to the church for some land at Nauvoo," her father said.

Hannah vaguely remembered the old farm back in Jackson County, where they lived when she was a girl. She could not think of that place without also remembering the awful day when the first of the Missouri mobs drove her family away from that farm, their lives saved only by the intervention of Oat Harmon's father. She nearly had forgotten that the family owned it and was astonished to think it was worth anything to them.

"Why would the church want that land?" Hannah asked.

"Because Joseph says someday we'll return there," her father said.

A few days later they bid farewell and thanks to their new friends at Quincy and joined hundreds of other Mormons journeying north along the river to the place called Nauvoo. They reached it at sunset on the second day. While her father went in search of news and some idea of where their land would be Hannah made camp in a dry area near the main camp. Clouds of mosquitoes floated above her. Nearby she saw people standing near fires letting the smoke drift into their faces and around them. Hannah soon learned why. Smoke was about the only thing that kept the mosquitoes away.

Children, oblivious to the insects, played in the dirt while their parents labored over fires cooking. Men with mules and horses were coming in from plowing the fields. As Hannah gathered wood for a fire she heard talk of an expedition to go upriver after timber. They planned to cut trees and float them downriver to Nauvoo. Someone had butchered a steer and large chunks of meat roasted on many campfires and food was being shared among the camps. The aroma floated on the breeze and made Hannah's mouth water. A kind woman with two small children walked to Hannah's fire and offered her a large chunk of the roasted meat.

"There's more here than our family needs tonight," she said. "Please take it."

As the evening darkened Hannah made out hundreds of campfires. Far across the river to the west she saw more. Above her the stars came out as the night blackened. Soon her father returned, his good arm carrying part of a loaf of bread someone had given him. He was more animated than she had seen him in months.

Despite the discomfort of the open camp and the biting of the mosquitoes, Hannah felt secure and at peace, a feeling she hadn't had in months. She wrapped herself in a blanket, lay down by the fire and fell asleep immediately.

# — 17 —

THE FIRST DAY SARAH CRIED AND SLEPT IN THE WAGON while Oat drove. The second day she sat next to him on the seat but she didn't speak much until the afternoon when Oat finally broke the silence.

"I hope you understand that it would not have been right for me to trade my horses for you," he said.

"I understand," she said. "They're valuable horses."

"I don't think you do understand," he said. "It doesn't matter how much the horses are worth. I don't hold with trading livestock for a person. It's not right."

"That's how John got me. He traded a mule to my father for me. So he owned me. I guess he could do what he wanted with me."

Oat gasped.

"People don't own other people," Oat insisted.

"What about slaves?"

"I don't hold with owning slaves."

"There's a lot of things you don't hold with, aren't there?"

"I suppose so."

Four days after leaving the Muller farm, the trail they followed led to the Mississippi River then veered north to a ferry that took them across the river to Quincy. He stopped overnight on the outskirts of the town. When he rose the next morning, Sarah was gone. He spent the day in Quincy waiting to see if Sarah would return, but she didn't. He scribbled a letter to his mother and mailed it before continuing on the next morning. A storekeeper at Quincy said the Mormons were settling on some swampy land to the north so Oat followed a freshly worn trail north along the river.

May 1, 1839
Dear Mother,
    I hesitate to send this letter because I know it will shock and worry you. So much has happened that I don't know where to begin.

    First, I am no longer in Jackson County. I sold the farm to Clovis Blackburn. Please don't be angry. I had good reasons to get away from there. You were right. The men who killed Papa want me dead too and they tried to kill me, but I got away.

    I helped the Mormon Joe Smith escape from Missouri. I did it mainly because it was in my best interest to help him and out of spite for Boggs. I'm glad I did it too. The story is too long to write in a letter. I will only say that I am safe for now. Smith offered to let me live among the Mormons for a time where I will be safe. I know you detest Mormons, but I will be safe there I think.

    I told Clovis to keep everything. I don't know exactly where I'll light, but when I find a permanent place I'll write again.

    I have learned many things in the past several weeks. Do you remember the old buffalo hunter Bufflehead? He turned out to be an evil man and not a friend as we supposed. He is a tormented soul. He confessed things to me hoping for forgiveness. He could not face you. I think you know that I speak of Papa's murder and I think you already knew in your heart. The money in your trunk came from him. I don't know how to explain everything in a letter, but I will try when I have more time. You were right about Lilburn Boggs. He is evil.

    I am now at the town of Quincy, Illinois, but I am traveling northward. Eventually, I plan to go into Iowa and get land to farm, but I may stay in Illinois too because Smith offered me sanctuary. I gave the bay to Clovis and he will pay me later if he can. If he doesn't that's all right because he's a good friend and he helped me. Love, Oat

    A half day out of Quincy the trail skirted a swampy bottomland. In many places the wheels of heavy wagons and the hooves of horses, mules and oxen gouged deep ruts in the moist earth. The Jacquard's hooves made loud sucking noises as they slogged through the mud. Clouds of mosquitoes hovered above the Jacquards. Despite the warm day Oat covered himself with a blanket to keep them from biting. The

Jacquards seemed oblivious to them. The horses' big tails swished back and forth through the air keeping the bugs stirred up but certainly not driving them away. Despite Oat's own flailing the mosquitoes remained a constant nuisance, constantly flying up his nose and into his eyes and ears. He could swat and kill ten at a time, but hundreds more instantly took their place.

Several miles north of Quincy Oat happened upon a wagon hopelessly mired in mud past its axles. The muck was so deep the wagon's box had sunk into it. Two spent mules strained to pull the wagon free, but it was stuck so deeply in the mud they couldn't budge it. One of the exhausted mules had collapsed and now lay in the mud too. A feeble elderly woman, wrapped in blankets, sat near a fire and a large pile of belongings they had removed from the wagon. A gray-haired man and a young woman labored with the animals. The old man pushed on the wagon while the woman whipped the mules, but nothing happened. The man and woman had smeared mud all over their faces and hands to ward off the mosquitoes and their clothing was slimed with mud. Oat saw from the man's bent stance that he was well past his prime and the woman was pregnant.

"Take a rest Maggie," the man said tiredly as Oat approached. "I'm afraid this wagon isn't going to come out of here."

He began to unhitch the mules as Oat's wagon squished to a stop nearby. The man and the woman peered up at Oat suspiciously.

"That's a good idea," Oat said, as he climbed down from his wagon seat. The idea of putting mud on his arms and neck to keep the mosquitoes off hadn't occurred to him, but the mosquitoes were so bothersome he was eager to try it. He scooped a handful of mud and smeared it on his bare skin. The old man watched Oat closely while leaning against one of the mules.

"We'll rest the mules for a while and try again," the young woman said, guiding him by the arm. "I'll dig some of that mud out of there."

Her voice, though sad, was lyrical and pleasant. Oat liked it and he couldn't take his eyes from her. Even with mud all over her arms and face and a scarf wrapped around her head and ears, his eyes were drawn to her. Despite her protruding belly, she moved about easily and gracefully.

"I'll pull this wagon out of here for you?" Oat said cheerfully.

"We don't need your help," she said firmly. "We can do this ourselves."

"You'll get this wagon out of this hole about the time the snow flies," Oat said. "My horses can pull it out now."

Her eyes lingered for several seconds on the Jacquards.

"People already have tried and gone on," the woman said. "We've worn out three teams of mules and a team of oxen and the wagon still won't budge. Go on. Leave."

Her stubbornness didn't set well with Oat and he felt his neck grow hot.

"Your grandparents are being eaten alive by mosquitoes. You should think about them for a minute and a little less about yourself."

"What'll it cost?" the woman said. There was anger in her voice and tears in her eyes. He suddenly realized she was afraid.

"A hot meal and a handful of sugar for my horses," he said softly.

She walked away toward her grandparents.

Oat walked around the wagon to get a closer look. He'd never seen a wagon stuck so securely. It had lodged in a particularly soft and sloppy hole. Mud oozed up around all four wheels enveloping the box. He wasn't sure that even the Jacquards could do anything.

"Do you know how far this muck lasts?" Oat asked.

"The trail is wet and muddy for about another quarter mile and then breaks onto the open dry prairie," the old man said tiredly. "Then its about ten miles to Nauvoo, or so I been told."

Oat drove his wagon ahead until he found a dry spot. He didn't want to get his own wagon stuck. He then unhitched the Jacquards and led them back to the mired wagon. By that time the older man had led the mules away. The young woman watched guardedly and the old woman still lay weakly on the ground near the fire.

Oat hitched the Jacquards to the wagon and climbed into the seat.

"Jack, Molly."

The big horses moved forward until the hitch tightened, then rocked back slightly.

"Ha," Oat yelled, and snapped the reins.

The huge beasts bent forward into their collars steadily increasing the forward pressure. For a moment Oat feared they would balk or pull the tongue off the wagon, then he heard a rush of air and the sucking of mud as the wagon box pulled free of the muck and moved forward. The man yelled and the woman clapped. The Jacquards moved the wagon forward until it was alongside their pile of belongings which Oat and the older man loaded while the young woman tended to her grandmother.

The rest of the day the two wagons moved together slowly through the swamp and about a mile out onto the prairie. The trail was easygoing once they were out of the swamp but the day was gone. They stopped alongside a small stream and the old man walked to Oat's wagon and extended his hand.

"I'm Orrin MacGregor," he said. "Me and my family deeply appreciate your help today and hope you will share our camp and eat with us tonight."

Oat accepted the offer and unhitched the Jacquards. After a long day in harness they liked to roll and both did so in the deep prairie grass.

Oat was hanging their harnesses on the wagon when the woman appeared. She had bathed and her face and arms were white and clean although her skin was lightly tanned. Her stomach bulged out under a clean dress and apron, but the scarf still covered her hair. Though she appeared more relaxed than earlier, she remained wary and hesitant.

"I was rude to you today and I am sorry," she said. "You were very kind to help us. My name's Maggie and I brought some sugar for your horses."

Oat caught Jack and Molly by the halters and led them to where Maggie stood.

"They're so big and gentle," she said. "I've never seen horses like this."

"This is Jack Jacquard," Oat said, introducing his horses and nodding toward the stallion. "And this is Molly Jacquard."

Maggie stroked Jack's nose and extended a handful of sugar to Molly, who blew half of it onto the ground as she sniffed it and then lapped the rest of it up. Jack repeated the process including losing most of it on the ground. But they liked it and eagerly licked up all that Maggie held in her apron.

Oat didn't have to ask to know the MacGregors were Mormons. As they sat together around the cooking fire, Oat learned that they came from Ohio. Maggie's father had been killed years earlier when a wagon rolled over him and her mother died of scarlet fever a year later. She was raised by her grandparents. Missionaries had converted them to Mormonism.

"We wanted to be with the rest of the saints so we traveled all last summer and got to Missouri just in time to be driven away," Old man MacGregor said. He sighed and shook his head.

"Our supplies were gone and we didn't have much to fall back on through the winter. The people at Quincy were very kind to us, but it was a bad winter. Permelia nearly died."

"Sometimes I think we never should have left Ohio."

Oat glanced at the old woman now sleeping again. She was thin, wrinkled and frail and Oat guessed she probably wouldn't live many more days. No mention was made of Maggie's husband.

When supper was over the MacGregors asked Oat to join them for their evening prayer. He felt a little awkward, but he knelt with them after Maggie awakened her grandmother. Orrin MacGregor prayed for everything — for happiness, for peace, for health, prosperity, that the mules would get stronger and the mosquitoes would go away. He prayed for Maggie, his wife Permelia and for Oat. And then he prayed for Joseph Smith.

"We thank thee Lord for freeing Joseph from jail and the awful, evil men of Missouri and that he has returned to live with his people again."

As MacGregor prayed on, Oat opened his eyes and watched Maggie in the flickering firelight. She was lovely, her skin fair, her overall appearance pleasant and feminine. She knelt with her head bowed and those sad, haunted eyes closed, her hands clasped together firmly in her lap as her arms encircled her unborn baby. The sight thrilled him and made him feel guilty at the same time. Where was her husband?

When her grandfather finished praying she looked up and their eyes met for a brief instant. She smiled, then turned away sadly.

# 18

THAT SUMMER, IN BETWEEN BOUTS OF THE FEVER, Hannah and her father built a log house with a sod roof. It wasn't as nice as their house in Far West that had a floor of lumber and cupboards, but that would come later when materials were available. Little lumber was available so they made do with the materials at hand — scrubby cottonwood trees, rocks and sod for the roof. It didn't look like much but it sheltered them from storms, heat and cold.

Hundreds of other houses of log, stone and sod sprang up along carefully surveyed streets. Stores were constructed. Men with great horses and mules and oxen dug canals and ditches and drained the swamp. When the ground dried the brush was burned. As the weather warmed and the land was cleared the plague of mosquitoes gradually dissipated. A wharf was built at the edge of the river and river boats began to dock there, bringing more people and goods for trade. A city rose out of the swamp.

In the outlying areas thousands of acres were broken out of sod and planted in crops. A sawmill was constructed near the river and rafts of pine logs from far upstream, cut by expeditions of loggers, were pulled out of the river and sawed into lumber.

Each day the people worked. It seemed they did nothing else. The women, even the children, worked often side-by-side in the fields with the men, constructing houses or stockpiling firewood. They worked from sunup to sundown, ate and fell asleep exhausted at night.

The only day of the week no one worked was Sunday. Hannah grew to love Sundays. Everyone met in the grove near the river because no meetinghouse had yet been built. Joseph or one of the other brethren preached and afterward sometimes they shared picnic lunches and visited. Hannah made new friends and renewed friendships from Far West.

But they remained a wounded people. The hurt from Missouri lingered and the loss of loved ones, friends and possessions left great bitterness. They hid their hurt well, but it was impossible to completely forget. One morning Hannah saw a woman, suddenly break down while walking with her children. She buried her face in her hands and wept uncontrollably, her shoulders convulsing while her small children gathered about her sad and confused. Somehow Hannah understood. Any woman who lived through the Far West misery would have understood.

Hannah developed a unique way of coping with her own anger and depression. Whenever she felt sad, she took the pistol and walked into the river bottoms away from town. There she fired round after round at driftwood floating atop the muddy water. She pretended her targets were Governor Boggs or some other puke. She felt much better after such excursions.

The fever made its rounds that summer. It touched everyone. Many died, mainly the old, the very young or the weak. Hannah spent a few nights sitting up with the Farnsworth and Browning children so the parents could get some much-needed sleep. Other than Sundays that was her only social outlet. There were other young women and men in the town and she liked to talk with them when the chance presented itself. But it wasn't often because there was so much work to do before winter. She wanted to laugh, talk and giggle and forget her troubles, but there wasn't time.

Toward the end of summer Hannah noticed a man about her own age who seemed vaguely familiar. She saw him often. He was hard to miss because he always had two enormous gray horses either pulling a plow or a loaded wagon. Something about him jarred her memory, but wouldn't surface. He was a tall, lanky man with big calloused hands. Mud always covered his face and arms. She supposed he smeared it on to keep away the mosquitoes, but it gave him an odd, almost ghoulish look, which repelled her. She wondered if he bathed and how he looked when clean. He didn't seem to know her either, nevertheless, the way he walked and some of his mannerisms were familiar and she was certain she had met him before, but could not place him. Over the past few years there had been so many things and people that she wanted to forget that it was hard to dredge through her memories to find his place in them. It required too much energy and caused too many heartaches.

Still, as the summer wore on the impression that she knew him nagged at her constantly. Finally, one day in late September as she hung freshly washed clothing out to dry the problem bothered her to the point she decided to do something about it.

"I'm just going to go ask him who he is," she said to herself aloud. "This is silly. I can't stand it anymore."

After washing her face in a pan of water, she fixed her hair as best she could for she had no brush or comb and straightened her skirt as she went out the door.

Down the street she met a tall, angular aging man with a droopy mustache and a wrinkled face, a former Quaker from Pennsylvania named Biddle, who walked in the opposite direction.

"Brother Biddle," she said. "You've seen that man who works those two big gray horses. Do you know his name and have you seen him today?"

Brother Biddle shook his head.

"I'm sorry. I don't know his name," he said. "But I saw him and his horses walking east of town this morning."

Hannah started off resolutely and hadn't gone ten steps when a name suddenly popped into her thoughts.

Oat Harmon.

She immediately remembered a shy boy with whom she had been friends many summers before. What was it? Five years? Six years? It seemed like a lifetime. She remembered with great clarity how Oat's father drove away the mob when her family was attacked in Jackson County. She even remembered the gray colts now. It was him. She knew it. And then the tears started. How could she not have known Oat? How could he not know her? Or did he? If he did, why hadn't he said anything?

Oatie Harmon.

Her thoughts raced. She should have recognized him the first day she saw him. But he was out of place, out of context and covered with mud. He should be in Missouri. In Jackson County. Why is he here? Is he now a Mormon? What brought him here? He's a man now.

She looked at herself. She looked nothing like she had that

summer years before. Oatie didn't remember her for the same reason she hadn't recognized him.

She set out to find him.

# — 19 —

THE CHILDREN WHO PLAYED AT THE EDGE OF THE RIVER near the wharf called Oat the mud man.

Each morning after breakfast Oat smeared his arms, face and neck with mud to keep the mosquitoes away. The children laughed as they watched and some imitated him. Oat wondered what their mothers thought when they came home with mud smeared all over their arms and faces.

The summer was hot and satisfying for Oat. For some reason the fever never hit him like it did most of the others in town. He often wondered why and whether he had a natural immunity to it. Everyone else suffered for a few days at least and some got so sick they died. But as the summer wore on the problem lessened.

The Jacquards got stronger everyday. They never ate better or worked harder. They each got four to five gallons of oats per day and all the grass they could eat. They used a tremendous amount of feed, but they needed it and were worth every ounce of oats they consumed.

The minute he and the Jacquards entered Nauvoo there had been more than enough work to do. He got so busy he didn't have a chance to leave. Behind the giant horses he plowed fields, tore out stumps, dislodged immovable rocks, skidded poles and logs for fences and houses, and when skiffs arrived from upriver he pulled slick, wet logs from the water of the Mississippi to the saw mill. Anything that required brute power and strength he and the Jacquards did it.

Most of the work he did for other people, not for himself. Not having a family to support left him free to do that. The people lived in poverty and there was a tremendous need for animals like Oat's to do heavy work. Pay was almost never negotiated. If someone asked for help he took the Jacquards and did it. The people, for the most part, were poor and destitute and he knew they had no money. So he simply asked for food for himself and his horses. Nevertheless his wealth grew. Appreciative individuals paid him with whatever they could spare. By summer's end he had accumulated two calves from a farmer whose field he plowed, a pig for building a fence and corral, a set of tools for pulling a winter's supply of firewood out of the river bottoms for a neighbor. A blacksmith assembled a pair of new reinforced harnesses for the Jacquards after Oat cleared stumps away, burned and plowed five acres of land for him. He also had a large pile of newly cut lumber with his name on it because each morning before he did anything else he pulled enough logs out of the river to keep the mill busy that day.

He talked to Joseph Smith only two days after his arrival in Nauvoo. Smith and a group of three other men busied themselves surveying the city's streets and dividing up the land for houses and stores. Smith was like a general, energetic, rugged, raw, forceful and honest to the point of being obnoxious. Oat was on his way to the Jones place, moving a plow to break out some land for planting. He stood for a moment watching Smith curiously. He never knew a man with such a presence.

Upon seeing Oat, Smith immediately laid down his tools and left the others to continue the surveying.

"Brother Harmon," he said. "I'm so glad to see you well and I'm happy to see that you escaped Missouri alive."

The fact that Smith remembered his name warmed Oat as did the salutation even though Oat still was not accustomed to hearing people call him Brother Harmon. He had no intention of becoming a Mormon, yet everyone he'd met since arriving at Nauvoo treated him as though he was.

"You were right sir," Oat said. "Boggs wanted to cut my throat so I figured it would be safer here than in Jackson County."

Smith laughed.

"Well you are welcome to stay and partake of Nauvoo's poverty freely," he said. "I must tell you that Hyrum and I have not told anyone of your part in helping us escape, only in the most general of terms, not because we don't appreciate what you did, but because we fear that if we use your name you'll become a target of their hate too and we would be sad to see that happen."

"I appreciate your thoughtfulness," Oat said, "but they know my name and what I did. They just don't know where I am. Are you out of danger here?"

Smith shrugged.

"I feel safer here than anywhere else but in times past it has been so-called friends and colleagues who have set the hounds of Hell after me. That very well may happen again. I am safe as long as friends don't betray me."

Oat thought of Bufflehead and nodded.

"I know what you mean," Oat said. "It's distressing and terrible when friends turn on you."

Smith gazed silently at Oat for a long moment. Oat felt a little uneasy, but the look was such a friendly affectionate gaze that he couldn't turn away.

"I know you understand," Smith said. "I know very well. I must be getting back to my work now. There's so much to do. Your mother is well and happy."

"I suppose she is sir," Oat said, wondering why Smith would mention his mother having never met her. "I haven't seen or heard from her for some time."

Smith smiled and turned back to him a moment longer.

"You promised to write your mother, Oat. She is well, happy and healthy, but she worries about you. And with good cause. She is a fine woman. She prays daily that she will hear from you. You should let her know you are okay."

As Smith walked away, Oat puzzled over what he'd said. Smith didn't know his mother. She was in Baltimore. But how did he know Oat promised to write her when he was settled? It seemed arrogant for him to say what he had said, yet it had been said warmly and kindly and Oat thought about Smith's gentle rebuke all day.

That night he wrote a long letter to his mother telling her of his arrival at Nauvoo and enquiring about her welfare. He mailed it the next day. At mid-summer he received a reply:

My Dear Otis,

    Thank God you are safe. I have been frightened to death for you and worried that something awful happened and that I would never know what became of you. I received the letter you sent from Quincy and I would have written long before now but I did not know where to send a letter. Shame on you for not telling me where you were.

    Do not worry about the farm. It is of little consequence if you are safe. I had long suspected that Boggs was behind your father's death, but I never thought that Bufflehead would have been the one to actually kill Andrew. I hope he dies a horrible death and then rots for eternity in Hell. I am sorry that I have such uncharitable feelings, but I cannot help it. He was a trusted friend. We invited him into our home and shared our family and love with him. For him to betray Andrew and us in such a way is unforgivable. I threw the money he gave you into Chesapeake Bay.

    Uncle John has a cancer and is dying although he's fighting hard. He sends his regards and wishes he could have known you better especially after all the stories I have told him about you. He doesn't get out of bed much any more, nor does he require much nursing, but it is good to talk with both him and Emily. We have so much to catch up on and they pepper me with questions about the west and about our life there and about you.

    I have begun working as a nurse. I mainly change bandages and help birth babies. I love that most. Seeing the little ones come into the world is a joy for me. Oat, I hope that one day I will have some grandchildren. Are you listening? I love babies so much and I want to hold my own grandchildren and rock them and hug them. I hope you are keeping your promise to find a wife and have children before I die. It is a selfish dream I have, but I know it will make you happy too.

    In that vein I must tell you that I have been seeing a man since I arrived here. He is a friend of the family, in fact he is our minister. His wife died a year ago.

    Please write to me as often as you can. I pray that the best is in store for you. With all my love, Mother

    Oat often thought, as he worked, about his mother's admonition to get married. She said it as though it was an easy thing to do. Sometimes, when he got extremely lonely, he wished it could happen soon. He knew it was time. Though busy, he felt a huge void in his life.

He thought about Maggie a lot in his lonely times. She puzzled him. She nor her family ever mentioned Maggie's husband, or even if she had one. That was odd. He sensed that the question would be unwelcome. Yet, she was going to have a baby. That was about as obvious as anything could be, but neither she nor her grandparents mentioned it or made any attempt to explain. It was so peculiar.

His feelings for Maggie made him feel guilty. She was the only woman his age he really knew and she was pretty and he liked her. He believed she liked him too but she remained distant. Since arriving in Nauvoo, she sometimes mended torn clothing for him and fixed meals when he helped her grandfather, but she never went out of her way to speak to him.

One evening not long after getting his mother's letter, Oat came home to the small lean-to he had built for shelter on the prairie east of Nauvoo near the MacGregor land. He found Maggie's grandfather waiting.

Orrin MacGregor helped him unharness and care for the Jacquards and then handed Oat a plate of bread and cabbage.

"The wife's feeling a bit better today," he said. "She improves some days, but on others she's worse. I worry about her."

Oat and MacGregor sat down in the hut.

"Maggie thinks highly of you," MacGregor said suddenly in a sad, serious tone that startled Oat.

"I like her too," Oat said. "But she avoids me. It's like she doesn't want to talk to me."

MacGregor's gray head nodded sadly and Oat saw tears.

"Maggie had her baby today," he said. "A big strong boy."

Oat sat the plate aside. It was the first time that any of the MacGregors acknowledged that Maggie was going to have a baby or had said anything about Maggie's situation.

"Where is Maggie's husband?" Oat asked.

"She has no husband and has never been married," MacGregor answered quickly.

"Oh," Oat said, a little shocked. He didn't know what to say so he waited as MacGregor searched for words to explain.

"I hope you won't think poorly of Maggie," he said, looking at Oat painfully. "It wasn't her fault. She did nothing wrong. We got to Far West last September, only a bit before the trouble began. It was my fault. I didn't even think about it. I should have protected her better. She was such a pretty, happy girl. I didn't think the mob would be cruel to her."

He wiped a tear from his eye and went on.

"Three of 'em. The wife was there, but they knocked her silly. I was away with the other men that had been marched out of town. Maggie fought 'em and that's probably why they got so awful rough with her."

He made a gesture with his hand toward his ear.

"They sliced up her ear and cut her hair. They beat her up so badly that we almost lost her. She was just beginning to recover when she found she was going to have a baby. Sometimes I wonder if it would have been better if she had died."

The story shook Oat. His heart ached for Maggie. He remembered the trip to Gallatin with Creech and Glaze. Blackguards. Devils. He now understood the troubled, faraway look in her eyes.

"I prayed and prayed the babe would be stillborn," MacGregor continued. "That's a terrible thing to admit, but I worry so about Maggie. She's so young, her parents are gone and I'm old and I won't be on this earth many more years. Who'll take care of her when I'm gone? I don't know."

They sat quietly for many minutes. Oat knew all the Mormons suffered badly in Missouri, but Maggie's predicament troubled him more than any other. There might have been others like her, but if there were it wasn't commonly known. Oat didn't know what to say. Finally, MacGregor rose.

"I best be getting on home," MacGregor said. "I came here because I know Maggie wishes things were different too. She's never said it but I know she worries that you and others think poorly of her because she's got a babe out of wedlock. I knew she wouldn't try to explain it to you so I decided I would."

Oat helped the MacGregor family get their farm started that summer, assisting in building a small house and plowing their fields. They accepted his help and Maggie and her grandparents treated him like a member of their family although Maggie continued to keep her distance. She spent her time caring for her baby, whom she named Abraham, but called Abe, and had Oat not known he never would have guessed how the baby was conceived, for she doted on him and took every precaution for his care.

Scores of other young women inhabited Nauvoo. Oat often saw them as he drove or led his horses through the streets. He would have liked to talk with them, but when he saw one he wanted to talk to he had his usual covering of mud to ward off mosquitoes. The mud was equally effective in warding off girls. He suspected that he looked quite odd and as a result he was shy about striking up a conversation with a girl while he was so dirty. But he kept smearing on the mud because not even his intense desire to talk with some of them could overcome the discomfort the insects caused.

One particular woman, however, caught his attention one day as he drove from the lumber mill past her with a wagonload of lumber. She had a fine-boned face and a striking, slender figure. Her brown hair hung down around her shoulders and she carried a small bag. She looked familiar, but he didn't remember her and, he realized, if he had known a woman as pretty as her, he certainly would have remembered. She met his gaze with a frown and appeared about to say something, but then the wagon rumbled past and the opportunity was gone.

Oat vowed to himself, however, that the next time he saw her, mud or not, he would ask her name, but a month passed and he did not see her again.

In September, more than four months after arriving in Nauvoo, he sat alone in the shade of a grove of aspen trees eating a lunch of dried meat and cornbread Maggie prepared. The morning's work involved cutting and dragging firewood for the MacGregors. The Jacquards grazed nearby. It was a beautiful afternoon. The days had cooled. Leaves on the trees were changing colors and the promise of fall was in the air. The mosquitoes were gone mostly and only the week before Oat ceased wearing mud.

After finishing his lunch, Oat reclined against a tree about to close his eyes when he saw her, the woman he had seen in town, walking the skid trail he used. She walked confidently, her head up and eyes alert.

For several seconds he watched her before she saw him or rather before she saw the Jacquards. She stopped when she saw them and searched the area until her eyes fell on Oat. A smile spread over her face and she stepped forward confidently walking straight toward him not taking her eyes away for a second.

Oat froze. His heart pounded in his chest. She walked resolutely forward, the most pleasant familiar look on her face. Oat wanted her to go and stay at the same time. She was a beautiful creature, laughing eyes and full lips yet at that moment she appeared more fearsome than the men who chased him out of Missouri. She had a full sixty yards to walk after she spotted him but she covered the distance in no time at all. She suddenly stood before him. Oat, surprised and awestruck, couldn't stand. His tongue was bound. All he could do was stare. She sat on the ground not three feet from him, brushed a strand of hair back and smoothed her dress so her ankles didn't show. Then she looked him squarely in the face and smiled the most beautiful smile he ever saw. A dimple appeared on her right cheek.

"Hello Oatie," she said quietly, and those two words hit him like a club.

A veil lifted and the memories flooded back. He couldn't believe he hadn't recognized her. The pigtails and the little girl voice were gone and she had the rounded curves of a mature young woman, but she definitely was Hannah.

"Hannah?"

She nodded and then giggles, laughs, smiles and tears spilled out all at once. For the rest of the afternoon they sat under the tree and talked and laughed. It was like he had seen her only yesterday, but there was so much to say. They recounted the experiences of the past six sad years and cried for each other. And when the sun dropped in the West she helped him hitch the Jacquards to the pile of logs he had cut during the morning and together they walked back into Nauvoo.

When they arrived at the MacGregor place. Oat introduced Hannah to Maggie and her family and told them what had happened. Maggie talked with them for a while, then politely excused herself and quietly disappeared.

# 20

That fall Oat purchased a small farm a few miles east of Nauvoo. It wasn't as far out as the MacGregor place, but it was fertile land with a stream running along the southern edge.

He looked on the little farm as a temporary set-up. He did not intend to stay long in Nauvoo but he felt comfortable living among the Mormons at present. They were amiable, hard-working people and they held no ill will toward him even though he hailed from Missouri and rebuffed all their attempts to convert him to their religion. He continued chewing tobacco and occasionally drinking when he could get it, habits Hannah hated. Eventually he planned to leave Nauvoo to settle elsewhere.

He worked the Jacquards hard, clearing the land and plowing fields in preparation for spring planting. With that chore complete, he built a small house and a barn with some of the lumber he stockpiled during the summer.

By November Oat had long since admitted to himself that he was in love with Hannah. Their reunion seemed providential. They spent long hours together walking along the river and talking, getting to know one another all over again. To Oat marriage to Hannah seemed the most logical and right thing in the world, an event that was inescapable. Certain she felt the same, he decided to propose to her.

The Sunday just before Christmas a storm dusted Nauvoo with a light coat of snow. Oat walked to the Wheatley home in the early afternoon and invited Hannah to walk with him. She bundled herself in her warmest clothing and walked beside him through Nauvoo to the wharf and then south along the river. When they reached a secluded area away from town, Oat took her hand and knelt in the snow.

"I love you Hannah," he said earnestly.

Oat expected her to happily express the same feelings for him, but she didn't.

"Oat," she said, smiling back at him. "I'm flattered."

Oat expected a more enthusiastic response. Thinking she was taken off-guard, surprised by the suddenness of his statement, he plunged ahead.

"Will you marry me?"

Oat expected her to joyfully throw her arms around his neck, kiss him and say yes. She didn't. Instead she gazed sadly off across the river for a long moment and shook her head.

"No."

Oat was stunned. Not in his worst dreams had he expected her to refuse his proposal. He steadied himself against an aspen tree and tried to clear his head, but it didn't work. He was dazed.

"Will you take me home now?" Hannah said, after a moment of silence. They retraced their footsteps, walking in silence.

"Why Hannah?" Oat asked finally. "I thought you felt the same as I do."

Hannah faced him.

"Oat, you are one of the dearest people in my life but I won't marry you."

"Why?"

"You're a puke. You drink. You chew. You spit. You are contemptuous of my beliefs. You patronize me and that's worse than criticizing openly. I won't marry a puke."

Oat was familiar with the term Mormons used when referring to Missourians. He even suspected that some Mormons called him a puke, but had never been called a puke to his face and certainly had never expected to be rebuked and rejected so forcefully by Hannah.

They walked into sight of the Wheatley cabin where they could see Hannah's father struggling with an armload of firewood.

"Hannah, would you ever change your mind?" Oat asked.

Tears formed in Hannah's eyes and ran down her cheeks.

"Yes I would Oat," she said. "But I'll be honest with you. That would require some changes in you. Big changes. In Missouri, my family lost everything because we were Mormons. To marry outside my faith now would be a betrayal. Papa would be hurt and I would regret it all my life. And, it would be an insult to my dead mother and brothers. You don't seem to understand that. And your inability or refusal to understand it offends me."

Oat left the Wheatley farm confused and angry. He briefly thought about packing up and leaving Nauvoo, but knew if he did he'd be back in a week to see Hannah again. The rest of the day he walked about Nauvoo trying to make sense of Hannah and Mormons. At dusk he found himself knocking at Joseph Smith's door.

Joseph's wife Emma answered and invited him into a cozy room and seated him near a fireplace. She took Oat's coat and hung it on a peg in the corner. Joseph appeared a moment later.

"Otis Harmon," he said heartily shaking Oat's hand. "Welcome." he said, seating himself near Oat. "What can I do for you?"

Oat briefly explained about himself and Hannah, how he had known her when they were children in Jackson County and that earlier in the day she refused his marriage proposal.

"She thinks you are a prophet and frankly I don't," he said.

Joseph nodded and listened. Oat went on.

"I know all the stories. How you claim to have seen God and Jesus and angels and that you were given golden plates to translate. But I grew up in Missouri and heard so many bad things about you. I just want to look you in the eye and hear you say it's true."

Joseph leaned forward in his chair and locked his gaze with Oat's.

"It's all true. I swear it. One of the reasons you can't understand is that you treat these things so lightly. You've never seriously considered the testimonies you've heard. Like most Missourians, you've dismissed them out of hand. God doesn't just give it to you. You have to make an effort to believe. If you don't, you'll never see."

An uneasy silence ensued.

"God commanded me to re-establish his church on the earth. It's been gone since the apostles were killed. This is His work."

Oat remembered how the Missourians laughed at those claims. He shook his head.

"I'm sorry to have bothered you," Oat said. "I'll go now. Thanks for talking to me."

Oat walked home, his thoughts flitting back and forth between Hannah and Joseph. He read some from a copy of the Book of Mormon Hannah loaned him, but didn't get far. He tried to pray like he had heard Hannah pray, but got no answer. No angels, no feelings, no visions, no voices. Total silence.

The following Tuesday a letter arrived for Oat. It came from Carthage and did not have a return address.

"To Oat Harmon," it read. "I apologize for bothering you with this matter but you are the only one I know who might possibly help me. I am in jail at Carthage and am in need of someone to speak in my behalf. Will you help me? Sarah."

Oat often made trips to Carthage with loads of lumber or bricks and it so happened that only a few days before he had accepted a job to haul a load of bricks from a new kiln at Nauvoo to Carthage. It was Oat's third load in two weeks for the same man. The next day he loaded his wagon and made his way to Carthage.

At the place designated for him to unload the bricks a group of men had gathered and there was an unusual amount of interest in the stack of bricks. The well-to-do mill owner who hired Oat explained that he moved the location of the house approximately fifty yards down the road. The pile of bricks Oat delivered in his previous trips was being moved. A matched team of massive black horses stood near the stack.

"We got us a wager going on," the mill owner said. "Frank Willard, who owns that team says his horses can pull that whole pile on the sled to the new spot. "Some of these men think he can, some say he can't. There's a lot of money being thrown around."

The contest intrigued Oat. Instead of a wagon with wheels, a large sled with wooden runners was parked alongside the bricks with the black work horses harnessed to it. Ten men stacked the bricks on the sled. Another twenty men watched and made side bets as the load grew taller and the sled got heavier.

The horses stood about a hand taller than the Jacquards because they had longer legs. It was the first time Oat had seen horses larger than his. They were grand animals. Their long legs were white up to their knees and white blazes stretched down their foreheads from their ears to their noses.

Oat got down from his wagon and stepped closer. The sled's runners sank into the soft dirt as more weight was added. Oat had no idea how much the loaded sled weighed but knew it was thousands of pounds. Still, he didn't think the horses would have much trouble pulling it. Knowing the strength of his own horses and seeing the load, he expected Willard easily would be a hundred dollars richer within minutes.

Oat judged it would take some time to get all the bricks loaded onto the sled so he walked to the jail to see about Sarah. The idea of a woman in jail troubled him and he wondered what she could have done to get herself in such a fix.

The jailer led Oat up a flight of stairs to the jail's second story and unlocked a door. Sarah sat on a bed in a far corner of a stark room with only the bed and a lone chair as furniture.

"I'll be back in ten minutes," the jailer said. He left, shutting and locking the door behind him.

"How did this happen?" Oat asked, sitting down on the chair.

"I'm a thief and I owe money," she said. "I didn't want to trouble you any more after we got to Quincy so I left and tried to find work. I did okay through the summer, but there isn't much work around here for a woman this time of year."

She hung her head and stared at the floor.

"I suppose I should have stayed with John," she said. "At least I had a roof over my head and food to eat. And I didn't feel like a slut."

"He beat you."

"Yes, well I got work at a tavern because that's all there was. I was beaten there too. Last week a customer left a bag of money sitting out on a table. I stole it and got caught. That's why I'm here."

"How much was it?"

"It was less than twenty dollars and he got it all back, but now the judge says I owe the man that much more plus a fine. All told I owe seventy five dollars," she said still looking down. "I'm sorry to ask but you're the only decent man I know. Is there any way you can help me?"

Oat squirmed. He liked Sarah and wanted to help her, but he

didn't have that much money.

"I'll go talk to the judge," he said. "Maybe we can make some kind of arrangement. What will you do if I can get you out?"

"I'm going back to Ohio," she said. "I have a sister there. She'll give me a place to stay until I get on my feet."

Oat left the jail and found the judge standing in the crowd waiting to watch the black work team move the brick load. The jailer pointed the judge out.

"He's the one in the suit who's half drunk," the jailer said. "He's always half drunk."

Oat spotted him, a soft-looking man with a scowling demeanor, well dressed and out of place among the hard and coarse farmers who had gathered to watch the pulling contest. As Oat approached, the judge must have sensed some purpose in his advance.

"What do you want?"

"I want to help the woman you're holding in the jail," Oat said. "What can I do to get her out of there?"

"Pay me seventy five dollars," the judge said.

"I don't have seventy five dollars," Oat said. "Will you take my word that the money will be paid and let her go? She can't pay when she's locked up."

The judge stared at Oat contemptuously and laughed.

"She'll pay one way or another," he said. "I don't take credit from thieves."

"I'm not a thief," Oat said. "I'll pay you the money as soon as I can."

"You look to me like a no-account Mormon and in my book that's the same as a thief," the judge responded. "Don't bother me unless you have seventy five dollars."

The judge reminded Oat of Boggs, the same haughty look, disdainful stare and derisive attitude. His heart sank as the judge walked away. How could he help Sarah if the judge wouldn't even talk to him?

A few moments later Willard stepped to the side of the load and took the reins of his team. The black horses stiffened and prepared to start. Willard slapped the end of the reins on their backs and yelled "ha." The blacks plunged ahead. The load moved about an inch, then stopped, the blacks stymied. Willard whipped his horses again with the same result. Over the next five minutes Willard tried to start the load several times, with no success. It soon became evident the team had more style than muscle. They soon balked and stood with heads hanging as Willard beat them. Willard finally threw his hands in the air signaling defeat. Half the onlookers cheered, the other half watched quietly.

Oat walked slowly around the sled inspecting the runners. They sat on soft, loose dirt. Nothing held them. The load should have moved. Oat frowned purposely and shook his head. The well-to-do mill owner caught his eye and walked to him.

"What's the matter?" he asked.

"Nothing," Oat shrugged. "I'm just puzzled why this load didn't move. My horses could pull it."

Oat made the statement loud enough that several men standing nearby heard. The crowd quieted. Oat suddenly stood at the center of attention, fifty men staring at him.

"Hey Mormon, what did you say?" Willard yelled. Embarrassed and stung by his failure he lashed out.

"He said his horses could pull this load that your horses obviously can't," the mill owner yelled so all heard.

"Did you say that?" Willard said, staring hatefully at Oat.

Oat nodded. He could imagine what was going on inside Willard's head. He was thinking he could win his one hundred dollars back if he could shame this young sucker into another wager.

"Well," Willard said, slowly and deliberately, so all could hear, "If my horses can't pull it I doubt any can. I've got a hundred dollars says yours can't either."

A tense silence settled over the group. Oat's heart fluttered and he felt warm blood rush to his face. His father once warned him about running off at the mouth and doing foolish things. Betting was foolish, but he wanted to help Sarah. Doubt seized him. The enormousness of the load of bricks suddenly appalled him. He had great faith in his horses' strength and believed they could do it, but never had he allowed himself into such a predicament.

"I don't have a hundred dollars to bet," Oat said.

"Then you should keep your mouth shut," Willard said, shaking his fist in Oat's face. "You Mormons are all alike. Always making great claims you can't back up. That puny team of yours couldn't pull half this load."

All eyes settled on the Jacquards. They stood about fifty yards off ears pricked forward as if they understood every word. Jack pawed the ground.

"I don't have a hundred dollars," Oat repeated. Willard played right into his hands.

"You sniveling coward," Willard yelled. "You got those worthless horses yer so damn proud of. You can bet them. I'll bet this hundred dollars against your team that you can't move that load."

Willard's insults stung Oat. He only wanted to win enough money to help Sarah, but Willard's meanness rankled him.

"That's not an even bet sir," Oat said loudly. "If I bet my horses you'll have to bet two hundred dollars."

Two hundred dollars. Oat couldn't believe he said it. A buzz went through the crowd. Men dug into their pockets and gathered around Willard. Like a pack of wolves, they smelled blood. After seeing the black team balk, not a man in the crowd believed the Jacquards capable of the feat. The doubters looked on smiling, laughing inwardly, thinking Oat was being shamed into the wager. Their confidence that the load wouldn't move unnerved Oat and he began to doubt too. He looked at the sled again, still slowly sinking in the soft dirt, and watched the magnificent black team being unhitched and led away. The task grew more impossible by the second. Willard jubilantly emerged from a group of men who had gathered round him.

"Here's it is. Two hundred dollars," he said. "Now big mouth. Let's see you move that load.

Oat hesitated. If he lost the Jacquards in a silly bet he would never forgive himself. He knew he should walk away, but his pride wouldn't allow it. Other men joined Willard, mocking him. He nearly retreated until he remembered the helplessness he had seen in Sarah face. He had to help her and this was his best chance to do it.

Oat walked to his horses and unhitched them from his wagon. The massive animals felt the excitement and tension generated by the crowd. They danced and pranced as he led them to the sled. In perfect condition, not an ounce of superfluous flesh adorned either of their massive frames. Their furry coats shone with the sheen of silk. Down their necks to their withers, their manes bristled and waved. While they didn't stand as tall as the blacks, they were heavier, more compact. Every inch of their bodies spoke power. Their heavy fore legs and haunches moved easily, thousands of pounds of muscle and grit rippling underneath the skin.

The crowd fell silent. They could not help but see that the Jacquards were extraordinary animals, but for them to move thousands of pounds of bricks seemed impossible in their eyes. Nevertheless, the nervous movements of men who suddenly wondered if they bet too much twitched throughout the crowd.

"Jack, Molly, tighten it up," Oat called.

The Jacquards tightened their harnesses and eased back a few inches.

"Ha!" Oat's voice cracked the tense silence.

The Jacquards shot forward in perfect unison. The load trembled, then inched forward slowly and jerkily. The first five yards the jerking continued as the Jacquard's huge haunches exploded into the work. The jerking perceptibly diminished; as the sled gained momentum until it moved steadily forward.

Men gasped and breathed again. Oat walked alongside the load happily encouraging Jack and Molly. As they neared the flag that marked the end of the fifty yards the mill owner and those who had not bet against the Jacquards cheered. When the Jacquards reached the designated spot, Oat stopped them. Men gathered round him, slapping him on the back and patting the horses.

One offered to buy the Jacquards then and there. Others had noticed that Jack was a stud and asked to let them breed their mares to him. During the backslapping and revelry, a sullen and defeated Willard handed Oat a wad of bills and walked away. Finally, after almost an hour of excited talking the crowd dispersed and Oat finally unloaded the wagonload of bricks he brought from Nauvoo.

Oat found the judge at a tavern drinking. He handed the judge the seventy five dollars. Without saying anything, the judge pocketed the money, stood and walked with Oat to the jail where he told the jailer to release Sarah. Soon, Oat and Sarah stood outside the jail. Sarah carried a small bag.

"Will you give me a ride away from here?" she asked.

"Sure," Oat said. "Put your bag in the back and climb aboard. I'll take you to Nauvoo."

"Why?"

"You can get a room there until you decide what to do. And if you want you could catch a riverboat to St. Louis, maybe even New Orleans."

"How? I don't . . ." she said.

Oat handed her the remaining money he had won in the bet.

"Use this to get a start."

With wide eyes, she counted the money.

"Where did you get all this money?" she asked.

Oat explained the pulling contest and the bet with Willard. Sarah was dumbfounded.

"Let me get this straight. You risked the horses you wouldn't trade for me on a two hundred dollar bet to get me out of jail."

"It was pretty much a sure thing all along, but it did make me nervous," he said.

They rode quietly for a mile before she spoke again.

"So you're a Mormon now," Sarah said.

"Naw," Oat said.

"You look like a Mormon."

"People keep saying that. I'm not a Mormon," Oat said. "What does a Mormon look like?"

"Sort of like you."

"Well, I ain't a Mormon and don't plan on becoming one."

Sarah nodded.

"I heard lots of men at the tavern say Joe Smith is an outstanding liar," she said. "I suppose he is."

"I think he's a decent man," Oat said.

Sarah looked at him quizzically.

"You know him?" she asked.

"Yes I do."

She frowned and sat quietly for several moments.

"You married?" she asked finally.

"No."

"Any prospects?"

"You sure are nosy," he said.

"Sorry," she said. "I just was wondering. You don't volunteer much so I had to ask."

They rode quietly for several miles before Oat spoke.

"I asked a woman to marry me a few days ago. She refused because I'm not a Mormon."

Sarah wrinkled her brow, then sat quietly for several moments.

"Well, you've been making people think you're a Mormon all day long," she said. "Maybe you can fool her too."

Oat was baptized in the Mississippi River a month later on a day when a sheet of ice an inch thick covered the Mississippi. He still wasn't sure about Joseph Smith, but he decided to keep that to himself. In a way, he felt like a fraud, but he decided he'd rather fake being a Mormon than try to live without Hannah.

The cold temperature and ice pleased Hannah. She regretted it wasn't colder because she wanted him to suffer for his stubbornness.

Hannah's father baptized him. They used axes to break a hole in the ice large enough for two men to stand in waist deep. While Joseph, Hannah and a few others looked on as witnesses, Jerome Wheatley recited the baptismal prayer and pushed Oat under the icy water. Large chunks of ice clunked against Oat's head as he came up gasping and shivering. Hannah clapped as Oat's hair immediately froze into icicles and his nostrils froze shut making it necessary to breath through his mouth. The onlookers covered him with blankets and congratulated him while helping him into the wagon where Hannah held the reins to the Jacquards.

"You deserve this," she told Oat unsympathetically as his teeth chattered. "If the baptism doesn't take, this should freeze the Missouri hell out of you."

She slapped the Jacquards on the rumps with the reins and started them back toward the Wheatley house where a warm fire burned.

"I think God is reminding you of your stubbornness," Hannah

teased. "If you weren't so knotheaded you would have been baptized last summer when it was warm."

After changing out of his wet clothing at the Wheatley house, Hannah's father and the other men laid their hands on Oat's head and confirmed him a member of the church while Hannah heated a large blanket near the fire. Oat continued to shiver until Hannah draped the blanket over his shoulders. The warmth felt so good as it spread over his body. He felt peaceful. He lay down on the floor near the fire enjoying the warmth and fell asleep.

# — 21 —

OAT AND HANNAH MARRIED AT NAUVOO ON THE FIRST day of spring. They stood near the spot Joseph had designated for the construction of a temple. In a small, quiet ceremony they exchanged vows and accepted Joseph's blessings of "posterity and happiness forever if you remain faithful."

It was the happiest time of Oat's life to that point. His regretted that his mother could not be there. He wrote and told her of Hannah and their plans, but left out the part that he had been baptized a Mormon. That detail would anger her so he planned to break that to her later at a more convenient time when he would have time to explain and soften the blow. He knew she would not be happy about it and would ask many questions. He wanted to answer them in person. He received a reply a week before the wedding.

His mother remembered Hannah and the Wheatley family and regretted that because of the distances and travel time between them she would be unable to attend the wedding, but promised to visit as soon as circumstances allowed. Oat was a little unsettled by what she had not written. She did not write that she was happy for him, nor did she mention the obvious, that Hannah and her family were Mormons. Nor did she criticize the Mormons in any way.

He remembered her admonition at one time: "Mormons are trouble. Don't marry a Mormon girl."

Oat's and Hannah's life together in Nauvoo began happily and peacefully. They built a new larger house for themselves and their expected family right next to the smaller one Oat built the preceding year. The small house they arranged for Hannah's father, whose health, despite their precautions and care, continued to fail though he appeared to be happy as long as he could be near Hannah.

Joseph had sent missionaries to England, Canada and the eastern states and converts arrived almost every day. Many came overland by wagon or they walked. Others arrived on riverboats, disembarking at Nauvoo's wharf where they were greeted warmly by Joseph and other church leaders, who gave them instructions and information on where they could obtain land to farm and build homes.

The newcomers made a huge impact on the city. Where only a year earlier the area had been nothing more than a swampy bottomland, now Nauvoo blossomed into a full-blown city. Grist and lumber mills, potteries, tanneries, foundries, blacksmiths, bakeries, slaughter houses, small factories, shops and stores sprang up. Brickyards were developed and home building became one of the biggest industries of all.

Each household had a garden. The residents planted fruit trees and raised livestock and poultry. Every space in Nauvoo was put to use as a tide of immigrants poured into the city.

Joseph recognized, almost immediately, the individual strengths and talents of the new converts, and he used them to the community's advantage in public works, temple building and even politics.

One such convert, John C. Bennett, arrived in Nauvoo in the fall of eighteen forty. Seeing the man's energy and political talents, Joseph set him to work seeking a charter for the new city. Bennett, a handsome, likeable and persuasive man, proved extremely effective in his assignment. The political situation in Illinois proved to be beneficial to the Mormons as both political parties actively sought the Mormon vote. Using those circumstances to his advantage, Bennett deftly maneuvered the city's charter through the Illinois legislature obtaining rights and advantages that few other cities in the entire country enjoyed. As a result the city had its own municipal court and its own military force.

Not all Joseph's efforts met with success, however. While Bennett lobbied for the Nauvoo Charter, Joseph traveled to Washington D.C. and petitioned President Martin Van Buren for redress for the Missouri atrocities. The president, preoccupied with the raging national debate over slavery, rebuffed him. The United States government would not extend any help to the Mormons for their losses and Joseph returned disappointed and frustrated.

Nevertheless, as the months wore on schools were developed and classes were taught in homes and public buildings. Soon there were plays, lectures, art exhibits, concerts, banquets and dances. Nauvoo became quite a merry place.

Oat and Hannah made many new friends as new neighbors arrived and built homes. Their closest neighbors were the Trasks, who had traveled overland all the way from Canada the previous fall and winter. They purchased a piece of land along the northeastern border of the Harmons' property.

George Trask, a tall, slender man with a thin, pointed face and a nervous laugh, immediately regretted his decision to move to Nauvoo. He and his wife Geneva had one child who was less than a year old. The Trasks were unexcited and uninspired by the challenge of building a new home.

"What a god-forsaken place this is, don't you think?" George said to Oat, a few days after arriving. "Had I only known I would have stayed in Canada."

"You'll get used to it. The soil's good and productive once you break through the sod," Oat said encouragingly. "The people are kind."

Trask rolled his eyes and sighed.

"I hope so, but I have my doubts."

The Trasks had a benefactor and friend named William Law. Law led the Trasks and a few others cross-country from Canada to Nauvoo and, being a wealthy man, helped them obtain land.

Oat met Law on one of his early visits to the Trask place, when he arrived with the Jacquards and his plow to help George break out a few acres of ground for planting.

"Big horses," Law said, circling the Jacquards. "What breed?"

"Percheron," Oat said.

"Percheron," Law repeated. "Never heard of that breed. How old?"

"It's a French breed. The mare's nine; the stud's eight."

"What will you take for them?"

"Pardon me?"

"What's your price for the horses? I need some plow horses and I want to buy them."

Law's tone didn't set well with Oat.

"They're not for sale," Oat said.

Law inspected the horses, running his hands over their backs, even trying to inspect Jack's teeth, but Jack snorted and sprayed Law. Oat laughed out loud.

"So what's the price?" Law queried again wiping his face with a handkerchief.

"They're not for sale," Oat repeated.

"Oh come on man," Law pressed on, while standing to Molly's right. "Everything's for sale. We just have to find the right price."

Oat looked back over the fields toward his house trying to think what he would be willing to take for his horses. He didn't know how much money Law had, but it wasn't enough. By happenstance, Molly, standing calmly in harness next to Jack, came to his aid. Shifting her weight from her left side to her right she moved her right foot about six inches stepping on Law's toes. She then stood like a statue. Law screamed and beat on the big mare, but she didn't move. She simply swished her big tail at him. Law was finally freed a few seconds later when Oat led the two big horses forward.

The incident ended Law's interest in the Jacquards for he never again approached Oat about buying them.

At times, the sheer immensity of the task of clearing land, plowing fields and all the countless related tasks discouraged the Trasks to the point of immobility. It was as if the very thought of work exhausted them, the problems of homesteading too big and insurmountable. With the Jacquards as healthy as ever and his own farm in good shape, Oat and Hannah helped the Trasks plant crops and build their house. Oat noticed that the sight of his two massive percherons in full harness breathed life and hope into the Trasks. He understood that. They did the same for him.

Other neighbors joined in from time to time to help the Trasks through their difficulties and by mid-May the Trask farm was ready for the growing season. Their fields had been planted, the four log walls of the house were up and Oat and George fashioned a roof of prairie sod and grass. They dug a well near the house and built a fence around a two-acre pasture for the Trask's mules and milk cow. Oat was proud of the work they had accomplished, but the Trasks, while grateful for the help didn't share the Harmons' enthusiasm for the area or the work needed to make it habitable. Nevertheless the two couples spent most Sunday afternoons together after church services.

Their discussions nearly always led to a debate on church doctrine and Joseph Smith. The Trasks, right from the first made it clear they converted to the church only at the urging of Law, who often visited them. They clung to their former faith and both liked to goad Hannah by ridiculing Joseph. Hannah took the jabs personally and often was furious by the time the two couples parted company. Oat stayed aloof during these discussions, but felt his feelings changing gradually.

"They say Joseph is a fallen prophet," George said one morning as he and Oat weeded and hilled corn.

"They? Who are they?" Oat asked

"People I know, high up people in the church."

"And why do these people say Joseph is a fallen prophet?"

"Mostly they think that all the power and influence Joseph has as the leader of the church has corrupted him."

"Oh," Oat said. "Sounds like you agree."

"They think Joseph needs to be replaced before he causes any further damage," George went on.

"And let me guess," Oat said. "The people who say these things think they can do a better job leading the church than Joseph."

"Yeah," George said. "And they probably could."

"If I were you George," Oat said, "I think I'd back off a little on this fallen prophet idea. I have my doubts too, but I know Joseph well enough that I can say he's not a bad man like you seem to want to believe."

George shook his head.

"You should hear the things they say he did in Missouri. He stole horses and cut the heads off people who opposed him."

"Damn it, George," Oat said. "I'm from Missouri. I've heard all those rumors. And I know what happened to Joseph there. If he was half as mean as Governor Boggs I'd be worried, but he isn't. You're listening to the wrong people."

Oat had a good idea it was William Law who kept George stirred up. He wondered why. Because he was wealthy, Law wielded a good amount of influence in the community and within the church but after his own experiences with Law, Oat decided to never trust him.

Publicly George and his wife supported Joseph. They attended church services and were friendly with the Smiths and other church leaders. On occasion George joked with Joseph and once in a testimony meeting even stood and declared his loyalty to Joseph and the church. But in private George remained unconvinced and critical.

# 22

MAGGIE HAD LITTLE USE FOR OR INTEREST IN MEN. she ignored and snubbed any man who showed more than a passing interest. In fact, the only men Oat knew that she spoke to were her grandfather and himself. Hannah shared Oat's concerns for the MacGregors, but Maggie's behavior didn't seem odd to her.

"She had an awful experience and it may take a long time for her to get over it, if she ever does," Hannah said. "I can understand. So far all men have done for her is put her through hell."

"But she needs to find a father for her son so he'll have a name," Oat argued.

"The Lord will take care of it," Hannah said.

That was a common response for Hannah, but Oat still worried. The Lord sometimes took his sweet time getting around to some things. He wanted to help Maggie, but had no idea how to go about it.

When Abe reached his first birthday and began to walk by himself Maggie took him with her about town, to church and everywhere else. He was a handsome child with blond hair, blue eyes and a natural, innocent curiosity that seldom was satisfied. He toddled industriously beside her as quickly as his small legs would carry him. And when they wore out, Maggie carried him.

Orrin MacGregor tolerated the child for Maggie's sake, but he was distrustful and reserved.

"I wonder what'll become of the boy," he said one day to Oat when he stopped to borrow one of the Jacquards for an afternoon. "He comes from bad seed."

The comment nagged at Oat and he wondered the rest of the day whether it was possible for the boy to inherit an evil disposition even if he didn't know his father. For Maggie's sake he hoped not, because it was evident that she truly loved the boy. She doted on Abe from sunup to sundown. He was well fed, clean and she always knew where he was. She obviously held no ill will to the child and plainly didn't blame Abe for her own misfortunes.

"Do you think Abe will turn out badly?" Oat asked Hannah the same day.

"Why would he?" she asked.

"Because of his father. Do you think he'll be bad because his father was bad?"

Hannah shook her head.

"Abe will turn out the way he chooses to turn out. He has as much chance to grow into a fine man as anyone does. With a mother that loves him like Maggie does, I'd say he has more than a fighting chance."

Maggie, still only seventeen years old, worked like a man beside her grandfather. As her grandmother's health deteriorated, the management of the MacGregor home fell to her. She nursed the old woman as well as her child, hoed weeds in the corn and tended a vegetable garden. She cooked, washed laundry, carried water and split firewood, the same as all the other women in Nauvoo. When her grandmother died, Maggie's burden became noticeably lighter.

Despite her predicament, Maggie did not isolate herself. In Jackson County, Oat knew of women, who on having children out of wedlock, were ashamed to appear in public. Not Maggie. She and Abe were as visible as anyone in town and for the most part the populace accepted them. Her story was known by many of the people who had come out of Missouri though Maggie herself never felt obligated to explain it. Those who knew what happened did not condemn her and accepted the child. Those who condemned her, she ignored as much as possible.

Maggie persuaded another immigrant, a middle-aged Englishwoman, to tutor her, and it was not unusual to see her hiking barefoot through the fields with a book in one arm and Abe in the other. On several occasions upon stopping to check on the MacGregors, Oat found Maggie reading to Abe, slowly sounding out the words of a story in the Bible or some other book she had borrowed. As she learned to read, some of the heavy Scottish brogue disappeared from her speech.

Maggie's hair grew to shoulder length and once it was that long she no longer wore a scarf. She usually walked to Sunday meetings with her grandfather, holding Abe and rocking him gently. Oat always noticed her and it saddened him to see how she struggled with her circumstances. He often took time from his own work to help the MacGregors and grew to feel quite protective of them. The old man aged quickly after his wife's death. Oat worried not only about Maggie's welfare, but about how she would be treated as Nauvoo grew.

Snide comments dropped here and there troubled Oat. Geneva Trask was Maggie's most vocal critic.

"Can you believe the gall of that woman?" Geneva said one Sunday evening after church services. "A woman like that should not be allowed in the church. She should not receive the sacrament."

Hannah defended Maggie.

"She was forced," Hannah said. "At Far West. It's not her fault. We need to love her, not condemn her."

But Geneva remained unsympathetic. Having not been subjected to the hardships in Missouri, she had no understanding or compassion despite Oat and Hannah's explanation.

"Sure she was forced," Geneva said, rolling her eyes. "I will not fellowship with a woman who has a bastard child."

If Maggie knew of Geneva Trask's feelings or comments she never let it alter her behavior. She attended services on Sundays, carrying Abe around as if there was nothing unusual about her circumstances. The Trasks and others mistook her presence as brazen insolence.

The Trasks knew and were openly critical of Oat's close ties to the MacGregors.

"Oat, if you keep visiting those MacGregor people, the whole city is going to think you're having an affair with that woman," Geneva said. "In fact, some already do."

"Well, I'm not," Oat said. "Maybe you can straighten out anyone who tells you that." But in his heart, Oat knew that if a rumor like that circulated, Geneva would be the source.

The Harmons began to see the Trasks less and less, even though they remained outwardly cordial. Hannah made special efforts to maintain their friendship. She presented them with gifts of baked pies and bread and Oat continued to help George in the fields. Both wondered if their friendship with Maggie affected their friendship, or if it was something else.

# 23

AFTER THE ILLINOIS LEGISLATURE APPROVED THE Nauvoo city charter, Joseph set about the task of building a temple. He spoke of it constantly saying the Lord would use it to endow his people with power. The temple project grew into a huge undertaking. The massive building would occupy the highest portion of ground in the city and take years to complete. The cornerstones had been laid that spring and the citizens of the city went to work on it with the same zeal they had used to build the city in the midst of the swamp. Faithful church members contributed one in every ten days to its construction.

Members donated money, building materials, labor, anything they could spare. Some did so at great sacrifice giving valuable keepsakes and heirlooms they had carried out of Missouri with great difficulty. Oat and Hannah gave up the extra money they had saved and worked at the temple site. At first Oat did it to maintain the illusion of being a Mormon, but as time wore on Oat noticed a change in himself.

To this point, he secretly never had considered himself a Mormon even though he'd been baptized and given up tobacco and alcohol. He'd done it for Hannah, not because he really believed.

Then, one day someone called him Brother Harmon, and it sounded natural. Deep down he realized he had changed. As he thought about the changes that had occurred within, he suddenly realized he did believe. The whole thing suddenly made sense. He thought of his mother. He still had not told her. How would he explain it? She would be scandalized. She might disown him. But the changes and his increasing love for Hannah brought peacefulness to his life he'd never known before.

That spring Molly's colt was two years old and Oat worked him in harness alongside his mother, who was nearly ready to give birth to another colt. The two-year-old was as light colored as its mother, but had a dark star in its forehead. Its legs were sound and Oat judged he would grow as large as Jack Jacquard one day. Oat received several offers for him from various brethren who needed a horse, but so far he had turned them all down. The colt was a prize and with the new foal Molly was carrying, Oat would have a second team to work in a few short years.

The unwelcome idea of giving the colt as tithing first entered his mind one Sunday as the presiding bishop pled for donations so that the work on the temple could go forward. Oat sullenly fought with himself about it for days, never mentioning it to Hannah. He had such big plans for the young horse. Jack and Molly, though still strong and able, were nearly ten years old. Though they still had several good years, eventually he would have to replace them. Other than Jack and Molly the colt was his most valuable possession, but the thought wouldn't leave. It pestered him all day long and kept him awake at night. Finally, Oat succumbed and told Hannah.

"I thought of the same thing, but it's really your decision," she said.

At dawn on the fourth day after the Sunday meeting Oat caught the colt and led it to the barn. He brushed its coat and combed its mane and tail. He and Hannah led the colt into Nauvoo to the temple office where Oat nearly choked as he patted the colt's front shoulder and handed the halter rope to the bishop.

"For the temple," he said quietly.

The bishop took the rope and nodded.

Oat and Hannah walked home silently.

"Are you sorry you gave the horse?" she asked as they neared their house.

"I don't know," he said. "It was almost like giving Jack away. It will be a while before I know."

Oat never knew how much money the church got when it sold the colt, but he figured it was a fair amount. Any regrets, however, completely disappeared two weeks later, when Molly gave birth to twin foals, both with dark stars in their foreheads.

A month later after one of Joseph's vigorous sermons, Oat stood in the shade of a sycamore waiting for Hannah who was fussing over a neighbor's new baby. While he waited Joseph appeared at his side.

"Brother Oat, you didn't go to sleep during my sermon today," he said. "I take that as a compliment."

"You should because I was tired," Oat said.

"You've changed. I heard about your donation of that young horse. It raised a nice sum of money."

Oat stared at the ground, a little embarrassed, remembering how he struggled with his decision. He tried to change the subject.

"You had more to say today, but you ran out of time. Sometimes I think you want to say more than you do."

"I do hold back at times," Joseph replied.

"Why?" Oat asked.

"You may not be ready to hear it all. When God reveals knowledge, it's normally accompanied by a commandment to put that knowledge to work in our lives. If we don't we could fall under condemnation."

"I want to know more," Oat said.

"Maybe you do, maybe you don't," Joseph said, shaking his head. "Sometimes the Lord asks difficult things. If he asked you to radically alter your life in a way that might offend your family and neighbors and make your life more difficult, could you do it?"

Oat thought about that for a moment. He didn't worry much about what most people thought except for his mother and she was in Baltimore. He couldn't imagine anything that the Lord could ask that would make his life too difficult.

"If I knew it came from God," Oat said.

"That's the key, isn't it?"

"If it came from God through you, I could do it," Oat said.

"I hope you can Oat. You'll get a chance to prove it."

# 24

WHEN HER FATHER DIED, HANNAH CRIED FOR WEEKS. Oat could do little to console her. Her father had not been an old man, but he never fully regained the use of his arm after being shot on his trek out of Missouri with Hannah. Hannah thought, probably quite accurately, that he had lost his enthusiasm for living after her mother and brothers died. He lost weight and grew weak, only a shell of the man he once had been. In October he passed away after suffering with a fever for more than a week.

Many fresh graves populated the Nauvoo Cemetery that autumn. Young and old alike had died of fever that summer and funerals occurred daily. At the graveside, Joseph reminded those present that death is not the end. Despite his comforting words Hannah remained inconsolable, not so much because of his death, she told Oat, but because the last years of his life had been so hard. She became distant and angry at times and Oat worried about her constantly.

Each day Hannah removed her pistol from its hiding place beneath a board she pried up in a corner of the house. She held it and caressed it. Somehow it soothed her and kept her most bitter demons at bay. She never told Oat about it, but whenever she walked alone she took it with her. Every few weeks she walked into the river bottoms where she shot it time and again. With practice she became a fairly good shot, although she often winced when she pulled the trigger and the gun boomed and bucked in her hands.

The gun made Hannah feel powerful. She grew to love its roar and the smell of gun smoke. Her targets were old dead logs and rocks. Squirrels, rabbits, turkeys, and deer were plentiful in the river bottoms, but she never shot at live targets knowing that if she killed anything she'd have to cook it and then Oat would ask questions. She remembered how awful she felt the one time she nearly killed a badger. She believed, however, that if she ever was attacked by another filthy, foul-smelling, tobacco-stained, Missouri puke she could gut-shoot him and happily watch him bleed to death. She hoped, even prayed, for the opportunity.

Hannah wondered what Oat would think if he knew about the gun and what she did when he worked in the fields without her. And her thoughts. They scared her sometimes. At first she prayed and tried to remove the anger and bitterness, but her heart wasn't ready. The hate remained. So after a time she fed them and continued to walk into the river bottoms with the pistol. Maybe she never would need the gun. But she had a feeling that someday she would. And if the day came, she promised herself that she would be ready.

One morning not long after her father's death Hannah walked into the river bottoms to her favorite place to shoot the gun. The spot was secluded, shaded and cool. On arriving at the location she loaded the pistol, aimed at a piece of floating deadwood and squeezed the trigger. The gun boomed and the ball hit the wood dead center. It flew to into several pieces. A second later she heard the frightened, alarmed cry of a woman.

"Hannah. Hannah. Are you all right? Hannah."

Someone ran toward her crashing through bushes and over dry branches and downed trees continuing to call out to her.

"Hannah. Hannah."

Hannah was so startled by the commotion that she hid behind a tree and quickly reloaded the pistol. She thought she was alone. Suddenly Maggie appeared with a large club in her hand, her eyes as big as dollars.

"Hannah!"

Hannah stepped from behind the tree so that Maggie could see her, still hiding the gun behind her back.

"Are you okay?"

"Yes. I'm fine," she replied. "Why?"

"I heard a shot and thought someone was trying to hurt you. Did you not hear a gunshot?"

Sheepishly, Hannah relaxed her arms and let Maggie see the pistol.

"Oh," Maggie said, her mouth dropping open.

"You came to help me?" Hannah asked, amused. "You heard a gunshot and you were going to club whoever was shooting at me?'

Maggie nodded and dropped the club.

"I didn't think. It just scared me."

"It's okay. How did you know I was here?" Hannah asked. "I thought I was alone."

"I followed you," Maggie said, embarrassed. "I had no idea you had a gun."

"It's okay," Hannah said. "I'm taking some target practice. Want to try it?"

"I have never shot a gun before," Maggie said.

Hannah sat down on the ground where she had a clear view of the river. Seeing another piece of driftwood, she took careful aim and squeezed the trigger. The gun exploded, but the ball missed the wood. Hannah carefully loaded the pistol and handed it to Maggie.

"Here. Try it," Hannah said.

Taking the gun, Maggie sat on the ground next to Hannah and aimed the gun as she had seen Hannah do. Pointing in the general direction of a floating log, she pulled the trigger. The gun boomed and jumped in her hands. The ball hit the water far out in the river. Her eyes widened and she stared at Hannah.

"Oat doesn't know you have a gun does he? Where did you get it?"

"A puke shot my father in the shoulder with it when we were coming out of Missouri and while he was reloading I smashed him in the head with a rock. Then I took his gun and his horse."

"I wish I would have had a gun at Far West," Maggie said.

"I wish I would have too," Hannah said. "I could have helped my mother."

"Your mother? What happened?" asked Maggie.

Hannah had never told anyone the entire story about that day in Far West because she'd never trusted anyone enough. She loved Oat but didn't think he would understand. It was so delicate and awful. Intuitively, she knew Maggie would. So she told her. She wanted to confess how she had hidden beneath the floor while her mother was ravaged and how she felt so guilty about not coming out of her hiding place to try to help her mother. But there was no one she trusted enough or who she thought would understand. It was a burden she had carried a long while and it felt good to finally let it all out. As Maggie listened, tears ran down her cheeks.

"If you had come out, they would have done the same to you and your mother's sacrifice for you would have been for nothing."

"Do you think my mother thinks poorly of me for not helping her?" Hannah asked as she wept.

"No, no, no," Maggie said. "I think she's probably grateful that you let her do that for you. That's what mothers do. I would do it for my child even knowing how awful . . ." Her voice trailed off and she began to cry.

Hannah wrapped her arms around Maggie.

"It must have been awful."

Maggie nodded and soon she was pouring out her own terrible story and for an hour they talked and cried together.

"They were evil," Maggie said. "I cut one of them with a rock. He beat me and I thought he was going to cut my throat, but he only cut away a piece of my ear. The others stopped him after that because they weren't through with me."

Later, Maggie and Hannah took turns shooting the pistol. Hannah taught Maggie her game of pretending the logs were pukes. They fired the gun again and again until they were out of powder and then walked back to Nauvoo together.

"Why did you follow me today?" Hannah asked, as they parted to their own homes.

"Grandpa said I needed to go somewhere by myself and said he'd watch Abe. When I saw you this morning I was curious so I followed. Please forgive me. I didn't intend to disturb you. It was fun."

"We'll do it again," Hannah said. "Just don't tell Oat."

"I won't," Maggie said. "I have never told anyone about what happened to me. And I haven't laughed so hard in a long while. It felt good."

As the months passed, Nauvoo became a teeming community

of thousands. Its long, straight streets were lined mainly with log cabins, but there also were some brick homes. On the highest hill the partially constructed walls of the temple rose above the skyline and could be seen from a great distance.

One morning in late March, Hannah joined Geneva Trask for a morning stroll that took them along the river past the lumber mill to the general store.

"How is our little soiled dove friend Maggie?" Geneva asked as they walked. "Does she have another bun in the oven yet?"

Geneva never missed an opportunity to belittle Maggie and her contempt seemed to grow daily.

"I wish you wouldn't speak of Maggie that way," Hannah replied. "She's in a difficult situation. Her grandfather's health is failing, but her son is well. Considering her circumstances, I think she's doing okay."

"Is she? I guess Oat checks on her quite often, doesn't he?"

"Yes, he does."

"I know," said Geneva. "George has commented that Oat seems to visit the MacGregors quite a lot."

"They are our friends. He helps a lot of folks. He helps you and George."

"Yes, and I appreciate that, but in this case I think you should keep a real close eye on Oat. You don't want him helping Maggie with too many things. Desperate women sometimes do desperate things."

"Thanks for your concern Geneva," Hannah said, "though I think it's a bit misplaced."

They walked on in silence.

It was a beautiful spring day and many people were enjoying the sunshine and the agreeable weather. The store was doing a brisk business. Hannah purchased a bag of salt, a spool of thread and a needle for mending Oat's pants in which he constantly tore holes. She also replenished her supply of powder for her pistol. Geneva, not needing to make any purchases, waited outside. When Hannah exited the store she found Geneva in conversation with a prominent and important-looking man she did not know.

"Hannah," Geneva said. "This is my friend, Mayor John Bennett."

Bennett bent forward in a garish, overdone bow. Hannah immediately felt ill at ease.

"It's a pleasure to make the acquaintance of such a beautiful woman," Bennett said rising, his eyes slowly moving over her body from head to toe.

Hannah blushed. It reminded her of being ogled by the pukes in Missouri. She certainly had heard of John Bennett. Everyone knew how he had worked untiringly with the Legislature to obtain a charter for Nauvoo a few years before. Since then he had become prominent not only in the affairs of the city, but also in the church. He had been elected mayor and was one of Joseph's closest associates.

"It's a pleasure to meet you too sir," she said. "I had no idea Geneva had such important friends."

After a few moments of small talk, Bennett invited them to walk with him. They strolled slowly up the street into a section of town where new houses had been built that Hannah never had seen before. So many people were building houses that it was impossible to keep track of them all.

As they walked, Bennett guided the conversation smoothly from one topic to the next. He complimented Hannah at every opportunity saying how he liked the way she had done her hair, how gracefully she walked, the fine features of her face and hands. Soon he asked about Oat, their farm, their house, and even asked her to describe the rooms of her house. Hannah soon wearied of all the questions and thought some of them were a little too personal. After almost a half-hour of constant questioning Hannah wanted to escape.

"I really must be getting along home," she said to Geneva. "Do you want to walk with me?"

"I believe I'll go a little farther with the mayor," Geneva said. "If time allows I'll be along."

Bennett took Hannah's hand, kissed it and again bowed with a great flourish.

"I hope your husband realizes what a lucky man he is," he said. "I am certain none of the angels Joseph has spoken of are as beautiful as you."

Hannah left them and made her way home, uneasy about the

things Geneva had said about Oat and Maggie and her encounter with Bennett. Something was in the wind. Why would Geneva say such things?

A few days later, Geneva visited Hannah. It was the first time in weeks she had come to the Harmon place on a social call. She was all smiles and talk, happily bouncing from one subject to another. She made a few sly, biting comments about Maggie, but mostly wanted to discuss Mayor Bennett, for whom she had formed a great infatuation.

"Isn't he just the most adorable man?" she purred. "He's so knowledgeable and capable. Where would we be without him? He got us the Nauvoo Charter. He has friends all over Illinois. We are so fortunate to have him here. Don't you think?"

"He's very charming Geneva," Hannah said. "But don't you find him a bit flirtatious?"

"Oh no Hannah. You are so prudish and judgmental. You really must get over that. That's just his way. We're invited to his house tomorrow. You've got to come with me. There will be other women there. We're going to organize a women's committee to plan city celebrations. It will be great fun."

Hannah had other plans, but after an hour of relentless coaxing she finally gave in and agreed to go, but with reservations.

"I have to tell you Geneva, that he makes me very uneasy," Hannah said, "I'll go with you but only because you're my friend. What time?"

"Ten-thirty. Come to my place at ten and we'll walk together."

The next day Hannah and Geneva, dressed in their Sunday best, arrived at Bennett's home promptly at ten-thirty. Bennett answered the door to their knock, dressed casually, and invited them into an empty room.

"Where are the others?" Hannah asked immediately.

"I don't know," Geneva said looking questioningly at Bennett. "Where are they John?"

"You are early. The others haven't arrived yet," Bennett said. "There may have been some confusion about the time. Sit down and I'm sure they'll be here shortly."

Hannah placed her bag on the floor and sat down in a rocking chair. Geneva sat in a nearby chair and they all waited together. Bennett began talking about some of his friends in the legislature. Geneva listened enraptured.

"Surely they all couldn't have forgotten," Hannah said after ten minutes. "Something must be wrong?"

Geneva walked to the door and peered out.

"I'll walk to Sister Kimball's and see what's keeping her."

"I'll go with you," Hannah said.

"No please," Geneva said. "Wait here. I'll be right back."

Geneva disappeared, quickly closing the door behind her and leaving Hannah and Bennett alone. Minutes passed and Geneva didn't return. No other women arrived. Bennett had gone quiet and now leered suggestively at her. Hannah became extremely nervous and decided to leave. As she picked up her bag, Bennett moved near and touched her arm.

"Hannah, you are very beautiful. I feel I have known you always and that we were meant to be together."

"I don't feel that way," Hannah said. "And I'm married."

"A few nights ago, after I met you, I had a vision," he said. "I saw the two of us walking arm in arm under a rainbow. Spiritually, I feel extremely close to you, so close that it's like I feel married to you. When that happens between a man and a woman God understands if they're intimate. I believe you are my spiritual wife."

"No," she said. "I don't think so sir."

Hannah tried to stand, but Bennett held her firmly. He moved closer and gripped her shoulders. Hannah's mind whirled. Where was Geneva?

"Geneva could return any time," she said.

"She's my spiritual wife too," he said. "She won't be back this morning."

It all suddenly became clear to Hannah. Geneva had lured her to his house.

"Please let me go sir. I am not your wife, spiritually or otherwise."

He pawed at the front of her dress, holding her left sleeve and trying to kiss her on the lips but she turned her face away, kicking and struggling. They fell onto the floor. In the struggle he ripped the sleeve of her dress. For an instant he lost his grip. She raked her fingernails across his face barely missing his eyes. He rolled away as she got to her feet and picked up her bag. He smiled and wiped blood from his face.

"It's okay Hannah," he said, grinning wickedly as he got to his feet. "I like to wrestle."

As he reached for her. Hannah pulled the pistol from her bag and pointed it at his head. He stopped abruptly.

"You touch me again and I'll put a hole in your head," she said.

"You won't shoot," Bennett said, suppressing a laugh.

She expertly pulled back the hammer and tightened her grip on the gun. She wanted so badly to shoot, to make someone pay for the anger and hate that suddenly surged through her. The hellish memories of her past flashed through her mind and she felt her chin quiver.

"Sir, you have no idea how close you are to dying," she said, her voice cracking. Her finger tightened on the trigger. She struggled for control. Bennett stiffened and backed away.

"Don't shoot. Control yourself woman." Bennett cowered, not able to look at her. It saved his life.

Stepping backward Hannah reached for the door, opened it and stepped outside. She tucked the gun in her bag and walked away from Bennett's house her anger and embarrassment growing by the second. Bennett did not follow. The sleeve of her dress flopped down to her elbow leaving her shoulder bare. She tried to fix it so that it wasn't obvious but it was useless. She walked on bravely while tears streamed down her face. She hated being betrayed. By a friend. A friend had done this to her. Luckily, no one was in the street. She thought about finding Geneva and confronting her. No. She was too angry. But she had to do something. What? Bennett was an important man in the city and in the church. Whom could she talk to? Who could help? Who would believe her?

She sat down under a tree out of sight trying to control her emotions, but found herself weeping uncontrollably. A hand touched her shoulder and she looked up into a kind, familiar face.

"Sister, what's wrong? What happened to you?"

It was Emma Smith, Joseph's wife. She knelt next to Hannah. Taking a shawl from her own shoulders she draped it over Hannah's bare shoulder and then helped Hannah up.

"Come with me," she said.

Emma's presence calmed Hannah. She didn't know Emma well, but she trusted her instinctively. They walked quietly together until they reached the Smith home. By then Hannah was ready to talk. Emma guided her to a chair, and then listened intently as Hannah told her story.

"Wait here," she said when Hannah finished. "I'll be right back."

Stepping outside she flagged down a passing horseman and spoke to him. The rider galloped away. Twenty minutes later Joseph rode up to the house on a saddle horse. He dismounted and hurried inside. Seeing Hannah he bent forward.

"What has happened?"

"Tell him everything you told me," Emma said to Hannah. "He can help you."

Hannah repeated the details of the incident and as she did Joseph leaned back dejectedly in his chair.

"You may not be the first this has happened to," Joseph said quietly. "I received a letter several weeks ago that said John has a wife and children in Ohio. I first thought it was just rumors. They weren't. There have been others. I have reports that Bennett and the Trask woman were carrying on, and I've even heard stories which I again thought were way off the mark, but apparently weren't, of her luring other women to Bennett. You are the first to come forward and give me a firsthand account."

Hannah tied up her loose strings with Geneva that very afternoon. Soon after arriving home she walked straight to the Trask place and pounded on the door.

Geneva swung open the door belligerently and eyed Hannah meanly.

"What do you want?"

"I want to know why you left me alone with John Bennett," Hannah said.

"Because John wanted you. After he met you the other day you're all he talked about, how beautiful you are, your eyes, your hair, your mouth. He asked me to bring you to him so I did."

"We're friends. How could you do that to me?"

Geneva snickered and shook her head.

"Us? Friends? You're no friend of mine you low-born wench. I have nothing but contempt for you. You are naïve and stupid. You believe everything Ol' Joe says. I have no patience with such incredible idiots. So tell me. How did you like John? Did you two have fun after I left?"

Hannah struggled to control her rage as she felt the blood rush to her face. The feeling was familiar. She remembered the same feeling when she and her father encountered the puke when coming out of Missouri. She remembered the satisfaction of knocking the puke to the ground with the rock. She wanted to hurt Geneva.

"After you left? After you abandoned me and left me alone with that lecherous maniac, he wanted to wrestle."

"I'll bet he did and I'll bet he had his way too."

Hannah shook her head.

"He lost interest when I showed him my toy."

"Your toy?" Geneva said, raising her eyebrows wryly. "What toy?"

Hannah pulled the pistol from her bag. Pointing it at Geneva's head, she slowly drew back the hammer as she had done with Bennett. With great satisfaction she watched the smugness drain from Geneva's face. The temptation to shoot rose up inside her again.

"I'm not a sweet little woman. I'm a raging lunatic," Hannah screamed at her. "Something inside me snaps when I'm betrayed by people I trust. I hate it. It's happened too much. Way too much."

The urge to kill Geneva nearly overcame Hannah. Her hands trembled and the gun barrel shook. She felt tears running down her face. Geneva covered her head and sank to the floor. Without lowering the gun, Hannah squeezed the trigger. The gun boomed and the ball tore a hole in the log wall behind the cowering woman. Geneva remained on the floor screaming and begging for Hannah not to kill her. Hannah watched for several moments with great satisfaction, then slammed the door and stalked home.

# 25

WHEN GEORGE TRASK SAW THE HOLE IN HIS WALL HE immediately found the sheriff. After hearing Geneva's version of the event, the sheriff and George rode straight to the Harmon place and demanded that Hannah give them the gun. Oat had not yet returned from the fields and Hannah refused.

"George Trask, you've got worse problems than my pistol," she said. "You best go back home and ask your wife a few more questions."

"All I need to know is that you've been shooting a pistol in my house and I'm here to get that gun."

"You ain't gonna get it."

The sheriff and George then searched out Oat, who was returning from the fields with the Jacquards. They informed him that unless the gun was turned over he would be arrested.

Oat thought the whole thing was some sort of weird joke, until he saw Hannah standing defiantly in front of the house. He knew by her demeanor something was horribly wrong.

"I'm sorry Oat," she said.

"Do you have a gun?" Oat asked.

Hannah nodded.

"Did you shoot it at Geneva Trask?"

"Yes, but unfortunately I missed. Didn't touch her."

"Where's the gun?"

"It's hidden and you ain't getting it."

"Where did you get it?"

"I took it from the puke who shot my father."

"Give it to me."

"No. And don't ask again."

Oat had never seen this side of Hannah. She was adamant about keeping the pistol. It soon became apparent that no amount of coaxing would get it from her. The sheriff was equally perplexed. He could see that Oat couldn't get the pistol from Hannah so he didn't feel right arresting Oat. And he had never arrested a woman and wouldn't know what to do with her if he did. Luckily, Joseph arrived suddenly and the problem took on new dimensions for the sheriff.

"I think I can shed some light on this situation if you'll let me," he said to the sheriff.

"By all means," the sheriff said.

Joseph put his arm on the sheriff's shoulder and the two of them walked about a hundred yards together slowly as Joseph spoke in low tones. Oat, Hannah and George watched them intently. About five minutes later they walked back, the sheriff shaking his head.

"Brother Trask," Joseph called out. "Will you take a walk with me?"

"Yeah," George said. "I want to know what all the secrets are."

Joseph put his arm over George's shoulders like he had the sheriff and they began to walk. The conversation didn't go as well as it had with the sheriff. George grew agitated as he listened. Then, he brushed Joseph's arm away.

"I don't believe that," he yelled. He stalked angrily back to his horse, mounted and rode away. Joseph walked back to Oat and Hannah.

"Have you told Oat what happened?" he asked Hannah.

She shook her head and then told Oat, Joseph and the sheriff how she had been lured to Bennett's house by Geneva, how she had escaped and her subsequent visit to the Trask home.

"I suppose I should feel sorry about shooting the gun in their house," she said defiantly. "But I'm not. And don't ask for the gun because its hidden and I won't give it up."

In normal times, the news that a woman with a pistol had shot up a neighbor's house would have consumed Nauvoo. It hardly caused a ripple. George and Geneva Trask said no more about the incident and made no demands of the sheriff. In the end, few people actually heard about the shooting because more dramatic and controversial events captured their attention.

Within days, Bennett was excommunicated from the church and forced to resign as mayor. The incident with Hannah was just the tip of a scandalous iceberg. To this point Bennett had been adored and respected by nearly everyone in the city. In addition to his duties as mayor, he had been serving as assistant president of the church in the absence of Sidney Rigdon, who had returned to his home in Pittsburgh.

Bennett's excommunication came at a bad time for the church. Businessmen and leaders in neighboring towns had hoped to profit from the influx of Mormons to the area. But the Mormons traded almost exclusively amongst themselves and developed a thriving economy from which the neighboring communities didn't benefit. Nauvoo grew and the Mormons built their own businesses. Jealousy grew. The newcomers attracted the suspicions and hate from the older communities. Anti-Mormon sentiment and hate began to blossom. Bennett was happy to add fuel to their vivid imaginations. Prominent residents of nearby communities began to accuse the church of all sorts of black deeds from petty theft of tools to murder and conspiracy to take over the state government.

Oat encountered George in the fields between their places a few weeks later.

"I heard Bennett's getting quite a following over in Warsaw," George said. "I'm afraid your friend Joseph will regret this. Bennett throws around plenty of weight in this state."

"Isn't Joseph your friend too, George?" Oat asked sharply.

"I obviously am not as good a friend as you and Hannah are. And I find him to be something of a hypocrite, especially in this Bennett thing."

"Hypocrite. Why?"

"Oh come on Oat, you know. People have been talking about it for months."

The polygamy rumors usually were printed in newspapers in neighboring towns whose editors were avowed enemies of the church. The rumors were troubling.

"George, I don't want to hear about polygamy," Oat said. "Joseph is my friend. About every week I hear some new rumor about some awful thing he has done or said. Mostly they're not true."

"Okay, you don't want to hear about the polygamy abomination. Did you hear about Boggs?"

"What about Boggs?"

"Somebody tried to kill him," George said. "He was at home and somebody shot him through a window. He's still alive though."

Oat suppressed an urge to jump up and down and cheer. Practically every man and woman he knew hated Boggs. No tears would be shed for him at Nauvoo. If he died there likely would be wild celebrations.

"Happened a few weeks ago and he's apparently going to live." George said. "Going to be hell to pay Oat."

As far as Oat was concerned the only bad part of George's story was the former Missouri governor survived.

"Why?"

"Some people say that whoever did it acted on orders from your friend Joseph."

Oat sighed and shook his head.

"I used to live in Jackson County, George," Oat said. "I knew Boggs, even had dealings with him. He had my father murdered and he tried to kill me. He was governor four years and made more enemies than just the Mormons, including me. I have a better reason to kill Boggs than Joseph does. I doubt Joseph had anything to do with it."

When Oat arrived home, Hannah was preparing supper.

The news about Boggs didn't phase her.

"I wish whoever did it was a better shot," she said simply. "I would have finished the job."

Hannah's bitterness toward Missouri never ebbed and Oat knew she nurtured an overpowering desire for revenge. Whenever she spoke of "that day in Far West" her eyes narrowed and her jaw clenched. At least once every few months she awoke in the middle of the night bathed in sweat and sobbing. And though he questioned her about it and knew that something awful had happened, she never told him the entire story. The only hint came once when she said: "I love you Oat, but you wouldn't understand."

It was ironic she had married Oat because as far as she was

concerned all Missourians were pukes. She never showed the pistol to Oat, probably fearing he would take it. After hearing how she used it to defend herself against Bennett and to scare the wits out of Geneva Trask, Oat didn't mind that she had it, but he never told her that.

Once Oat learned about the pistol, Hannah enjoyed telling how she got it. She took great pains describing the sound of the stone hitting the puke in the head with a "dull, hollow pop like when you thump a melon" and she liked to tell how the man fell forward onto his face. She embellished the story each time she told it, and always wondered aloud about that puke saying he probably got mad as a hornet when he came to and found his horse missing. The story always made her grin broadly. It was so out of character from every other aspect of her personality that it worried Oat.

Whenever she told the story Oat remembered the dead man he found coming out of Missouri. He never told Hannah about the body. He figured she had enough to worry about.

# 26

THAT NOVEMBER HANNAH ANNOUNCED SHE WAS GOING to have a baby. The news brought a sigh of relief to Oat. Hannah craved children. When she saw babies at church she begged to hold them. When opportunities to watch small children arose she readily accepted and could occupy them for hours playing the small pointless games they invented. Some nights Oat awakened to Hannah's quiet sobs and when he asked what was wrong the answer was always the same.

"It's nothing. I'm okay. Sorry to wake you."

But he knew why. Her sadness infected him. Oat wanted a child too. He wanted to be a father. He wanted as many children as Hannah could bear, boys or girls, it didn't matter which, the more the better. He wanted a large close-knit, strong family, the type of family he had often seen but never experienced.

After nearly fourteen months, neither could imagine why it had taken so long but the wait was forgotten as a mood of contentment and happiness settled around them. The days and weeks passed. Oat doted on Hannah at every opportunity except for the days when he left to work on the temple.

For her part Hannah enjoyed the attention, though to Oat's chagrin, she pursued her normal activities. She carried water, split wood and chased livestock every day. She liked to prove that she could do almost anything that Oat could, including harness and work the Jacquards. In many ways she puzzled him. She had been hurt in Missouri, not physically, much deeper in a way he couldn't quite determine. He often wondered if her efforts to prove herself physically were an attempt to hide something she had resolved to bury deep inside.

"I'm not afraid of many things Oat," she said once. "Not after

Missouri. I just hate a lot more."

Oat often stopped what he was doing in the fields just to watch her walk about the yard as she did her chores. The work that brought Geneva Trask down into bed weekly was nothing to Hannah. Her bearing thrilled him, the grace, the inner strength, the natural sway of her hips, the confidence in her face. At times as Oat watched he would smile and thank God he was so blessed. Yet sometimes a wild fierceness would come over her and her eyes would seem like those of a trapped animal. Over time he came to realize that Hannah fought a battle of which he knew very little.

By the following spring Hannah's stomach was huge. Often as they sat together after supper Hannah would pull his hand to her stomach. She smiled and her eyes danced as they both felt the baby squirm and kick. He loved her all the more for it.

As close as Hannah could predict, the baby would be born sometime in July. The month of June was unbearably hot and Hannah, her stomach swollen to the bursting point, was miserable. She couldn't relax and sleep was elusive.

One hot afternoon toward the end of the month, Hannah sat in the shade of the house, her feet in a bucket of water and a damp cloth on her brow. It was too hot for work and the animals had taken refuge in the shade. The Jacquards stood head to tail under a large elm about a hundred yards west of the house, their giant tails swishing back and forth to ward off the flies. Oat sat near Hannah trying to make her comfortable.

That was the day Joseph chose to visit.

They saw the dust from his carriage while it still was a ways off and both hoped it was no one coming to see them. When Hannah saw the occupant of the carriage she nearly fainted. Struggling to her feet she attempted to escape into the house before he saw her but it was too late.

"Don't go," he called to her. "Please sit down."

Hannah slumped back into her chair, suddenly too exhausted to care how she looked even though the most prominent and revered man in their part of the world had come to visit.

Joseph stopped the carriage and climbed down. He stepped into the shade and went to Hannah, taking her hand and patting it gently.

"Please forgive me for coming today. I know its hot and miserable and its a dirty trick for me to do this to you, but I must speak to both of you."

Joseph presence charged the atmosphere. Oat felt refreshed and noticed that Hannah perked up too. The air wasn't any cooler, but the company was livelier.

"Don't apologize," Hannah said. "You are always welcome."

Joseph arranged his chair so his back was to the house and leaned back.

"You have a beautiful farm. I've seen you and those big horses at work on the temple too. Your help is very much appreciated."

Whatever Joseph had come to talk about, it made him nervous, something Oat had never seen before. The past months had been hard for him. His Missouri enemies were trying everything they could dream of to extradite him to stand trial for the shooting of Boggs. Bennett and Boggs had joined forces to discredit and arrest him, but so far he had outmaneuvered them. Bennett had published a sleazy tract about Joseph and the church and now was lecturing in every town where he could find an audience.

But persecution was second nature to Joseph. He had lived his entire life with it. Oat sensed something else weighing heavily on the man and he guessed that it had to do with rumors circulating throughout Nauvoo. The city was restless. According to rumor, even some of the inner circle in the church's hierarchy were conspiring against Joseph.

"I'll warn you that this won't be easy on either of you," Joseph said, fixing his gaze on Oat. "Do you remember the conversation we had about receiving new knowledge from God and how we are under an obligation to live by it."

"Yes, I remember that," Oat said. "I'm surprised you do."

"I wouldn't be here if you hadn't said what you did," Joseph said. "I have some things to teach you, but I caution you that once I tell you this, you'll be under an obligation to live by it."

Oat and Hannah looked back and forth at each other. Oat felt a sense of excitement and a grand curiosity, tempered by a feeling of foreboding.

Oat imagined Joseph would ask him to go to New England or perhaps even to England on a mission for the church. Other brethren had been called to fill similar missions. The thought of leaving Hannah and a new child for a long period distressed him, but others had done it. He and Hannah already had resolved to do their part if asked.

"I believe I can," Oat said. Joseph took a long deep look into Oat's eyes. Then Joseph turned to Hannah.

"Hannah, can you?"

Hannah looked back at Joseph for a long moment before saying anything. He waited patiently and as the time passed Oat got the impression that Hannah knew already what he was about to tell them.

Finally she said: "Yes, I can do it."

"You've read the Old Testament, haven't you Oat?" Joseph said.

Oat nodded. He and Hannah had struggled through it the previous winter.

"Many of the old patriarchs had more than one wife. Some had many wives. The Lord wants you to do the same."

Shocked, Oat looked at Hannah. Her face was a stone. He couldn't read a thing in her eyes. For the next hour Joseph explained the doctrine of plural marriage using Bible scriptures and his own persuasive personality. Oat asked questions and Hannah listened, following every word. Oat watched her closely, trying to read her thoughts by studying her eyes and face, but could see nothing. Finally Joseph finished.

"I didn't expect this," he said, looking forlornly at Joseph. "I thought you were going to send me on a mission."

"I know," he said. "but we need you here. You may be the best farmer in Nauvoo. You and Hannah must accept and live by this doctrine."

They sat uneasily. Hannah hadn't spoken and her silence bothered Oat.

"So it's true," Oat said. "You have other wives besides Emma?"

Joseph nodded.

"When will Oat need to marry again?" Hannah asked suddenly. "And who will it be?"

Joseph leaned back again against the wall of the house.

"Normally I would say that would be up to the two of you, but I have a suggestion," he said.

Oat braced himself. Joseph's suggestions carried more weight than most men's commandments.

"You know about Brother MacGregor, don't you?" he asked.

Both Oat and Hannah were painfully aware of the MacGregor family's plight. Orrin had collapsed while working alone in the fields east of the Harmon farm. It had occurred only a few days earlier. When Maggie found him, she had come to Oat and Hannah for help.

"He can speak slowly, but he can't walk. He can't take care of his farm anymore and Maggie has her child to care for and now her grandfather. You know the situation. Maggie can take care of them, but she can't handle the farm too. Their house isn't much more than a shed and Brother MacGregor will die soon."

Hannah visited Maggie only the day before. She returned home depressed and worried. It didn't take a prophet to see that Maggie's future was bleak. Oat had begun tending the MacGregor's crops.

"I visited Brother MacGregor last night," Joseph went on. "He can barely speak, but he made me promise to care for Maggie when he dies. I promised him that I would even though I didn't know how I was going to keep it. I worried and prayed about it all the way home and I fell asleep troubled."

Joseph paused and took a sip of water.

"I had a dream. I saw you and your two big horses. Hannah rode one of the horses. Maggie was on the other. This morning I went back to the MacGregor place again. He's worse than yesterday. He didn't know me, but I spoke to Maggie and I told her generally the same thing I told you except I didn't tell her about the dream and I didn't mention you. I believe the Lord wants you to marry her Oat."

Oat liked Maggie. If not for Hannah, he would have asked her to marry him despite her problems, but it hadn't happened that way. He looked at Hannah, so miserable yet so brave and suddenly felt very guilty.

Oat stood up. The afternoon shadows had extended into early evening and a cool breeze now blew from the Northwest.

"Can we talk about this?" he asked Joseph.

Joseph nodded: "Pray about it too."

Oat and Hannah stood silently in deep thought until Joseph's carriage disappeared in a cloud of dust. Then Oat walked to the barn to do his evening chores while Hannah prepared their evening meal.

After a troubled hour Oat returned to the house to find supper on the table and Hannah waiting for him. He sat down and stared at the tabletop for several moments before looking up to see Hannah watching him.

"You're troubled Oat," she said.

He nodded: "I can't do it Hannah."

"Why?"

"First of all, my mother would disown me."

"If I can accept it, so can your mother. You don't live with your mother. You live with me."

"She has a child," he said sternly and as he uttered the words he saw his young wife wince. She looked away and her chin quivered. After a moment she composed herself then slowly, deliberately, cleared her dishes from the table and placed them on the stove. It seemed as though she was taking great effort to control herself. Then she started for the door.

Oat rose from his chair and stood in her path. She extended her arms and held him at arm's length.

"I could be just like Maggie," she said quietly. "The only reason I am not is because at Far West I had a mother who protected me. Maggie didn't. She and my mother, and I don't know how many other women went through hell there. It wasn't Maggie's fault she had that baby alone."

"I'm sorry," Oat said. "I didn't mean to sound judgmental."

"Do you believe Joseph is a prophet?" she asked.

"Yes I do," he said.

"So do I," she said. "It is the basis of all my hopes. If he is not a prophet, then all the things my Mama and Papa suffered and that I have suffered have been for nothing. If he is not, then this is a useless, wicked world that may as well not exist because it would hold no hope."

"I believe Joseph is a prophet," Oat said.

"Then do what he asked."

Tears welled up in her eyes.

"But Hannah I thought it would make you unhappy and hurt you if I . . ."

"Don't worry about me," she cut him off. "I am much stronger than you apparently think. This is nothing compared to what's happened before. I've lost my home twice, Oat. I saw my mother suffer and die. She and my three little brothers lie in cold lonesome graves somewhere between here and Far West. My daddy went to his grave because of a wound he got trying to protect me. They gave everything and did everything asked of them until they couldn't anymore. And I will not soil their memories by refusing to do something the prophet asks because it might offend your mother or some witch like Geneva Trask."

"Hannah, I just want to be with you," Oat said. "I don't want anyone else."

Hannah opened the door.

"Maggie and her child need a home. I like Maggie. She's my friend and we understand each other. If I have any choice on the woman I share my food, my home and my husband with, then I want it to be her."

The next few days passed silently between Hannah and Oat. They didn't speak of Joseph's visit. Despite the heat, Oat spent the time hoeing and hilling corn, working methodically while deep in thought, avoiding much time at the house and trying to work out the confusing set of problems that had been set before him.

Despite the heat Hannah walked with Oat to visit the MacGregors and then stayed a few hours to watch Abe and tend to Orrin's need while Maggie got some rest.

Early on the third day after Joseph's visit, Maggie and Abe walked into their yard and told them her grandfather had died the night before. Maggie eyes were red, but she was calm.

"Grandpa is at peace now," she said solemnly. "I don't have to worry about him any more. He's in a good place."

Later, Oat walked to the cemetery and dug the grave for his friend.

Joseph conducted a graveside funeral service the next day and later Oat filled in the grave. Arriving home later in the afternoon he found Hannah in their kitchen with supper on the table. They ate in the same tense silence they had shared since Joseph's visit. He didn't like it. As he had thought and worried about his predicament he realized if Hannah was agreeable, he could do what he had been asked to do.

"Are you certain you understand your feelings about what Joseph asked us to do?" he asked Hannah.

"I understand what he told us and I know how I feel," she replied.

"Are you still agreeable?"

"Nothing's changed. I can do what he asked?"

"Then I'm going to go see what Maggie thinks of Joseph's idea," Oat said. "Do you want to come with me?"

"No," she said. "I would be in the way. You best do that yourself."

At Maggie's front door Oat heard singing inside and it wasn't hard to discern Maggie's strong voice in the melody.

Oat knocked, while studying the poor condition of the house. A moment later Maggie appeared in the doorway. She smiled brightly.

"May I come in?" he said.

"Abe's asleep," she said, stepping outside. They walked slowly away from the house. Oat squirmed uneasily and searched for words. Maggie rescued him.

"You came to ask me to be your second wife, didn't you?" Maggie said abruptly.

"How did you know?" Oat asked.

"After Joseph's visit a few days ago I have been expecting someone to come. I'm glad it's you and not someone else."

He took her hand and she faced him.

"I'll make you a good home and I'll love you," he said.

"The most important thing to me Oat is that my son grows up having a father and a name," she said. "I don't want him to know about my troubles. Are you willing to be a father to my son? Will you love him, give him your name and treat him like your own son?"

"Yes," he said.

"Are you sure you want me? Most men wouldn't."

"I want you. You are a lovely woman. Do you want to be a second wife?" he asked. "Most women wouldn't."

"To you?" she said. "Yes, You're a gentle, kind man."

"Then I'm sure," he said. "I love Hannah very much, but I love you too. And I have been worried about you for some time now. I would be very unhappy if you were to marry someone else."

"How does Hannah feel about this?"

"I wouldn't be here if Hannah hadn't pushed me out the door."

Maggie smiled: "Hannah's a generous person. She's like a big sister to me."

They stopped walking near the edge of a wheat field about thirty yards from the house. Oat took her by the hand and knelt on one knee, the same as when he proposed to Hannah.

"Maggie, will you marry me?" he said.

"Will you love me as much as you love Hannah?"

"Yes."

"Will you look at me the way you look at her?"

"Yes."

"Then, yes, I will marry you."

The next Thursday morning dawned bright and cheery. In the late afternoon Oat returned to the house to find a note from Hannah: "I have gone to help Maggie get ready for tonight. Don't be late."

During the preceding days she insisted that Maggie move into the little house, the one Hannah's father had lived in until his death. The preceding winter Oat had made it into a tack room and shop. It was right next to their house, was warm and comfortable and had enough room for both Maggie and Abe. The tack could go back to the barn. The house was considerably better quarters than the sod house Maggie and Abe had been living in. Oat, Hannah and Maggie worked all week transporting Maggie's belongings and getting it ready.

Oat was concerned that Hannah had walked into town. It was a fair distance and that may not be good for her in her condition, but she was gone and there was nothing to do about it now. He ate a lunch of cold stew and bread and then harnessed the Jacquards. He found his best clothes lying on the bed. He washed and put them on. He arrived at Joseph's red, brick store just after seven o'clock.

Joseph met him at the door, escorted him to the second floor of the building, then shut and locked the door so they would not be disturbed. Hannah and Maggie already were waiting as was Joseph's brother Hyrum. Maggie stood side-by-side with Hannah, dressed in white, as radiant and pretty as any bride he ever had seen. Maggie had made arrangements for Abe to be tended for the night by the old Englishwoman who tutored her. Hannah, still swollen with child, smiled at him.

"You look very handsome," Hannah whispered softly when he got close.

Oat and Hannah had been sealed several months prior so Oat was familiar with the ceremony. He led Maggie to the altar where they kneeled. Joseph spoke for several minutes about the new and everlasting covenant as they knelt together. Oat didn't hear much of what he said. The emotions and thoughts inside his head were such a jumble that he couldn't really think. He glanced at Hannah from time to time for reassurance. She smiled back at him. He would never understand that.

Joseph soon pronounced the same words and blessings he had pronounced upon Hannah and Oat months earlier finally sealing them together for time and eternity. When he finished Joseph leaned forward and said: "You may kiss your wife now Brother Harmon."

Oat leaned forward and kissed Maggie lightly. Upon standing he and Maggie shook hands with and accepted congratulations from Joseph and Hyrum. Then with darkness closing around them, Oat seated himself between his two wives and drove home.

# 27

THE BABY CAME THAT NIGHT. THE MINUTE THEY ARRIVED home Hannah went into labor. Oat carried her into the house and laid her on the bed. Maggie helped her get undressed while Oat left immediately to get the midwife who lived three miles away. Hattie Christensen, a gruff and outspoken woman who previously had lived in eastern Pennsylvania, took her time getting ready to go.

"Don't be worried," she said. "It's her first. We'll be there in plenty of time."

But when he and Sister Christensen arrived back at the Harmon farm well after dark, it was all over. The strong wailing of a tiny baby lilted through the evening air as Oat reined in the Jacquards in front of the house and hurried inside. He found Hannah lying with the child beside her. Maggie sat on a chair near the bed sponging Hannah's brow.

"I tried to wait for you Oat, but he just wouldn't wait," she said smiling weakly as Oat knelt at the bedside. "Maggie helped me."

The baby boy grimaced and squirmed. Oat reached out and touched its hands. The child's tiny hand closed ever so softly around his calloused finger.

"My timing was very bad," Hannah said to Maggie as Oat examined the child.

"Please don't apologize," Maggie said. "You should rest now. Sister Christensen and I will take care of the baby."

"I'm very cold," Hannah said, shivering. Oat spread additional bedding over her and then sat near holding Hannah's hand until she drifted off to sleep.

Maggie picked up the child and she and the midwife bathed it in warm water while it squirmed and cried. Oat's eyes remained glued to it the entire time, awed by the realization that he was now a father and that he had taken part in the creation of a new living soul. It appeared so fragile, small and helpless. He was afraid to touch it at first, but its small cries and the grotesque faces it made magnetized him. This was his son, his flesh and blood, his future. After they were finished, Maggie wrapped the boy in a small blanket and placed him in Oat's arms.

"You two should get a little better acquainted," she said.

While Oat rocked the baby, Maggie and the midwife made beds for themselves on the floor. Oat rocked the baby for almost an hour as Maggie and the older woman drifted off to sleep and then placed it in a small crib he and Hannah had built for it. Returning to his chair, he sat down and fell asleep.

He was awakened at dawn with Maggie frantically shaking his arm.

"Oat, Hannah's got an awful fever."

Sister Christensen stood over Hannah, a hand on her brow, and a worried look on her face.

"She burning up," the midwife said.

The three worked frantically for the next hour sponging Hannah's body with cool, wet rags. Hannah moaned and moved when the rags touched her skin, but she didn't awaken completely. Then she vomited.

"You best go get a doctor," Sister Christensen said finally to Oat. "She's delirious. We'll take care of her while you're gone."

Oat rushed out of the house to find the Jacquards standing before him in full harness. In all the excitement the night before he had forgotten to unharness them. They had stood obediently in the same spot all night patiently waiting for him to put them away and feed them. He felt a rush of affection for the huge beasts.

"Jack, Molly, I'm sorry," he said out loud to them, but inside he was glad they were ready. The Jacquards sensed the urgency of the moment and held up a hard gallop all the way into Nauvoo, blowing hard when Oat pulled them to a stop at Dr. Jensen's home. And when the doctor and Oat emerged from the house they galloped all the way back. This time Oat didn't forget them. The doctor insisted Oat stay outside the house while he examined Hannah, so while he waited Oat unharnessed the horses, watered and fed them generously and then brushed them. As he released them into the pasture the doctor came out of the house.

"Hannah has severe ague," he said, shaking his head. "It's life threatening because she's weak right now. I've given her quinine, but right now about all we can do is help her fight the fever."

The doctor stayed for a few hours until a carriage arrived to take him on another call. He promised to return soon.

For the next four days Hannah alternated between chills and fever. She would get extremely hot and delirious and during these bouts both Oat and Maggie wiped cool, wet cloths over her skin. Then the fever would break and she shivered for hours. Then the entire process repeated itself. She hardly noticed when the baby nursed and her breathing was labored. The doctor, Sister Christensen and several neighbors visited during this time, some bringing food, some offering ideas that might help. But there was little anyone could do but wait and see if Hannah's strength would hold out.

On the evening of the fourth day Joseph and Hyrum paid a brief visit. Joseph entered the room quietly and went straight to Hannah. Placing his hands on her head, he blessed her and told her she would survive to raise many children.

"She will be fine," he said to Oat as he rose. "Have faith."

Only a few minutes later he and Hyrum left as quickly and as quietly as they had come.

Maggie's presence was a stroke of good fortune. She cared for the new child, as well as Abe who now was four years old. She fed the baby goats milk the Lott family had thoughtfully brought by when Hannah couldn't nurse. She also prepared their meals, and helped Oat bathe Hannah and change her bed, caring for her when Oat milked the cow and fed the horses. Five days after the baby's birth, Oat awakened in his chair to find Hannah sitting up in bed nursing the baby. Her eyes, though tired, were clear and she smiled at him.

"What shall we name him?" she asked.

He rose from his chair and went to the bed where he sat down on the edge near her.

"Do you have a suggestion?"

She nodded: "Andrew Jerome Harmon. After our fathers."

"I like that," he said.

She kissed him on the cheek.

"I'm going to be okay," she said.

During the next few weeks Hannah steadily improved gaining strength each day and slowly taking up her work again. Oat returned to the fields and their lives assumed a certain rhythm. Oat soon realized his life would never be the same again because his family had more than doubled in one day. The new baby cried often in the middle of the night causing them to lose sleep and during their waking hours soaked up constant attention which they happily gave. While the child was a joy, it was also a task. Maggie and Abe added another dimension that took some getting used to. Abe adopted Oat easily the first time he was hoisted onto Molly's back. A short ride around the yard turned into an hour of smiles and giggling. He cried when he had to get down. Maggie was shy and quiet in a way Oat never had known her to be. She divided up the household duties with Hannah and was always willing to help with the baby. As Hannah gained back her strength and resumed most of the household tasks, Maggie worked with Oat in the fields.

# 28

AFTER FOUR YEARS IN THE MOUNTAINS, THE CLUSTER of stores and houses that made up the township of Independence looked odd to Glaze. The place had changed radically during his absence. The city was larger and there were many more people, mostly settlers, including women and children. All appeared determined to go west. They wore cotton or wool clothing although an occasional beaver skin hat could be seen bobbing up and down the street even though it was said they no longer were in style. For the most part style did not matter to the people who lived on the edge of the frontier. And if it did, the more weighty matters of survival soon made it seem meaningless.

West of town thousands of these settlers, some quite starched and strait-laced, were quartered in an immense encampment, and would have looked like an army preparing for battle had it not been for the children. For days, as Glaze and Tucker rode eastward across the prairie leading their pack animals, they met dozens of wagons going in the opposite direction toward the lonesome, far-off places from which they had just returned.

In front of the courthouse Glaze tied the chestnut. The hitching rail brought to his memory the vicious fight the animal had gotten into with Oat Harmon's big gray the last time it stood here. Spitting a stream of tobacco juice onto the ground, he walked inside. Tucker kept going down the street to the nearest tavern. Tucker, Pepper and the two trappers Glaze met in Independence the day Otis Harmon escaped from Jackson County had been the only white men with whom he had conversed for four years, except for those they met at rendezvous. Though his retreat into the west had been eventful and memorable, it now was time to settle unfinished business. That business concerned Governor Boggs, it concerned Joe Smith and it most certainly concerned Otis Harmon — if Glaze could find him.

Four years earlier, Glaze had pursued Harmon for days after Harmon and his big horses had destroyed the ferry, a sight which he still couldn't believe he had seen and which provoked Tucker to call him a liar whenever he mentioned it. He and the others rode downstream to the next ferry, but by the time they crossed the river that night it was dark and by morning a heavy rain had washed away Harmon's tracks. Harmon got away clean.

Remembering the governor's state of mind the last time he saw him, Glaze had been afraid of what Boggs might do in a fit of anger, so he prudently decided to give the governor some distance and time to cool off. He hid out in the Missouri River bottoms near Tucker's place and waited for Tucker, Pepper and Ward to return from Gallatin and join him. Otherwise, he worried he might end up like old Turvey, floating belly down in the Missouri with his head cut off.

Going west seemed like the perfect solution. Tucker and Pepper both were delighted with the idea. Old Ward wasn't, so he stayed in Missouri saying he was too old to be chased by Indians. With the two buffalo hunters, Glaze, Tucker and Pepper traversed lonesome prairies and rugged, frigid mountains. They trapped beaver, hunted buffalo and fought Indians. Significantly, all survived except Pepper. Pepper, tremendously fat and hideously slow, was killed in an Indian ambush along the Flathead River the second year out. A Blackfeet hunting party surprised Glaze and Pepper as they skinned a buffalo near an aspen grove one evening at dusk. Luckily for Glaze the chestnut stud was only three steps away. Glaze mounted and easily outran the Indian ponies. Pepper tried to reach his horse too and had been far too slow. The Blackfeet literally skinned him alive. Glaze heard and remembered the screams, but dared not return until a week later after finding Tucker and the others. A pair of grizzlies were feeding on Pepper's carcass and Glaze and Tucker saw no point in fighting with the beasts over the remains. Pepper was dead and it didn't matter much to them whether he was buried or eaten by bears. In fact, the bears saved them the trouble of burying him.

Inside the courthouse Glaze confronted a clerkish looking man with big glasses and suspenders.

"Governor Boggs still live in the same place he did four years ago?" Glaze asked as the clerk grimaced and squirmed. Glaze wanted to get squared up with the governor so he wouldn't have to watch his back all the time. He hoped four years would have taken the edge off the man's anger.

"Boggs is no longer governor," the clerk said hardly looking up from his ledger. "He was defeated in the last election by Thomas Reynolds. He took the defeat very hard but he's still active in politics. At least he was until he was shot last year."

"Shot?" Glaze repeated.

The clerk shuffled a pile of papers and looked up.

"Yup. Last year Mr. Boggs was shot and nearly killed in his own home. Everyone thought he would die, but he didn't."

Glaze tapped his fingernail on the counter that separated him from the clerk while he digested the information.

"Who shot him?"

"Most people think Porter Rockwell did it for Joe Smith."

Rockwell shoot Boggs? Rockwell was one of Smith's close friends and had a reputation as a topnotch gunman. It was a well-known fact in Missouri that Rockwell would do anything for Smith.

"Who do you think did it?"

"Me?" the clerk acted surprised but didn't look up. "Don't know. The Mormons certainly hate Boggs."

"Is he at home?" Glaze asked.

"I don't know," the clerk said, still not looking up.

Glaze walked out of the courthouse and down the street to the tavern where Tucker's horses stood tied to another hitching rail. Inside Tucker already was telling tales of their exploits in the west. A group of locals had gathered around and were being royally entertained. Tucker stopped his storytelling long enough to acknowledge Glaze.

"Hey Glaze," he shouted. "You remember old man Ward, who used to drive wagon for us all the time. You know, Creech's uncle. He died a year ago. These guys say his skin and eyes turned yellow and then he just up and died, just like 'Ol Joe said he would. You remember that?"

Glaze didn't want to hear it. Thoughts of Joe Smith had

tormented him for four years and after Pepper had been killed Tucker talked for three days about how Ol' Joe prophesied that Pepper would be scalped and eaten by bears. Glaze hated Smith and didn't care if anything Ol' Joe said came to pass or not. It didn't make any difference only perhaps to rankle him further. He sat down and asked for beer.

Tucker returned to his story and Glaze listened for a while. He had heard Tucker spin yarns for hours on end and never tired of it. Tucker could make a trip to the privy sound like an exotic adventure. The men all were thirsty for stories and information about the high mountains. Many either had been there and returned or expected to go there someday and they eagerly asked question after question then listened intently to Tucker's answers which usually resulted in some wild, yet not altogether false tale. They shared a jug of corn whiskey and spit into a brass pot in the middle of the floor thoroughly enjoying themselves.

Glaze sat apart from them, but he listened and occasionally Tucker would point at Glaze when telling a story and the men would turn and look at him. For an hour Glaze listened as Tucker told about the spouts of hot water they had seen shooting out of the ground on the Yellowstone and the grizzlies and hostile Indians they fought. Even Glaze was amazed as he listened. He had lived these tales, but still it was captivating to hear Tucker relate them. He remembered details and made up parts that made them more interesting. The men sat about him intently hanging on every word. The Indian stories intrigued them most so Tucker told how Pepper was killed. Though he hadn't been there he could tell the story better than Glaze. Later he related tale after tale of their encounters with the tribes.

"Just this spring coming out of winter camp me and Glaze surprised a small camp of Cheyenne just this side of the Yellowstone. Not often that you can surprise an Indian, but we did. They put up a hell of a fight. We killed two bucks and a squaw and the rest ran into the brush while we helped ourselves to their food, horses and furs."

Tucker described their booty and then sat pensively for a few seconds, his brow wrinkled.

"We found two small injuns hiding under blankets in one of the tepees, quiet as a pair of gophers, barely able to walk. Must have been kids of the dead squaw. Anyway, when we found 'em and kicked 'em outside they started crawling all over the squaw's body and bawling and making a racket you probably heard here in Independence. We knocked 'em around a bit trying to get 'em to shut up, but it just got worse."

Tucker took a long swig of beer and then held the mug out.

"Glaze finally got fed up with their noise. It was awful loud and it was hard for a man to concentrate especially when you're familiar to silence. So Glaze there grabbed each one of them by the hair of the head like this."

Tucker held his mug of beer out and grabbed another mug that was sitting on the table. He held them out in front demonstrating how Glaze had held the two young Indians.

"He knew how to shut em up."

Tucker became quiet. The men leaned forward trying to hear.

"How?" one of listeners asked after several seconds of silence.

Tucker slammed the two mugs together sending beer and glass shards spraying around the room, then slapped his leg with a loud guffaw. The glass cut his hands and he bled but he was oblivious to it and continued to laugh and slap his thigh. The onlookers gaped at him, then at Glaze. Glaze glared back, then stood up and walked out while Tucker drunkenly laughed and laughed.

After identifying himself at the Boggs home, Glaze waited ten minutes before a woman showed him into a room where Boggs lay in a bed reading a St. Louis newspaper. He was fully dressed and appeared to have recovered from his wound, but he didn't move very quickly. When Glaze entered Boggs threw the newspaper onto the floor and glared at him.

"I was hoping you was dead," he said.

"Nope. Went west for a while," Glaze said as Boggs scowled.

"If you'd done your job right when you had the chance this wouldn't have happened to me and I'd probably still be governor," he said sitting up slowly.

"Like I said the last time I saw you, it wasn't my fault. Somebody tipped Harmon off."

Boggs grimaced as he shifted his weight on the bed.

"You still think that, do you?"

"I know that," Glaze said. "Fact is that's why I came to see you.

To straighten that out once and for all."

"Okay then," Boggs said settling into a position that apparently was comfortable. "Straighten it out."

Glaze sat down on a chair near the bed.

"I saw Bufflehead at Rendezvous on the Green River two years ago."

Boggs jerked his head around sharply and made another face.

"Did you talk to him?"

"No, not at Rendezvous. There were too many other things going on and I had business. He didn't know me anyway."

Glaze unsheathed his hunting knife and cleaned his fingernails with the point while Boggs watched and listened.

"When Rendezvous broke up Bufflehead moved north toward the Yellowstone with a few Shoshones and another white man. We followed 'em 'bout a half day behind. Me and Tucker. Anyway I kept an eye on him for several weeks until winter closed in and he moved out by himself to lay out his traps. That's when I talked to him."

Boggs reached to a bedstand for a cup which he sipped at as he listened, his eyes still fastened on Glaze. He said nothing.

"He was putting out a bear trap when I walked up on him. He was getting pretty old and not too sharp. He didn't see or hear me. I'm surprised he survived as long as he did in Indian country. He was baiting the trap and had both his hands in just the wrong spot when I tripped it. Trap nearly cut his hands off at the wrists. Anyway, he was bound up like an animal with both hands caught."

Boggs stared back at him without blinking and took another sip from his cup. Glaze shifted around on his chair.

"He begged me to let him loose and I told him I would if he'd tell me what he had told Oat Harmon. It took him a while, but he finally remembered. He told Harmon about you and me and about the ambush and how we were going to kill everybody. That's how Harmon was tipped off."

"You could have made up this entire story," Boggs said, shaking his head. "You've told me nothing that's convinced me you even saw Bufflehead let alone made him talk to you."

Glaze shrugged: "Not so far. But Bufflehead told me a few other little tidbits. He told me that he killed Harmon's father years ago and that you paid him fifty dollars to do it. Now, that's something I hadn't known before. Does that convince you?"

Boggs met his gaze obviously impressed.

"Maybe," he said. "Did you let him go?"

"No point in it," Glaze said, shaking his head. "His wrists were broken and he would have bled to death anyway so I left him."

"You could have put him out of his misery."

"Waste of powder," Glaze said, shaking his head. "What's the matter? You suddenly have a soft spot for Bufflehead?"

Boggs closed his eyes tiredly, leaned back on a pillow and smiled.

"Far as I'm concerned Bufflehead got what he deserved. I just wanted to be sure he's dead."

"He is," Glaze said. "That trap was chained to a tree. Bufflehead is still there. Least his bones are."

Boggs opened his eyes and gestured at his wound.

"Smith did this to me," he said. "I want him dead. You owe me. I could still send you to the gallows."

Glaze knew Boggs' teeth were still plenty sharp. He might seem helpless, but he had power. He wasn't governor but he had many people beholden to him, some of them in the same way Glaze was indebted to him.

"Smith's in Illinois. He couldn't have shot you."

"He had somebody do it for him."

"Anybody could have shot you. You have lots of enemies."

Glaze doubted Smith had done it, but it was a convenient explanation. If anyone had cause to kill Boggs, it was Smith. And it was easy to fix the blame on the Mormons because they were hated far and wide and got blamed for every unexplained mystery. Glaze suspected that if someone cared enough to investigate thoroughly the truth would be far different from what Boggs said. But public opinion in Missouri being what it was an investigator could get himself shot in the back if he tried. Best to just accept Boggs' word at face value and let it ride. Anyway, Glaze had as much desire to see Smith dead as Boggs. It was a matter of pride for Glaze. Smith and Otis Harmon were the only men he ever had set out to kill who were still alive. He planned to remedy that situation. That was reason enough for him.

"I'm gonna need some money," Glaze said.

"That's not a problem. Guarantee that you'll kill Smith and you'll get all the money you need."

Glaze shrugged.

"Five hundred will do for starters."

"It's him or me," Boggs insisted tiredly. "And you owe me. I don't care how you do it or how long it takes."

# 29

Glaze crossed the Mississippi on the ferry at Quincy in late February. In the preceding months he spent many long hours with Boggs. Boggs' hatred for the Mormons and Joe Smith had deepened because of the shooting. The former Missouri governor had been corresponding with an alienated Mormon by the name of John Bennett, who apparently had a falling out with Ol' Joe and now was as eager as Boggs to kill him. And there were others. Boggs had opened correspondence with other governors and even someone within the U.S. Postmaster General's office in Washington D.C. Bennett had informed Boggs that there now were hundreds of men in Illinois willing to participate in Ol' Joe's demise. Boggs had given Glaze a list of names.

None of these men, Glaze suspected, knew how to conduct a killing. Killing, however, was Glaze's specialty and that's why he made the journey.

Bennett and a newspaper man named William Sharp had organized some anti-Mormon meetings in Warsaw, a small Illinois town south of Nauvoo, where Glaze was told to meet them. Boggs told him that Bennett and Sharp apparently had a spy, a leading man in the Mormon Church, who was one of Smith's confidantes. And Glaze and Boggs obtained promises from other Missourians to come running with their guns loaded when the time was right. They only needed to know when. The net was closing around Ol' Joe again.

Glaze left Quincy about midmorning speaking to no one except the owner of the ferry, who told him how to get to Warsaw. Warsaw was twelve miles to the north and he wanted to be there before nightfall. An anti-Mormon meeting was planned and Glaze wanted to see if the sentiment against the Mormons was as great as he had been told.

At Warsaw he stabled his horse, took a room at the only hotel in town and about seven o'clock entered a hall a few blocks away from the hotel where the clerk had directed him.

The hall, relatively small, held about two hundred and fifty people, mostly men. Every seat was filled and men stood in the side aisles and at the rear. Many were armed with pistols, bottles of whiskey or both. A few women sat near the front. Lamps lit the room, and a cloud of tobacco smoke wafted through the hall.

Glaze pushed and shoved his way through the back of the room and made his way to the front where he spied an empty chair. Three men in formal attire sat to his right. Although it had been cold outside the press of human bodies in heavy clothing took the chill from the room.

He squinted at the handbill that had been given to him on entering the hall. He couldn't read it but he heard someone say there were three speakers. It would be a long evening, as bad as going to church. The crowd was worked up already. As the three speakers entered the room, applause and cheers greeted them. Glaze didn't recognize any of them.

A minister prayed and a quartet of Warsaw women sang an off-key hymn. Then the first speaker, a Baptist preacher from Livingston, Missouri, took thirty-five minutes reciting embellished anecdotes of atrocities committed by the Mormons before their expulsion from Missouri. The preacher said Smith cut off the heads of anyone who disagreed with him, but never mentioned any specific names or places. The stories brought the audience to its feet with howls of rage. Glaze laughed out loud. Most of the deeds mentioned he knew to be true because he had committed them himself so they would be blamed on the Mormons.

The second speaker was Sharp, the newspaperman. His speech was rather boring though it didn't matter because the crowd already was worked up. It was like a tent revival meeting, Glaze thought, but instead of the crowd shouting hallelujahs and amens, they were screaming "kill him" or "hang him high" or "let's cut his damn throat." Sharp recited his versions of the history of the Mormons, saying they were unfit neighbors, unable to remain in any one place for long because of their obnoxious beliefs and attitudes.

"Joe Smith is corrupt. He threatens our freedom." he screamed to the crowd's foot-stomping delight. "He hopes to dominate the entire country and world, combine church and state and reign like old King George of England. If we wanted that we wouldn't have had the Revolutionary War."

Glaze was delighted by the crowd's reaction. They believed every word. They wanted to believe, shouted their approval and cheered delightedly. After about twenty minutes, Sharp sat down.

Silence set in as the third and final speaker rose and walked slowly to the podium. He was John Bennett, the excommunicated Mormon. All eyes fastened on him as he slowly removed a document from his pocket. Unfolding it carefully he placed it on the podium and then reached into another pocket for his reading glasses. Every eye was on the piece of paper.

"Some of you know that I spent a few years among the Mormons," he said quietly. Every ear strained to hear because he spoke so softly. "But," he said more loudly, "I was there with my eyes open. I had heard of the illicit conduct of the man we all know as Joe Smith. I wanted to see for myself what a man who claims to be God's prophet is really like and what he teaches because I suspected he was a fraud."

The hall was hushed. The men and women in the room were titillated. Glaze turned and gazed over the crowd. So many sweaty faces bearing expressions of righteous zeal.

"I was baptized a Mormon and received their priesthood, but please know that I was not deceived. I knew every moment what I was doing. I infiltrated them successfully. I was elected mayor of Nauvoo, became major general of the Nauvoo Legion and was appointed assistant president of the Mormon Church. I sat in meeting after meeting with Joe Smith and spent a great deal of time in his home. I was privy to almost every one of Joe Smith's dark and sinister acts. And I can tell you ladies and gentlemen, Joe Smith is no ordinary man. He is clever. He is evil. He is powerful. You have cause to fear."

A shiver swept through the hall. Bennett moved out from behind the podium.

"Now, I want to show something to you," he said reaching for the paper and holding it up. "With this piece of paper I can prove to you that Joe Smith is a false prophet."

Bennett adjusted his glasses as a murmur rippled through the hall. He waited for silence.

"This is one of Joe Smith's supposed revelations," he said. " I copied it as evidence from the Mormons' Book of Commandments while I was in Nauvoo. It's dated Dec. 25, 1832. Please note that date. That was almost twelve long years ago when most of the Mormons lived in Ohio."

Bennett began to read from the paper.

'Verily thus saith the Lord concerning the wars that will shortly come to pass, beginning at the rebellion of South Carolina, which will eventually terminate in the death and misery of many souls; And the time will come that war will be poured out upon all nations, beginning at this place. For behold, the Southern states shall be divided against the Northern States, and the Southern States will call on other nations, even the nation of Great Britain, as it is called, and they shall also call upon other nations, in order to defend themselves against other nations; and then war shall be poured out upon all nations. And it shall come to pass after many days, slaves shall rise up against their masters, who shall be marshaled and disciplined for war.'"

Bennett dropped his arm to his side and let the paper dangle loosely.

"If Joe Smith is a prophet then he's a pretty bad one. I haven't heard about any war like the one he describes here. Have you?"

"No," a man in the fifth row back shouted.

"Do you really expect to?" he yelled.

Almost in unison the crowd shouted "NO!"

Bennett reached out to the podium and steadied himself.

"I have heard Joe Smith say that the Mormon Church will roll forth until it fills the whole earth crushing all other nations and kingdoms before it. Do you want that?"

"NO!" the crowd was becoming louder and unruly. Some scowled and hissed for silence wanting to hear more from the man who knew so much about Mormons.

"Well ladies and gentlemen that is exactly what Joe Smith intends to do. The Mormons are gathering more people to their cause daily. They have a legion of men well trained and armed to the teeth with weapons provided by our own state militia. They could lay waste to this town tonight and you couldn't stop them."

Men and women glanced at one another fearfully.

"And now the rumors. You probably have heard the rumors. I wish they were just rumors, but they are not."

Bennett shook his head sadly, grimly refolding the paper he had read from and stuffing it back into his pocket.

"I hesitate to make mention of these awful stories because we have many of the fairer sex amongst us tonight, but it must be said outright so all understand."

Bennett now let them see his righteousness. His eyes were afire now, his hands trembling, clenched white in wrath.

"When I was in Nauvoo, I tried to dissuade Joe Smith from this course, but he persisted and now secretly advocates and teaches a doctrine he calls plural marriage, but which is actually the enslavement of white women for the entertainment of Joe Smith and his lieutenants. It's called polygamy and it's a moral outrage. Every upright human being should rebel against this moral travesty. Will you allow this to go on?"

A man several rows back of Glaze stood up and began a stomping chant: "No! No! No! No!" Others soon joined in and within seconds the entire room was on its feet chanting "No! No! No! No!"

Bennett kept shouting. His deep voice could still be heard.

"Joe Smith is a renegade and a despot. He must be stopped one way or the other. The Mormons must be stopped. Burned. Destroyed. Exterminated."

Glaze stood on his feet with the rest of the crowd clapping, stomping and cheering for almost ten minutes. Then the meeting slowly broke up and people began to file out the door in the back. But there were small groups of men throughout the hall still talking, drinking, working themselves into an angry frenzy. From Glaze's perspective, the meeting was a rousing success.

He made his way to the front of the room where he saw Sharp and Bennett speaking to a circle of men who had surrounded them talking excitedly. Glaze introduced himself to both Bennett and Sharp at the same time.

"Boggs wrote to me about you," Bennett said.

"The governor wants Ol' Joe dead and I'm here to help," Glaze said. "Fact is, I intend to be the one who puts a bullet through his heart."

"You're certainly welcome to help us."

"From what I saw tonight you don't need much help," Glaze said. "You already appear to have an army."

"Their fire will die soon," Sharp said. "They need to be organized and whipped up again. We're meeting two nights from now with some key people up north. You're invited. Be there if you're serious."

The meeting place was a tavern several miles north of Carthage. Glaze was early. He didn't like the smell but figured he'd get used to it.

The tavern owner and his wife kept a pig pen nearby and when the wind shifted just right the stink drifted right into the tavern. The tavern's mistress kept a pot of beans and pork hot and served it generously with a half loaf of warm bread. It was unexpectedly tasty considering the smell and the dark environment inside. There was only one small inadequate window to give light and air to the whole enterprise so two lanterns hung from the ceiling on either end of the spacious room to add light and the door was propped open to keep air circulating though it didn't seem fresh or clean.

Glaze ate alone in one corner.

Four tavern inmates caught his attention immediately because of the mixed aroma of alcohol, body odor and animals that followed them. All chewed tobacco and were content to spit the juice right onto the floor. They took a table in a far corner sharing a jug of homemade corn liquor. They laughed boisterously and teased the old woman who waited on their table and obviously enjoyed their attention. Glaze knew they probably infested the place every night of the year and would be the last ones out when the doors were locked in the wee hours of the morning.

In the darkest corner a strange man rocked back and forth in a chair though its four wooden legs were planted firmly on the floor. He wrung his hands and occasionally he would call out "kill him, kill him." Then he would erupt into a slow, solemn roar of laughter that would fill the entire room and interrupt the merriment at the middle table. The man's laugh was out of place, mistimed, overdone. It shook Glaze's nerves and even the regulars each time looked at the man derisively, but returned to their revelry without saying anything. Glaze assumed from their behavior that the man must be known to them and hold some place of respect in their minds or they would not tolerate such rude behavior. For his part, when he wasn't laughing, the strange man stared at the table top, ignoring everyone and everything.

When Glaze finished eating he pushed his plate away. Even though it had been several hours since the sun had set he was still early. The meeting was scheduled for midnight. That meant that the key people must not want to be seen.

At the stroke of midnight Sharp entered the tavern and beckoned to Glaze.

"The meeting's in the back room," he said. "Everyone else is there. There's another entrance because some of them are shy."

He ushered Glaze through an innocuous door at the back of the establishment and Glaze suddenly found himself in a room of impeccably dressed men. They had a more refined appearance than any men Glaze had seen since his youth in Georgia. All were seated around a table and all stared silently and suspiciously at him.

"Who is this?" one of them said. The speaker had delicate, dark, almost feminine features and shrewd eyes.

"This is Tyrone Glaze from Missouri," Sharp said. "Boggs sent him."

"Can he be trusted?" the speaker asked.

"Mr. Glaze has worked for Lilburn Boggs many years," Sharp said. "He participated in the Haun's Mill battle and the razing of Far West. He comes highly recommended by Boggs and I'm satisfied that he's one of us."

"Sounds as if he should have a seat of honor," the speaker said acidly.

Sharp identified each man for Glaze as the meeting proceeded. Glaze was startled when Sharp whispered that Thomas Ford, governor of Illinois was seated at the table. Then, remembering Boggs, he thought it not that unusual. In fact the only thing that seemed odd to Glaze was that everyone, including Ford, deferred to the man who had taken charge of the meeting. They did not question or challenge him. He maintained complete control.

Besides Sharp and the speaker, there was Bennett and a judge from Carthage. Levi Williams and Robert Smith, commanders of the Warsaw and Carthage militias, were there, as were several other members of the militias. The last to be introduced were four Mormons. They included an extremely nervous fellow named George Trask, a square-jawed bulldog of a man named Frances Higbee who was a judge in Nauvoo, and the most prominent of the four, William and Wilson Law. The Law brothers brought with them most impressive credentials. Wilson Law was the commanding officer of the Nauvoo Legion and William Law was in the Mormon Church's First Presidency, second counselor to Ol' Joe Smith himself.

"I want to make something perfectly clear from the start," the mysterious man said. "We are not laying a plan to capture Joe Smith, or to injure him or to discredit him. Those things all have been tried before with varying degrees of success. Our purpose here is to lay out a plan to kill him, to assassinate him, to put an end to his life. If there is anyone here who does not have the stomach for what I just stated, let's hear from him now."

"If we didn't have the stomach for it we wouldn't be here," Glaze said.

The speaker looked at Glaze and then casually glanced around the room as though meetings of this sort were an everyday occurrence for him.

"I act under the direction and authority of not only the illustrious Illinois Governor Thomas Ford," he said, nodding to the governor and pausing for effect, "but also with the approval of certain people who occupy the highest offices in the land."

"What exactly do you mean when you say highest officers in the land? Are you saying the president is in on this?" Higbee asked.

"You may draw your own conclusions," the speaker said. "I am not going to say anything further about that, but I can guarantee that none of you and no one who helps you ever will be punished for killing Joseph Smith."

The speaker then took charge of a disjointed, rambling, unimaginative discussion of how best to kill Smith. It took two hours for the group to agree on the outline of a plan: Draw Smith away from his friends in Nauvoo, isolate him and destroy him. It sounded simple enough, but Glaze knew from experience it would be complex. Smith would not be an easy man to kill.

"We must seize on any pretense we can to jail the man outside of Nauvoo," the speaker said. "The Nauvoo Charter gives him almost as much power as the governor himself. We have no power over him there. Once he's jailed, anywhere outside of Nauvoo, preferably in Carthage, we must not hesitate. We must combine our various powers to hold him and destroy him. He is intelligent and creative. We won't be able to hold him long."

The Law brothers and Trask, given their proximity to Smith, were assigned to track Ol' Joe's whereabouts and inform the others.

"Smith is wary," Wilson Law said. "There have been so many attempts already to capture him that he's like a spooked animal. And he's very perceptive. If we do anything out of the ordinary, he'll sense it."

The men lapsed into an uneasy silence. The meeting had about run its course.

"We have another plan we are developing with other Mormons who feel as we do," William Law said abruptly. "There are almost two hundred of us. This all may be unnecessary if our plot succeeds."

"I truly doubt that you will be successful," the speaker said. "If there are more than twenty people involved, someone will rat you out. Just be certain that no one besides those in this room know of this plan. We will enforce a strict code of secrecy because of the reputations of those who know about our plans. If anyone in this room speaks of this plan with anyone besides those who are here, he will be hunted down and killed. Does everyone understand that?"

"I don't see a need for all this secrecy," Glaze said. "From everything I have seen the entire damned country is lining up against Smith and probably will cheer for us when we're through."

"You may be right, but please don't forget that what we are planning to do is called murder in all the law books," the speaker said.

George Trask, who had been relatively quiet all evening, responded too.

"There are some who will do anything for Smith," he said. "They honestly believe he is God's prophet. Otis Harmon, my neighbor, would tear me apart if he knew I was in on a plan like this."

Glaze immediately forgot the point he was making.

"Otis Harmon?"

Trask nodded.

"Did this Otis Harmon you know once live near Independence?"

"Yes," Trask said.

"I owe him," Glaze said. "I want you to show me where he lives."

"That brings up another topic. In Missouri Governor Boggs used midnight raids to his advantage," the speaker said, smiling. "Do you have some experience in those types of things, Mr. Glaze?"

Glaze smiled and nodded.

"Good then," he said. "We want you to find a few men to help you. Conduct some raids. Put the fear of god in them. Burn some houses. Let them know there's a cost to being a Mormon."

The speaker then turned to William and Wilson Law.

"We have before discussed the idea of starting a newspaper in Nauvoo. It would be a useful tool in spreading dissension among the Mormons themselves. We'll print anything that's embarrassing or harmful to Smith. Use a few of Mr. Sharp's articles. He has a flair for that sort of thing. The public has a tendency to believe things that appear in print even if the truth is twisted a little."

"If that becomes necessary we'll consider it," Law said.

The speaker bristled and his face grew dark.

"Do more than just consider it," he hissed. "We have funds at our disposal. Use them."

"And Mr. Trask," the speaker went on. "I would like to meet your friend Otis Harman. It may be that Mr. Harmon has more in common with us than you think."

# 30

THE KNOT IN LIBBIE HARMON'S STOMACH GREW AS the riverboat churned upriver. She peered over the railing and into the muddy Mississippi hoping her stomach would settle. Her intuition told her something was wrong, but she couldn't tell what.

The reverend, her husband, stood several feet away conversing with fellow passengers, most of whom were completing the last leg of a journey that had begun in England. They were giddy with excitement. The reverend was trying to convince them that what they were doing was wrong and she could see his frustration level rising because he was having scant luck. All the new converts appeared perfectly at ease and comfortable with their decision to go to Nauvoo and be Mormons.

The reverend's efforts mattered little to her. He was a good man and finally had succumbed to her pleadings to accompany her to Nauvoo to see Oat. This was a sort of honeymoon voyage for them. Despite that, her thoughts were focused almost entirely on Oat. She missed him. She yearned to see him. It had been nearly five years since he had put her on the boat near Independence. Guilt now racked her for many reasons – for leaving him alone in Missouri, for staying too long at Independence in the first place. She now abused herself for not having returned to Baltimore years ago while Oat was still young and she had the power to influence him. She could have gotten him into a good school, taught him to be a gentleman and molded him into something. He could have been anything with the proper instruction and guidance. What would happen to him now?

She thought of his youth and shook her head. In her estimation Oat didn't have much of a chance. He had grown up like a wild animal in Missouri, no education except what she had taught him about reading, writing and math. His only social outlets were with the backward, prejudiced old settlers of Missouri who weren't any more educated than most farm animals and she shuddered to think of what they might have taught him beyond chewing and drinking.

And then there was the matter of his father. Oat had worshipped Andrew, and Andrew had doted on Oat. From the time he was old enough to walk Oat had resembled his father in features and mannerisms and by the time he was eighteen Oat was a physical replica of the man she had married. He never shirked a chore and he worked as if his very life, and her life, depended on him completing the task at hand.

Andrew's death had been a blow from which she would never recover. He was a beautiful man, rugged, independent, and yet so intent to have a wife and family. She would never love another man like she had loved Andrew. It had been youthful indulgence to wed and follow that man to the edge of the frontier. He had been so enthusiastic and strong-willed that he convinced her the hardships would be few and the rewards abundant. He had been wrong. Her heart broke every time she thought of the two young sons they had buried. Even now, tears formed when she thought of them. After Andrew's death she had not been a good mother to her remaining son.

The morning after Andrew had been murdered. Oat had found his father lying on his back with a bloody hole in his chest. What a nightmare for a twelve-year-old boy. He had come running back to the house crying only to face another horror, seeing his mother collapse after telling her that his father was dead. How had that shaped him?

He had become a man that very instant. He dug his father's grave, comforted his mother and assumed all the chores. She had done what she could after the shock wore off. She shouldered her part, but Oat held the farm together. He developed a true kinship with the big horses Andrew had traded for the previous year. He didn't know much about training horses, but he had trained them and they trusted him. Somehow she knew Andrew was a part of that. She didn't know how, but she believed Andrew was close for Oat, a sort of guardian angel, guiding him past the roughest patches of life. He had to have been. She hadn't.

She became so bitter upon Andrew's death that she hated everyone. Even God. And it was all because of the Mormons. Because

Andrew and Oat had gone to the Wheatley place that morning. And she had followed. She wished that day never had occurred. Boggs had been there and Andrew had defied and embarrassed the lieutenant governor as only Andrew could. She had thought for a brief moment that morning that Andrew would kill Boggs. She wished now that he had. Maybe things would have turned out different, in some way better. They couldn't have turned out much worse.

Now she had an opportunity. Maybe today she could right a few wrongs and be a proper mother to her son. Even though he was all grown up now and could easily take care of himself, she felt there were things she needed to do. She wanted to hug him and tell him she loved him and how sorry she was for those years when she had been so bitter and angry.

She looked up, suddenly aware that the boat was approaching Nauvoo. A huge building became visible on a hill. That, undoubtedly, was the temple the Mormons were building and that she had heard so much about on their trip upriver. Oat had mentioned it in his letters. That meant she would be seeing Oat very soon. The knot in her stomach tightened.

# 31

IN APRIL, OAT RECEIVED A LETTER FROM HIS MOTHER that threw him into a fit of worry. He had been corresponding every few months with her since he had been living in Nauvoo and had written to her about his marriage to Hannah and the birth of their son. But he still hadn't told her about his marriage to Maggie. That had been more than nine months earlier and now Maggie was big with child and due to give birth any day.

His mother's letter imparted intriguing and terrifying bits of news. The intriguing part was that she had remarried to a Methodist preacher from Baltimore. Oat was happy for her and glad to know that she was carrying on with life and not pining away about the past like she had often done at the farm near Independence.

She also wrote that she and her new husband, the Rev. James Winter, were coming to Nauvoo for a visit. They were leaving immediately from Baltimore and would arrive by riverboat at Nauvoo probably only a few days after he received her letter.

"I want to see my daughter-in-law and meet my new grandson," she wrote. "Most of all I want to see you. It has been much too long."

Oat wanted to see his mother too, but worried that she would be appalled by the fact that he had two wives and that she wouldn't accept them. She wouldn't understand. He knew it.

He thought over various options. He could send Maggie away while his mother was here, but that wouldn't work. Maggie was ready to deliver a child and needed him. And he couldn't send Hannah away. His mother already knew of Hannah and Andy. He asked Hannah and Maggie for suggestions, but didn't get any sympathy.

"I won't live a lie or try to deceive her," Hannah said. "We'll tell her exactly how things are. If she accepts us that's wonderful. If she can't accept us, then that's just too bad. We're your family."

"Easy for you to say," Oat said. "You don't know my mother."

"I remember her," Hannah said, "From when we were little. She was a kind, thoughtful woman. It will be okay Oat."

"She'll love us Oat," Maggie had said comfortingly. "She raised you and you love us."

Their words didn't ease his worrying, but maybe they were right. When his mother arrived he would try to explain and let her figure out the rest. He didn't have to wait long for the opportunity.

At noon the following day a carriage turned up the lane on its way to the house. Oat, who was dunging out the barn, watched it as a feeling of foreboding grew in his heart. The carriage clattered to a stop in front of the house and two people emerged. He easily recognized the silhouette of his mother and felt a surge of affection. She looked much the same as she had the last time he saw her at Independence. Next to her stood a short, round, well-dressed man who wore spectacles on the end of his nose.

Oat emerged from the barn and rushed to his mother. They hugged before a word was said.

"Oat, this is my husband, the Rev. James Winter," she said.

Oat and the reverend were shaking hands when the door of the house flew open and Hannah burst out.

"Oat, go get Sister Christensen," she called excitedly. "Maggie's started. The baby's coming . . ." Her voice trailed off as she saw Oat's mother. Oat's feet suddenly felt fastened to the ground. His mother looked at him.

"We're having a baby?" she asked.

They all heard a moan from inside the house. Hannah hurried back inside as Andy toddled into the doorway followed by Abe who came out. My children pick such opportune moments to arrive, Oat thought. His mother rushed past him to the door, stopping to pick up Andy and give him a hearty hug and a kiss on the cheek. She then handed him to Oat.

"This isn't any place for you right now," she said. "Take these children and leave."

Oat remembered that his mother helped deliver many children while in Missouri and worked as a nurse in Baltimore. Just the same he harnessed the Jacquards and he, Andy and Abe went to get Sister Christensen. The reverend found a spot of shade near the house and started reading a Bible he carried with him. By the time Oat returned with the old Englishwoman, the baby had been born. He heard its tiny cries as he pulled the Jacquards to a stop in front of the house.

"We're getting pretty good at this," he said, looking at the older woman seated next to him in the wagon.

While Sister Christensen hurried inside to help, Oat sat down near his new stepfather and waited. The reverend had seated himself on a block of wood in the shade of Maggie's room. He set aside his reading when Oat sat down near him.

"We drove through Nauvoo on our way here from the boat today," the reverend said in a low patronizing tone. "These Mormons are busy people aren't they?"

"Yes. It's a good place to live. Mostly, the people are kind and friendly."

The reverend's brow wrinkled.

"Your mother said you knew Joseph Smith, that you helped Smith escape from the law in Missouri."

"That I did."

The reverend shook his head and wagged his finger at him sagely.

"That was a mistake."

"No, it wasn't," Oat said. "It was one of the best things I've ever done."

The reverend cocked his head and looked back at Oat quizzically.

"You speak like you're one of them."

"One of who?"

"The Mormons, like you're a Mormon."

"I am a Mormon."

The reverend shook his head again.

"So, Joe Smith tricked you too. Your mother will be sad and ashamed. You should have told her. Smith is evil and corrupt and you should never believe a thing he says."

"Do you know Joseph?"

"No. Never met him, but I've read about him in the newspapers."

"I know him personally," Oat said. "I don't make my judgments from what's in the papers. He's my friend. You would do well to follow him too."

Oat stood and walked into the house.

Inside, Hannah and his mother stood near Maggie who was holding a tiny, wrinkled baby girl. As Oat approached, his mother picked up the baby, wrapped it in a small blanket and went to the rocking chair where she sang to it. Oat went first to Maggie, who smiled at him weakly.

"I'm going to be fine Oat," she said, closing her eyes. "All I want to do now is sleep."

Oat sat down near his mother, who was looking at him rather oddly. She stopped singing.

"It's so good to see you again," she said, smiling.

"I'm glad you came," he replied.

"I must say, however, that I'm a little confused," she said. "Where is this child's father?"

"I'm the father," Oat said uneasily. "She's your granddaughter."

His mother smiled and gazed down upon the child lovingly.

"I thought so," she said, then her brow wrinkled, "But I thought Hannah was your wife."

"She is," Oat said.

"But . . ."

"Maggie is too."

His mother stared at him for a long moment still rocking the child. For the rest of the day she said little. She was polite, but she held back and Oat knew her well enough to sense her disapproval. He didn't know what to say to her. She helped with the children, tended to Maggie and helped Hannah with the house chores. She said almost nothing, until she went outside and spoke to her husband the reverend, who remained outside reading most of the day. The reverend never did enter the house, refusing to do so after learning that Oat had two wives. But unlike his mother, the reverend had plenty to say when he got the chance and that chance came when Oat took a plate of food to him in the evening.

"You have soiled your family name Oat. And you're going to burn in hell for it," the reverend said. He obviously had been stewing on it all day.

Oat, however, was ready for an argument, having done a little stewing himself all day.

"Why?" he said defensively.

"Because adultery is a grievous sin and offensive to the Lord," his mother's husband said piously. "And you have brought a bastard child into this world."

Grabbing the reverend by the lapel, he pulled until he was nose to nose with the man.

"I have not committed adultery, sir," Oat said. "I am wedded to both Hannah and Maggie legally and lawfully. And my children are not bastards. They are innocent, pure souls and if I hear you refer to them as bastards again I shall pound your face in the dirt."

Oat released the reverend and returned to his house.

Oat's mother and the reverend left the next morning. The reverend made a bed in the barn for the night and his mother slept in the rocking chair, getting up occasionally to help Hannah tend the babies. She wouldn't accept the bed Oat prepared for her and never unpacked her bag. Oat drove them to the wharf at Nauvoo. They said little during the wagon ride.

"I wish you would stay longer," he said to his mother at the wharf.

She shook her head, tears in her eyes and said nothing. She boarded the riverboat without looking back at him.

His mother's rejection hurt Oat. He mourned about it many days when he realized he may never see her again.

Despite the hard feelings that had been engendered, Maggie and Oat named their daughter, Elizabeth, after Oat's mother, and naturally, within a few weeks Oat had shortened it to Libbie, though he vowed to himself he'd never tell his mother.

Two days after his mother left, Joseph and Emma unexpectedly paid a visit. Their carriage arrived in the late afternoon accompanied by two armed men, one who rode ahead and one who rode behind. While Emma visited inside Joseph sought out Oat who was in the barn repairing a harness. Oat noticed that the riders circled the farm warily.

"Who are they?" Oat asked.

"Bodyguards," Joseph said. "Hyrum won't let me go anywhere without protection these days."

The latest stories circulating about Nauvoo said hundreds of armed men were ready to attack the city and try to take Joseph by force. The sight of the two armed guards told him the rumors had some basis in fact.

"Are they enough?" he asked.

"I don't know, what do you think?" Joseph said. They were large, bearded and leathery. They didn't smile, obviously taking their assignment very seriously. Both held rifles easily in the crooks of their arms. Pistols and knives were tucked in their belts. They appeared ready for anything.

"I wouldn't insult them," Oat confessed.

"Nor I," said Joseph. "I'm glad their on my side."

They laughed uneasily.

"Despite the best efforts of all my good friends my life is becoming more insecure every day."

"Has it come to that again?" Oat asked.

"It has," Joseph said. "I can feel my enemies closing on me, but I'm going to fight them every step."

"Can I help you some way?"

Joseph shook his head.

"The ones who concern me most are the ones who should be my friends, who have sat with me in my own home, shook my hand daily and accepted my counsel. So-called friends. They are the ones who will do me in."

"I cannot imagine betraying a friend like that," Oat said.

"You'll have your chance Oat," Joseph said. "You will have the opportunity to give me up."

They talked a while longer about the farm and Joseph asked about Maggie, Hannah and the children.

"It's awkward," Oat told him bluntly. "My mother was here a

few days ago and she was offended when she found that I had two wives. She left angry. I should have prepared her. It caught her by surprise. I may never see her again."

"You'll see her again. She still loves you and she'll grow to understand the Lord's will in this," Joseph said. "One day you will have a great family in the Rocky Mountains."

"I have heard you say that before. Why would we go there?"

"Because it's the last place on earth we can go to be at peace. One day there will be thousands of elders living there and the church will become strong."

"You'll be there too," Oat said.

"Maybe, but if my enemies ever get their hands on me again, I will not survive it."

Joseph and Emma left not long after that, and behind them they left a feeling of melancholy. As Oat finished his work on the harness he had a definite feeling that something awful was about to happen.

# 32

ANOTHER MEETING BEGAN AT THE STROKE OF MIDNIGHT. George Trask waited nervously for his turn to take the oath and sign his name. As he waited, his eyes scanned the list of those who already had signed. He was close enough to see the signatures easily. At the top of the list was the name of William Law, then Wilson Law. Other signatures included those of Chauncey Higbee, Robert Foster, Joseph Jackson and a score of others. The man who stood nearest the signature sheet and who administered the oath to each man or woman who came forward was none other than Nauvoo Justice of the Peace Francis Higbee.

During the preceding months this group had met several times to discuss a change in leadership for the church. George had been happy to join them when William Law explained the group's purpose. But they were a minority in Nauvoo and they knew it. The majority of Nauvoo's citizens accepted Smith as a prophet. Trask shook his head and thought of Oat Harmon. Oat followed Smith like a sheep. He did the same things that Smith did. He even had two wives.

Earlier in the evening the group concluded that Joseph Smith was going to hell and if the church was to be saved he would have to die.

"He's a fallen prophet," William Law said. "He is teaching and living polygamy and he rules Nauvoo with an iron fist. He has too much power. We must be careful because in Missouri he cut off the heads of people who opposed him. The same fate awaits us if we are not vigilant."

Law's words carried a great deal of weight with many people because he knew Joseph personally, sat in council with him almost daily and was privy to the most guarded secrets of the church.

The claim that Smith cut off men's heads was incredible and

George asked Law about it the first time he made the claim in George's own house.

"I don't know if he did," Law said with a laugh. "I doubt it, but it's intriguing don't you think and people who hate Joseph want to believe it. Besides it serves my purpose and it makes Joseph angry whenever he hears the tale so I like to tell it as often as I can."

Outside in the darkness, armed men guarded the entrance to the house, allowing only those who knew the secret passwords to enter. Most of those present were men, but three women joined the company, heavily veiled so their identities would not be known readily. They also came forward and took the oath. One of them was his own wife, Geneva. Conspicuous because of their youth were two boys that George guessed to be fifteen or sixteen years old. One was William Law's house servant, the other apparently was the servant's friend. They stood nearby in a corner watching quietly as the parade of prominent Nauvoo citizens come forward and took the oath.

Presently, it was George's turn. He stepped forward, faced Higbee and placed his right hand on the Bible Higbee held.

"Are you ready?" Higbee asked.

"Yes."

"You solemnly swear, before God and all holy angels, and these your brethren by whom you are surrounded that you will give your life, your liberty, your influence, your all, for the destruction of Joseph Smith and his party, so help you God?"

"I do," George said firmly, then taking a quill pen in hand he signed his own name to the sheet as Higbee watched. When finished, Trask stood aside to allow the next one in line his turn. There was a long line behind him. The room was not large enough for everyone so after they signed many exited the house and disappeared into the darkness outside. But George stayed because Law asked him to. Finally after what seemed an interminably long time the last signature was in place. Higbee put down the Bible and rolled up the signature sheet. The remaining men, about twenty in all, stood up to leave.

"Wait a minute," Wilson Law said pointing. "Those two boys over there have not yet taken the pledge."

Twenty sets of eyes suddenly fastened on the two boys. Big arms reached out to them and they were gently, but firmly prodded forward in the flickering candlelight until they stood before Higbee who unrolled the sheet, replaced it on the table, and again had the Bible in hand.

"Are you ready?" he asked the first boy.

"No." The boy shook his head and stared at the floor. The room became so quiet that George could hear the wheezing of a fat man across the room.

"Are you ready?" Higbee asked the other boy.

The second boy shook his head. His refusal stunned George because he knew the boy worked for Law.

"Why?" Higbee asked the youths.

The boys shrugged and stared at the floor. Angry men closed around them cursing savagely.

"Why?" Higbee demanded.

"Joseph Smith never done nothin' to me," the first boy said. "I don't want to kill him. I thought this all was just in fun. I guess I'm too young to understand what it's all about. And I ain't gonna take no oath."

"And you?" Higbee asked the second boy.

Law's servant boy nodded defiantly.

"I ain't taking no oath either. Let us go."

The two boys tried to push through the group of men toward the door.

"Oh no you don't."

Wilson Law stood in the doorway and refused to let them out.

"You two boys know who we are and all of our plans. If you won't take that oath and become one of us, we're going to have to kill you. Now are you going to take the oath or not?"

The boys shook their heads.

Higbee, the Laws and Fosters quickly conferred in a corner while the other men held the terrified boys.

"We'll kill them in the cellar," William Law said. "Take them downstairs. George, do you have a sharp knife?"

George nodded and followed the group into the cellar.

In the cellar the two boys were held by three men each. Their arms and legs were pinned against a wall so they couldn't move and their heads were jerked back to expose their throats.

"We'll give you boys one last chance," Law said. "We don't want to kill you, but if you won't take the oath we have no choice. What do you say?"

Neither boy said anything.

"Cut their throats," Law said, motioning to George. George never had killed anyone before and this didn't seem right, but he was afraid to say no to Law. If he did they might cut his throat too.

"Wait a minute," a deep voice said. It was Higbee. "These boys' folks probably know where they are. It could be dangerous to kill them here. We may be found out. It would be best to take them somewhere else."

The group quickly saw the wisdom in Higbee's words so they carried the boys outside and pushed them along roughly in the darkness toward the river where they intended to do the deed, but once outside the house, the need to kill the boys suddenly seemed less critical. And the closer they got to the river the less certain the collective will of the group became. Finally, to George's relief, Law and Higbee let the boys go with simple death threats if they ever revealed what they had seen and heard. Once released the boys quickly disappeared into the brush and trees by the river.

The conspirators soon wished they had cut the two boys' throats. Within a few days all Nauvoo knew about the conspiracy to kill Joseph, the oaths, the death threats and the names of a large number of those involved. In mid-April the Laws and others prominent in the conspiracy were excommunicated from the church and their identities exposed in an edition of the Nauvoo newspaper, the Times and Seasons. George soon found, however, that his name was not associated with those of the other conspirators probably because the two boys had not known him and therefore could not identify him. He continued however to accompany the Laws on frequent midnight jaunts to Carthage and Warsaw for meetings with editor Sharpe and those involved in the governor's plot to kill Joseph. He enjoyed these meetings. He felt important being taken into the confidence of important people like Sharpe, Tyrone Glaze, the rich Law brothers and the mysterious man from Washington.

On one occasion Glaze rode back with George from Warsaw and spent a day at the Trask home. After dark the two of them scouted the Harmon place. Although George described the layout of Oat's place to him in detail Glaze had to see it for himself. In the darkness they crept close to the Harmon house and watched Oat, Maggie and Hannah moving around inside until the lights in the windows went out. Once in a while they could hear words and parts of sentences and occasionally the cry of a baby lilted through the evening air. Glaze stared at the house for more than an hour after that chewing at a wad of tobacco and spitting onto the ground in front of him. He studied the simple farm with its house, barns and sheds, saying nothing. Livestock were fenced together in a large pasture behind the house and they easily could see the outlines of Harmon's horses grazing quietly in the moonlight.

"How long has Harmon been here?" he asked finally.

"Bout five years."

"Not a bad place. I wouldn't mind owning it. Too good for a Mormon though."

"Yeah."

"He's married to both women?"

"Uh huh. Hannah and Maggie. Hannah was his first wife, but Maggie already had a bastard kid when she married him last summer. Hannah had one last summer and Maggie had her second one last week. It was kind of funny because Oat's mother showed up the same day from the east. She didn't even know Oat was a Mormon, let alone that he had two wives."

"Well, we're going to put a stop to that," Glaze said, shaking his head. "There's already too damn many Mormons around here."

In May, the Laws finally started their newspaper. They picked out a name before they even bought a press. They planned to call it the Nauvoo Expositor. With Sharp's assistance they purchased a press and type downriver and shipped it to Nauvoo by riverboat. It arrived at month's end. Sharp, Trask and Glaze helped the Laws move the press into a shop on Nauvoo's Main Street late one night so as not to attract attention. Later, George and Glaze rode their horses through Nauvoo's quiet streets.

"Not even one tavern or saloon," Glaze said, amazed. "No place for a man to relax and have a drink after a hard day's work."

They rode past Joseph's house and Trask pointed it out to Glaze.

"That's where Ol' Joe lives?" Glaze said. The lights were out and the house was dark. They reined their horses to a stop and studied the house.

"We could knock that door in, march in there and end this whole thing right now with one shot," Glaze said to George, who was uneasily looking over his shoulder.

"I'll bet you couldn't," a voice said. Whoever said it stood out of sight in the shadows.

The voice terrified George. But Glaze didn't seem to be affected. Sitting easily in his saddle he seemed amused.

"Who's gonna stop us?" Glaze called out to the voice.

"Me."

"Who's me?"

"Don't matter much does it? The only thing you need to know is that if you get off that horse I'll shoot your eyes out."

A door creaked open.

"Anything wrong out there Port?" George recognized Joseph's voice. It terrified him too.

"Naw. Just a couple of sightseers. Ain't that right boys?"

George and Glaze spurred their horses ahead quickly and didn't stop again until they reached George's place.

The midnight press move didn't fool many people. By noon the next day the whole town knew what the Laws were up to and men and women walked past and gawked curiously in the windows. The Laws spent the next week secluded in the shop writing and setting type. George stopped by a few times in the evenings, but the brothers were so engrossed in their task they hardly paid him any attention.

"Listen to this," William would say and then read an interminably long string of words that accused Joseph of practically every crime George could imagine and a few he couldn't. The brothers laughed and joked about their own cleverness and seemed in positively great spirits.

"When Ol' Joe reads this, it will drive him wild," William said. On June seventh, the first and last issue of the Nauvoo Expositor was published.

# 33

GLAZE WAS SUMMONED TO THE WARSAW SIGNAL newspaper office on the morning of June twelfth by Wilson Law who pounded for five minutes on his hotel room door. Glaze had been out all night on a wolf hunt to Ramus where he and a small group of Warsaw men burned two Mormon houses and ran off some cattle. He felt tired and cross.

Opening the door he grabbed Law by the hair and slammed the man's head against the door jam.

"What do you want?"

"They sent me to get you," Law said when his head finally cleared. "We're having a meeting at the Signal offices."

Glaze had become impatient with the snobbish, arrogant Laws. They could have ended this whole affair long ago, he thought, if they hadn't been such cowards. They must have had a hundred opportunities to shoot Smith in a church meeting. If they could just get out of Nauvoo there wouldn't be a jury in the whole country that would convict them. Glaze wanted to go back to Missouri and let these inept cowards fuss, fume and stew.

"He's beaten us again," William Law said disgustedly after Sharp and Glaze arrived at the office.

"Oh. That's a surprise," Glaze said acidly.

"How did it happen?" Sharp asked.

"After we published last week he must have called the city council together. Last night he declared our paper a public nuisance. The marshall destroyed the press and pied the type. We're out of business after only one issue."

Law continued to whine about the newspaper's destruction until

Glaze burst into a derisive laugh.

"The nerve of the man," Glaze said sarcastically. "Here you are publicly accusing him of major crimes he didn't commit, secretly plotting to kill him and then he comes along and without any warning at all he messes up your newspaper. Is there no justice in this world?"

Law's jaw dropped.

"I don't like your tone sir. Are we on the same side or not?"

"Unfortunately we are," Glaze said. "But it's been a long time since I gave a damn about what you and your backstabbing weasel of a brother think. Ol' Joe has more guts and brains in his little finger than you'll ever have. You're a couple of spineless women."

The Laws and Glaze glared back and forth at each other. William's chin quivered.

"What did you do when they destroyed the press?" Sharp asked, breaking the tension.

"We left for Carthage," Wilson said. "I truly believe our lives are in danger."

Glaze rolled his eyes and laughed.

"There are about fifteen thousand Mormons on this side of the river. You've moved freely amongst them for more than a month since they discovered your plot to kill Ol' Joe. And you're still alive. If they wanted to kill you you'd be dead."

More silence ensued.

"I guess we're finished. He has more lives than a cat. We'll never get him now."

"No. You're wrong," Sharp said. "He's given us the excuse we've been looking for. He destroyed a newspaper. Nobody does that in this country. He may have ended your newspaper publishing career, but he ordered the destruction of private property. He just made a huge mistake."

Within a few days the mysterious man from Washington appeared in Warsaw. The conspiracy surged forward. Sharp's newspaper accounts over the destruction of the Nauvoo Expositor stirred central Illinois into a bloody frenzy. Glaze increased the number of wolf hunts. A committee of prominent citizens was dispatched to enlist Governor Ford's assistance and demand Ol' Joe's arrest. This was more for show than anything else because the governor already was planning to come. The local militias in Carthage and Warsaw prepared to attack Nauvoo. Glaze sent a message to Boggs in Missouri and hundreds of Missourians streamed across the Mississippi to join the hunt for Ol' Joe, among them Glaze's old friend Tucker.

Meeting after meeting was held in dark backrooms at taverns and hotels in Carthage and Warsaw. Plans were laid and abandoned, discussed and argued. Almost every night, Glaze led armed groups of men against outlying Mormon farms burning houses, running off livestock, destroying crops and increasing the pressure on Ol' Joe. Their tactics worked. At Nauvoo, Ol' Joe declared Marshall Law and established a curfew. It was the type of situation Glaze loved, dangerous and fragile, like Missouri had been six years earlier.

One morning Glaze purchased one of Sharp's newspapers and had Tucker read it to him. He didn't like people knowing he couldn't read, but Tucker already knew and wouldn't tell anybody and Tucker wanted to know what Sharp was writing as badly as Glaze did.

Tucker read only one paragraph using his deep voice and storytelling abilities to emphasize every bombastic word.

"War and extermination are inevitable! Citizens arise, one and all!!!—Can you stand by, and suffer such INFERNAL DEVELS! to rob men of their property and rights without avenging them. We have no time for comment, every man will make his own. Let it be made with POWDER and BALL!!!!"

Laying down the paper, Tucker sipped from a cup of hot coffee and grinned.

# 34

During June, what the non-Mormons called wolf hunts increased.

Oat spent several sleepless nights worrying about an attack on his own farm. He kept the guns loaded and warned Hannah and Maggie to be ready, but no attack came. Though their farm was on the eastern outskirts of Nauvoo, it wasn't the farthest out and they were relatively close to the city, but he wasn't safe. He never had been so afraid, but then nothing like this ever had happened to him since he had a family.

Other nearby farms were raided. Livestock was stolen or scattered and crops trampled by horsemen. Roofs were pulled off some houses and barns were burned.

Rumors pulsed through Nauvoo that a thousand Missourians had crossed the Mississippi and now were preparing to attack Nauvoo. The Nauvoo Legion was put on alert and Joseph's proclamation of Marshall Law sent tensions even higher.

Maggie and Hannah went about their daily labors as though nothing different was happening, taking all the rumors in stride. He was always aware that both had been through this before at Far West though they didn't talk much about those times. Their courage made him feel a little silly.

One evening near dusk in mid-June, George Trask paid a visit. George drove a carriage, unusual because George didn't own a carriage. Seated next to him as they drove into the yard was a bespeckled man in a pressed black suit and polished shoes. Oat had never seen the man before but he recognized power when he saw it. Instinctively, he knew this man possessed it. His movements, or lack thereof, his gaze, the tilt of his head all bespoke authority. Oat knew because he had seen men like this before, because here was a man not unlike Lilburn W. Boggs.

George and Oat's friendship, though not good since the feud developed between Hannah and Geneva, had grown even colder over the past few months since the Laws were excommunicated and left the church. Oat knew George sided with William Law who was accused of plotting to murder Joseph and he now wondered how much involvement George had in that affair. He did know that George spent a lot of time away from home. The crops he planted that year were overrun with weeds.

Oat didn't invite the two men into the house but could feel both Hannah and Maggie staring out the window as he leaned against the top rail of his corral where Molly Jacquard and her newest colt munched on a bucket of oats. The colt was a male and had Jack's conformation. He was breeding stock, Molly's seventh. All had been sired by Jack, and Oat now trained the young team of twin percherons that Molly had birthed two years before.

George did not introduce the man seated next to him. George acted as if they never had a disagreement between them. He asked about the horses and the farm and crops and finally about the increasing tensions in Nauvoo. The man next to George sat quietly as George and Oat spoke. Oat sensed George had something on his mind and it didn't take long for it to come out.

"Oat," George said seriously. "You could put an end to this problem and make yourself a rich man at the same time."

"Me?" Oat said. "How could I do that?"

The man in the suit finally spoke. His voice was not unlike his appearance, very confident. This man was accustomed to giving orders.

"I asked George to bring me here," the man said. "I have a business proposition for you, quite a lucrative one. If you will help me I can make all of your troubles go away."

"I have a lot of problems," Oat said. "I need to build a new barn. I've got coons and bugs in my corn and the weeds never stop growing. There aren't enough hours in the day. How are your going to solve all those troubles?"

"Money."

Instinctively, Oat knew where the conversation was leading. He remembered Joseph telling him he'd have a chance to betray him, but his curiosity was aroused.

"Doesn't sound to me like it's anything I want to hear about," Oat said.

"You could listen."

"Okay," Oat said. "Let's hear your proposition."

George got out of the carriage and climbed onto the top rail of the corral, facing Oat.

"Joseph likes you Oat. And he trusts you. He'd do anything you asked him to do. Wouldn't he?"

"He's my friend. If I needed him he'd help me?"

"It's more than that," George said. "He owes you. You helped him get out of Missouri."

"Yes, I did." Oat said.

"Well, here's the deal. You go into Nauvoo tomorrow and tell Joseph that Andy's sick and needs a blessing. Ask Joseph to come here tomorrow night about this time. That's all you have to do."

The man in the suit got out of the carriage, walked around the horses and stood before Oat. In one hand he held a heavy bag, in the other he held several gold coins which he displayed in his palm.

"This is a thousand dollars. If you do what George just asked I'll give you this bag plus as much land as you could ever hope to farm. And anything else you might like."

The man put all the coins into the bag and handed it to Oat. Oat hefted it and as he did he remembered Bufflehead and the hellish, haunted look in the man's eyes. He handed back the money.

"The governor and officers of this state and all neighboring states, as well as the most powerful people in this whole country would be beholden to you Oat, if you do this. You'll be a hero. Who knows. You might even become governor one day. All you have to do is bring Joseph Smith here tomorrow night."

"And you would have about a hundred men hiding in the cornfield ready to kill him," Oat said, accusingly.

"We wouldn't kill him Oat," George said. "We'd take him to jail first. He'd get a fair trial."

"All I have to do is sell my soul?" Oat replied. "George, you're a liar. And you're in the company of this snake. What do you think I am? A stinking Judas?"

"We're just giving you an opportunity to do the right thing and make some money at the same time."

Oat felt the bile rising in his throat. Why would George ever think that he would consider becoming a traitor? A thousand dollars was a lot of money. He'd never seen that much money. Probably never would. But he wasn't even tempted by it. The memory of his dead father, of Bufflehead, of the hell his mother had gone through flashed through his mind. The more he thought about it, standing there looking at George and the smirking stranger, the angrier he got. He tried to speak and say something intelligent, but the words weren't there. His tongue was tied.

"So what's it gonna be Oat?" George asked.

Oat pulled George from the top rail of the corral and hit him in the face. The blow knocked George to the ground. Oat then pushed the stranger backward until he fell backward onto his rear. Then Oat rolled him around on the ground until the man's clean suit was covered with dirt.

"I can't think of anything else to say," Oat yelled finally. "But George, if you ever come back, bring a gun."

George helped the suited man get to his feet and the two of them got into the carriage.

"You just made the biggest mistake of your life," the stranger said menacingly. "This isn't over."

As June wore on there were reports of legal wrangling and political deals. They heard that Joseph had been charged with rioting for ordering the Nauvoo Expositor destroyed, then that the charges had been thrown out of court and then that he had been charged again. The latest rumor was that Governor Thomas Ford was bringing a force to Nauvoo to arrest Joseph and that there would be a fight. There were so many rumors that Oat couldn't keep up with it all. And then, a few days later, there was still another report that Joseph and Hyrum had fled across the Mississippi and were going West.

The next day was Oat's day to work at the temple. At sunrise he arrived with the Jacquards to find a large group assembled but little work being done. Rumor was that Joseph had decided to go to Carthage and face the charges against him. Less than an hour later, a procession of about fifteen men on horses appeared including Joseph and Hyrum.

It had rained the day before, but the sun was shining as the group made its way to the temple grounds and stopped. Joseph dismounted and walked about the grounds for a few moments casually inspecting the work.

He appeared distracted, deep in thought, but at the same time he obviously enjoyed the view of the grounds and of the city which lay out below him. He paused and shook hands with almost every worker.

"You're been a fine friend since the moment I met you," he said when he came to Oat. "I treasure your friendship. You have a lot of work to do but I think you have a grand life ahead of you. God will bless you for your loyalty."

"Thanks Joseph," Oat said. "I hope all goes well in Carthage."

Joseph said similar things to others as he made his way about the temple site. Then remounting his horse, he waved good-by and he and the procession filed off the hill in the direction of Carthage.

# — 35 —

**G**LAZE CAREFULLY POURED A MEASURE OF POWDER down the muzzle of his rifle. Putting his hand into his pouch he selected a ball and dropped it in on top of the powder. The ramrod went in next and he tamped the powder and ball mixture in tight. He leaned the gun against a nearby tree and sat down in the shade.

Around him scores of men did the same. It was probably the hottest day of the year so far. Some of the men were drinking. Others sat quietly in the shade sweating. Others talked excitedly and looked nervously toward the jail down the street. About twenty yards away a militia officer spoke to a group of men who wanted to go home. The wafflers weren't sure that killing Ol' Joe was the right thing to do. The militia had been discharged officially by the governor earlier in the day, but unofficially they were told to remain in Carthage.

"We've gone to too much trouble to get Ol' Joe here to let him get away now," the officer said loudly and angrily. "He ain't going home this time boys. Don't be puny yellow cowards and go running home. Even the governor's okay with this."

Ford was in town doing his part. He entered Carthage with a posse a few days before Smith gave himself up. Glaze watched the governor ride into town while men stood around and cheered him. Ford acted like some damned French emperor on a mission to save the peasants. He sent his posse on to Nauvoo to arrest Smith, but not surprisingly and to his embarrassment, it had not been successful. But he was popular with the men in town. When Ol' Joe surrendered, Ford had met with him and yesterday paraded Smith in front of the assembled militia, introducing the Smith brothers as generals. That nearly caused the murder then and there.

Ford left early that morning on a covert mission to assure the Mormons that Smith was safe. Another midnight meeting had been held the night before to finalize plans for the killing. Glaze attended because he had become the informal spokesman for the Missouri contingent. Everyone was worried the Nauvoo Legion would show up in the middle of the party. And with good cause. The Nauvoo Legion had enough well-trained men under arms to raze the entire countryside from Carthage to Warsaw.

In the same tavern where Glaze first met the governor, he sat across a wooden table from Ford and the man from Washington. Together they had devised the plan for the following day.

"I will go to Nauvoo tomorrow with my men," Ford said. "I'll keep the Mormons occupied for the day. They actually are very trusting people. We'll go take a look at their temple, tell them Smith is just fine and probably get a nice meal."

"You're going to miss all the fun," Glaze said.

"He needs to be somewhere else when we kill Smith," the Washington man said, "otherwise everyone will assume he's involved. If he's in Nauvoo we can turn suspicion away from his, at least for a while. If he's connected to the killing there will be a public outcry."

Looking at Glaze the Washington man frowned.

"Can we be certain your men have the nerve to carry this out?" he asked.

"You just tell me when," Glaze responded.

Ford then appointed the Carthage Greys to guard Smith. Glaze appreciated that stroke of genius. Ford was a lot like Boggs. The Greys were among the most rabid of all the anti-Mormons who had gathered in Carthage.

"Like leaving a pack of hungry wolves to guard raw meat," he told Tucker.

As they sat in the brutal heat, someone said loudly that Ford was probably being served a cool drink by Holy Joe's wife about now. That brought a number of nervous laughs and guffaws.

Tucker had gotten tired of listening to the militia officer and now sat down in the shade next to him. George Trask followed Tucker around like a lost puppy.

"Are we going to do this or are we going to sit here and sweat for another four hours?" Tucker asked.

"We'll do it soon. Won't be long now. Think about how Ol' Joe must be sweating about now."

"He looked plenty cool yesterday," Tucker said.

The day before Glaze and Tucker paid a personal visit to 'Ol Joe and his brother. It had been late evening, almost dark. The brothers recognized Glaze immediately.

"You came all the way from Independence just to kill us," Ol' Joe said sarcastically. "I guess we should feel honored. Have we changed much since Missouri?"

"You're older and you've put on weight," Glaze said.

"So have you," Ol' Joe said. "Would you like to know what I see?"

Glaze declined, but Tucker quickly said, "Yeah, what do you see?"

Smith didn't even hesitate.

"I see two bloodthirsty murderers who should have been hanged long ago and if there wasn't a corrupt government in Missouri you would have been. Since you spent your lives murdering others you shall have your fill of blood to your entire satisfaction. You will see and experience unimaginable carnage. You will fight people you now think are your friends and you shall be filled with regret and sorrow. You will wish you had never been born."

Ol' Joe ended his little speech with his eyes resting directly on Glaze.

"You told me that once before," Glaze said unimpressed. "But I'll prophecy to you too Joe. I prophesy that I will outlive you."

Ol' Joe turned away and didn't say anything more to Glaze or Tucker and they soon left. Ol' Joe's words however gave Glaze an odd feeling for a while, one he was not used to, but it soon departed about the time he and Tucker left the jail and went about their preparations.

At sunup that morning, Glaze had stood near the jail speaking with one of the Carthage Greys. Glaze had just told the man about the time several years before in Missouri when he had taken Ol' Joe to Gallatin and how Ol' Joe told Creech he wouldn't live to see the sun set only a few hours before Creech had been crushed to death by his own horse.

At that moment one of Smith's friends, who stayed with him in the jail overnight, exited the jail.

"What was the gunfire last night?" he asked the militia man.

"None of your damn business," the Carthage Grey said.

Glaze knew. One of the Missourians got drunk and fired his rifle at the jail, but Glaze didn't feel inclined to tell the man that. Let Ol' Joe worry.

"You best get out of here. We're not going to let Ol' Joe escape alive, and if you don't want to die with him you had better leave before sundown. I can prophesy better than Ol' Joe. Neither he, his brother, or anyone who remains with them will see the sun set today."

That had been a good ten hours earlier and now the sun was on its downward arc.

"We best get it done before the sun sets today or our Carthage friend is going to look like a sap," Glaze said to Tucker as they waited.

Sharp, the Law brothers, Williams and the other leaders huddled under another tree about forty yards away having a heated discussion. The words got louder and angrier. Sharp shook a fist in Law's face. Everyone was waiting on them.

"I don't like the looks of that," Glaze said to Tucker as he watched the men argue. "I thought those guys got everything worked out last night. I'd better make sure they're not turning yellow."

As he walked toward the tree where the group argued he heard singing coming from the jail. All of the men quieted immediately and Glaze stopped and listened. It was the strong, solid voice of a man singing a sad haunting melody. Glaze was too far away to make out the words, but it sent chills up and down his spine despite the heat. As the singing continued Glaze finished his stroll to where Sharp sat.

"We gonna do this or not?" he asked. "What's the problem?"

"Can you believe it? Law's getting cold feet, but we straightened him out," Sharp said. "We're waiting for the guard to change. Blacken your face."

Glaze walked back to his tree. Stopping near a fire ring he scooped up a handful of charcoal. He mixed it with some gunpowder and water and smeared it on his face. Tucker did the same.

The singing started again.

A little past four o'clock the guard at the jail changed. The Carthage Greys, who had been sitting near Glaze, got up and marched off to the jail to relieve the men who now guarded the jail. These last Greys had special orders and Glaze watched as Sharp and Williams patted some of the boys on the back and sent them off.

The time went quickly after that. Glaze often thought that time always moved more quickly when someone was about to die. A while later Glaze saw a man running back, one of the guards who had just been sent. He spoke quickly and excitedly to Williams. Seconds later he heard Williams rousing the men.

"All right boys," he yelled. "They're on the second floor of the jail. Let's get our work done."

Glaze moved into line in the street behind Williams and the other men. Every face was painted black and was set toward the jail. No one spoke. On William's signal the men walked quickly and purposely forward.

The guards at the jail did exactly what they had been told to do. They raised their guns and fired over the heads of the approaching men and then joined the attackers. The shots were the signal for the attack. The men broke into a trot, quickly surrounded the building and began shooting into it. A large group burst through the outside door and charged up the stairs to the upper room that held the prisoners.

Glaze stayed outside. He trotted purposely to the south side where he could see a window on the second story. Tucker was at his side. There was movement inside and most of the men already were firing up through the window. Some of the poorer shots hit the frame and splinters flew everywhere. At least a hundred shots were fired in the space of only a few seconds. Glaze took his time. Positioning himself about thirty yards from the jail, he knelt down, raised his gun and drew a fine bead on the open window.

There was a sudden stillness. Many of the men already had fired and were reloading. It was almost quiet. Suddenly a figure appeared in Glaze's gun sights and filled the window frame. In a split-second Glaze knew instinctively that it was Ol' Joe.

"What if he is a prophet?" It was the first time the thought had troubled him. Ol' Joe was a big proud-looking man with wide shoulders and a clean-shaven face. It occurred to Glaze in that quarter-second that he had been hunting Smith for years and suddenly that hunt was over. This seemed too easy. He always had known innately that he would kill Smith. He had sworn to do so. But it was one of those things that even though he knew he would do it he wasn't prepared for the doubts that suddenly popped into his head. But it was too late to turn back now. His whole life had pointed to this. Now it was happening. He couldn't turn back.

As his finger tightened on the trigger, Glaze saw Smith's eyes scanning the group of men below him and they rested squarely on Glaze. For another split-second their eyes locked together and then the gun exploded. Glaze saw the bullet hit Smith squarely in the chest. Tucker fired and hit him too. A second later more bullets hit him in the back from inside the jail, but it didn't matter by then. By sheer force of will, Smith clung to the window sill for a second. He said something that didn't reach Glaze's ears because of more gunfire. Then he fell. He was dead before he hit the ground.

A moment later the jail emptied. Several men dragged the body of Hyrum Smith down the stairs and outside. Both bodies were leaned against the building and some of the men, including Trask, shot them again. There could be no mistake now. The Mormon leaders were dead.

"Cut their heads off," someone yelled.

Glaze remembered he promised Smith he would put his head on a pole. Reaching to his side he pulled out his hunting knife and approached the bodies. He would have decapitated the Smiths but for a chilling yell that echoed through the Carthage streets.

"The Mormons are coming."

Glaze never knew any emotion as intense as the fear that seized him at that moment. Nor, apparently, had the other men. The armed force, that only a few moments before had bravely stormed the jail and killed two men, evaporated. Glaze ran like a spooked deer out of town and into the brush where the chestnut was tied. Mounting, he rode hard away from town finally circling southward. He didn't feel completely safe until it was dark and he was in Warsaw.

# 36

By late July the corn was eight feet tall and still growing. Oat worked from dawn to sunset daily fighting an endless battle against weeds, birds and raccoons. Despite the pests' best efforts, however, it appeared he would have a good crop.

The work kept his mind off other things. A gloomy pall had settled over Nauvoo since Joseph's murder. Many people had lost hope in Joseph's vision of a latter-day Kingdom of God. They feared that without Joseph there could not be a kingdom, that it now was time to just give up.

A few alternatives remained. William Law started his own church and Sidney Rigdon had returned from Pittsburgh, where he had been living the past few years. He went door-to-door throughout Nauvoo and even stopped to visit Oat and his family. He described a vision he received the exact day and hour that Joseph was murdered.

"I was instructed to become a guardian to the church," he said, sitting at the table in their home. "The Lord has shown me what to do and how to build up the church until he can raise up another like Joseph."

Later as they ate supper Oat voiced misgivings about Rigdon.

"I know he was first counselor to Joseph," he said. "But I don't have much confidence in him."

Hannah and Maggie nodded in agreement.

"He wasn't very convincing," Hannah said. "I wonder if he really had a vision."

"We could have said the same thing about Joseph," Oat said.

"No," Maggie said quickly, shaking her head. "When Joseph taught us his eyes sparkled and my heart swelled."

"That's exactly right," Hannah said. "There was no question with Joseph. We all just knew."

Oat ate the rest of the meal in silence. Later he walked through the corn, thinking and wondering what to do. There seemed to be no good alternative. He wanted to keep his family together, but the outcry against the Mormons and especially the practice of plural marriage was growing throughout the country. If his family stayed together it had to be with like-minded people.

George paid a visit that night, and this time he brought a gun.

"What you going to do now Oat?" George said, seated on his horse near the corral where Oat had thrown him into the dirt. "Looks as though the ol' church is going to crumble into the dust. And great shall be the fall thereof."

The smugness in George's voice didn't set well with Oat.

"I plan to go on living just the same way George," Oat said. "There ain't no good reason to change now."

"President Law invites you to come to his church now," he said, puffing out his chest. "I'm one of the high priests in it. If you do you'll have protection from the wolf hunts and you won't have to work on that stupid temple any more."

Oat said nothing.

"You'll have to give up one of your wives though," he said. "President Law don't hold with polygamy."

The anger surged through Oat.

"You know something George," Oat said, his voice rising. "I really don't care what William Law does or doesn't like. The man is a traitor and a murderer. I could never trust him and I certainly don't want to pray with him."

"He did something that a lot of us thought needed to be done," George said.

"You sound like you are happy they murdered Joseph," Oat said accusingly.

George couldn't resist the opportunity to boast.

"You think so little of me," George said. "Not only was I happy to see it, but I was happy to help."

"You were there?"

George nodded: "I was there cheering 'em on and shooting too. I didn't kill him, but I shot him and I'm proud of it."

Oat went numb. He felt the same he did when Bufflehead confessed to murdering his father.

"You are saying that just to try to upset me, aren't you?" Oat said.

"I'm not joking Oat," George said seriously. "I was tickled to death to help snuff out that lying slug. The world's a better place now."

"Use your gun or leave George," Oat said walking toward him. He intended to pull George to the ground and beat him.

"Come on Oat, we're friends," George protested. "Don't run me off again."

"We aren't friends any more George. Get out of here."

George wheeled his horse and rode away. Four days later he returned with the wolf hunters.

It was unusual to conduct a wolf hunt during broad daylight. Glaze and Tucker preferred the cover of darkness. At night the raiders struck quickly and disappeared in seconds. There was little chance of being discovered or followed. Glaze decided to make an exception for Otis Harmon. This was a payback a long time in coming and he wanted to see well enough to do the job right. He also wanted Harmon to know who did it. They would hit the Harmon place at midmorning in broad daylight. Because he didn't want to attract a lot of attention he took only three other men, Tucker, another hard case from Warsaw named Fenton whom Tucker had befriended and George Trask. Trask told him there was only Harmon, two women and three small children.

Still, they traveled mostly at night congregating at Trask's place at daybreak. Harmon's place was only a short distance away. Trask's wife Geneva remained inside and didn't ask questions as they checked their weapons and waited. Glaze intended to kill Harmon and told the other men.

"Do what you want with the women," Glaze said. "I don't care. This is an old score and I'm going to finish it today. Harmon's mine."

Tucker and Fenton grinned. Trask looked a little shocked, but didn't say anything.

"What should we do with the pups?" Tucker asked, referring to Harmon's kids.

Glaze, busy tightening the cinch on his saddle, didn't seem to hear so Tucker repeated the question.

"What should we do with the pups?"

Glaze finished tightening the cinch, tucked in the loose straps and pulled at the stirrup so that it fell back into place. Turning, he stared back at Tucker.

"You know what to do with them," he said. "Nits make lice."

When the sun rose high enough in the sky they moved out skirting the Trask corn patch and hugging a string of trees that gave good cover. It only took a few moments to get to the Harmon place moving at a slow gallop. Glaze rode the big chestnut stud. Though it was more than ten years old now it was powerful and still carried him with ease. They circled the north edge and came in from the west. Breaking out of the trees they moved across some cleared ground and up a little rise. Suddenly the Harmon place was before them, a few buildings made of wood that would burn easily, a fenced pasture with some work horses, a vegetable garden near the house, a cow, a calf, some pigs.

The women were outside. One was washing laundry. The other was pulling water from the well. Two young boys played in the dirt nearby. Harmon was nowhere in sight. They rode straight through the yard reining in their horses at the edge of a large corn patch that covered several acres to the east. The corn stood so high that even seated on his horse Glaze could not see over it. He remembered the face of the woman at the well. He had seen her before. She recognized him too because she dropped a piece of clothing she held, looked toward the other woman and said something he couldn't hear.

"This the Otis Harmon place?" Glaze asked.

"You know it is." One of the women replied. " The yellow dog on the horse next to you led you here."

"Is that any way for a good Mormon woman to speak to her neighbor?" Glaze said. "Is Brother Harmon here or is he out looking for another wife?"

Her eyes rested on their guns and loathing spread over her face.

"I reckon he's out looking for another wife," she said, shoving the smallest boy toward the house.

"Maybe this will bring him back," Glaze said.

Aiming his rifle at the milk cow standing near the barn, he fired. The cow dropped to its knees and rolled onto its side as the women looked on helplessly and the children began to cry. Fenton and Tucker fired at the pigs and calf then got off their horses and approached the women. Glaze and Trask held the horses, swiveling their heads from one side to the other and waiting for Harmon's appearance. Glaze reloaded.

Oat had just finished cutting down a tree he intended to use for firewood. He was trying to hitch Jack Jacquard to it and pull it back to the house, but Jack was acting up again. He pawed the ground, nickered and blew, and he wouldn't stand still. His neck bowed like it did when he mated. Over the preceding few years Jack had grown heavier and more surly. He nearly killed a young gelding that strayed onto Oat's property a few months earlier. Oat worked him less and less as he became more bullheaded. His main duty now was as stud.

"What in the world is wrong with you Jack?" Oat said crossly to the big horse.

No sooner had he uttered the words than a rifle report boomed across the field. A few seconds later two more reports sounded in his ears. He could not see who was firing because the corn patch lay between him and the source of the sound. The shots came from the direction of his house.

"No," Oat said aloud, not wanting to believe the thoughts that flashed into his mind. But he knew instantly. Dropping the hitch he jumped onto Jack's back. Slow as Jack was he could get him back to the house faster than Oat could run. Jack didn't need much urging. He lunged forward eagerly whistling and snorting. He smelled something, probably other horses. Oat whipped the big horse and soon Jack was galloping toward the corn patch that blocked the house from view.

It seemed to Oat that it took ages to reach the corn. Jack Jacquard didn't slow a bit as the tall corn stalks beat into his face. He cleared a swath five feet wide as he thundered forward. Oat heard voices and laughing now. Jack was tall enough that Oat's head was above the corn and as he moved closer his head stuck up out of the corn. Still he couldn't see anything but the roof of the house.

He tried to slow Jack Jacquard by pulling the harness reins. He feared the big horse would trample Hannah or Maggie or one of the children when he broke out of the corn patch into the yard. But he couldn't pull hard enough. Jack, wild with rage, shook his big head and screamed as he ran. He had the bit in his teeth. For the first time in his life Oat had lost control of him. The only thing he could do was hang on.

Hannah intuitively had known this day would come again. She wondered if the shots would bring Oat and, if they did, would he be in time? And when he arrived what could he do? He wasn't armed. He was only one man. Four armed pukes stood in their yard, spoiling for a fight. She had tried to prepare for it by placing various weapons in strategic locations both inside and outside the house. A rusty old knife lay under a block in the woodpile, but it was several yards away. A bucket of round, smooth rocks sat on the ground nearer the well. All were about the size of her closed fist. She inched toward the bucket.

Maggie had done the same. She whittled a long branch into a spear that leaned against the house was a stick. The blunt end had a wicked looking knot that she smoothed and polished. Hannah had watched her doing it.

"What's that for?" she had asked.

"It's for clubbing and skewering pukes," Maggie replied.

"Good idea."

Hannah's first thought, however, was for the pistol, lying hidden in the house. She was the only one who knew its location. She wished she had told Maggie because Maggie stood nearer the doorway and would have had a better chance to get it if she knew where it was. Oat's rifles were loaded but they hung high on a wall in the kitchen. And there was no time now. Hannah snatched up two stones, one in each hand.

The puke approaching her grinned showing the few teeth he had.

"Oooh, this one's gonna fight," he laughed.

The first rock hit him in the chin and sent him staggering backward. The second hit him in the ribs causing him to howl with pain.

The other puke was big and he didn't take Maggie seriously either. She had picked up the pointed stick and held it in front of her. From his belt he drew a large hunting knife and flashed it about so she could see, and showing off for the other men who were watching. For just a brief instant he turned his head to watch when Hannah hit his companion with the stone. When he did Maggie lunged driving the point of the stick into his upper thigh and then jumping back. He lashed out with the blade in a long arcing swing missing her throat by inches. He clasped his thigh and screamed in rage, again taking his eyes from her. She swung the blunt end of the club and hit him in the side of the head laying him out flat on the ground.

Glaze and Trask laughed at their companions.

"Those little women too much for you boys?" Trask yelled.

"You need some help Tucker?" Glaze heckled.

Tucker was angry. Staggering to his feet, he charged at Maggie, grabbing the stick when she lunged at him again. With the back of his hand he knocked her to the ground where she writhed in pain. The other puke reached Hannah a second later. His big fist caught her in the jaw, knocking her senseless. It was several seconds before her head cleared. When it did she saw the puke who hit her rubbing his back.

"Now we have some fun," the puke said reaching for Maggie. "Glaze, haven't we seen this wench before?"

Hannah wanted to go to Maggie and though she could think and see what was happening around her she could barely move. Her hands and feet were numb. The leader, sat with his rifle pointed straight in the air watching, apparently waiting for Oat. Trask looked on solemnly, but didn't move.

Andy crawled away from the house and now walked toward Hannah crying pitifully. Abe stood against the house, his eyes round and frightened. Hannah could guess what the men would do to her and Maggie, but what would they do to Andy and Abe? And Libbie slept in the house. What would they do to her? It was the most terrifying moment of her life. She was helpless again. Dear God, she thought, please help us.

A moment later she heard a terrible sound. At first she thought it was because of the blow she had suffered. As her head cleared, she heard it again. She looked about, but saw nothing. The noise confused their attackers too. They also looked all around puzzled, brows wrinkling. And then everyone realized, almost at the same instant, that the noise came from the corn patch.

When Jack Jacquard and Oat burst out of the corn patch Jack was on a dead run and though he wasn't a fast horse there was no stopping his forward momentum. Oat gulped in the scene. Hannah, Maggie, Andy and Abe were near the house and out of the big horse's path, though Hannah and Maggie lay on the ground. Two men with knives stood near them. Four saddle horses stood right in Jack Jacquard's path. Two had riders. One was George Trask and, even though it had been years since he had seen the man, Oat instantly recognized Tyrone Glaze as the other. He rode the same chestnut stud that Jack had thrashed years before.

Jack charged straight at the chestnut. It didn't matter that three other horses blocked him. They went down like a row of cornstalks, George Trask in their midst. George's horse toppled over backwards into the rock wall of the well. Oat heard bones snap and George scream in pain. One of the men on the ground tried to limp out of the way as another of the horses stumbled backward and fell onto him and then trampled him as it got back up quickly. Glaze's stud went down too, but as it did Glaze leveled his rifle and fired. The bullet, intended for Oat, was stopped by Jack's big neck. It broke Oat's heart to see it. The chestnut stud reared and fell over backward as Jack's massive bulk slammed into it. Glaze hit the ground directly under the stud and the weight drove the air from his chest leaving him gasping on the ground. Jack crumpled slowly to the ground.

Oat slid off Jack's back landing not ten yards from the only attacker left standing. Oat now remembered him too — Tucker. He was a big man, as tall as Oat, but much heavier. And he had a knife. As Tucker charged at him Oat backed toward the barn. Out of the corner of his eye Oat saw Hannah race into the house with Andy in her arms. She grabbed Abe too on the way in the door. Maggie, now on her feet too, wielded a club with a knot on the end. With a good solid swing she slammed it against the head of the man who had just been trampled. He rolled over and didn't move.

Tucker lunged forward. Oat grabbed the hand with the knife. The blade nicked his hand drawing an instant stream of blood. Oat pinned the man's wrist against the barn wall then, ignoring his assailant's flailing fist, bit into the fleshy part of his arm as hard as he could. He tasted blood and saw the knife drop.

As his breath returned Glaze rolled onto his stomach. He saw Harmon and Tucker struggling near the barn. He and his men had been completely surprised by Harmon charging out of the corn patch on his big horse. Glaze heard Trask moan behind him, but he couldn't see Fenton. He and his men were in poor shape.

"This fight ain't over," he said aloud to himself.

He slowly drew his pistol from his belt. Harmon's back was to him, not twenty yards away and he was busy with Tucker. Glaze saw Tucker's knife drop after Harmon pinned him against the barn, but they still struggled, until only a few seconds later one of Harmon's women bludgeoned Tucker in the back of the head with a club. Tucker went down hard. Coldcocked.

"I'll bet you think yer going to live," Glaze said under his breath. Aiming his pistol at Harmon's back, he pulled back the hammer.

When Maggie clubbed Tucker's head, the big man dropped like a rock. Oat immediately turned in a circle, looking for Glaze and instantly saw him lying in the dirt like a coiled rattlesnake, a goofy smile on his face. Oat froze and waited for the bullet, but Glaze hesitated. He laughed.

"Gotcha Harmon."

Glaze didn't see Hannah, who exited the house behind him barefoot. She held the pistol Oat had wanted to take from her. The same gun she shot up the Trask house with, that the sheriff wanted and that Joseph said she ought to keep. Oat thought it odd to see her with a gun, but at that second he was happy she had it. His eyes shifted to Glaze.

"I've waited a long time to kill you," Glaze said. He rested the pistol barrel on his left arm and carefully aimed.

He took too long. Hannah ran around the well leaped over Trask and landed with both of her knees planted squarely in Glaze's back. For the second time in less than five minutes, the air was knocked from Glaze's lungs. His pistol slipped from his hands and he lay gasping in the dirt.

Hannah sat on his back, grabbed a handful of his hair and jerked his head back until his chin was nearly a foot off the ground. She stuck the end of the pistol barrel against the back of his neck at the base of his skull.

Hannah's jaw was clenched, her lips pursed rigid, her eyes wild and terrifying. Oat could hear her teeth grinding. Whenever Glaze tried to move, if only a little, she jerked his head back further and pushed the pistol barrel forward.

"It's okay Hannah," Oat said. " He can't hurt us now."

"Get away from me," she screamed. "I'm going to kill this puke."

Oat recoiled in surprise and horror. The thunder of more hooves pounded in their ears as two men on horses charged into the yard. It was Brother Jones and another brother Oat didn't recognize. They had guns.

"We heard shooting . . ." Jones said. Jones had a head of curly red hair everyone liked to tease him about and he had a big, loud voice. But his voice trailed off when he spotted Hannah on Glaze's back. He and the other man hushed and silence fell over the yard. They, Oat and Maggie looked on spellbound. Pure carnage surrounded them. The cow, calf, a pig and Jack Jacquard lay dead and bleeding. Glaze's stud limped off toward the corn patch. The three other attackers lay in various positions. Trask moaned and the other two men moved slowly, reviving groggily, but conscious enough to dare not move now that Jones had arrived.

Hannah tightened her grip to the point that she tore a handful of hair free. Glaze's face slammed into the ground. His nose spurted blood. She instantly grabbed another fistful of hair and whipped his head back into the same painful position. Tears streamed down Hannah's face.

"This is for Mama and Papa," she said directly into his ear. "And it's for my little brothers and everybody else you miserable pukes have murdered."

She thumbed back the hammer on the pistol and her eyes widened and became almost lifeless. Oat held his breath and watched Hannah's trigger finger twitch. He didn't try to speak to her. He knew this was a moment she long had waited and wished for. She wanted this. No one, maybe not even God, would fault her for killing this man. He deserved it. Oat tensed for the inevitable blast of blood and brains.

After a long moment, however, Hannah loosened her grip. She closed her eyes and her chin sank. She let go of Glaze's hair and his face slammed into the ground again. He moaned as Jones swarmed over him and bound him. Standing, she handed the pistol to Oat.

"That man's a puke. I should gut shoot him and party while he bleeds to death, but I can't do it," she said. "I always thought I could, but I can't."

"He'll pay," Oat said. "One way or the other he'll pay."

"I hope so."

# — 37 —

AUGUST 30, 1844

Dear Mama,
    You may be wondering about us and though your feelings were perfectly clear about how you felt when you last visited, I thought I'd write and tell you how we are, just in case you still have some kind feelings toward me or perhaps a change of heart. We are fine. We have been through some trouble. A mob attacked us at our farm. It was awful, but we got through it okay thanks mainly to Jack Jacquard. The babies, Hannah, Maggie and myself are okay, but Jack is dead, killed by one of our attackers. He sired many colts of which I still own three. They will be good horses, but there never will be another Jack Jacquard. We buried him in the corn patch. It took me a full day to dig a hole deep enough and it was one of the saddest days of my whole life. He was like a brother and I loved him. We lost our milk cow too, but our good neighbors have given us milk for the babies and cream for making butter and now we have plenty of dry beef to eat from our dead cow.
    Our neighbor George Trask turned out to be a traitor to us sort of like Bufflehead. He was one of those who attacked us, but they weren't expecting the fight they got. They spent a week in the Nauvoo jail and then were turned over to the sheriff at Carthage. We found out later they were turned loose a few minutes after they got to Carthage. All around us mobs have been attacking the homes of our neighbors by night, burning them and running off livestock and destroying crops. They call them wolf hunts. I have moved my family into Nauvoo because I fear they may be hurt if we stay at the farm. The new house is small but the mobs dare not

come into Nauvoo. They are cowards who mainly attack the outlying farms at night with their faces blackened.

Many people now think all might now be lost for our cause. They think that Joseph was the only thing that held us all together. At first I felt the same. I thought about moving some place safe where no one would know that we were Mormons, but where would that be? I don't know. I thought that Jesus must have given up on us and taken Joseph away for that reason. Now I know different.

We've had many visitors lately.

Many try to persuade us to follow them. One is Sidney Rigdon, who was a leader in the church for many years. When Joseph and Hyrum were killed he lived in Pittsburgh. Then he came back here to take over.

He came to our home. And there have been others.

You probably have never heard of Brigham Young, but he is well-known in the church because he is the president of the Quorum of the Twelve Apostles. I don't know Brigham Young well. Until lately, about all I knew is that he was in Boston on a mission when Joseph was killed. I have heard his name often, but until I saw him at our home I couldn't even have described him to you. Now I can. He is a strong man, bearded, with a solemn, pious face.

He is not a great orator, like Joseph, or Rigdon, nor is there anything about him that is very memorable.

He appeared at our house in the evening alone, after supper. We invited him in and all sat together around the kitchen table. As we sat talking a change occurred. When Brigham spoke it wasn't Brigham's voice I heard, it was Joseph's. I know that sounds crazy, but that is what happened. I don't even remember what he said, just the familiar words and tones that used to flow off Joseph's tongue. They were there again and even though I knew that Joseph was dead, it seemed to me as though Joseph was sitting there speaking to us.

Hannah and Maggie experienced the same thing. Since that day I have heard many others speak of the same experience. After he left that night I broke down and cried. I had been so worried about what to do and then to finally know was such a relief.

The Lord has gotten his point across to me. I will remain a Mormon.

We have decided to stay here. There is talk the church may move West sometime soon to a place where we can live in peace. If so, we will go. Please do not worry about me and your grandchildren. We could not be in a better place and God will protect us and make us strong. God bless you with his spirit that you may know that what I have said is true. I will not trouble you with many letters, but I felt you should know we are okay. I love you, Otis

# 38

APRIL 6, 1862 — NORTH OF CORINTH, TENNESSEE

Captain Tyrone Glaze strode easily along through the woods with more than two hundred men marching to his right and behind. Thousands more advanced on all sides. It was a beautiful, cool, clear spring morning just a little after dawn. And it was quiet so far, but a big fight was brewing. Glaze had been told the northern army was up ahead and he and his men had been ordered to join the attack.

His outfit was a combination of stragglers from other units that had been shot up in earlier battles. Or they were green and had never seen a battle. All were intensely loyal to the Confederacy. They had merged with the army at Corinth. For weeks they trained or sat as the army gathered in volunteers. During that time Glaze had been appointed captain of his regiment by General Sydney Johnston. Then, finally, during the first days of April the army moved slowly and ponderously northward finally ready to engage the enemy and its drunken General Grant.

The countryside was wooded, well covered with trees — hickory, locust, sycamore, oak and a variety of bushes and briars. The men clamored into and out of ravines and hollows, but they couldn't see far ahead. For the past few days that's all they had done. Once in a while they would hear sporadic musket fire, but mostly just the clomping, trudging, grunting sounds of thousands of marching men.

Glaze paused as he and his men scrambled through a thicket and out of a small draw. Tucker bent over and panted from the effort. Both he and Tucker were near fifty years old now and things like this weren't easy any more.

"Damn, I'm getting tired of this walking," Tucker said. "When ya think we're gonna fight?"

Glaze shrugged and continued on. A few moments later the sounds of sporadic gunfire far ahead filled the forest. The intensity increased until there was a constant popping in the air.

"That's more than picket line fire," Glaze said. The men around him laughed and cheered.

"We're finally going to have some fun," Tucker said. "Like the old times when we went after the Mormons."

Glaze grinned. It had been a long time since he and Tucker did anything like this. It reminded him of the wolf hunts.

For the past eighteen years he and Tucker had been inseparable. Neither had married. For a few years, after killing Ol' Joe Smith they wandered the plains hunting buffalo and living with the Indians. Both kept squaws for a year or so before returning to Missouri. After that they worked on river boats traveling up and down the Mississippi between St. Louis and New Orleans countless times. They stole horses and robbed a few banks when opportunities came along. Finally, they signed on as scouts for a federal army the government formed in to send to Utah against the Mormons who had congregated in Utah. The army needed men who knew the western mountains. It was a perfect job for Glaze and Tucker. That army had been called back when the tensions between the north and south became serious.

The gunfire around him intensified as the men surged forward hoping to get into the fight. They were mostly farm boys who never had been in mortal danger. That soon would change.

All morning they advanced never getting a chance to fire a shot. The Yankees fell back. In some places the Yanks fled so quickly they left their tents and knapsacks. They came upon other southern soldiers who had stopped to eat the breakfast that the Yankee soldiers left behind in their haste. They walked over the bodies of dead and wounded men, both Yanks and Rebs, mostly Yanks. The dead were contorted into awkward positions with grotesque looks on their faces. Some of the wounded cried out pitifully. Others stared at them dazed, frightened and quiet.

Now Glaze's men didn't seem so anxious to get into the fight, but there was no intermission in the sound of the battle ahead now. The chatter of small arms was constant and now was mingled with the whining song of grape shot, the hum of cannon balls and the roaring and explosion of bombshells. Smoke from guns and fire filled the air around them leaving an eerie, smoky haze over the battlefield.

About mid-afternoon they came to the edge of a clearing where several thousand Confederate troops had grouped for an attack. As the front lines came into sight a bugler sounded attack and the troops moved forward in a gray mass howling like mad dogs. Glaze's men rushed forward to join the attack but were ordered to halt by a major on horseback.

"Form up here men and we'll send another wave at 'em in a minute," the major yelled over the din.

Glaze's men took cover and watched the Confederate advance get shot to pieces. Across the way a few hundred yards a small rise ran along a line of brush and briars where there appeared to be a deeply rutted road. The Yanks had settled in behind the bushes along the road, thousands of them. The open ground between the Confederate and the Yankee lines was littered with the bodies of dead and wounded men. This time the men on the ground were dressed in gray or dirty, light yellow uniforms. As the new attack advanced musket fire erupted from the brush and hundreds of gray-clad soldiers crumpled to the ground. Volley after volley was fired and hundreds more fell. Some continued forward until they were shot down, others turned and ran back until they reached their own lines and the disgusted stares of the soldiers who were forming for a new charge.

General Johnston galloped past. The general was fearless and an inspiration to the entire army. He and Glaze had gotten acquainted during the Mormon campaign in the West. They spent some time together a few weeks earlier reminiscing about the western campaign. It hadn't turned out the way either had hoped. Johnston had wanted glory. Though he didn't say it in so many words, Glaze knew he was disappointed there had not been an open, pitched battle with the Mormons. For his part Glaze wanted one more chance to kill Oat Harmon, but never got it.

Tucker appeared at Glaze's side, a wry smile on his face.

"They're finally getting some artillery set up over yonder," he said smiling and tossing his head back to the right. "That'll soften em up. They're saying those are Illinois and Ohio units over there across the way. Wonder if there's anybody we know?"

Glaze looked across the field at the Yankee lines. Their friends and accomplices during the Mormon trouble could be over there. They were relatively quiet for now. He could see blue-coated soldiers moving about, officers shouting orders and moving men, preparing to receive another charge. It fascinated him to think that he might know some of the men he would soon be shooting at and trying to kill, men from Warsaw and Carthage, maybe hundreds of the men from the militias that participated in the killing of the Smiths. Levi Williams was probably long since dead and men like William Law, William Sharp and John Bennett undoubtedly had concocted ways to stay out of fights like this. They were the types of schemers who could do that. But the no-names were over there, men like Fenton, Foster and Trask. They probably were wondering if Glaze and Tucker were staring back at them. On impulse Glaze stood up and waved his hat over his head at the Union lines.

"Hey you Carthage Greys. You can't hit nothin'."

His cheer was greeted by about a dozen musket shots that fell far short. He crouched back down beside Tucker laughing.

As they waited over the next several minutes, tensions increased and Glaze's thoughts for some odd reason wandered until he remembered old Governor Boggs. The old boy had pulled up stakes in Missouri and went west to California about the same time the Mormons trekked into the Utah territory. Glaze always had thought that funny and wondered if the old governor killed any more Mormons out West. Just before the war broke out Missouri newspapers had published notices that the former governor had died at his home in California at the age of sixty-eight.

"I wonder if I'll ever live to be sixty-eight," Glaze said to himself, wondering aloud. His thoughts of Boggs reminded him of Illinois Governor Tom Ford. Ford was dead too. He died about five years after helping take care of Ol' Joe Smith.

The Confederate artillery started up and shells began to fall on the Yankee lines. Glaze and his men waited as the intense bombardment continued for about a half hour. Smoke billowed up from the union lines and Glaze heard the screams and howls of wounded men. A low-hanging haze of gun power smoke settled in over the fields. Then the order was passed. Charge.

Glaze stood and moved forward, his men forming in lines and moving forward with him. Hundreds of other men moved out of the trees and the attack began. At first they trotted, but then broke into a run, shouting and yelling. Glaze heard Tucker scream at the top of his lungs and he yelled too. As he moved closer he could see the enemy better. They lay crouched on their bellies aiming their rifles. They were ready. The artillery bombardment hadn't changed much. Hundreds of guns were pointed at them. Glaze panicked. He thought he saw an opening in the Yankee line to his right just past a small pond. There was brush there and no soldiers that he could see. He'd have to run through the water.

Glaze heard a Yankee officer give the order to fire. A fusillade of bullets slammed into the Confederate charge. Some men went down silently, others screamed. Glaze continued forward untouched. Tucker still was at his right. Another volley discharged and more men wilted to the ground, but at least half of the advance remained on its feet. As Glaze splashed through the pond about twenty yards from the opening he hoped to gain he realized to his horror that it wasn't a brush-covered opening at all. The Yankees had hidden three cannons in the brush. The cannons undoubtedly were loaded with canisters full of thousands of pieces of metal and chain, but there was nothing to do but charge ahead now. Tucker ran ahead of him still screaming like a wild man. He was ten feet from the brush when the Yanks touched off the cannons. The discharge tore Tucker into a hundred pieces before Glaze's eyes and then everything went black.

Glaze revived before sundown in the middle of a pile of bodies. All around he heard the groans and cries of wounded and dying men. So many bodies had fallen so closely together that there was hardly any ground visible. The bodies, both living and dead, lay in grotesque positions all about the field. There was movement all around him, but it wasn't significant movement, just the painful twitching of dying men. The stench of burned flesh and hair filled the air. A foul taste filled his mouth and he yearned for a drink of water. Movement brought great pain. A gash and burn on his face sent throbs through his head and his left eye felt heavy and swollen. His arms were intact, but he felt wounds in both legs below the knees and blood oozed from an ugly shrapnel hole in his stomach. Looking close, he saw that his right leg had been broken by a bullet just below the knee. The left leg was broken too, but he couldn't feel it.

The pond was only five yards away and at least ten dead men lay between him and the edge of the water. Whenever he moved pain shot through him, but his need for water soon overcame the pain. He climbed over the mangled bodies between himself and the pond, wallowing through the bloody mud dragging his useless limbs behind. The pain was nearly unbearable, but he didn't care. All he could think of was his thirst. He had to have water. Rain began to fall in a steady drizzle and a cold breeze started up. The rain water, mixed with his own blood and that of those around him, formed into puddles beneath him and soaked into his pants and shirt as he inched through the mire.

At the edge of the pond he pushed away a decapitated body. The pool was ringed by men who had crawled to the water's edge only to drink and die. Some lay partially submerged. A few floated in the middle of the pool. The water itself was deep red. Glaze closed his eyes, put his face in the water and drank deeply. The water even tasted like blood. When he had drunk his fill, he sat up with great difficulty and looked around. He felt the stomach wound, just below the ribs on his left side. It bled steadily. No matter how hard he pressed or squeezed blood trickled between his fingers.

He heard cannon and musket fire off in the distance. The battle wasn't over; it had just shifted somewhere else. He surveyed the battlefield. Immediately around him were hundreds of bodies. Most were dead but some were alive. A few, like himself, sat up dazed. Others staggered around. Pitiful cries for help filled his ears, tragic because there was no help.

A familiar-looking Yankee soldier staggered slowly across the field to the pool's edge. He clutched at his stomach with both hands. The portions of his face that weren't covered with dirt or blood were ghostly white. He had lost his hat and he carried no weapon. Wading into the water until it came to his waist he knelt, still clutching his stomach. In this position only a portion of his head and shoulders was visible above the water, but he could bend forward and drink. He drank the same blood-polluted water that Glaze had, then with difficulty stood again and walked out of the pool. When he got to the pool's edge only a few yards from

Glaze he sat down. It was only then that Glaze remembered his name.

"Hello Trask."

The Yankee looked around wildly until his eyes rested on Glaze. He stared for a long moment.

"Glaze," he mouthed. He undid his coat and shirt, revealing a six-inch slit in his stomach through which his bloody entrails pushed out. He held them in his hands pathetically.

"A reb opened me up with a bayonet when I wasn't looking," he said. "I had to stuff my guts back in." He paused a moment, still confused and disoriented. "Was it you?"

Glaze shook his head.

Holding his stomach, Trask rocked back and forth.

"How bad you hurt?" he asked.

"Bad enough to be dead by morning," Glaze said. "I'm bleeding to death like you."

They sat in silence for several moments. Glaze picked up a rifle that lay nearby at his side and tossed it out of his way. Then he arranged his left leg in the place where it had been.

"That the gun that killed Joseph Smith?" Trask asked absently.

Glaze shook his head. Among Missourians and even many from Illinois, it was widely known who fired the shot that killed Ol' Joe. It had given Glaze a sort of celebrity status even though Glaze had not dared proclaim it openly.

"Naw," he said, shaking his head slowly. "I sold that gun years ago to a Missourian from Clay County. Paid me two hundred dollars for it."

"What did he do with it?"

"I don't know," Glaze said. It didn't seem important now. "Where are we?"

"I'm not exactly sure. There was a little church back over yonder named Shiloh Chapel."

Trask tipped his head backwards and to the left in the direction of the church. It now took great effort to speak so Glaze didn't say much.

"We've reaped the whirlwind haven't we?" Trask said after a momentary silence.

"Done what?" Glaze asked.

"The whirlwind, you know. Sew the wind. Reap the whirlwind." When Glaze continued to gaze back at him with a blank stare, he continued: "We shouldn't a killed the Smiths. If we hadn't maybe this wouldn't have happened. I've had nightmares almost every night since we did it."

Glaze said nothing and Trask began to cry.

"I knew better. He didn't do nothing wrong. And I knew better."

Trask whimpered and cried, rocking back and forth.

"What day is it?" Glaze asked a few moments later. It was getting dark now. Too dark.

"Sunday," Trask whispered. He had fallen over onto his side, but his hands still pinched the wound in his stomach.

"I know that," Glaze said crossly. "What day of the year?"

Trask thought for a moment.

"It's April sixth," he said finally. And then he began to cry again softly.

A little while later Trask stopped crying. Glaze could barely see him because it now was so dark. He heard a low rattle in Trask's throat, saw the man's hands weaken and then he saw Trask's bowels gush out.

Glaze tried to get up but was too weak. He fell over onto his side resting his head on the leg of a dead man. How could this happen to him? He was Tyrone Glaze. He was invincible. Until now, no blade or bullet ever had pierced him.

Faces flashed before his eyes. He saw the Mexican lad in Texas, Turvey, the boy in the blacksmith shop at Haun's Mill, two Indian children and others that he had murdered himself or helped others murder. Then he saw Joe Smith, staring at him from the second floor of the Carthage Jail.

Out on the battlefield he suddenly heard laughter, loud raucous laughter that went on and on. He had heard that type of laughter before somewhere, but couldn't remember where. It was so odd and out of place. So much suffering and someone laughing like he had just pulled an incredible joke on them. The laughter never stopped, it just faded away.

For the first time in his life Glaze felt remorse and sorrow for the murders and the awful things he had done. He suddenly understood how awful they were. He'd never believed in God, until now. Now, with his life about to end, God's presence on the earth was so obvious he wondered why he'd never seen it before. He wondered if he should pray, but having never done it, he didn't know how. He looked about him again. He lay in the midst of the worst carnage he had ever seen, significant because he had seen so much bloodshed in his life. The sight of the men around him was so awful he closed his eyes, but he could not shut out the smell of blood, singed hair, burned flesh and the wailing, moaning sounds of the crying men all around him.

Sew the wind, reap the whirlwind. Trask said that. Live by the sword, die by the sword. The pain from both his legs throbbed more painfully as did the wounds in his head and stomach. He thought of Ol' Joe's words to him and tried to fight them, but he couldn't. He knew he was dying. But the worst of it was fear, an awful fear. He wasn't ready to die. He wished he could take back his whole life, start over and live it again, but he knew it was too late now. Despite having sworn he would never do it and still hating Ol' Joe who had said he would, Glaze wished he had never been born.

Glaze alternated in and out of consciousness for some time after that. He dreamed awful dreams and thought he saw the devil standing near him. And there were many others, among them Boggs, Creech and Tucker. Trask had joined them now.

Rain splattering onto his face awoke him one last time. Thirsty again, he wallowed through the mud and blood to the pond and drank. His clothing now was soaked almost entirely with blood. Once there he couldn't move out of the pond and he couldn't hold his head up.

The next day, the grave diggers couldn't tell if he'd drowned or bled to death. They didn't care.

# 39

AUGUST 19, 1865 — LEHI, UTAH TERRITORY

The snake struck out at the two boys and the little girl and the dogs, but it was surrounded. Each time it struck two sticks hit it in the back and a dog would lunge and it had to recoil and strike again. The children laughed and poked. The snake was a diamond back rattler, about seven feet long and as thick as the largest child's thigh. It had been crossing the front yard, over a surface of dry packed dirt and rock, heading for a patch of sagebrush on the west side of the house when the children and dogs intercepted and surrounded it.

The boys and the girl circled the big rattler, giving little heed to the danger they faced if the snake reached one of them, innocently offering the soft flesh of their small legs as a target for the serpent, laughing and stumbling backwards when the snake struck out, then getting back up and joining the attack again. The game went on for several minutes before an older sister appeared in the front yard, saw the snake and screamed.

"Snake, Mom, snake."

A second later the children's mother appeared in the doorway of the house, a small child in her arms. Her eyes showed concern, but not surprise, worry but not fear. Bird-feet wrinkles were etched into the corners of those eyes and were now stretching outward. She read the situation with one glance

Setting the child on the porch she strode quickly down the steps snatching up a shovel that leaned against the porch railing. In three long, but quick steps she reached the circle, pushed one of the boys out of the way and brought the shovel blade down on the snake about an inch behind its head pinning it to the ground and cutting its head halfway off.

Then using the heel of her shoe she ground its head into the dirt while the children watched. When she was certain it was dead, she grabbed the oldest boy and spanked his rear five sharp strokes and then worked her way through the others doing the same. The three-year-old girl was last but she was spanked just as hard as the oldest boy. Soon they all were crying pitifully.

The woman grabbed the snake by the head and shook it in their faces.

"You don't play with snakes because they can kill you. And because they can kill you we have to kill them. And whatever we kill we eat. This is your supper."

She walked back to the house snake in hand and hung it on the outside wall so the kids could see it. A minute later she came out of the house with a knife and skinned it while they watched. She cut off the head and the rattles, throwing the head to the dogs. The rattles she handed to the small girl.

"This part's okay to play with," the woman said, picking the child up and kissing her on the cheek. "I don't ever want to see you playing with rattlesnakes again."

The girl shook the rattles and smiled. The woman set the girl down and hugged the two boys, who wiped away their tears and brightened immediately.

"Ma look."

The older daughter pointed northward at something far away. About a mile north on the trail leading away from the farm a solitary figure stood at the crest of a hill silhouetted against a purple background of sagebrush.

"Do ya think it's her?"

The woman and her daughter watched as the figure picked up a bag and slowly trudged onward along the trail toward them.

"Yes, it's her," the woman said as she studied the oncoming figure. "She's one of the few people her age who's too proud to ask for a ride but able to make the walk. She'll be here in about ten minutes. Better go tell your father and Maggie."

The girl raced off toward the fields where her father and her older brothers and sisters were busy cutting and shocking grain. On her way she would stop at Maggie's house which was only a hundred yards away.

Minutes later the area between the two houses began to fill with people. Maggie walked from the other house slowly, holding the hand of a two-year-old boy who was taking small, but very quick steps. She let go of the toddler and sat down on the porch.

"Mornin' Hannah."

Hannah picked up her baby and sat next to Maggie.

"Where'd ya find the fresh meat?" Maggie asked, gesturing toward the rattler.

"I caught the kids playing with it. I'm gonna make 'em eat it for supper tonight. Maybe they won't be so anxious to play with snakes again."

They sat quietly together watching the smaller children play. As they waited Oat drove a partially loaded wagon into the yard pulled by two large gray percheron mares, both descendants of Jack and Molly Jacquard. Three young men and four young women, their sons and daughters, of various ages who had been helping their father in the fields, got out of the wagon. The girl who had gone to get them was with them. The boys, strong and wiry, weren't wearing shirts because of the hot weather. Abe, the oldest, was now twenty-five years old and only a week earlier had proposed to the daughter of one of their neighbors. The boys' shoulders and backs glistened like copper. The girls wore long skirts down to their ankles. Their arms and faces were the same color as their brothers' backs.

"Seventeen. Nineteen if you count Adam and David," Maggie said. "What do you think she'll say when she sees all this?"

A child had been born to one or the other of them almost every year since they had reached the Salt Lake Valley. And each had a son who had died in infancy and occupied solitary, unmarked graves somewhere between Winter Quarters, Iowa, and Salt Lake City.

Hannah shrugged: "She knows about us. If she can't accept it by now I suspect she'll go back to Baltimore."

For twenty years, communications between Oat and his mother had been non-existent. Oat wrote many times but there never was an answer. The lack of response troubled Oat for years and Hannah and Maggie speculated between themselves that perhaps she had died. And then out of the blue, four days earlier Oat received a letter.

"Dearest Otis," it began. "I arrived in Salt Lake City two days ago. I intend to visit you as soon as these old legs will carry me there. Please do not come for me. I must walk. I've made it this far and it's my penance for being such an awful mother."

The letter went on to explain that the reverend had died of heart failure, that Emily had died and was now buried next to Oat's uncle John. Oat, his hands shaking, had read the letter to both Hannah and Maggie, then had broken down and cried. It was the first time Hannah or Maggie had seen him cry since the deaths of their infant children on the trek across the plains to the Salt Lake Basin.

"I just hope this visit goes better than her last one," Maggie said, and then both she and Hannah laughed.

"Couldn't go much worse," Hannah said between giggles.

"I'm gonna go meet her," Oat said, walking quickly past Hannah and Maggie up the trail. He hadn't changed much physically over the past twenty years. His tall, lanky frame had filled out some, but he worked too hard to put on much weight. His thick, full head of hair was graying, but she didn't think he'd changed that much. He limped now because one of his big horses had stepped on his foot a week earlier and smashed one of his toes. It hurt him, but he had crops to harvest so he ignored the pain. Each morning he arose and attacked the day with enthusiasm and determination. He accomplished more in one day that some men did in an entire week and as a result he provided a good life for Hannah, Maggie and all their children. Times got tough once in a while and there wasn't much money, but they always had food.

"Wait," Hannah said. "We'll come too."

She and Maggie fell in beside Oat and soon the entire family was walking down the trail to meet their visitor. The children were uncommonly quiet. They never had seen their grandmother and didn't know quite what to expect. They only had heard stories, told reverently and often with sadness. They didn't have to go far. Down a small hill and around a bend in the trail they came face-to-face with Libbie Harmon.

She had heard them coming and had placed her bag on the ground and was brushing the dust from her clothing and face but she wasn't able to get it all. She had aged. Her hair was completely gray and her shoulders stooped. When she saw Oat she held out her arms to him and started to cry. They embraced and hugged tightly for a long moment as the children, Hannah and Maggie drew around them.

"When I got to Salt Lake City I went to see Brigham Young," she said finally. "He helped me discover where you lived and told me how to get here."

The children had surrounded their father and grandmother and Libbie Harmon turned a full circle studying the tanned faces staring back at her from the tallest boys to the smallest girls.

"Oat," she said, "Which ones are my grandchildren?"

Oat frowned and his brow wrinkled. Running his right hand nervously through his hair, he looked around at his children, and then at his wives, imploring them to help him pick which ones to offer up as grandchildren. Hannah and Maggie smiled and said nothing.

"They're all yours ma," he said finally. "Every last one of them." Then, as his mother's mouth dropped open he introduced his children, one at a time as they came forward and hugged their grandmother.

That evening after supper Libbie Harmon sat with Oat and Andy in a shaded tree near the well. Andrew wanted to know all about his grandfather, whom he was named after and asked the old woman question after question which she obligingly answered. Afterward Oat brought his mother up-to-date on their lives. Oat told her of their struggles in getting established, the poor crops, the hard work, the disappointments and the successes.

"Are you happy?" she asked when he finished.

He looked back at her thoughtfully.

"Yes," he said. "I truly am happy."

"Are Hannah and Maggie happy?"

"I think so. Life isn't easy but they seem content."

"You need to make sure they are happy. They are unusual women and they have given you a beautiful family."

They sat quietly for a few minutes watching the children run back and forth around the house playing in the cool of the evening.

"I'm glad you came here," she said after a long moment. "The war has been awful. Horrible battles. So many dead. So many wounded. I'm glad you missed it. It's peaceful here."

"We've had our troubles here too," he said. "Indians. And the government."

She gazed eastward to the mountains where Mount Timpanogos rose abruptly from the valley floor. Shadows crept up the mountain as the sun set in the west.

"I stopped at Independence on my way here. I wanted to see the graves of your father and brothers. I found their graves, but there's nothing left of the old farm. The house and buildings are gone, burned to the ground in the war, just piles of ashes. I didn't see many houses that still are standing. Everything was ruined in the war. So much death and misery. If we had been living there we would have been wiped out and probably killed. I don't know what became of Clovis and his family."

"They're in Oregon," Oat said. "Clovis sent me money when he sold the farm and moved west. That was years ago. Early fifties."

Catherine crawled out of the house and over to the feet of her grandmother, who lifted the child and cuddled her.

"I didn't tell you I was coming because I didn't know if I could make it here. It's a long way. I traveled with a wagon train most of the way and I had a horse, but it drowned crossing a river in Wyoming so I had to walk the rest of the way."

Oat shook his head.

"I would have come and gotten you if you had written, ma," he said.

"I wasn't sure of that. It has been so long and I had ripped up your letters without reading them so many times that I wondered if you could ever forgive me. I had to do it myself and I wasn't sure I'd make it so I didn't write until I got to Salt Lake City.

"I was angry with you for a long time. I wanted a big family, children, grandchildren, everything, but your father was killed, your brothers were dead and you were the only one left and you wouldn't go to Baltimore with me. Then I visited you and you had become a Mormon and had two wives. It was a shock.

"The reverend hated you. When we returned to Baltimore after visiting, he preached sermon after sermon about how awful Mormons are and he used you as his prime example. He built up such a hate. And I have to admit I didn't understand. I was ashamed. Over all these years I was bitter at God. I thought he cheated me. Today, when I saw all those grandchildren I finally realized that he didn't. Maybe he was trying to give me more than I was ready to receive. But I still don't understand how it all happened. Can you explain it to me?"

"I'm not sure I can," Oat said. "It's a long story and it will take a lot of explaining. It could take a long time."

"I don't know how much time I have left," she said, shaking her gray head. "The past few years I have felt so old and alone. I have worried that I would die without any family around. If you don't mind having me I'll stay here. It seems so good to be near you. And you don't know how proud I am of all these grandchildren. I want to get to know you again and all of them too. I don't have anywhere else to go."

"Ma," Oat said, taking her hand. "This is your home now. I want you to stay."

She squeezed Catherine: "The main thing I want to do is hug these babies. They are beautiful children Oat."

The temperature was cooling now that the sun had set. A wagon rumbled into the yard driven by a young man with a woman seated next to him. The woman held an infant child.

"I have a surprise for you," Oat said as the man helped the woman down from the wagon. They walked forward toward Oat and his mother. The young woman had long auburn hair pulled back and tied with a bow. She handed the child to Oat and then embraced the old woman.

"Hello Grandma," she said.

"Grandma?" Oat's mother said. "Are you one of my grandchildren too?"

"You should remember her Ma?" Oat said. "You helped deliver her in Nauvoo."

"You are that baby?" Oat's mother said, looking at the young woman with wonder. "What is your name?"

"My name is Libbie," she said. "Mama and Papa named me after you."

Tears formed in Libbie Harmon's eyes and dripped down her cheeks.

"She's married now," Oat said, pointing to his son-in-law. "And this is their first child, your first great granddaughter."

Young Libbie took the child from her father and presented it to her grandmother, who carefully took the infant into her arms.

"She's only a month old," young Libbie explained. "This Sunday at church we'll name her and bless her. Her formal name will be Elizabeth, but we'll call her Libbie."

THE END